Praise For The Fire In Their Eyes

Winner: NYC Big Book Awards 2025, Medical Thriller

Distinguished Favourite: The Independent Press Awards, Visionary Fiction

Finalist in the Chanticleer Global Thriller Awards 2025

"An anthropological thriller that arcs back and forth through time, *The Fire In Their Eyes* is a fast moving and absorbing read, and a worthy sequel to the excellent *Bone Lines*. At its heart lie questions about the nature of humanity and of human knowledge and its application, about information and misinformation, making it very much a novel for our time." *Jane Johnson, author and editor*

"*The Fire in their Eyes* is an engrossing, urgent polyphonic novel about the connections between the planet's deep past and our present unstable, unpredictable world, driven by a memorable cast of characters. A joy to read." *Jude Cook, novelist and literary critic*

"This engaging sequel to *Bone Lines* eloquently conjures the far-reaching effects of prehistoric life on today's realities while exploring intersections of science, faith and human nature along the way. A brave polemic for our times." *Nicole Swengley, journalist and author of The Portrait Girl*

"A powerful, thought-provoking read that beautifully captures the spirit and beliefs of our ancient ancestors, whilst also giving a snapshot of the philosophical and scientific thoughts of today." *Emily Pankhurst, book blogger*

Praise For Bone Lines

"Terrific scope and a powerful narrative that keeps you turning the pages, while throwing up profound questions about humankind. Bravo – a great debut!" *Jane Johnson, author and editor*

"Gracefully written, carefully researched, *Bone Lines* reaches far across time to relate the interwoven stories of two women – a genetic scientist addressing the complexities of contemporary experience, and one of our earliest ancestors as she engages in a physical and spiritual ordeal of survival... A brave and moving adventure of the imagination." *Lindsay Clarke, prize-winning author of The Chymical Wedding*

"Gripping read and a fascinating premise. I loved the authoritative tone, and the idea of a simultaneous closeness and distance across huge swathes of time." *Lulu Allison, author*

"A brilliant, genre-defying read, Bone Lines deftly unravels the wonder of oneness." *Barbara Bos, Editor, Women Writers, Women's Books.*

"A monument to the timelessness of human nature, and a work of art. Bretherton ignites her characters with a life, complexity, a personality with which any number of readers will identify and empathise with." *Naomi Moore, Editor, New Orbit literary magazine*

"Opening up new worlds... what powerful fiction does best... a novel to be appreciated on many different levels. Ambitious and brave yet effortlessly pulled off... Like Sapiens... if fictionalised and seen through the eyes of two fierce and admirable women." *Zero Filter Books blog*

About the author

Born in Hong Kong to a pair of Liverpudlians (and something of a nomad ever since) Stephanie now lives on a cliff in Cornwall, in deep gratitude for her coastal perch. Before returning to her first love of writing fiction, Stephanie spent many years pursuing alternative forms of storytelling, from stage to screen and media to marketing. Meanwhile, an enduring love affair with words has led her down many a wormhole on the written page.

Drawn to what connects rather than separates, Stephanie is fascinated by the spaces between absolutes and opposites, between science and spirituality, nature and culture. This lifelong curiosity – and occasional conflict – has been channelled into her debut novel, *Bone Lines*, and its follow-up, *The Fire in Their Eyes*, book two in *The Children of Sarah* series.

Stephanie also writes short stories, such as *Human Error* and *Entropy* published in Breakthrough Books' *Taking Liberties* and *Order and Chaos* anthologies respectively and *The Right Kind of Medicine* for *Sunshine Superhighway* from Jay Henge. Various other works in progress keep her busy with authorly procrastination.

Published in Great Britain in 2025 by Breakthrough Books.

www.breakthroughbookcollective.com

Paperback ISBN: 978-1-0687185-7-1

Cover design and typesetting by Jamie Chipperfield

Cover images: Flames photograph © Keith Brodie, Cracked Ice courtesy of Unsplash

*To all the ancient storytellers of our precious planet,
since the first spoken, gestured or handmade words.
And all who honour their legacy.*

The Fire In Their Eyes, while being book two in *The Children of Sarah* series, is a stand alone novel. However, for those who may wish to refresh or familiarise themselves with certain characters first met in *Bone Lines*, a brief introduction to key players in both books can be found at https://stephaniebretherton.com/glossary/

THE FIRE IN THEIR EYES

Book Two in *The Children of Sarah* series

STEPHANIE BRETHERTON

Breakthrough Books

Somewhere

The infernal noise does not belong here, in this ancient, undefiled place.

The clanging and grinding of metal parts. A screeching mammoth tormented by an industrious swarm. A ravenous entity seeking knowledge equal to its survival. A hive mind awakened long ago and driven to remember how – and why – it was made.

The drill goes down, the ice comes up.

Other things listen and sigh. Yet more things stir and wonder if their time has come, again.

-1-

HERE AND THERE

The dawn brings an unfamiliar chill, a new wind has turned inward from the north. She rises before the rest of the clan, draws the remains of an old bear skin around her shoulders – the ragged smaller share that was left to her so long ago – and walks toward the river.

The others scold her for this dangerous habit. The four-legged hunters dream about an old woman such as you, they say, an old woman foolish enough to fetch water alone. To please them, she carries a spear, even if it proves more useful for walking than for killing.

She has no fear for her own safety from tooth or claw, no dread of her brothers and sisters in a different skin. The loss from such a deadly encounter haunts her daily, it is true, but like her mother before her she understands her fellow creatures. She can feel them, hear them, smell them. And unless foolishly distracted, she sees what they will do before they choose it for themselves.

It is not her fate to fill the belly of a beast, this much she knows, this much her mother had ensured by the reluctant sacrifice of her own spirit animal. Her path to the river will remain untroubled by any prowler.

Yet the shiver of the morning mist has stirred a different kind of fear. An ancient depth of ice, crackling in her bones. The others can neither share nor appreciate such terror, but The Old Woman remembers what it is to be cold, so cold a body can barely move. She was no more than a waddling child through that dark, endless winter, but certain marks are carved on the spirit for life.

Fear is a particular thing. Necessary and yet so often futile. She refuses to suffer it in the worthless and limiting ways. Pain is another matter. She feels her own, more and more – but mostly that of others. This is her gift, her curse.

Nevertheless, The Old Woman understands what fear can do. She has seen more loss and injury than any of her clan, whether warrior, hunter or longtooth, yet has never concerned herself with the claim that comes for every living thing. The claim that will come for her, soon enough.

Death has taken much from her, it is true. It has drunk from her heart too many times, but she has never indulged the fear of its embrace. Not even when the risks were sharper, when her children and her grandchildren needed her most. And even as her love for the living world grows stronger and sweeter by the day, The Old Woman knows she must – as everything must – leave it all behind in time. She knows what lies beyond and where this love will carry her.

Now she must collect water to carry back through the scrub, the rich red earth of her narrow path no more than a dull brown in the lingering mist. She aches for the morning sun, for more light, but she knows this way to water and could walk it eyes closed. Her fellow creatures seem quiet, no squawking yet at the dawn, perhaps they too are waiting for a true sense of the day. The stillness turns her back within.

But what she feels this morning is not some sharp or reflexive fear, it is a deeper sense of unease, a new and nagging visitor. It is not lashed to the smallness of her own shrinking life nor bound by the weariness of her body. This gathering dread is for the many – too many? – children yet to come, and what they may choose. What they may forget. What they may ravage in the void of that forgetting and in the hunger of their foolishness.

The First Mother has foreseen the power of her children, it is true. She came close to taking it all back from them, to putting them away from her forever. With fire and then with ice. Was she right to have forgiven them, to have granted them another chance?

The Old Woman chews on such thoughts whenever she feels a penetrating chill, from within or without. Perhaps it would have been better if none had survived those lightless seasons of ash. Better if there had been none left to suffer – in the way that her kind so love to do – and none left to cause any suffering?

She and her blessed band, the new family her mother had discovered at the end of an impossible journey, had somehow survived. Perhaps there were others, far from here, somewhere? Her kind had been reprieved, it seemed, if only by the handful. And why not? The Old Woman knows, all too well, that a mother must forgive.

And yet, how much pain can a mother withstand? Even The First Mother? Will she come with all her fire and fury once again, or only the unbearable cold of a heart so neglected it beats in stony silence, withered and twisted beyond all care?

As the morning chill abates, so do such worries. The heat of the rising sun is melting the mist as The Old Woman reaches the river. She breathes in its warmth, down into her complaining bones, then aims for a certain cut, that jagged corner of the red-brown bank where the water is shallow and clear. A spot where no snapping jaws can lurk unseen, where she can fill all the bladders she has strung about her waist by tucking her back safely toward the damp earth, eyes forward and open to whatever may approach.

Has she shared this knowledge yet? No, perhaps not. She must remember to tell another, at least one other, and show some sensible soul the safety of this place. Tonight, when they gather, she will find a way to impart a morsel of this wisdom – and, in time, of everything she knows.

It is true that some no longer hear her stories, no longer believe her. A few of the restless young, a finger-count of the careless, those who cannot find the time or the will to imagine another yesterday, a different tomorrow.

They listen kindly, they nod and smile. For, despite how they wonder at her wisdom when she acts in ways they cannot understand, she is revered among the clan. She remains the one they turn to in sadness or in pain. But her tales of the great walk, so far, so long ago, settle now like soot at the pit of a dying fire. Lost so easily to a thoughtless wind.

Her own fire is fading too, this she must accept, even if her ways of understanding grow only deeper. Who will take the cloak of this precious gift from her when the time is right? Who is brave and wise enough to wear it? There is so much still to pass along.

In truth, sometimes The Old Woman questions how much of her memory is clear. She does not doubt the feelings, but the details... have they altered with the years? Are they her own or are they borrowed from her mother?

Her mother. The Stranger. Now passed into myth. Yet she feels her still, hears her voice, draws from her strength.

There is no use in wondering, or in doubting. She knows she has further to walk, whether by crooked foot or in waking dream before she can follow her ancestors through the beckoning cave. All the pathways must be remembered, the lights of the heavens marked – in her own mind and in the minds of all who still believe. There are stories to be told.

⌒⌘⌒

'Hello?'

'Eloise.'

'Darius,' she whispers, adrenalin surging, 'What is it, why on earth are you calling at this hour?'

She might not have responded to the humming vibration at her bedside, had she not seen DARIUS light up so importantly on her screen. His had been only the second name, after MUMANDDAD, that she'd entered into her very first mobile phone, at a time when she'd had no patience for changing letter case or making spaces on the old-school keyboards. Even after multiple upgrades and saved SIM memory, she's never bothered correcting those early shortcuts – and capitals somehow suited Darius. She's never had the heart to delete her parents' old landline, even if no such call would ever come again.

But a call from Darius, especially when abroad and on a dig, always feels significant and full of portent, for good or bad. She recalls those many cryptic demands that *'we have to talk,*

Eloise. When I get back this time. We really have to talk.' The worst call of her life had come from Darius, too, the news of her father's accident during his last expedition. How Professor Kluft had seemingly chosen not to call for help, nor to reach for his haemophiliac's first aid kit, but had allowed himself to bleed out, unable to live any longer without her mother.

And yet Darius had also made the most significant call of her career. The news of the Mount Kenya discovery, the remarkable set of ancient remains that would ultimately become known as 'Sarah.' The project that would define the career of one Dr Eloise Kluft.

So, yes, Eloise knows she will always answer his calls – even this late at night – just as she will always open an email and always read a text despite the emotional trigger of registering his name. The formality of being addressed in full rather than with his preferred diminutive of 'Lolo' also feels significant.

'Is something wrong, Darius?'

'Oh, no. No, my love. Something is very, very right.'

'Hold on. Let me get up.'

She is fully awake now, sitting up, reaching for her reading glasses, if unsure why. Her stomach tightens. His resounding voice still raises a vortex of emotion, and she can clearly visualise the commanding if not-quite-handsome face of her first meaningful crush, exactly as she'd first encountered him, framed by copious black hair and a trim goatee, as he confidently assisted her father at one of his lectures. A vision that remains compelling, both for everything this first love had awakened in her, and for everything it had carved out of her.

Concerned not to waken the sleeping soul that now shares this once neat and spacious bedroom, Eloise pads down to the kitchen, and without turning on the light – she need not be reminded of its persistent shabbiness – she feels for and finds the quarter glass of wine abandoned earlier beside the sink. Neglected wine is now a common occurrence, unfinished like so many lesser personal plans, kitchen refurbishment included. She has other, more compelling distractions these days.

'OK. You have my full attention now. What is it, Darius? Where are you?'

'Back on Mount Kenya. We've found something.'

'What... where?'

'At the Sarah site. And now the ice is gone, we may find even more.'

'Another bone?'

'No, a claw. But not just any claw, Lolo. A huge claw. A claw that we really don't think has any place there at all. Not by itself, not naturally.'

Eloise walks into the unlit living room, sips her wine and immediately regrets it. 'Really? Oh wow. Do you think it has something to do with her, with Sarah? Was it near where the other bones were found?'

'Yes. Yes, very close. Though we need to be careful, we don't know nearly enough yet. And we won't know anything until we can age the claw. If it comes in at around 74 thousand years, we'll know it's a possibility. But there's more, Eloise. The claw has markings. It's been carved.'

'Bloody hell!'

'I know.'

⚬⚬⚬

Which tale to share with them tonight? The air is cool and clean. The dying Sun has singed the skyline into a furious glow, puffing out his chest like a warrior in defiance of his fear. Perhaps an evening such as this demands the playfulness of the Fire Spirit? Something to chase away that persistent northerly wind? Something to bring both warmth – and a touch of mischief?

They love her stories about the one who can change. From him to her and everything in between. From woman to animal, bird to fish, ghost to living flesh. But what purpose shall her wayward flame-walker serve this evening, she wonders, where shall it take them? Upwards perhaps, to the brightest star, to pursue it through a tiny tear in the pelt of the night and explore what can be learned from the whitest light behind? Or perhaps it will pull them downwards, somewhere deep beneath the earth? There are the secrets about its cousin, the wind, that this formless liar must reveal to her.

She places her hands to the ground, gazes to the sky. It is the soil who speaks first.

The Old Woman now asks the clan to look into the fire. The first one to see the face of the spirit must call out its name – and then she must catch it by the tail. There is a gasp and a cry, and she has him now. Yes, tonight the flame is a man, and a beauty at that. Oh, this is a naughty one. One who wants to be loved but at little cost to himself. Well, she has played with his kind before. She knows this game.

⚇

'Oh, come on stupid brain, get into bloody gear!'

A vigorous massage of the forehead fails in its intent. Eloise is familiar with frustration in her lab work, with the surges and setbacks of trial and error. Experiment. Measure. Repeat. But this gridlock of the grey matter is something else, both unwelcome and of a disturbingly different nature. Is this, she wonders, what they refer to as writer's block?

Shoving her laptop to the back of the antique roll-top desk, she stands up with an ache in her knees and paces across an unhelpful Persian rug, which, she feels, really ought to be more inspiring. Its thinner patches testify to the help it gave her father in finishing various tomes on archaeology.

Abandoning the task to make tea instead, Eloise curses as she returns and trips over nothing at all, the brew spilling darkly down a clean white shirt. At least she is alone and can relieve her vexation out loud. Clenching her jaw, she takes advantage of this temporary solitude to hiss-swear for a second round, this time with an extra serving of both volume and venom.

When in company, Eloise does her best to subdue the fiery irritability of the 'hormonic possession' that has blighted this stage of her life, if all too often she fails and must seek forgiveness. Today, however, it is neither her habitual clumsiness nor the petulance of technology that is torturing her. A lack of motivation then, or simply fear? Or the deep weariness of the sticky, cerebral molasses that seeps now through every irregular cycle? Whatever it is, the words simply will not come.

Why is this bloody foreword proving so difficult?

Eloise wants to understand. To be able to control and fix. The latest draft of *The Sarah Project* is now ready for her editor, with its revelations about archaic DNA, the various puzzle pieces that have coalesced into a thrilling picture of one remarkable human life – and the ancient era in which it had been lived – together with its hypotheses and insights into how such a distant past might be pertinent to our present challenges.

But its author, the renowned geneticist Dr Eloise Kluft, is struggling to switch the tone and content of her prose to something more... *personal.* Her publisher has requested a foreword with a more intimate and engaging context, allowing for some of the emotive touches that have been kept clear of the primary text. Something to chime with the smiling and slightly too glamorous 'head shot' they have taken of her for the back cover. The shoot for which she'd returned any greying strands in her now age-appropriately bobbed hair to their original blonde, and for which she'd permitted the makeup artist to 'bring out the Norwegian DNA' in her pale blue eyes, to highlight the contours of a face that remained as well-defined as her runner's form, even if surrendering more and more to the effects of gravity. Eloise had drawn the contractual line, however, at a character-erasing facelift courtesy of Photoshop, having long since made peace with every well-earned wrinkle.

Two cups of tea later, it dawns that the reason she's struggling with the introduction is because she knows neither where to begin nor where to end, in terms of the impact this extraordinary story has had upon her life. Sarah changed everything.

The entire experience – from the thrilling discovery of the skull to fighting for the DNA project, from its challenges and revelations to its unexpected hazards and traumas – had catapulted Eloise into the vitality of the here and now. Into a new determination, acquired from investigating the ancient past, to live more fully in the present and to grasp all of its opportunities.

Even so, she remains unable to compose even the first sentence of the deadline-looming foreword. It's a distracting relief, then, to hear the notification of a new message landing brightly in her inbox, and, in spite of herself, to feel that flicker of pleasure in identifying its sender. The grainy thumbnail portrait that flashes up cannot diminish a familiar, off-centre smile, the sculpted features behind black-framed spectacles, the dark eyes that had once looked at her less as one looks at a colleague and more as if seeking confirmation of their teasing chemistry. She can hear KC's calm, Midwestern tones as she reads.

TO: DrEloiseKluft@children.of.sarah.org
FROM: DrKCHarmon@viro.paleo.ac

Hey Eloise!

I'm sorry it's been so long and I wish this could be nothing more than a friendly hello and we'd have time to catch up, but I need to talk to you about something serious - and very urgent - and need to know when you're available for a secure call?

Thanks, KC

PS. I could use a pint of IPA and a bowl of "proper" chips about now. This misplaced Anglophile misses London!

PS again. I know you, and I know this is going to worry you, but don't worry too much, it's nothing personal (not yet, anyway) this is "business". Talk soon.

The journey below ground in the company of the Fire Spirit had not been as light-hearted as she'd hoped. She withholds her feelings from the others. There is little yet they need to know, only a new form of an old warning – that the brightest, hottest and most entrancing flame will happily scorch a careless heart before it burns itself out.

For now, she has shared only the needful reminder that not everything enticing is what it seems. Nor can it last. That one must look again with different eyes. That one must listen for the lies beneath the loveliest song. That the trickster succeeds by telling you what you most want to hear. How special you are.

And she is reminded of another truth as she claws her way upwards from sleep toward the morning light. In the bowel of the beast lies both poison and power, and each must be returned to the earth to make new life. She had felt that power again, under the ground, but she'd tasted the poison too, and now she understands. Something is coming.

The garden is cool and quiet, holding its breath. As Eloise is contemplating what she may miss of the coming spring, the resonant gong of an incoming SMS gives her a start. She remains unaccustomed to receiving so many texts, to communicating life and love in this easy, shorthand way. The culture – and the fraught, complex language of relationship – had been so very different when she was with Darius.

The message is, of course, from Tom.

Hey, just heard from the social, the next family court date re getting Josh back for good has been postponed again. Probably just as well considering your trip. Shame it couldn't have been before you go. Can't believe you're going before valentines!
Still, thanks for doing all this court stuff at all. Makes such a difference that you are 'here' (wherever you will actually be!) for us both. Luvya xxx

Looking at Tom's kiss-laden 'Luvya' her heart both lifts and falls.

She feels the persistent stab of how hard it will be to leave. Not this fond if weary old home, the one they'll all leave behind soon enough, along with London, whenever the farmhouse is renovated and ready. When her suddenly acquired family would be all under one roof at last – maybe by early summer? Eloise knows how blessed she is to have such options, the financial cushion of inheritance. But to leave Tom, if only for a few days or weeks, is a prospect loaded with pain. Once, this upcoming journey might have thrilled her towards a purpose, towards someone she looked forward to seeing again. Now she enjoys a life too full to leave behind so freely.

Tom's anxious expression as she'd begun to plan and pack, check and double-check her itinerary. His obvious fear. His struggle to understand this sudden, urgent departure, without her being able to tell him anything other than, 'It's vital work. Please just trust me.'

The way he keeps interrupting her busyness just to hold her. To search in her eyes.

Eloise has reassured him, promised, cajoled. This will be nothing like the last time they parted. And the agony but seeming necessity of that. The black hole of the years in between. Everything is different now. She *will* be back. This is work, only work, and it is essential for all of them, that's all she can say. She cannot delay, but she will miss him every day. She will call, FaceTime, email, or whatever way she can communicate, every day.

She will fly back in time for the next meeting with social services, the next family court date. But she'll also ask her dear friend John Evesham to provide a reference, to speak for them if need be and to show up in his reverential dog collar, all dressed to impress. They *will* get him back. Josh, Tom's beloved son.

She promised.

-2-

MANCHESTER

'Oh not again, Max! Will you never get bored of how good you look on the telly?'

About to leave for a night shift, Jessica leaned over the back of the saggy, brown corduroy sofa to kiss her husband goodbye, but found him rewinding through *The Story of Sarah* to enjoy his fifteen minutes of documentary fame once more.

Max pressed pause, twisted his long, lean torso around to look at her, tilted up his handsome head and pushed his surf-locks back to adopt a mocking, selfie-style pose.

'If I'm going to make a career out of this, babe, I need to know what works best. I have to work on my camera face.'

'A *career*? On telly? What about your bloody astrophysics doctorate? You know, the one I've been working so hard to help you afford?'

'They go hand in hand, sweetness. I need to be "Dr Max Michaelson" if I'm going to score any high-profile boffin gigs. They like their talking heads to come with titles, you know.'

'Shit. You're serious, aren't you?'

'Why not?'

'Oh God. You are. Are you? I'm never quite sure whether you mean anything you say. It's that Aussie inflection. It hides a multitude of piss-takes.'

'Well, TV would pay a shitload more than babysitting undergrads, babe. And then maybe you wouldn't have to wipe up the shit and dribble from all the night shufflers.'

'Oh, fuck you, Max. How dare you belittle my work? Or my patients. My profession is just as valid as yours.'

'Ah look, sorry babe, no offence. You know I appreciate every minute you have to spend in that nuthouse.'

'Yeah, right. God, I don't know why I bother.'

Jess had all but given up on tutoring Max on his 'problematic' expressions, praying only that he would never use such banter in front of her colleagues. Or his. She didn't know why they all forgave him so easily and excused his sharper edges. It wasn't excusable at all, but he played his charm for all it was worth.

She turned to leave, but caught sight of the screen again. 'Did you ever hear anything more about her? Dr Kluft?' She indicated the white-coated woman now held in half-blinking freeze-frame on a TV Jess had always felt was too large and ostentatious for their modest two-up-two-down. 'Was she OK after that hostage thing?'

'Yeah, she was fine. Far as I know.'

'A drama like that, though. It affects you one way or another. Some people end up with PTSD, others do alright. Some even thrive. Get their priorities sorted.'

Jess wondered whether she should tell Max about Calumn Berryman, the arsonist and fundamentalist cult member who had held Dr Kluft – and the bones of 'Sarah' – hostage. It was an odd coincidence, for sure, him ending up on her ward, but she knew Max would only ask too many questions, which could only compromise patient confidentiality.

'Why wouldn't she thrive?' asked Max. 'Life's what you make of it, babe. I mean, I did alright after my little mountaineering-slash-archaeology accident on Mount Kenya. The tumble into that glacier, finding those bones. Best thing that ever happened to me.'

'The best thing? *Ever*? Are you sure?'

'Apart from you, angel, eh. Naturally.'

How did he do it? Make up for everything with a blue-eyed wink, a shake of his sunburnt curls and a flash of that tigerish grin? 'Right. That'll cost you breakfast, you bastard. See you in the morning.'

'Wait... where's my kiss?'

TO: calumnberryman@patient-secure.hmhosp.org
FROM: revjohnevesham@bettering.world.org

Dear Calumn

Thank you for inviting me to the hospital and for seeing me. I can appreciate this was not easy for you. I accept that you do not wish to talk about the events with Dr Kluft and the bones of "Sarah" nor about the "family" you felt you belonged to at the time and who had encouraged those actions, but should that ever change, please consider my ears (and my heart and, I hope, my understanding) open. But also completely discreet!

Your loyalty to that group, despite how they have abandoned you, is commendable. You clearly have a great capacity for devotion. I only hope we can explore that together in ways that are less harmful and more fruitful for you. I look forward to seeing you again next month.

Yours faithfully,
Rev. John Evesham

'Can you see it now?'

'Oh, yes, yes. How far?' Jess asked, moving herself against Max with the joy of discovery, their pre-dawn breakfast abandoned for a different form of communion, skin to skin, eyes to the heavens.

'Sirius?' he answered. 'About eight light years.'

'Eight years. We weren't even aware of each other when that light first left home.'

'No.'

'Thank God.'

'For what?'

'That you were there. Here. Now.'

'And you, babe. But "God" didn't have anything to do with it.'

'Well, you know what I mean, Max. It's amazing.'

'Everything's amazing, babe. And the more you look, the more you see.'

Max turned Jessica's warm body around to face him and kissed her forehead, lifted her hand and kissed her fingers, her wedding ring, the one he had chosen immediately on seeing it, knowing it was exactly right. 'You see this finger? This beautiful finger? In every moment billions of neutrinos pass through it, right the way through it, and you're not even aware of it, you don't even feel it.'

'I feel you.'

'Ah, but do you? We never really touch you know. It's just atoms repelling each other. That's what you feel.'

'Oh, Max. Don't spoil it.'

Max pulled her away from the telescope, away from the window and back to the bed.

Some might have described his Jess as ordinary. Her sensual appeal was subtle, saved for those who could really see her. She wore no make-up, let her lush brown hair fall wherever it wanted. But beneath her comfortable clothes lay curves that Monroe might once have envied, silked in skin so smooth he never tired of touching it. Her gentle face didn't demand a second look at first meeting, but it had become, for Max, his very own Da Vinci.

Jess was not undamaged. A traumatic childhood had found her and her sister torn between the warring factions of a deeply devout mother, who had refused a divorce, and an estranged father, embittered by his captivity and cruelly familiar with the comforts of the bottle and the bordello. Yet Jess had embarked on marriage with characteristic optimism and the same dedication she'd poured into becoming a nurse.

Specialised in psychiatric care, she worked long shifts and was often hidden from Max under a coating of other people's pain, but she always found her way back to him again. Jess always bobbed up to the surface. The first time he'd seen her, she'd been battered by a wave at Bondi and rolled to shore, bemused and bedraggled but laughing, her bikini dredged with sand, half exposing one outstanding breast and a round sweep of plump, pink cheek.

It had all been so easy. They met, dated, fell in love. While many – those tarnished by experience and who could never understand the ruby rarity of a love that just comes, just fits – accused them of marrying in haste, a few feared they were doing so to clear the path to visas between Australia and England. But Max and Jess were never in doubt.

Her sister was one of those who didn't seem so sure. This bothered Max, not only because he was accustomed to instant popularity, but because Jess and her sister were so very alike. How could one love him, unquestioning, and the other not even seem to like him much?

Manda had not yet forgiven him for the rushed civil ceremony on Sydney Harbour on New Year's Eve, feeling that free fireworks were a poor substitute for Jess having her family at her wedding. Now they were settled back in the UK, Manda was gradually warming up, beginning to trust him, and this made Jess happy. It was surprisingly easy to make Jess happy.

Her mother was a different story. Not only was Max not a Catholic – neither, actively, were either of her girls – but he had no religious fervour at all, except for the majesty of the universe and a determination to be its new Einstein. Max's faith was in his own potential.

Perhaps he would identify the 'dark' dimensions gobbling up gravity and making it so inexplicably weak. Maybe find the planets that could bear evolved life. Or continue Dirac's trajectory of marrying mutually shy relativity with quantum theory. Stare directly into the fathomless eye of a black hole and see so much more than the different heat colours, so much more than a fuzzy ball of string (theory)... perhaps find a form of quantum computer there... and all the stolen information it had consumed waiting within.

Or, in pure fantasy, he might test Susskind's theory that all the information from every 'reality' was scrambled and reflected like a two-dimensional holograph at the very edge of the universe.

There would be something to make his mark, for sure. Jessica's love was the sweetest reward Max could imagine, but it was a goal already achieved, if not without its niggles. And Jess was not *entirely* his. The subtle, triangular tug of war between partner, family and profession – for both of them – was already setting up some unwelcome strains. His family ties and responsibilities were far enough away not to pull so persuasively. Hers were closer, in every way.

The way Max saw it, he protected Jess from her mother's catechism of negativity and guilt, even if Mrs Wallace saw only unwelcome heckling from the gallery and interference with the audience to her tragedy. Max Michaelson had not been part of the script.

'What if we had never met?' asked Jess.

'Sssh...' He moved over her.

'No, but really, can you imagine?'

'We were meant to meet.'

'You don't believe in fate, Max.'

'No. But I believe in this.'

❧

TO: revjohnevesham@bettering.world.org

FROM: calumnberryman@patient-secure.hmhosp.org

Dear Rev Evesham

Thanks. I am willing to see u again. Nurse Jessica (the only one in here I can bare, she is touched by the Holy

Spirit, u kno, u can see that too, cant u?) well she
thinks it will do me good. But as aggreed pls dont ask
me about the others. I let them down with my weakness,
they are right to turn their faces from me. I failed
them but I wont betray them.

Calumn B.

That moment over the Barrier Reef, on their honeymoon, when she had found herself in the middle of a morphing field of minnows. Tiny, glistening, silent, but so connected they moved as a single mass. Jess had swum into them deliberately on the outbreath, expecting them to scatter away and then rejoin, hoping only for an instant in their midst before they evaded her perceived predation. But the school had simply re-formed around her stillness, as she kept her lungs empty and equalised her float. Then she was part of them for seconds that stretched into the stoppage of time. She felt their resonance, their communication, their absolute unity.

When life became too frenetic, Jess would close her eyes and go back to this and know what she needed to know. It was an escape that was essential to her working life. Each patient presented their own challenges but sometimes the hardest to help were the relatives. Those who had changed the nappies, shared a bed, or fed at the breast of the one now lost in a wilderness they could not access. With a broken leg, even cancer, they would have known what to do, how to comfort and connect, but so many of the residents here lived in a world beyond reason or recognition.

Jess understood all too well that to detach, to not feel guilty or responsible, to know that it was the illness talking or the imbalance acting and not the person you love, was desperately difficult.

Tonight, the ward was heavy with unhappiness and the medicated quiet could not contain the sense of something festering. At least she didn't have to attend to any of those in solitary, to the looming bulk of one Eddie Briggs in particular. She was in no mood for his vulgarity and barely withheld lust for violence. Nevertheless, she had almost completed the early rounds of her night shift when she came to the paint-peeling door that always gave her pause, even if it was left open once she was through and with a security guard in the corridor.

Calumn was ready, quiet, his sleeves rolled up in acquiescence. Today would not be a day when he refused his treatment. Even better, he was seated. This was a relief as his emaciated height, prominent bones and awkward limbs not only felt otherworldly at times, but made administering to his needs somehow more challenging, as though she might easily damage him. Jess was relieved.

Calumn looked at her. 'You are with child.'

Jess nearly dropped the insulin. She felt her stomach clench against a rising swell of nausea.

'Yes. Yes, I am. But I'm not showing yet. How did you know?'

'The child is special. But he must be consecrated to God. Otherwise he will be in great danger. Do you understand?'

-3-

HERE AND THERE

'**I**f it came from the ice, maybe we can get help from ice. What about exhuming some victims of the Spanish flu from any frozen ground left in Greenland? They had a number of cases there. Let's see if we can isolate the virus, see if it's similar?'

An unidentified male voice is echoing from out of view. The effect is no less disconcerting to Eloise than much of her experience so far, since arriving in the Norwegian Arctic to meet KC at the quarantined research station. Their first video call with smiling, lab-coated colleagues half a world away, and certain mysterious powers-that-be off screen, is doing little to put her at ease. She glances at KC, huddled beside her in front of the iPad, after the mystery member of the off-site committee has offered his suggestion.

KC nods and so she replies. 'It's worth a try but the Spanish flu is probably still too recent. The deepest part of the ice core that was pulled up for the geological survey is over 70,000 years old. If it did somehow come from that, unlikely as it seems – if that's what our patients are dying from here – then we're dealing with something way beyond any living or recorded memory.'

'Having said that, we don't have time not to try, even if it's a long shot,' offers KC. 'Can we get an executive order to dig them up?'

'I thought the quarantine was successful?' asks the voice, its indistinguishable accent heavy with authority and concern, 'I thought it was isolated?'

'We think so, but we can't be one hundred percent sure,' answers KC. 'Since the emergency team got here, of course we're observing Biosecurity Level Four, but we can't be sure what happened before the alarm call. It's possible Patient Zero had some kind of contact with indigenous herders, but we haven't traced them. He died in delirium talking about dogs and reindeer but we can't be sure if he'd had actual contact or was hallucinating. No one from the original team who's lucid enough seems to think that's the case and there's nothing in the field logs. But then the herders have been much further north than usual for this time of year. Especially after the anthrax unleashed by the last crazy permafrost melt killed off so many of their deer.'

'So how do we know it didn't come from the herders?' asks the voice, a darkly clad elbow belonging to its owner now visible in a corner of the screen.

'Because all those who've died or have become ill had direct contact with the core ice, or else with each other.' KC continues, 'There's no record of any indigenous contact with anyone else here and there are no reports of sickness among the Sami before the outbreak, or since.'

'Could they be immune carriers, or asymptomatic?'

Why won't the speaker reveal himself? Eloise wonders, imagining KC thinks the same. She leans in closer for the comforting pressure of another, familiar shoulder.

KC takes this as encouragement to keep answering. 'Possible, but unlikely. We're trying to get permission to take bloods and swabs from that community. But if it *is* like a flu, which subtly mutates every season, or Covid which mutates even more quickly, then any adaptive immunity probably wouldn't last, unless it was somehow genetically conferred.'

Surely anyone party to a call such as this would know that?

'Is it flu? I mean we know it's not another corona, right?'

Ah, there he is, peering down from a corner of the screen: a 'suit' Eloise doesn't recognise. Younger than he sounds. But not a scientist? Not even fully briefed, it seemed. And with relations so strained in international public health, his presence is perplexing.

Eloise answers him. 'It looks a little like some flu-causing viruses, both in its structure and as it presents, bar a few notable extra symptoms: A sandpaper rash, photophobia, diarrhoea, one case of jaundice. It's almost like a pick-and-mix of old enemies. But no, this thing is different enough to anything we've seen before, so we shouldn't consider it a flu or try to assign an easy identity...'

'You think this is old, then? Not a new zoonotic?'

'It's certainly a possibility,' confirms KC. 'I mean, that's partly why Dr Kluft and I are here, right, to have paleogenetics as part of the virology team? Because we might be looking at archaic DNA?'

⚭

```
Encrypted Status Report:


STRICTLY CONFIDENTIAL


To: Eugene Vanterpool, Director, UKGenIn


Dear Eugene


You may be relieved to hear from me, at last? So, this
is what we know and what I am now permitted to share
with you, and you only:


Twenty-five days ago a researcher in an international
Arctic lab came down with a "cold". Except it wasn't
a cold, it wasn't even a bad case of man-flu. Within
two days all three of his dormitory mates had it too,
and the woman who worked beside him. He, and soon after
all the other infected, were immediately quarantined
in sickbay by the remaining team.


Then two more came down with it, and then another
three more, leaving only six unaffected and keeping the
station running. An emergency intervention including
hazmatted medics arrived within eight hours of the
alarm call and quarantined even the healthy to their
```

dormitories, setting up separate facilities for the research team to follow, which includes myself and Dr KC Harmon, whom you know well.

After three days of sickness and after apparently rallying, Patient Zero succumbed to a rapid cascade of organ failure and internal haemorrhaging and died on day five. Dehydration and weakness from a couple of days trying to fight or ignore the sickness may have played a part, but then two others followed a similar tragic course.

The remainder have been stabilised, for now. Case Fatality Rate of 50% so far. Not unusual in the early days of an outbreak but extremely worrying nonetheless, especially in previously healthy people. The international team here, courtesy of the Norwegian government and military, includes virologists, microbiologists, geneticists, infection control experts, investigators, data analysts, and of course medics, all observing the correct levels of biosecurity.

Lessons learned from Wuhan! I still can't believe they were working only at BSL2 in their coronavirus research, with no protection against airborne transmission, and that the Defuse funding from the US was ok with that, just to save money.

Of course, we don't know what happened there after they cut off from their foreign partners in 2017, but what a way to explode trust in scientists! And now with everything that's happening to gut publicly owned science in the US… we have such an uphill battle on our hands.

The source of infection with the new virus here cannot

be traced to the station's food or water supplies. As far as can be ascertained, Patient Zero had no recorded or reported contact with any animals or birds, certainly not in the immediate vicinity of the station. It didn't come from contact outside the lab (we don't think).

It may have come from an ice core sample he had defrosted and was working on. His lab mate said he was not always so scrupulous about protocols and had a habit of snacking at every break. The boredom factor of this isolated location can bring out certain comfort behaviours, apparently.

A failure of judgment of course, a very human error, maybe a bit of lingering 'brain fog' from even before this new infection, but then this is not a virology lab and they weren't working with known pathogens. Nevertheless, any ancient ice or permafrost needs great care in handling, and this may prove to be another mistake the science community cannot afford.

Back to the facts: The ice core is approximately 74,000 years old. A virus has been isolated from the patients and is subtly different to anything we've seen before.

As you are aware, I have samples and readouts of Sarah's DNA with me, and now I have informed you of the date of the ice core sample, you will understand why. Although Sarah was found in Africa, ancient human DNA may yet be of use here for comparative purposes. We also have DNA samples from the deceased here and the very sick and the one who seems to be fighting it most successfully.

We're working every hour within safety guidelines. There's no reason to believe this has, or could, or will spread any further but there's an urgent attempt to contact any other human populations in a wide radius and check for signs of sickness.

One sample of the ice core, however, may have been sent to another lab. The records Patient Zero kept were unclear, he was already becoming ill. All contact between this research station and every other it collaborates with are being traced. We have to learn better from so many failures with Covid and be religious about the mantra of test, trace and isolate - and immediate quarantines. Even without the cooperation of key superpowers!

Apart from the paleo connection, my main focus, as ever, is immunity. Despite the time pressures, the day-to-day work, as you will well understand, is slow, methodical, repetitive and requires absolute precision, from titration and incubation to the paradigm plate-reader. I will update as and when appropriate and approved, but I think it's safe to assume I will not be back at my desk in the very near future.

Dr Eloise Kluft

The Old Woman remains disturbed by notions that have taken root but will not take recognisable shape. She cannot know what approaches but feels it crawling closer to the clan every day. The nights are no less restive. The strangest sensation is one she can name only as arousal. She has not experienced a stirring of this kind for many seasons, but the pretty limbs of the flame-walker that had danced to life that evening around the campfire seem to have awakened feelings long buried.

The young, who imagine the earth and all its pleasures have been made for themselves alone, would laugh at her for expressing or acting on such compulsions. Yet she had shared a lasting passion with her mate until his sudden passing and knew many other mothers and fathers in the clan who kept their desires alive, either with their life-mates or with other agreed partners.

Then she realises it's not that kind of longing. This is something other, even if it begins in the pit of her belly to raise a heat that flushes upon her skin. It is an appetite, yes, but one that neither feast nor coupling could satisfy.

It is the sense of something calling to her, waiting for her, wanting her. It is the call to leave behind all that divides her from the realms of the spirit and fall back into its endless river. A call she is so tempted to answer. Not yet, surely? They have need of her here for a little while longer.

⫘⫘

```
TO: tom2tattoo@finte.mail.com
FROM: DrEloiseKluft@children.of.sarah.org
```

My darling Tom

It's too early to Facetime, but I need to get this down before it dissipates. I know other people's dreams are never as compelling as they feel to the dreamer and it's impossible to translate the weirdly 'real' sensations of that subjective state, but I'm compelled to try.

Last night I dreamt of Sarah.

It's hardly the first time she's meandered through my nightscapes - usually embodying the challenges we faced in unravelling her secrets - but this was new. An extraordinary 'close encounter.'

Perhaps the finished reconstruction has made her more real to me? That muscular yet elegant form, the lustrous brown skin, the mass of black hair, the proud, prominent bone structure, the inclination to daring that's written into her DNA… and now also her visualised and gloriously expressive form. But Sarah has always been a powerful presence to me, even when no more than a mysterious set of archaic remains in my laboratory.

I know you didn't share that journey with me, but thanks again for being the first audience for my book - my 'average punter' sample as you would put it - and for all the interest you've taken in my work. Nevertheless, I do feel that Sarah somehow *connects* us. Without her I may never have been open to a second chance with you, or what we have now. I may never have abandoned my preconceptions as to what constitutes a 'suitable' relationship, may never have looked past the obstacles and the differences, in age or otherwise and - yes, I'm going to say it - 'listened to my heart.'

But I saw her, Tom, so clearly. She was in her world and yet also in mine. More than that, I *felt* her. She was so vigorous, yet so vulnerable. She was cold, but not yet on the mountain. She was suffering from something, some kind of illness, but I knew this was not what killed her, this was something she'd managed to overcome. She didn't speak to me, but I understood what she was trying to tell me.

I don't know if you've ever dreamed of flying, but if so you might understand the exhilaration I enjoyed, and the disappointment I felt on waking. I was at once unmoored and unrestrained, as if anything was possible yet everything was at stake. And while I still can't tell you about my 'mission' here, I can say that her presence in my subconscious confirmed the tantalising notion that Sarah somehow holds a vital key to the work we're doing right now.

I miss you madly, in every way, but the simple holding most of all. The way we so easily connect and share in

```
each other. I can't remember the last time I properly
laughed but I know it must have been with you.


I love you. You must know that by now. As you must
always have known, even when I turned away.


Bye for now, my beloved,
xEx
```

Days tumble into days, and even if she cannot shake the conflicting sensations that have gripped her, solace can be found in familiar routines and in the company of the innocent.

They gather drowsily now on the cool, red earth, inviting the warmth of the yellow rays that have reached above the boundary of darkness. The children have come to her while their parents go about the tasks that keep their offspring alive. Some giggle as they rediscover the day, some squabble over a piece of honeycomb, some pick the grit from their eyes, noses or navels. But soon, as she squats in stillness, breathing deeply and steadily from the delicious morning air and cradling the little ones within those circles of breath, they fall into silence – until she asks one of them to begin.

Every morning The Old Woman listens to the dreams of the children. Their natural wisdom must be encouraged, their fears soothed, but there are other reasons for this ritual. The young ones may be allowed to hear and to remember what their parents have forgotten, they may become the voices of those no longer held back by the heavy weight of skin and bone, those not separated from the greater world by a single, lonely body.

Their parents have other distractions. When a stomach is hungry, a heart is angry, or a womb is yearning to be filled, then eyes may search, muscles may strain and skin may tingle, but ears are too often closed.

Some of the children remember their dreams and some forget, too concerned with the promises of the morning. Some pretend to remember to win her favour. She listens even so – imagination also deserves its rewards. The boy she has chosen to talk about his dream today seems both excited and troubled by his nocturnal reunion with his other self.

He stands, faces the sun, allows it to cast the darkness of his own shape behind him, then reaches around to scoop up the dirt that lies in that darkness and rubs it over his face. The Old Woman understands. Freed from the luminous bonds of the daytime to take control of the night, the boy's shadow has become his nocturnal guide. He tells them now how he and his shadow have ventured beyond the clearing, beyond the shelter of the forest and into the waving grass where the fast ones run.

This is not unusual; most of the boys long to make this same journey with their fathers. Many of the girls too. The girls of her own mother's line, for sure. Particularly the grandchild who is so like that tall, wild-haired Stranger, the one who had walked here from the north, miraculously, the infant at her back carried safely from the ice and the ravenous and the tribes of the lost.

The Old Woman sees her own mother in every serious stride taken by the dark, lithe legs of that woman's great-granddaughter and in every toss of The Tall Girl's untamed mane. Those tight curls come from the girl's father, though the length and thickness of her hair are marks of The Stranger's making. That name, the name the tribe had given to the woman who had walked so far, had stuck, even years after her arrival.

Had she ever felt her mother to be a stranger? Perhaps. There had been a deep wound in that woman. Such losses, such terrors, such efforts, such hunger. She had never been fully whole, as much as her daughter with her light touch of healing had tried to help. Scars were borne that even a child with her own powerful gifts, unformed and emerging, was unable to heal.

There were inner grooves to echo the outer scars rubbed deep into her mother's shoulders and back. Scars that had been carved by carrying a growing child in a series of roughly made baskets over such distances, along with everything needed to ensure their survival. Marks that made her daughter believe she must do everything possible to earn the precious life such efforts, such suffering, had granted her.

The Old Woman looks again at her own granddaughter, sitting among the other children, listening to the little boy's dream. The Tall Girl's burning eyes belong not to that brave, suffering Stranger, nor to any from the tribe she had been welcomed into, but to another still – and this particular distinction has been The Old Woman's to give.

Indeed, all of her own children and grandchildren have claimed these same eyes of fire that she alone had brought here, bound upon The Stranger's back, delivered from somewhere beneath the rising sun on behalf of a father she would never know. A sparkling sign that sets all of her surviving line apart, in ways both useful and dangerous.

The Tall Girl has been gifted the fiery eyes and the speed of a distant paternal line, it is true, but she also carries the courage and strength of her maternal ancestry. This is good, this is necessary, for those limbs and that long and muscled back have borne an extra burden since infancy. The weight of another beloved soul, one that her grandmother, The Old Woman, pines for every day. The one who gave his life to save this child, leaving a wound that still twists within, even if she rarely has the freedom to weep for this, or indeed for anything, without worrying the clan.

But now she must turn her attention away from her own thoughts and memories and listen once more. The boy, the chosen dreamer, is telling them of his flight across the grass. While The Old Woman had pondered the survival of her own line for a distracted moment – and the ache of a loss she cannot release, as much as she ought to – the boy and his shadow have since changed into a hawk as they continue their starlit adventure.

He stretches his arms wide, feathers his slender fingers, turns his face to the ground. This is good, an intriguing turn. The vision of a bird is always a boon. What can he see from up there? A new star shape to guide them? A group of celestial brothers to match those blessed seven sisters? Or perhaps an old hunting trail waiting to be rediscovered? She listens more intently now, just as she should.

Recollections of those lost can wait for the loneliness of the night, to warm the tired skin that no longer wraps so close about her bones nor seems to be fully her own, which no longer shines as it once did, plump and bright and full of inviting hope. And yet, these most tender of memories love her no less in return, for all the inescapable decay.

The boy has never been close to ice before, so how can he describe it? The world has been turned like a turtle, he says. The sky is now below. The earth is like a cloud, completely white, like a heavy-skied day before the summer rains, but brighter than such clouds, so much brighter. Sparkling white like the top of the mountain. Like their distant, sacred mountain.

The Old Woman shivers as he shares his vision. Not only at the thought of a land formed entirely of bright, solid cloud, but at the reminder of her mother's mountain. Her mother's grave? A place of both power and pain for both of them, if in different ways.

The boy may not understand what his dream has shown him, but he recognises the physical sensations that were also part of the experience. He explains how one morning in another season – a true morning, belonging to the waking hours – he had jumped into a rock pool fed by a high-tumbling waterfall, too early for the sun to have blunted the stony blade of its dark and chilly water, so he knows how such searing cold can steal away the breath, stop the limbs, hurt the bones. The air in his dream, he reveals, had felt the same.

The Old Woman leans in and listens closely as he tells her more about how he and his shadow, having borrowed the wings of the mighty bird, had flown much further than any dreaming child she could remember. To places even she has never seen, waking or sleeping, or at least that she could recall.

This is a land that never sees the night, the boy tells her, and yet never sees the day. Both, or perhaps neither, he is unsure. And while this makes no sense, she feels it must be possible, that such a place of never-ending ice is more than possible, it is essential –

and not only to the world of dreams. A land where life is hard and death is easy, but somewhere so precious it would mean a slow and brutal death for all that lived, if ever its own life were lost.

Her own visions of late have shared the sensations of this chill but are not as crystalline. Ah, the clear eyes of youth, both within and without. Nor are her visitations, illuminated by the brightness of ice. Rather, she sees these very children at her feet as though stalked by a shadow, a shape she cannot yet see. Neither beast, nor spirit, nor man. Or perhaps this is some form of man, after all? One not truly alive and yet not quite dead?

These thoughts make no sense. But the threat is dark and cold and empty, this much she knows. It comes from something with a hunger beyond satisfaction, something drained not of blood, but of the true essence of the heart.

4

MANCHESTER

C ould Calumn know about her single degree of separation from his 'nemesis', Dr Kluft? How? Jess used her maiden name at work, never spoke about Max or her personal life, certainly nothing about his discovery of 'Sarah'. Was Calumn simply messing with her head when he'd pronounced that strange intuition about her pregnancy? Or had one of her colleagues let something slip about Max and his now infamous climbing accident on Mount Kenya? Jess wasn't sure that anyone below her paygrade was even aware of all these coincidental connections.

Her seniors, of course, knew that she'd once met Calumn's hostage victim during the making of a documentary, and that it was her own adventurer husband who'd found the very bones that Calumn had tried to burn – the very bones that had opened the door to Max's small-screen ambitions.

She'd declared a potential conflict of interest, but the board had felt that as long as Calumn remained unaware, and Jess had no qualms, this should not recuse her from his care. She had their trust. Though she also wondered whether this peculiar web of events and players might have indeed fascinated them, with the seductive thrill of proximity to a sense of 'fate'?

Then again, there were simple, practical considerations. Yes, it had been acknowledged that Calumn's persecution complex could only regress should he ever discover her connection to Dr Kluft, but they were too short-staffed, too lacking in nurses of her experience and calibre – or willingness to work here – to re-assign or relocate her. She'd been assured they had every confidence both in her discretion and detachment.

But *should* they have such confidence? Should she? Jess was rattled, it was true, but she had never before let any personal remarks or micro-aggressions discourage her from helping a patient. She was not about to give in now. This was her career, her passion. She wanted to come back to it after maternity leave – and at the level she'd left it.

So, should she tell Max about this bizarre connection, especially now, after Calumn's unnerving comments, his creepy prediction about their child? Max would laugh it off as nonsense at first, but then he would worry. He worried about her working life enough as it was.

Yes, she had to admit she'd been adversely affected by the conversation, but she wasn't exactly frightened. She felt no particular fear of Calumn, only concern and, yes, a certain wariness and discomfort. But then she needed to remain risk-alert to *all* of her patients. Jess realised nonetheless that she'd be wise to talk to someone about it. Not Max, though. And not management. Not yet.

'Consecrated to God.' Even for Calumn that had been a peculiarly specific phrase. He was neither Catholic nor High Church as far as she was aware, and if anything was probably prejudiced against such papist 'sorcery'. True, he had a formality about his manner, but talk of sacraments seemed almost idolatrous and even indulgent for one so austere.

As she got ready to leave for work, Jess decided to take a closer look at the pastor who'd recently visited Calumn at his specific request. Although this had been greenlit through a different department, she'd asked admin for the basics about his visitor at the time. John Evesham had been cleared as having no connections to the cult of which Calumn had been a member. What's more he was an approved and experienced prison and hospital visitor, with an impressive reputation and set of references.

But now she wondered why Calumn had requested *this* particular minister, and why Reverend Evesham had been so willing to travel up from London to oblige. There was an assigned chaplain already attending the facility, so this new, external arrangement seemed conspicuous. Internet access for patients was limited, pre-approved and monitored, so how had Calumn come to know of him? Some further investigation seemed in order and Jess resolved to make this her admin priority for tonight's shift. Maybe it was time to take another look at the available records from Calumn's legal defence and pre-trial diagnosis.

Max's phone vibrated but he resisted pulling it from his pocket and instead gave Jess her requisite hug before work. She seemed to hold on a little longer and closer than she normally would, and he knew he should have asked her what was up, but his phone was feeling hotter than usual in his jeans.

He'd been a touch more careful with that device of late, especially in proximity to his wife. Marcy, the director from the Sarah documentary, was now on speed dial but under the name 'Carl (climbing)'. Max wasn't sure why he'd chosen such subterfuge, there was nothing going on there, nothing ever likely to. He didn't need to scratch the kind of itches many men suffered. Jess was enough for him. Jess was everything. But there was *something* about Marcy, a sense of being at ease with an adventurous sexuality which created a frisson he did not discourage. More to the point, Marcy could become particularly useful to him.

She certainly had a compelling authority, not only courtesy of her sharp-shouldered, jacket-over-jeans signature look and even sharper haircut, but also because of her occupancy of the director's chair. This aura of confidence was appealing, if not an irresistible turn on, because Max knew ambition when he saw it and recognised in Marcy a fellow traveller. That woman was going places, and with a camera… hopefully to the kind of locations where he might tag along as 'the talent.'

He kept his contact with Marcy clear of Jess because he'd anticipated his wife's negative reaction to his small-screen aspirations. She would never put a leash on him, nor on his dreams, but Jess certainly had her insecurities, especially when it came to the reliability of men – and men who travelled for work in particular. Max had no desire to cause his beloved any unnecessary worry or pain.

Nevertheless, as soon as she was safely through the front door, he retrieved his phone from his pocket and pressed send on the saved draft of a message to Marcy. It was little more than a friendly 'hey, how ya goin'?' followed by further compliments on the stellar job she'd done with *The Story of Sarah*, which he'd recently rewatched. And an invitation to lunch if ever she happened to be in Manchester or if he was down in London.

⚭

```
TO: calumnberryman@patient-secure.hmhosp.org
FROM: RevJohnEvesham@bettering.world.org


Dear Calumn


I do plan to come and see you again, but it may not be
as soon as hoped. A certain administrative wrinkle has
arisen, which I'm sure I'll be able to iron out. It is
my mistake, so I hope you will forgive me.


In the meantime, it might not hurt if you were
to reassure your care team, and Sister Wallace in
particular, of your continued enthusiasm for our
contact? I have every intention of doing my best to
keep visiting you. Your wellbeing matters to me very
much and you remain in my prayers.


In fact, I have even invested in a new umbrella
in consideration of Manchester's often monsoon-like
micro-climate and in anticipation of many further
visits. I did get thoroughly soaked on my way back to
the train station last time, which made for a rather
soggy journey home! I will be in touch again as soon
```

as I have news.

Yours, John.

SMS: From 'Carl (Climbing)'

Hey Max! Or is it Dr Max yet? Great to hear from you! How's it hanging? (If that's what I'm supposed to ask a surf bro?) And thanks again. The Sarah story was a complete joy to work on and it was so lovely to meet you and Jessica. Actually, this is great timing because I was thinking of getting in touch. Possible Horizon commission for the beeb! Probably better discussed over a phone call? Or Zoom? Let me know when's good for you?
Marcy x

One of the few positives about night shifts was a quieter pool during the weekday, and Jess could usually find a women's only session. No would-be Olympians splashing their clumsy strokes into her path, with perfect timing for a mouthful of warm public water. Today she had three lanes to herself and could access that rhythmic loss of thought that carried her into tranquillity. This was her medium, this was where she belonged.

Her father had taught her to swim. A navy diver, he'd found the one skill that might be truly useful to his girls, whenever he was around. Kicking a ball about was never on the agenda. He had no particular prejudices about what females could or couldn't do, but there was no sign of those talents in either of his girls. He had neither the aptitude nor the availability for overseeing homework or for story reading. Or, indeed, for moral instruction. That was their mother's domain.

Jess thought of him every time she was in the water. That brief shore-based posting at HMS Tamar in Hong Kong had been the finest time of their lives. All together. Manda had been too young to remember much but for seven-year-old Jess it had been formative. Only two years in basic quarters right before the handover, but such magic.

The lights on the harbour, the smells and the sounds and the tastes and the wild, wet heat. Beaches and boats and clubhouses, all with ready-made friends and accompanied by the music of her mother's laughter, now so rarely heard. Jess remembered diving from her father's broad shoulders, slippery with suntan oil, into the clear, cooling waters. Then closing her ears to the late-night shouts and accusations, the smashed cocktail glasses and launched ashtrays.

Those days had given Jess the travel bug that had bypassed her sister, whose quintessential Englishness tied her more closely to their mother. Manda had been happy to slip into stability as a kindergarten teacher in Bristol until she had children of her own, whenever 'the one' came along. But he was taking his time. Jess knew that Manda suffered from daddy issues which had often affected her choices, one way or another. Their father's last postcard was from Manila. He had found a way to exploit some poor woman over there and settled into a life of tropical dissolution.

For now, Jess let each length of the pool wash away her worries. Her high-maintenance mother. How time had diminished her, reduced her once sparkling personality to an evaporated residue of regret. The progressive arthritis, a gnawing condition that had also been her grandmother's, twisting up her once elegant, bejewelled hands. How pain changes the brain. Would this be her own fate too, one day?

But each stroke was cleansing. Warm water was always the antidote to anxiety, diluting her concerns, if some were more stubborn than others today. Despite the effects of her swim, Calumn kept coming to mind. The way he could elicit both sympathy and cold shivers in a single encounter. More than that, she realised, it was his unresolved connections to the cult that had staged the hostage drama with Dr Kluft and the bones. Were they still a threat, she wondered... to anyone? She had written to John Evesham asking for more information about why he in particular had been summoned to Manchester to minister to Calumn.

Thoughts of work were a distraction, however, from her primary concern. Her pregnancy. Or rather, the lingering fear of its new and arcane experience. A startling development, which at first had terrified her, but which now seemed to be settling into something powerfully *natural*. Jess had done her research. Mental healthcare staff were trained to look out for signs of psychological stress in their own lives and she knew she had a responsibility to address it.

Yes, perhaps the 'illumination' now invading her waking hours could be related to several casebook problems requiring treatment or management, but it didn't *feel* like any of them. Jess sensed her work would be *helped* rather than hindered by it. Convinced that it wasn't a disorder, or worse, she was allowing the metamorphosis to unfold. Even as it brought with it an enhanced awareness that might be easier to live without.

And with another reflexive flash, she saw the horror. Eddie Briggs was coming out of maximum security. The first steps toward a wider release, as in the terms of his original sentencing he had served his time. Jess knew his ultimate release must not happen, but not how to prevent it. She had developed the vague notion that only some sort of 'sacrifice' would suffice.

She supposed that in other times, the savagery of a man like Briggs would have been celebrated. The value of a weapon so liberated from fear, remorse or inhibition would have been without measure to the Vikings, Visigoths or Mongol hordes. The ideal tool for striking terror into the heart of the enemy, his useful viciousness hewn out and honed, then unleashed in victorious abandon.

Briggs might have been a hero, a true Norse 'Berserker'. But now he was just another berserk misfit, caged and sedated because no one understood what to do with him. Nature knew precisely how to handle the irreparably broken or the out of control, but social evolution had backed itself into a corner when it came to the choice between compassionate civility and decisive, merciless eradication.

Jess understood why. She could never have wielded the axe herself so how could she expect anyone else to? How could she deny any soul the chance of seeking the ultimate pardon? To help, to support, to meaningfully contribute was precisely why she had gone into nursing in the first place, and then specialised in such a challenging field.

She felt her strokes losing their rhythm. Thoughts of Briggs, images of this huge, grinning, life-beaten man were raising her heart rate and not in the steady way intended by her swim. She calmed herself with the knowledge that he remained safely in seclusion, for now. But confinement was difficult and costly to manage and the isolation offered little hope of rehabilitation. The only person apart from the staff whom he was currently permitted to see, through tempered glass, was his mother. Jess had no idea what part this faded woman may or may not have played in her son's deformation, or why Mrs Briggs stuck it out when her son treated her as he did, but she was moved by her perseverance.

Jess wondered what else might run in the Briggs family, apart from such obvious unhappiness. Perhaps they were carriers of the so-called 'warrior gene'. That tiny and ancient troublemaker, a double helping of which in the male of the species could condemn the bearer to a life of violence and impulsiveness, if all the right (or rather, wrong) childhood conditions were in place. She knew there might never be answers to such questions about Briggs, nor might they make a difference to the immediate problem – the fast-approaching plans to phase him back into the common areas and communal life.

Those who'd invested so much conviction in his care were persuaded Briggs was submitting to their regime. Improving. Jess wholeheartedly believed in the possibility of healing, especially when patients were equally invested. She resented all the cliches, tropes and fears that marked out as 'different' – as either too vulnerable or too dangerous for full social inclusion – any soul suffering from one of the many debilitating conditions across the broad spectrum of mental health.

She knew there were so many they could help – whether or not they had crossed the kind of lines that demanded secure care – and that such help *must* be attempted, *must* be available. Many illnesses, after all, were no more than a magnification or misfiring of a mental state that may once have been in balance and of use.

And yet, against all her compassionate, redemptive impulses, Jess had come to think that a reliable enough 'repair' was beyond the reach of an unlucky few. That for some patients, the true 'inmates' of their conditions, the best that could be done was to keep them – and vitally, all others – protected from real and present danger.

Briggs, she was convinced, was among that tragic group. At least until psychiatric medicine could regenerate the part of his brain that restored his empathy or accountability. Jess had no desire to see the poor soul degraded. She understood that without some socialisation, without humane care, there was little hope for him, but he could never be let off the leash without risk. For Jess, increasingly, the needs of the individual did not outweigh the greater good.

The board, on the other hand, was too easily impressed. Briggs had started writing poetry, remarkable perhaps for a man who had rejected – and been rejected by – the educational establishment since the age of twelve. Jess had nothing against poetry. On the contrary, she was partial to a bit of Blake or Rumi, some Rilke or some Oliver. Anything transcendent, uplifting, sublime.

The verse produced by Briggs, however, was crass and juvenile – even if the 'experts' failed to judge it beyond the merit of its effort. But Jess read only simmering rage between its lines. She saw only hazard around his scarred and famished heart, his wounded, malformed mind. Yes, she could physically *see* it now, she could actually *feel* it. Though of course, she couldn't possibly tell anyone about her strange new 'gift'.

Spears of light pierce the swell, teasing colour from the coral as he watches Jess investigate under a crusted shelf. He sees her startle as the rock she thought would make a steady grip emerges from stony impersonation to become an octopus once more and escape her probing touch.

Max checks his gauge. His air is running low. Time to follow the bubbles back toward the surface, slowly. He turns to signal to Jess that they must go up, but he cannot see her. He kicks down toward the shelf. He knows what he will find, he has found this before. But he cannot wake himself, not yet. Not until he has seen her.

Jess is not there beside him when, at last, he opens his eyes, so he cannot calm his racing pulse by feeling for her, cannot slow his breathing by matching it to hers, cannot reassure himself that she breathes at all. He remembers now that she's on nights again.

Only more of the same element could chase away the aquatic horror of the vision that has stalked him into the morning. A cold shower, a hot drink. Remembering there is nothing to fear, not for Jess when she's in the water. She's at home there – it's her happy place, her safe place.

Anyway, she'd be on the ward by now, finishing her rounds. And despite another spike in his pulse there is surely nothing to fear about that either. Security is good at the hospital. Isn't it?

5

HERE AND THERE

TO: Revjohnevesham@bettering.world.org
FROM: DrEloiseKluft@children.of.sarah.org

Dear John

Thanks for your kind enquiry after my well-being - and
for looking in on Tom. He told me you'd dropped by and
met our rescue puppy! Gorgeous, isn't she? This really
is an appalling time for me to be away, from a personal
perspective at least. I can't tell you anything about
the nature of my current project, but I know you'll
understand that it's important.

All those years deliberately and often happily alone
and now, just when "family" has found me again, it's
lost me to the kind of work which kept me from its
comforts and distractions for so long!

Speaking of family, Tom says you reminded him of me
in certain ways. Something to do with how we express
ourselves, or the way we think. And while we do
occupy opposite poles when it comes to certain matters
(though not crucial questions of ethics) we do have
much in common, not least our peripatetic and singular
childhoods. And so much time spent in the company of
academic adults… which perhaps explains our love for
drinking too long at the philosophical bar? Tom says
he felt as though he'd met the sibling I never had!

Thank you for offering to provide a reference for us in our suit for full custody of Joshua. I'm hoping it will be a formality. His mother has been located, at last, but apparently won't object. I don't think social services will feel continued foster care is preferable to a stable home with his natural father and his de facto stepmother.

I can't wait for you to meet Josh. He's a delightful little boy, despite his recent hardships. A little guarded, naturally, but bright and sensitive and kind. He and Tom are the reason this work matters to me more than ever. Having lost those seven years with him, it's agony to be apart, but his and Josh's safety mean more right now than easy comforts. For someone who seemed such a jack-the-lad when we first met in the park, Tom has settled into domestic stability surprisingly happily, and it's such a relief to exhale into our lives *together*.

Thanks also for letting me know that you've been visiting Calumn in the secure hospital. The news did bring me up short, I must admit, and I had a few involuntary reactions to Mr Calumn Berryman wandering across my imagination again.

Understandable, I suppose, given the trauma of those events, but I'm fascinated to hear of his progress. I do hope he - and you - can make some? I wonder if he will say anything about the cult and about *her*? Or why he let himself get sucked into that madness? Was he always inclined to arson, did he always want to burn this wicked world - and 'witches' such as me?

And there I was thinking the life scientific was a way to avoid such superstitious nonsense. For something I

have no faith in, fate can have a very chastening sense
of humour!

I don't suppose you'll be able to answer any of the
above. No more than I can divulge the details of my
secondment here, other than to say I'm working with KC
again. But then I must respect confidentiality, whether
in a priest or a doctor, and in that way our professions
are perhaps quite similar? Another reason why you and
I are the unlikeliest if firmest of friends.

Signing off as very tired now and not quite
acclimatised. I can't tell you where I am. Suffice to
say it's an unfamiliar kind of "homecoming" - and it's
COLD. Ah well, at least somewhere still is! So I'm off
now to enjoy the comforts of a cosy if rather compact
bed, but I'll be in touch again soon.

Yours gratefully, Eloise

She shivers as she wakens but the air is warm. What inner chill causes the hair on her arms to rise? Yes, she has the sense of something now... or maybe this is a borrowed memory?

It is a huge axe head coming down with force. No... it is the swift slicing of a throat. No, an opening scar across an angry forehead. It smells like something from her infancy, her mother's milk... no, her mother's sweat, her mother's fear, and something other. Like a wounded animal, surprised by a spear but not yet ready to accept its fate. It smells of ash, it smells of burning meat. It is the wrong kind of bones at the bottom of a long dead fire. It is a cry of hunger... no, of rage... no, of grief. It is a sickness of the stomach... no... the itch of an insect bite... no, a poisoning of the blood.

Why will it not come clear? How can she prepare for what approaches if her inner sight is failing her?

TO: dreloisekluft@children.of.sarah.org
FROM: RevJohnEvesham@bettering.world.org

Dear Eloise

Your email found me very well, thank you, though as
ever our contact stimulates much contemplation. I am
certainly intrigued by your location. Do keep warm
wherever you are. I always say you can't beat a hot water
bottle, my mother swore by them, a simple comfort that
made the English winters more bearable after her move to
my father's homeland from her native Rajasthan. She said
that putting up with the cold and damp felt like a fair
exchange for soothing all her expat husband's sunburns!
Their research work, and somewhat frowned-upon romance,
weren't the only reasons they had spent so much time
sequestered inside the University.

Luckily, I've inherited my mother's melanin, though as
a child I wasn't always made to feel so lucky about
that fact by school friends over here. Just to confuse
the bigots, I also inherited her ecumenically-inclined
Christianity and the blue-grey of her "Bollywood" eyes.
Well, that's my attempt at a more glamorous answer to
the frequent questions about my heritage!

I do, however, suffer from the heat in the same way
that my father did. You'd have thought enough Indian
holidays with the relatives would have cured me of
that, but alas. Speaking of heat, we're having another
eerily early spring. I was in short sleeves the other
day, though I'm sure that news is of no comfort to you.

But enough of me. Let me put your mind to rest on other matters.

Tom is fine, if lonely, and seems to be coping well, and I have met young Josh! Let me play at prophecy and predict that he'll grow into a wonderful young man, and a musical one at that. I heard him compose his own little song as we walked on Hampstead Heath (in your honour) and the lad is a natural. A couple of scars, understandably, after his separation from both parents.

I do hope he and Tom can learn to forgive his mother in time. Both for the events that caused Tom to flee for his own safety, and for all that followed. Such a shame about her problems. The disease of addiction capitalises on a deep personal chasm and, unsurprisingly, having an unplanned child (as delighted as we all are that Josh is in the world) was not the solution for that poor girl. Nor could seeking validation in the company of dangerous men be a viable antidote to her failed relationship with Tom, despite his best efforts at a hands-on fatherhood. I have no doubt that you both can help to prevent such a chasm forming in young Josh.

Tom is a lovely man! I see more of his particular qualities each time we meet. Yes, he's made his mistakes (haven't we all?) and, yes, I can see why some of your peers might be scratching their heads at your pairing, but the heart has its own mind and recognises a kindred spirit in another. As the child of what was often considered an "odd couple" I am more naturally inclined to see past any superficial differences - and snobberies - and go straight to the *heart* of the matter.

I see as deep a kindness in Tom as in you, and your bond makes perfect sense to me. What's more, there's a lightness to his personality that I'm hoping counterbalances your own tendency to overthink? Forgive me for saying so, it's only because I recognise the trait - but I wager you've earned some fun and laughter in your life by now?

Secondly, your question about Calumn. I've seen him only once so far but plan to see him regularly if I'm permitted to keep visiting the secure hospital. I feel I owe him that journey to Manchester, somehow.

Though he says very little - about anything! I'm not sure whether he blames me somehow for the failure of his mission to hold you and the bones of Sarah to religious ransom. Perhaps he thinks my invitation to pray actually triggered his diabetic seizure and so *I* am the true villain of his story. No enemy more dangerous than the one that comes dressed as a potential friend, after all, even if I'm a touch more "establishment" than the wilder fringes his group inhabits.

On the other hand, a part of him may feel my intervention was on some level divine. Perhaps beneath all his professed loyalty he feels a kind of relief that his assignment failed and that he's been rescued from the clutches of the cult?

I do feel that his vulnerability, gullibility and fascination for fire were horribly manipulated and it riles me. The twisting of words meant for love and redemption into a manifesto of judgement and blame is a hideous blasphemy to me. I saw too much of that in my childhood. But then, hatred is a rather lucrative commodity, is it not?

I have no more information about his shadowy group, however, nor of "Madame Scarlet" as you call her (yes, indeed, a guillotine-watcher if ever there was one. I wonder if she knits?) But as you say, I remain bound by confidentiality, legal obligations notwithstanding.

Now, before I forget, I must thank you for your donation to the refugee fund, generous as ever. Tom has also offered to make a collection among his fellow design students at evening class and at the tattoo parlour. Though how we'll keep up with the ever-growing need, especially while the warmongers profit and as climate breakdown increases, Lord only knows.

Hopefully we can all learn to live lighter lives and appreciate the simple things - and each other. Perhaps Covid had a couple of silver linings, after all? Then again, perhaps it only cast a cold light on the differences between so many of us. Especially now when mask-wearers have actually become the outcasts! I mean, what ever happened to "you do you"!?

But no, I prefer to keep seeing all the many kindnesses, large and small, and to keep hoping. You know how I cherish our meeting as fellow Samaritans, don't you? And what a wonderful crew we had on our shift!

And on that note, wishing you love, light, peace and every blessing… and fortitude for what sounds like a challenging endeavour.

Yours,
John.

The girl who ate her yellowfruit in the rain? Yes, time to bring out that old story again. It is only in the telling and retelling of their stories that the deeper truth trickles through the changing streams and the heart remembers.

One or two of the older children will have heard it before. The Tall Girl with the wild and sunburnt mane, surely. And it seems she does remember, smiling now as her grandmother begins, knowing perhaps that this is not so much a story as a sharp memory of what it is to fear for your place, to fear a return to isolation and hunger.

The Old Woman takes the gift of her granddaughter's secret smile and continues. She tells them about a certain young girl who is too fond of the yellowfruit, far too fond. During the season in which it grows ripe, the clan move deeper into the forest, to the slender trees from which it hangs, rich and round and impossibly tempting.

They must move quickly as the monkeys and the birds also have a taste for its treasures and there will be a rush to gather it in time. The trees are hard to climb, their bark slippery, their branches not strong, and so much of the higher fruit is left to those same monkeys and birds while the whole clan moves quickly to gather what they can from the lower branches, catching the tender-fleshed, easily-bruised fruit into nets woven tightly from the vines nearby.

They eat some as they go, for this fruit will not last long. It is a fleeting if precious joy belonging to days that come not quickly enough and leave again too soon. Even so, the children are prevented from gorging themselves all at once. Their young stomachs will complain, often messily, and far too close by for the camp to bear, while a kind of nectar-driven madness comes upon them which few of the mothers can abide.

Oh, but the sweetness, the tenderness of the yellowfruit! The juice, the bright sensations of bliss bursting on a thirsty tongue, awakening all the hidden places of a watering mouth! The storyteller smiles to herself, knowing the mouths of her audience are watering now too.

But for some, as The Old Woman continues, this ecstasy cannot be resisted. For one girl in particular, who wakes herself at night to creep to where the nets have been strung, high up between two trunks, away from the earth-crawlers. Can she be blamed? This poor girl spent the first years of her life knowing little of such sweetness, feeding on whatever her mother could find or kill to keep them both alive during those long, barren, dusty days while they searched for this new family. Little wonder she has a lifelong weakness for such honeyed pleasures now.

The clan might always expect to lose some unguarded fruit at night to the most fearless of the monkeys, or those bats who could find their way into the dark spaces within the nets, and before the clan could strip out and dry what flesh could be preserved by the sun. The girl thinks she will be able to blame these same creatures, while she silently takes so much more than her fair share.

But she has forgotten one thing. The mess the fruit makes when eaten. The rivers of golden juice that run down her chin, her arms, her chest. There is no denying her shame come morning. The only punishment delivered, however, is all those stomach-clenching looks of disappointment. She has taken what is not hers, taken from her friends. The shame.

It should have been enough. She should have learned her lesson the first time. But the temptation is too much and the shame too easily forgotten when the yellowfruit season comes around again. This time she is assisted in her crime with the blessing of rain, a showering gift from the sky spirits, sent to wash away all evidence of her sins.

The little girl climbs the tree, reaches into the nets to take more fruit, slides down slowly, finds a clear space in the forest and stands enjoying her forbidden bounty in utter abandonment, drenched in delight. So rapt is she that she forgets how other creatures like to creep out in the rain. Things that swim up from the soil to escape from drowning.

She feels the sting, like a fine, hot arrowhead deep into her ankle and she knows: *scorpion*. Black or yellow? In the night rains, in the warm mud, it is impossible to tell. Will she die for her yellowfruit or merely suffer?

She runs back to her mother, wailing her confession. But it is too late to cut and suck above the sting. Now, they can only sit and wait. Hold each other tight and weep and sob to each other of their love.

There is silence among the clan for some time after they realise The Old Woman has finished her tale. They cannot believe or accept that this is the end of the story. But what happened, they cry, did she live or die?

What do you think she deserved? The Old Woman asks of them. Most, of course, shout out that the young girl should live, it was no more than a childish mistake! And of course, they are right. Even if it's the second time she has stolen from her friends. Surely now she will learn?

Indeed. But it's always useful for The Old Woman, the storyteller, to know who among the gathering has wished for a punishment far greater than a little girl's desperate regret and the terrible fear that death would take her too soon. Or perhaps worse, that she might be cast out. All for the stolen taste of a handful of yellowfruit. It is useful to see whose eyes call out for a more malicious revenge.

Yes. She must remain alert to every possible hazard, especially while this new and creeping shadow prowls across her nightscapes, drawing ever closer, yet still shrouded and unwilling to reveal either its face or voice.

⌾

(Saved to drafts)

Oh Tom, the lights!

I can hardly describe them, though I've waited my whole life to see them and still can't believe we slept through them that night back home! We understand so much now about how they form, what affects them, what happens to those charged particles when they dance wildly with the solar winds… and yet I felt like the first human to have ever gazed upward in awe when I saw them shimmer across the blanket of the night.

No wonder we began to worship gods, or the magic of the earth mother, or the ghosts of heroes gone before. These bewitching messengers from other worlds. We are all children again when confronted with the magnetic power of light against the darkness.

I thought about my superstitious Norse ancestors, how far into this incandescent wilderness they may have wandered, what they saw and what it meant to them. My father spoke of seeing the lights as a boy and how I wished I could have told him about my experience. Told him that I was *here*, now, in his homeland!

Of course, I also thought of the family I'm blessed with today. How I longed to have pressed my back against your chest, held your arms around my waist, felt your warm breath on my frozen cheek. Heard your gasps of joy. How I wish I could have shared all of that with you. And Josh too, of course!

Maybe one day. I hope. I might even pray. Yes, I, the agnostic, am tempted these days (or afraid enough) to offer any form of "higher power" the humble plea that we three may live long enough, well enough, worthily enough together to appreciate whatever wonder is left to us. Whether that power lies in nature, the life force, or even consciousness itself.

I cannot tell you what I fear, Tom. I cannot even send this email. It must, by necessity, remain in my drafts. Not only for security, or risk of revealing where I am, but because I can't quite tell myself what I fear. It

```
will not take clear form.
```

```
Love you Ex
```

Eloise knows there's little point in writing more so she clicks save and sets off in search of KC, hoping to indulge in pictures of the Aurora Borealis which neither of them can yet share with the ones they love.

She comes to the door of his pod and waits for a moment outside, suspecting he can sleep no more than she. She waits, as KC had once waited outside her hotel door only a few years ago, wondering if she might change her mind and respond to his clumsy if unclear overtures, knowing she too was lingering on the other side and wondering whether to open it again. Things are different between them now, settled to a friendship. Even so, Eloise is nervous about knocking.

Before she can make up her mind, the flimsy prefab door swings open. KC emerges from his capsule and they both jump back in shock. 'Oh, hi!' he says. 'Can't sleep either, huh?'

'Nope. Fancy a foul hot chocolate from the bad-tempered machine?'

'You read my mind.'

They walk together to the canteen, silently at first, then Eloise breaks the awkwardness.

'I'll be amazed if I don't put on weight while I'm here. Taste is the only sense we can really indulge – and because everything's so scrubbed down, it's only when we eat or drink that we actually get to smell anything. If it wasn't for the kaleidoscope of lights behind the Perspex walls, there wouldn't be much to look at either.'

'Yeah, that's to prevent sensory deprivation, which apparently can drive *some* people gaga.' KC looks at Eloise and smiles. She raises her eyebrows to acknowledge the joke at her expense. 'The brain starts compensating with its own inventions, you see, and filling in the gaps. Especially any brains with overactive imaginations.' This time she digs him in the ribs. 'No, but seriously, Eloise, we do have to watch out for that. I guess that's why they ship us out to see stuff like the Aurora when it's firing up?'

'It was amazing though, wasn't it?'

'Sure was. Unforgettable.'

'I think I might be *too* stimulated by it all, though. The lights, the work. I tried to email Tom just now but had no idea what to say... or what I *could* say. About anything.'

'I know.'

'I mean, we all knew more of this battle was coming, in one way or another. It was inevitable. And I've always understood that evolution isn't done with us quite yet. I just hoped it would be less destructive, less *inconvenient* than a constant war with a bunch of tiny little fuckers that are using *us* for their own evolution. Such human vanity, eh?'

'Yeah, but the pathogens have always come for us, haven't they? It's kinda why we do what we do, or at least why we jumped on this particular ship.'

'Except that, now, globalisation has given them a hell of a shortcut and a hotrod of a ride! Although, when you think about it, the Black Death ravaged Europe before a single engine was ignited, hitching its ride by flea, by rat, by ship, by donkey cart, by bolt of cloth, by human hand. And the Spanish flu took out a hundred million souls before the "package holiday" was even a glint in old Thomas Cook's beady eye.'

'Who now?'

'Oh, just someone with a lot to answer for. But the way we live now, KC, the population density, the speed and volume of travel, how poverty or greed compromises hygiene... food choices... pest control... water purity! And then there's all the habitat destruction, all the melting and the flooding. *Everything* is setting us up to encounter more sources of infection and this war of attrition isn't going to let up anytime soon.'

She takes a beat but then cannot resist summoning her nemesis. 'I mean, bloody Covid keeps coming back for more. It's beaten the crap out of us! Despite the weird amnesia and deafening silence about it these days. So many loved ones lost or disabled, so many with still much to live for, to offer.'

'True, but then Covid sacrificed super high fatality for super-infectiousness, at the acute stage anyway – and like any bully it went for the most vulnerable. But this new thing? Oh Lord, Eloise, the fatality rate in such healthy young adults is frankly terrifying.'

'I know. God, I know. But then Covid keeps creating whole new waves of the vulnerable,' she thinks of the explosion in new onset diabetes and all the cardiac, neuro, gastro, vascular, autoimmune and whatever other timebombs of health horrors are lurking in wait. 'It's done a brilliant job of softening us up or going after whatever predispositions we might have – whether we're aware of them or not – and I can't help wondering how many of our patients here might have been immuno-suppressed by previous infections? I mean, what if that's what's making them *so* ill, so quickly?'

After some prodding and poking, the machine has delivered. Eloise takes a sip then nearly spits it out. 'God, but this goo they like to call hot chocolate is truly ghastly, isn't it...?'

'And yet weirdly comforting,'

'...If you say so. But what I can never get my head around, KC – and what we might be up against with this new one if it isn't contained or tracked – is how public health has been so complicit in abandoning all caution, especially with a novel airborne virus. This mystifying regression in infection control. It's almost like, hey, why bother cleaning our drinking water anymore cause maybe a dose or two of cholera will clear up that mythical case of "immunity debt" we so conveniently invented for you? As if the only way to *not* get sick was to keep getting sick!'

'I hear ya, Dr Kluft. Not so much herd immunity as herd mentality.'

'I know, right? But immunity is so badly misunderstood. You can have the strongest constitution and still have some unknown vulnerability, or develop a new one with enough infections. And no amount of vitamins or a "wellness" lifestyle will protect you from that roll of the dice. Nor can we assume that any virus will behave like any other, or how well any individual – or system – will come through it. Not without years of study.

'Preaching to the choir, Eloise.'

'I know, I know,' she acknowledges, but she isn't done yet. 'But Covid was never "just another cold or flu". It's a nasty, systemic little bastard that you can catch again and again, that can attack any organ, and even kick off other latent viruses, even after so-called "mild" or asymptomatic cases. It's heartbreaking what we've done to ourselves, KC, and how we've bought in to all the bloody "hopium." It's almost as bad as what we've done to the planet. I mean, I used to think we had such potential as a species but now I wonder how we even got this far. And just look at how your own country has pressed replay-with-a-vengeance on its own particular tragedy!'

KC drains his paper cup, makes a face of disgust. Eloise has barely touched hers and continues her theme, not sure if his expression is about the beverage or his compatriots' embrace of an outright kleptocracy. 'And yet as much as we've ravaged her, Nature still finds her own way back to some kind of equilibrium, even if that's at the expense of the dominant species. So, maybe our new Arctic friend has come along to finish off what all the other diseases started?'

'You really can't resist the colourful thinking, can you, Eloise? You know it's not personal, right? You know it's just good old cause and effect.'

'I know. I'm sorry. But in my defence, we have just come back from a truly awesome *natural* experience. That's why I came looking for you, you know, not so you could listen to yet another rant from me. Though, there'll probably be a few more of them! Go on then, I'll show you mine if you show me yours?'

'Say what?'

'Pictures. Of the lights.'

'Oh, yeah. OK, good idea. Come on, let's pull up a perch.'

KC is a far better photographer than Eloise and she comes down with a serious case of camera envy. Nevertheless, she's thankful for this moment, even while acknowledging something else she can't yet share with Tom – how glad she is to have experienced the Aurora with *someone* she cares about, with a friend.

How close a friend – how close they came to being more than friends in those dry and distant years when she and Tom were apart – is also reserved for the drafts folder. No need to cause Tom any more concern, any more pain. That old temptation has long since faded. KC's marriage is safe, Tom's heart is safe. *Well,* she admits to herself, *as safe as any living thing can ever really be.*

-6-

MANCHESTER

TO: SisterJessicaWallace@staff-secure.hmhosp.org
FROM: RevJohnEvesham@bettering.world.org

Dear Jessica (I hope I may call you that?)

I would like to thank you once again for your kind assistance with Calumn Berryman. I do believe I can continue to help him, though your questions and concerns are perfectly reasonable. Your email asked for more detail about my connection to Dr Kluft? I realise I should have disclosed more of that at the time of my application to minister to him, following his expressed desire to confront his "mixed feelings" about my role in the failure of his mission.

In brief, I have known Dr Kluft for about 15 years, since we were Samaritan volunteers at the centre where I was her shift supervisor. We developed an interesting and stimulating friendship based on mutual respect but also mutually fascinating differences. I believe we recognised a natural fellowship despite our occasionally diametrical positions on certain matters.

However, believe it or not, it's purely coincidence that I happened to be the "Man of God' whom the police called upon to negotiate with Calumn during the hostage situation. You are, of course, familiar with his threats to burn the bones of "Sarah", the lab - and poor Dr Kluft with them? I am known to the Met and often called upon when needed. As you may know, I also minister at Pentonville Prison, as I did at Holloway before its closure, and I am Home Office approved.

I was aware when the police called me that it was to Dr Kluft's usual workplace, but was only apprised of the situation en route, and it was only on arrival that it became clear she was his intended victim. However, I think it was a happy coincidence from her point of view and that the presence of a familiar and friendly face was of great comfort during a terrifying ordeal.

Calumn's diabetic fit, which effectively ended the event, was the result of his refusal to be medicated, but it seemed Dr Kluft had suspected he was on the verge of such and so had drawn out their conversations. My instincts were to do the same while also trying to better understand and address his motivation, though the gamble was risky, considering the lighter he held ablaze and the kerosene pooling on the floor. It was a great relief to us all that it did not ignite when he collapsed.

I hope I can assure you all, however, of my impartiality in the matter. I do not blame Calumn, nor, I believe, does Dr Kluft (though naturally she is not his greatest fan). I am here only at his request, or rather grace - and only to help him - and by doing so to also help his care team.

I can assure you of absolute confidentiality. Dr Kluft is aware of my role - it seemed subterfuge was neither useful nor called for - but as someone who is also sworn to confidentiality in her profession, she completely understands my position.

Nevertheless, I must say that should Calumn ever wish
to divulge any information willingly which might assist
the police with their ongoing investigation, I would do
what I could to facilitate that and ensure the correct
legal procedures were observed.

This, however, would not be the objective of my pastoral
care for Calumn. My simple hope, my aim, is that I may
ease his considerable spiritual burdens.

Yours faithfully
Rev. John Evesham

It had been one of those quiet moments she cherished. The
ability to do nothing with the one you love felt to Jess as
important as having someone with whom to share all the fun.
But the reverie was all too soon disrupted.

'Ah, Christ, it's a bloody epidemic!'

'What, Max? What do you mean?'

Jess put down her book, shifted her position, a spasm of
tension returning to her lower back. It seemed none of their
eclectic array of eBay-sourced chairs was comfortable enough
anymore, especially when a front-loaded weight was added to the
equation. She might have joined Max on the sofa, but his energy
was that of a caged cat, hardly conducive to relaxing before a
shift.

'Of fucking stupidity. Christ. Idiocy must be the most
infectious condition on the flamin' planet.'

'Oh God, Max, you had me worried for a minute! That's
the last thing I need to hear when I'm expecting. None of us need
any more anxiety than we already have! What's got your boxers
in a bundle now?'

Max snarled and stared and scrolled.

'The funding's gone. As if Brexit didn't do enough bloody damage. As if losing foreign student income to all the hostile lies about immigration wasn't bad enough. My God those bastards nearly broke us – and now with this asset-stripping heist that's happening in the US – science... knowledge... centuries of enlightenment, it's all fighting for its life! But then those bastards over there took their cues well enough from us, didn't they?'

He had begun to gesticulate his vexation now. 'Yeah, that's right mate, you just go on dumbing everything down and weaponising stupidity. Deregulate us into a failed dystopian state. Defund vital programmes and cast doubt on the experts – unless of course they can give you a get-out-of-jail-free vaccine. Make the right noises about science funding but then trash the procurement processes so you can fatten the party coffers instead, or give some mate down the pub a nice financial return. Then just keep running down the NHS so you've got a better excuse to sell it off to your shady overseas paymasters...'

'Tell me about it, hun!' Jess needed no lectures on that nightmare. From binning the nursing bursaries to losing their valued EU colleagues, and then to all the PTSD and pandemic burnout, her working world was badly broken. Even if she and Max had managed to ignore the peer pressure and the misinformation and somehow keep themselves well. 'You know, if I still went to Confession, which of course my mother would love, I'd probably have to say a shitload of Hail Marys just for hating the Tories with every fibre of my being. Thank God we're finally shot of them.'

Max nodded but was in his own world of pain. 'Yeah, until "Deform" manage to hypnotise what's left of the hard-done-by haters. Because it's not just the fuckstick populists or the neoliberals or the disaster capitalists, is it? It's every bloody idiot who enabled them, whether they knew what they were doing or not.'

He was looking at his phone again but it wasn't giving him any comfort. 'We'll be paying that bill for decades, babe, because they made sure everyone was blaming each other while they picked our pockets and devastated anything that helps us think, or imagine, or create.' He looked up at her again. 'And it wasn't just science, was it? They shafted the arts and the musicians, then fucked the freelancers and the small-time entrepreneurs. Ah, but they made sure the billionaires and the media barons had their gold-lined bunkers nicely stocked up, eh? I tell you, babe, the best ruse ever invented was to distract the populace with some phony culture war just to stop them starting a bloody class war!'

Jess waited until she was sure Max had run out of invective. 'Feel better for that?'

'Not really, no.'

'Thought not. Me neither. You know, we can rant and rave and blame and stuff, but it's not fair to slag off everyone who's just trying to get by. There are so many frightened and unhappy people out there. I mean, they teach us really well how to *want* stuff but not how to handle the disappointment of not getting it. And despite all the bias and the groupthink, nobody likes the thought of being fooled or played. But they *do* need a little respect and compassion, Max, especially when the shit hits the fan. Trust me, I see it every day. So... go on then, enlighten me. What's erupted Mount Etna this time... you said something about funding?'

Max put down his phone but without relief. He leaned forward over his knees, head in his hands.

'The money's gone. For the hook up with the FRB telescope in Canada. The collaboration with Ligo and Caltech will probably be next. Christ. Bad enough we can't lead half our own European Space Agency projects anymore. But our kind of "out there" physics just takes too long for a return on investment. It doesn't look as lucrative as "save the day" pharma, or AI, or flaming superconductors. Crappy short termism as per bloody usual. Ah shit! This probably means my shot at the new docco has gone too. Buggerfuckery.'

'What documentary?'

'Oh, nothing. Just something maybe for the BBC. Only hypothetical at this stage, don't worry, babe. And probably no need to travel, they'd have filmed at the Lovell. Would've been great, but, eh. Shit. Not fair. I mean, our corporate overlords might not agree but to the science-minded public there's nothing sexier than mysterious, repeating radio signals from outer space. And come on, babe. Magnetars. I mean... Magnetars. The word alone is enough to get most space cadets wet.'

Jess was disturbed by this possibly accidental revelation about a new TV gig – why had he kept that quiet until now? – but sensed the mood was shifting and encouragement would be more constructive than interrogation.

'Oh, really, babe? Go on then. Say it again.'

'Magnetars.'

'No, sorry. Dry as a bone.'

'Oh, very funny. But I could always help you out with that? What time d'you have to leave...?'

⚕

```
TO: RevJohnEvesham@bettering.world.org
FROM: SisterJessicaWallace@staff-secure.hmhosp.org
```

Dear Rev Evesham

Thanks for your enlightening message. Coincidence is a funny thing indeed, I'm very familiar with it myself. (Someone once told me we should pay attention to it because it means we are "on the right track" - or something that my husband would scoff at, anyway!) One day I'll tell you about another weird connection in this particular web that might really surprise you.

In the meantime I'm pleased to say that your explanation and assurances are satisfactory and everyone on Calumn's care team is keen for you to carry on. Personally, I'm also looking forward to seeing you again and hopefully having a proper chat sometime?

Best,
Jessica Wallace RN, BSN

A precious few hours of magnification. Doors had always opened for Max, but he understood the privilege presented by all the facilities of Jodrell Bank and might have genuflected before the magnificence of the Lovell telescope, if it would not have made him ridiculous.

He was already considered something of an outrider, not always presenting the standard sobriety of approach or discussion. But although it was often meant with a pejorative edge, he didn't object to the nickname that marked him out for resentment in some quarters. The "Road Warrior" had an appropriate ring to it.

Max knew he bucked the trend for how a boffin was supposed to look or speak or behave, but his combo of edge and charm might just make him the televised "face" of astrophysics, even if those more qualified were overlooked. The Sarah show had put him on the map, made him connections. Connections such as Marcy and her new Magnetar doco, his place on that now in jeopardy.

Fuck that. He wasn't going to let it go. He *wanted* that Horizon gig. Needed to capitalise on his rising star before the sprog popped out and any spare time was lost to night-feeds, nappies and all that literal shit. So maybe he should give Marcy another call, turn on the charm, persuade her that the funding cut didn't matter?

She'd been a potential mentor since directing *The Story of Sarah* and had since recommended him through her network for a couple of brief commentary slots on Discovery. The fact they no longer had the FRB telescope time didn't have to rule him out of her new project though, surely?

Sarah.

What a lucky old beauty of a stumbled-upon-skeleton that girl had been for him. The Mount Kenya expedition had been a marvel, but he'd almost missed out altogether, especially when his father's Parkinson's was diagnosed and he'd nearly hopped on a Qantas back home instead. But that battling old bastard wouldn't hear of his son missing out, he'd always loved to live vicariously through his golden boy.

Luckily Jess, as ever, had been cool with the trip continuing as planned, even if that was before the baby.

He'd been raising the money for that climb for over two years, not easy on a post-grad's sparse resources and only tolerably taxing on his beer money. But at least the build-up had given him an opportunity to reach optimum fitness, and, as they'd made base camp and prepared for the ascent to one of the few remaining glaciers, he'd never felt more ready.

It was the adventure he needed before life got any more serious and it had delivered more than he could have hoped for. As the responsibilities of married life and the demands of his Astro Phd receded with each step above sea level, sparkling stellar nightscapes offered an invigorating reminder of all that inspired him.

The equipment was more than adequate, their guide experienced, the summit tantalising. No altitude sickness. Then the slip that changed everything. Cunningly disguised, the icy canyon had set an ambush for his ambition, the snap of the rope choking his previously unchallenged confidence. A few centimetres more and his ankle might have been shattered instead of badly sprained at the rocky base.

When the dizziness waned, he'd lunged with his crampons at the ice to steady the unwinding spin and achieve some purchase – but it wasn't a foothold he'd found when a small section of the wall came away. It was a humanoid skull.

How many times had he told that story since? He never grew tired of it. And, wasn't it his palpable enthusiasm, his natural gifts as a raconteur, his ability to translate tough theory into *lingua franca* for the average joe that made him both a good teacher – and a potentially *great* TV personality?

There was a shining future ahead, he had no doubt. Nothing was going to hold him back. Not funding, not overburdened schedules, not uni admin, not even family life. He could do it all, have it all. There was always an alternative route over or around any random hurdle. Or at least a salvageable silver lining. Like a set of priceless bones – and a break into television – lying beneath an almost broken ankle and an aborted climbing holiday.

7

HERE AND THERE

S he hears his footsteps, recognises them now, anticipates his knock, knowing he'll be concerned by her cryptic text.

'KC. Please come in.'

'So, what's this big secret, Eloise?'

'Thanks for coming. Close the door, would you? Thanks.'

KC does as instructed but seems unsure what to do next. Eloise occupies the only chair and he is hesitant to sit on her bunk, until she encourages him with a gesture.

'Please, make yourself comfortable.'

Although much has changed since the first time they worked together in London, when the electricity of *will they, won't they* still crackled between them, Eloise remains conscious of the extra dimension to their professional bond, if no longer concerned about colleagues noticing the apparent intimacy of their relationship. Hence the invitation to her private quarters. Even so – and even when comfortably ensconced in the sci-fi sleekness of its cocoon – she keeps her voice low.

'Sorry for the hush-hush summons here but there's something you need to know before anyone else.'

'Whatcha got?'

'A new mutation. In patient 5's DNA.'

'You're kidding?

'I kid you not, KC. There's a sequence that's suddenly become palindromic. It's only a tiny change but it's in the part of the genome we used to call "junk" – remember that folly? – and the GTCA lettering is now, somehow, symmetrical in either direction. It's almost as if the process that inspired *deliberate* gene editing with CRSPR CAS is randomly at work in her cells...

Almost the way bacteria splice in sections of DNA from invading viruses to make themselves immune. And it's much more than the protection of new antibodies in the blood or the lymph or the marrow – and not only epigenetic in expression either. This is a *germline* change, KC. Permanent. Inheritable.'

KC rocks back on the bunk. 'Wow. Wow. Ah heck, you know, sometimes I wish I'd acquired the British talent for swearing when I was over there. I could use something much stronger right now, but I guess my Mid-Western filter is way too ingrained.'

'Fuck me. Um, that's not an invitation, obviously.' Eloise reddened in spite of herself. 'But I think it might be the expression you're looking for?'

'Ok then. Fuck me! This is big.'

'Of course, it's happened before,' Eloise adds, as KC takes in her news. 'Viruses with the ability to alter human DNA. And we know that evolutionary changes have occurred among survivors of such bottlenecks in our ancient past, and not only through genetic drift and reduced diversity, but with actual *genomic* shifts as well. Nevertheless, it is unusual.'

KC nods in ruminative silence. Eloise continues. 'The question is, in this case, is it a good thing or a bad thing? Could it be conferring something useful like immunity – to something that's clearly very dangerous – or is it the next leg of the pathogenic arms race, whose effects we can't yet predict or understand? Has nature just levelled us up and handed us an empowering weapon, or could this ultimately weaken us? If this virus did get out and cause a pandemic, would those who survived be *different* somehow?'

'Well, I guess Patient 5 and her altered DNA have just become even more important than our index case. Whether or not she survives.'

'Yes, but there's more. Hold onto your metaphorical hat, my friend, because I had one of my hunches and did some digging... somewhere familiar. And sure enough, the new sequence? It's an exact match for a section of Sarah's DNA. One we haven't *yet* been able to match in any contemporary genomes.

But if Sarah had somehow inherited or even spontaneously acquired that sequence... and if she'd had a surviving line, well who knows where, when or how that might turn up?'

'Well, in that case, fuck me all over again. But why the secrecy, Eloise?'

She looks at him as she contemplates this question. KC is her one connection back to real life in this place. She feels so thankful for the simple fact of him. 'I don't know. Maybe I'm not that comfortable with the heavyweight military presence here. Though I think I trust them more than Mr Hotshot in his shiny suit on our Zoom calls, if you know what I mean? And now I'm really hoping we get another fighter among the patients, not only out of empathy, but because if this isn't just some weird anomaly – if it repeats itself – then we might really be onto something.'

'I hear ya.'

'It's also interesting that Patient 5 is the only continental African here, and one of only two women, with the other healthy one still in quarantine. Oh God. Don't let me start hoping that *she* gets sick too. Sometimes I hate myself. And this job.'

The one story The Old Woman is never asked to tell, even by the one who sits at its centre, is of the day that ripped her heart asunder. And yet the story will often tell itself, in the middle of a soulless night when the fit of her bones no longer makes sense and the slightest sound drags her to wakefulness, like a sand rat sniffing out predators on the angry air.

Her grandchild, The Tall Girl, was not so tall then. She barely stood above the rippling grass – barely stood at all. But all she needed was her smile to stretch up and fill the space around her. A giggle like the song of a bird, a giggle not heard so freely since that terrible day, too enchanting, too distracting. A sound that made her mother – and, unforgivably, her grandmother – forget their duty. A sound that caused the Seer to fail and become momentarily blind to the approaching danger.

But not the child's grandfather. He noticed the grass move in a way unnatural to the wind, a few men's length ahead of where she had toddled into its thickness to chase a butterfly. He had no spear in his hands as he was binding the carcass of a kill across his shoulders, but he threw the gutted buck to the ground and raced toward the movement.

Too late to shout and wave and prevent the pounce, but quick enough to cast the child out of its way, before huge claws wrapped this beloved man's back into a vicious embrace, before mighty teeth tore away the greater part of his neck.

The child's mother awoke from her rapture and ran to pick up the animal's intended, easier prey. Carrying her screaming child, she ran from the creature's wrath, ran from her own shame and shock. Seeing her daughter and her grandchild safe, the man's mate picked up his fallen spear and, screeching, ran to drive it deep into the grappling shoulder of the yellow beast.

As others rushed to help, the predator realised it had lost its kill – and perhaps its own life too. Screaming its fury to the sky, it leapt back into the grass, trailing blood from mouth and foreleg. Too late. Too late.

The Woman, feeling not so 'Old' at that time, dropped to the ground, gathered in and cradled her love, let his life spill over her, watched it drain away. This man she had known and loved for most of her own life. For all the life she remembered, all the life that mattered. The laughing little boy, met for the first time in grass such as this.

Better grass, grass that gave and did not take away. He was the first child, the first human other than her mother that she had ever seen. The one who cared nothing for her difference, for the strange blaze in her eyes and those of their children. The one who cared for everything she was, or ever would be. The one who loved even the gifts that distanced her from him in ways he would never understand. How would she live now, she had wailed to an empty world, without this other life?

Eloise is startled from an attempted nap by what she has come to recognise as KC's unique style of knocking.

'Hey. What's up? We haven't lost another patient, have we?'

'Nope. I bring you only good tidings this visit. We're outta here!'

'What do you mean?'

'Only for a few hours, but hey. Chopper's picking us up in 15. Permission has come through to take samples from the Sami herders. Apparently, their Shaman is a forward-thinking guy. Likes a side order of science with his reindeer meat. Or maybe the *spirit* moved him?'

'Woah, KC, sensitivity alert! Don't forget, we're all pretty much *their* guests up here.'

'Hey, chill out, Dr Kluft, no offence intended. I thought you could take a joke?'

'*Of* course I can, but this is *such* an important opportunity and I don't want anything to mess it up. I suppose I'm more excited than I should be, but this feels like an amazing chance to honour both my father's roots here *and* my mother's calling at the same time. God. She would have loved this.'

'Gotcha. So come on then, bundle up for the deep freeze. Here, you'll need these mittens too. But don't worry, they're purely synthetic. Nothing appropriated.'

'Ha! OK. I deserved that. But how the hell am I supposed to take samples wearing these?'

'Good point. I guess there'll be some kind of heated field tent? Hope so, anyways.'

'God. I hope so too. And that we get to have a proper chat with the shaman, because traditional Sami medicine is fascinating, KC. Did you know they'd hit upon things with parallels to modern pharmaceuticals and medical practices way before we did? Natural antiseptics and anti-pruritics, plus a kind of social distancing as infection control. Which might have *looked* like superstition to some, especially any observers from a Victorian point of view, but hey. And as for their DNA... Well, I probably don't have to tell you?'

'Refresh me. But keep getting ready while you do.'

'Ok, so, they were probably isolated up here throughout the last ice age, though of course there's been plenty of admixture since then with northern European DNA. But in about a third of the population the genome has this really intriguing motif of three specific mutations... Oh, and did you know that the Sami and the Berbers share a particular gene that suggests original connections with North Africa? Or maybe the same radiation out of the southwestern European refuge, and it's a gene that could confer resistance to certain diseases... Bloody buggery! Sorry, KC. Bloomin' zip's caught again! Oh God, help me on with this walking sleeping bag, would you?'

'Good Lord, Eloise, I don't know how you get yourself in such a twist. I swear you're the most uncoordinated person I've ever met. OK. There. All sealed up. Ha. "Seal" ... get it? But while we are on the subject, we shouldn't forget in all our excitement about anthropology and all, that it's not just human samples we need. We're still looking for viral spillover from any other species, so we gotta get some reindeer blood and some nasal swabs too – and any parasites we can scrape from them.'

'Good point. That'll be your job then. Can't offend a reindeer, I don't think. But the shaman is all mine, OK? Right. Let's hit the trail! Or rather, let's waddle down it.'

❊

The Old Woman knows this path as if it were drawn upon her skin. The quiet walk to her mother's tree is a ritual undertaken when each new moon hangs low in the daytime sky, whenever the clan returns to the summer camp. With a fresh pebble in her hand, carefully chosen, ready to be laid with all the others around its massive trunk.

The quiet walk. The clan will not allow The Old Woman to walk so far alone. A pair of hunters step beside her now, but they respect the silence of this task.

The Sun has not yet stretched his arms, but his slow awakening points a finger of purpose over the foot-worn trail through the high grass ahead, lending an ember-bright glow to its ageless dust. Long ago, in a similar season, she made this same trek at the turning of the dawn and the one who would become her mate looked into her eyes and gasped.

His smile was as open as the horizon as he told her of their colour. How at this moment they burned like the path enlightened at their feet. How they were the colour of the stone the elders cherished as they held it to the light to wonder at what life had been captured within. The stone for which her mother had named her, from the old tongue, a sound belonging to those whom The Stranger had loved but left behind in the great dying.

A secret name for the daughter of a stranger. Given as a blessing, in thanks for the seed-gift of another wanderer and what he'd bequeathed to the child of that fateful coupling. Eyes like the morning sun. Eyes like the wolf, the owl, the leopard. She is the daughter of two strangers who'd met briefly, passionately, painfully on a very different path, in a very different land. Lovers whose bones lay far apart from each other now, in places she may never know, never go.

And yet she is not abandoned. She feels those lives drum and whisper within her. Every day she recognises their many and lasting gifts, their echoes as they move about her in warm and vital flesh. Many more children have been born because of that distant encounter. And while she does not know for sure where either her mother or her father now lies, her destination today is as blessed and as good as any place in which to honour the lost.

Soon The Tall Girl will be old enough to take her place by her grandmother's side along this trail of red-yellow dust. To learn about her great-grandmother, The Stranger, to feel the deep stirring of her legacy. Surely this girl is the one who must take on the cloak? If so, then her awakening must soon begin. For the time is coming also to explain to the girl her womanly relationship to the Moon, how to mark the days she will need to remember, how to find and how to use a certain moss to soak up the gifts of that same sister Moon.

Yes, it is surely this young woman, this bearer of the flame who must learn how to walk the burning path. To share the burden of sight, of wisdom, of care.

Not because she is special, not even because it is her blood-right. Any soul could awaken to the gift. But there is a cost, a sacrifice demanded. In truth, the exchange is of nothing at all, nothing but illusion, a notion of comfort. Yes, there is some pain in making it and most fear the price, prefer the easier way. But The Tall Girl has already understood the nature of sacrifice. She lives now only because of that made by another. A grandfatherly life given to the long grass, to the great yellow beasts. This child has one foot already set upon the way, one eye already open.

When and how shall she prepare the girl? Perhaps it is time to take her out for a quiet walk and tell her of the honour she may choose to accept or not, of the call of her bloodline. How much should she tell her? How much had her own mother told her when it was her time?

The Old Woman tries to remember those shrouded days. It was not long before The Stranger had left her, had left the camp and the clan altogether on her last, lonely trek to the mountain. Two seasons before that The Stranger had taken her excited but wary child on a very particular quest, one of the last times they had been alone together, and soon to become her daughter's first experience of being truly alone. Despite all the time that had passed since, how could she ever forget the terror of that initiation?

The Old Woman recalls how her determined mother had marched her out, tired and complaining, for many days, until they reached the foot of a forested hill. They'd made camp and, exhausted, she'd slept long.

In the morning the fire was almost dead and her mother was gone. She had never felt such fear. But she knew enough to rekindle the fire, to keep the fungus The Stranger had left her smouldering and safe. She had no weapons, no tools, other than a small hand axe which might also work as a spearhead. Her mother had left her one fur and some lengths of gut. An almost-empty water bladder. And the powder of a certain plant.

Yes, it all comes clear and close to The Old Woman now. She is there in that moment once more, a terrified young girl who is not yet ready.

But this child-woman knows she must make herself ready. First, she must find and sharpen a suitable stick. Then she must walk back to the stream they had camped beside the night before. But where, exactly? Under the arm of The Hunter, yes, under his arm as it rose in the young night sky. Should she wait for nightfall? No, not safe. Perhaps it would be better to first make a kill? What, where?

She has neither her mother's skill nor understanding in these matters. But she knows how to find fruit. She can select and climb a tree like few others. And from such a height, perhaps she will also see the tell-tale cut between the trees, the snaking hint of the stream? Yes. She breathes again. She may not yet know all the ways of her mother, the right ways, but there is always *another* way. She must find her own.

That night, fruit-full, water replenished, a spear made and marked with her own signs, the fur bound and strung like a cocoon between two trees, the fire burning high, the girl feels a little less lost, a little less fearful. But not quite ready for the powder.

The Old Woman realises now, of course, that her mother must always have been close, unseen, unheard. But all she knew then was the cold fear of the hidden trail that she must walk – that only she could walk as a journey of her own creation – and it had sat in her taut young belly like a stone, heavy with purpose. Like one of the smooth rocks that her mother, The Stranger, would leave around her sacred, fat-trunked tree at every new moon.

True, she had known enough about what she must do if she took the powder... and what she must not. She must not eat but she must keep water close by and drink each time she came out of the fever or emptied her stomach. She must find and keep some fat and watery roots to roast soon after returning to the earthy, solid world in which they had grown. Her own growth would take her to a different world, for a while.

She must keep weapons nearby and trust her ability to use them if needed. She must stay warm, not cast aside her skins no matter how much she may burn with the desire to do so. No matter how much the spirit that walked within her own skin may change. She must accept whatever came and embrace it. For all was only from *herself* and of her own nature, after all.

Finally, she had decided, no further delays, no more fear.

The Old Woman feels every moment coming back to her now, animating her tired but tingling flesh.

The girl that she was pours the powder into a half shell and mixes it with water from her newly made gourd. She drinks.

She breathes. And breathes. And breathes. She relieves her stomach of its contents in a violent retch. And then she flies. Not on the wings of any creature she has ever seen, not through the air. It is a journey out of her own body, out of her own thoughts, out of her own understanding. Into her own truth.

⚕

The weather is not as kind as it could have been. There's no falling snow but she feels the looming threat of it, even if the slicing wind makes beautiful music with the bells adorning the herd. The chiming creates a haunting accompaniment to the *a cappella* folk chants their hosts offer them in welcome, once the helicopters have powered down.

The ceremonial patchwork and embroidery of their clothing is some of the finest craft Eloise has seen, and they seem so much warmer and happier in their furs and wool weavings than the ground crew in their hi-tech textiles.

The steaming breath of the reindeer, grey on grey against the heavy air, enhances the poetic sense of another world, another time. But the reek of the rutting bull the shaman is blessing as they are introduced brings Eloise back to reality, grounded in a sense she's been deprived of in the neutered, caustically clean and hermetically sealed environment of the research station. Even if the source of that reawakening in her sense of smell is less than enticing.

The taste of the curdled milk and blood sausage the shaman graciously offers is a further assault upon her subdued senses, but an experience that thrills her with memories of travels and indigenous encounters with her mother. She has taken off her full elastomeric face mask in order to honour this offering and to drink.

Meanwhile, a field tent is skilfully erected. Heaters on generators are blowing in warm air as the equipment is unpacked in sterile containers. Eloise replaces her respirator and walks inside the wind-whipped shelter with her host, as KC is guided by an ancient herder toward the shuffling and snorting animals selected for the sampling.

The shaman, younger than she had expected, shares his free and ready smile and seems eager to help, eager to talk despite every right to feel guarded about his people and their culture.

Her gloved hands are already numb but Eloise has rarely felt more alive.

He wanders in from the north, following that earlier chill wind. A solitary figure, little more than skin draping bone. Favouring one leg over the other, which he drags behind him, and on which a scar the shape of a spearhead has barely healed.

The Old Woman senses him before she sees him and sends out a handful of hunters to meet him. Could this be the peril she has been expecting, or merely a portent of what is yet to come?

It seems this solitary creature could be of little threat. Tribe? Unrecognisable. Matted hair falls over a low forehead and half-hides a drawn and haunted face. Not young. Too old to have survived alone? She sends more hunters out in a wide circle in case he is bait and others lay in wait. Her clan is fearful of him. She cannot yet tell whether they are wise to be.

And yet she *must* welcome him. She must help him. Is this not perhaps as her own mother might have looked when she first found this place and these people?

More than repaying a debt, this is the first stranger, the first true outsider the tribe has encountered since her mother's arrival, so she must take the time to learn everything there is to learn from this half-living soul.

She must know, is this the first edge of the spreading shadow from her night visions, or is this something fleeing from its dark embrace?

8

MANCHESTER

C alumn was making the good Reverend wait today, so Jess insisted on buying him a hot chocolate and sharing a moment or two of confession.

She'd begun to look forward to Calumn's regular visitor, even if her patient seemed to view it as some kind of penance, one that he must 'prepare for in prayer'. John Evesham travelled from London every fortnight to see him, nonetheless.

Sometimes he waited all day for an audience. While he waited he would visit other inmates who'd asked for him, and Jess was glad of whatever time she could steal with him in the small, yellow-speckled, pit-stop of the staff canteen. The two had already formed what she felt was an easy and valuable bond.

There was something about a priest. However much Jess had rejected the angst-ridden dogma of her upbringing, the presence of a man of God was somehow settling to her. Well, a man such as John, anyway.

Aware of the reasons she was drawn to such 'fatherly' attributes, Jess knew the pull extended beyond the pastoral and was clearly a response to the paternal vacuum in her own life. Even if – or perhaps because – John's intriguing Anglo-Indian colouring, ageing rocker's quiff and inner-city ministry lent him something edgier than the 'kindly country vicar' trope he could occasionally evoke. She felt she could listen to him all day and had even thought about recommending he started his own podcast.

Jess had often wondered whether John had a life partner or family of any kind, but he gave nothing away and she felt that at this stage of their relationship, if he wasn't offering any such information, it would be intrusive to enquire. She had started a conversation about her own spiritual life instead.

'Ah, Jessica, what you have, you see, is what the Jesuits would call "a deposit of faith." Regardless of all you've been through, all you've chosen to move away from, you still *feel*. Something. It's instinctive. Don't be afraid of that. Leave it where it rests and just draw from it when you can, when you need to, in whatever form you choose. In nature, in your relationship, in your work.'

Jess dipped her peppermint tea bag in and out of the chipped mug, waiting for the dark green to reach an infused richness that bordered on bitter. 'Yes, I suppose you're right. I mean, I don't understand complex science the way Max does, but when he tries to explain it to me, I feel such a sense of awe and inspiration. It's weird, but in a way, astronomy brings me closer to God than the church ever did.'

'Absolutely, I can see how that could happen. People of faith shouldn't be afraid to confront the scientific facts. If faith is meaningful it will survive. I don't believe it's purely coincidence that every human culture eventually develops a spiritual tradition. I mean, is this really nothing more than the natural processes of starting to think and ask questions? Or rather have we always been looking for God because, somehow, we sense that whatever it might be, it's always been looking for us?'

John's phone bleeped. He pulled it out of a saggy tweed pocket, glanced at it briefly, then turned it to silent and carried on. 'Personally, I wholeheartedly accept all the extraordinary discoveries that have replaced our mythical imaginings of how the world began and how we were made... and yet, still, I believe. No matter what I learn, I just cannot get rid of God. It's a lifelong love affair, you see, and people in love are so often driven to irrational behaviour, are they not?'

John smiled in his warm, self-effacing way.

'Yes. I do know what you mean.' Jess drank her tea, impatient for it to cool, moving the liquid quickly around her mouth so it wouldn't scald. 'You know I'm not convinced that Calumn will see you today, John.'

'Ah well, let's see. He *is* quite the enigma, though, isn't he? Sometimes he seems barely there, almost ghost-like. And he gives so little away that our conversations can be quite a challenge, though he does tend to say more in our correspondence.'

'Yes, that's been noted, and considered very good from a therapeutic point of view. At least he has *some* outlet now for self-expression and communication. But I'm sorry that he's stringing you along today, I think it's disrespectful. Like those people who are aways late and seem to be saying that their time is more important than yours.'

'Well, some things are more of a challenge to forgive than others, aren't they? It all depends on how we're wired, I suppose. But it's alright, I don't mind, really. I've a few hours until the last train and I can catch up with some online ministry in the meantime. In fact I'm working on a talk about my own multi-cultural life experiences for a Zoom conference on "Spiritual Intersectionality" – which I suppose is just another way of asking, "Why can't we all just get along?" Oh, I'm glad you're smiling, Jessica. I don't mean to be glib, and I do understand the need for sensitivity, but we also need to carry things lightly whenever we can. So, Jessica, I know you can't say too much, but in your opinion how's Calumn doing?'

She shrugged. 'Up and down. Sometimes he seems calm and surrendered, and so vulnerable. Then he goes all... altered. If I'm honest, he disturbs me, and I can't explain why. I understand his condition and there are others here far more prone to actual violence. I mean, without a match and some accelerant Calumn is more or less harmless but... oh, I don't know. The way he looks at me sometimes, right into me, right through me, like he knows something or sees something. And that weird semi-smile he wears.'

'Yes, I know. But that's just his fear looking at you, Jessica. And right into yours. Makes you question yourself, doesn't it? But he needs you to let him look, let him see. Perhaps if we're also not afraid to look at our own fears directly they can fade under the light? Not stare at them, not become fixed on them, but let them pass by like grey clouds, let them change shape and dissipate knowing that behind them is always blue sky.'

Jess took a breath, leaned in, decided to confide. 'John, I need to tell you something. It's hush-hush for now as it's still early days and I don't want anyone here to know yet, but I'm pregnant.'

'Oh, congratulations!' John exclaimed, as much as was possible in the requested hush-hush manner, 'That's wonderful news!'

'Thanks, yes, we're over the moon. It's earlier than planned and could mean a few financial hiccups, but we're very happy... despite the state of the world we'll be bringing it into.'

'Yes, I do understand any existential angst, I really do. But I'm sure you'll make wonderful parents, Jessica, and if humanity is going to not only survive but thrive, it will *need* children raised by wonderful parents. But is there something else worrying you?'

'Yes, yes there is. We're both in good health and we'll manage despite any worries... I mean, we're both pretty optimistic at the end of the day. It's just...'

'Yes?'

'Calumn.'

'Oh?' John leaned further in.

'I have no idea how he knew. I'm not showing yet, especially under my work clothes and with my usual curviness. I haven't been sick at work or anything – but he knows. He guessed somehow. And he said something really strange.'

'What?'

'He said that the baby was "special" and would be in danger if it wasn't "consecrated to God". He said, "*he* is special." I mean, how could he know?'

Jess noticed that John's breezy lightness was betrayed by a flicker of reactivity, a tensing in his shoulders, a tiny furrowing in his brow. But he soon recovered his smile.

'How odd! But please don't fret, Jessica. You're probably closer to Calumn than anyone else, and in his withheld way he's become attached. He feels that he knows you, and let's face it, he has little else to do than observe you closely. Is it possible he might have noticed small changes, subtle signs that you're not even aware of?'

'But why would he say that, about the baby being special?' Jess asked, expecting John to know somehow, to have all the answers, 'What does it mean?'

John took a beat to reply. 'Calumn is very cunning you know, perhaps more than any of us have realised. Perhaps it's his way of pulling back some power, some control?'

Jess frowned. 'But how does he know it's going to be a boy? We don't even know that yet and in fact we've decided we don't want to.'

John kept his voice and his breath steady. 'Maybe he just made a random guess. I mean, the odds are pretty good, aren't they? At least 50-50. And it might not be a boy, Jessica, he could just be playing with you.'

'Do you really think that's all it is? A cheeky guess and a bit of messing with my head?'

'Most likely, yes. Would you like me to ask him about it?'

'No. I don't want him to know he's got to me, 'specially if it is some kind of game. But...'

'What?'

'What if he's right? About... you know.'

John smiled again. It showered over her like summer rain. 'Every child is special, Jessica, every child is already sacred to God. And the risk of being alive means that every one of us is in a degree of danger, every day. He's toying with a mother's primal instincts, that's all.'

'Yes. Yes, of course. Thanks, I'm sure you're right.'

'But if it would help – not because of anything Calumn has said, but just for you if you want to – I'd be happy to baptise the baby? Something simple, whatever works for you. I have a rather customised ceremony, actually. More of a dedication or a moment of loving promise. And I do *not* subscribe to the doctrine of original sin! It's a dreadful Augustinian imposition that has no place in my spiritual view. I don't believe for a minute that we are all born with ready-blackened souls needing immediate priestly correction. Quite the opposite in fact. Anyway, have a think. Whatever you decide, you know that you are in my prayers.'

SMS TO: Jessica Wallace
FROM: Duty Desk
CONFIDENTIAL (please use code):

> Sister Wallace, sorry to bother you at home, and we didn't want to disturb any potential sleep with a phone call, but we must inform you of an incident with Calumn Berryman. During a random search, contraband has been discovered. The remains of an extinguished match deep in the creases of his bible. He has been moved to C wing while a complete strip down of his room and his person has been conducted. Calumn claims he has had this item for a while and refuses to divulge its source. No other method of ignition or flammable materials have been discovered, but on a body search we found he had wrapped lengths of masking tape, presumably from the craft room, around his arms.
> He would not say why he wanted this tape, but clearly it could represent either a self-harm risk or be intended for someone/something else and he did not feel he could go through the correct channels to request access to the tape outside of the art and craft room, or be supervised in its use. Team meeting tomorrow late afternoon to decide the course of action.

The half-light of dusk and Bowie in the distance on the downstairs speakers. After the twenty-week scan, Max and Jess had made the most of some rare time together, of the surrender to shared anticipation and the fusion into a singular sense of purpose. A long walk along the canal, a lazy lunch and then home to the ecstatic expression of all that sensational loss of self.

Jess pressed herself closer again now and listened, tuning in to the lyrical call to become extraordinary. This moment, this soft and suspended time afterwards, entwined. It was the right time to risk it. She wasn't ready to tell Max about her new sensory 'experiences' but there was something else, something more important it seemed to her now, that she needed to ask, to build up to broaching. She rested her head in the curve of his neck, stroked the ridges and outlines of his stomach.

'So, do you think the baby will have blue or brown eyes?'

'I don't know. We'll have to wait and see, eh? Brown probably, like yours, that's most likely the dominant gene. You haven't got any blue eyes in your family, have you?'

'No. I don't think so.'

'See, sometimes you get to be the boss.'

He tilted his face toward hers.

'Except they aren't just brown, are they, they're kind of hazel or something... those amazing little amber glints that you can only see in the right light, or when you really look up close.'

Jess smiled then turned her head forward, disentangled and sat up, but kept stroking his stomach.

'Max, we need to talk about something. Don't get upset, but I want my friend John to baptise the baby.'

'What? Ah, no way, Jess. Come on, we agreed? None of that hoodoo voodoo mumbo jumbo crap.'

'Max, this is important to me, please. I can't explain it, I just want this. Please.'

'Why?' he asked, both confused and annoyed.

'Just humour me on this, Max. Look, it doesn't have to be all traditional. Apparently it doesn't even have to be in a church. Please.'

'Oh shit. Well that's just wrecked the mood. But if we *are* getting into taboo subjects then there's something I need to discuss with you. I don't want you on nights anymore, Jess. Or even on the ward for that matter. Can't they put you in an admin role until the baby comes? I miss you too much and I'm worried. And I'm having weird dreams again. That diving one with the octopus, and another new one. Some big bald guy in an alleyway, and some tall thin bloke behind him, but I can't make either of them out. The thin guy keeps lighting a cigarette though.'

Jess suppressed a shiver. A big bald guy. Eddie Briggs? No, Max knew nothing about any of her patients. How could that man be anywhere near his subconscious? But the tall thin guy with the lighter? No – ridiculous. She shrugged it off. 'Oh, angel, I'm sorry you're having the horrors, but there's really no need. I don't tend to hang out in alleyways with strange men. And I'm not going diving anytime soon.'

'I know but that's not the point. Let's make a deal. I'll think about letting you have this primitive ritual of yours if you'll think about talking to work?'

'Ok, it's a deal. Now where were we?'

⌀⟨⊳⟩⊲

```
TO: calumnberryman@patient-secure.hmhosp.org
FROM: RevJohnEvesham@bettering.world.org


Dear Calumn


Thank you for letting me visit again, I'm touched
that I have your trust. Please don't worry about the
wait, I found plenty to occupy me. Thanks, also, for
your reading from Numbers in the good book. Though I
do struggle to find any goodness in Moses' vengeance
against the Midian. In such cycles of violence from one
people to another, each of whom believe themselves to
be "right" it's always the innocents who suffer. Thus,
the trauma is perpetuated.


I feel Christ was trying to turn us away from all that.
Moses was convinced that God was behind every one of his
actions, but how could He be? When one chooses to become
a leader of men, to take worldly power for oneself -
which Christ, as you remember, steadfastly refused to
do, despite every temptation - one then becomes too
```

open to corruption. I wonder, is it the mention of how they burned all the cities behind them that interests you in this story, Calumn, or the purification of their plunder afterwards by fire?

I doubt that any other species holds a grudge the way we do. Why is that? It's as if the drive for revenge bypasses every other circuit in the brain. Whether justified or not, all that anger and hatred is an intoxicant, stimulating the kind of mental states that we can become addicted to, and some will risk everything (even the environments that sustain us) in order to pursue that.

Anyway, something has occurred to me since our last meeting, and I wanted to remind you of this verse from John:

If anyone says, "I love God," and hates his brother, he is a liar; for he who does not love his brother whom he has seen cannot love God whom he has not seen.

Or, perhaps this one:

Whoever says he is in the light and hates his brother is still in darkness. Whoever loves his brother abides in the light, and in him there is no cause for stumbling. But whoever hates his brother is in the darkness and walks in the darkness, and does not know where he is going, because the darkness has blinded his eyes.

Now, I know you might claim that your "brothers" are only those who share your specific understanding of God, but isn't that a kind of arrogance? Surely our brothers are every single person that the Father has made? And if others choose to hate us, how then should we live with that? I return once more, as I so often do, to John: "If the world hates you, know that it has hated me before it hated you." Better, surely, that we all work to put aside all that hate? To look for what we have in common, the ways in which we all suffer? The conditions that bind and influence us all. Leave "vengeance" to One who sees the whole picture?

Until next time. I am relieved the board's review of your possession of contraband has not resulted in the suspension of our visits, but hopefully only a few milder restrictions that you'll easily bear. Apart from the more regular checks upon your person, which I know you will find uncomfortable. I would love to understand, however, why you felt the need to sequester that tape, if you ever feel you can tell me, in complete confidence of course.

Yours faithfully
John

9

HERE AND THERE

'I come bearing coffee,' announces KC, not looking as cheerful as he sounds. 'But also, I got good news and bad news. Bad news, that might also be good news. Bad news. Really bad news, I guess. Looks like it's a longer incubation period than we thought. They're stretching back the contact tracing for our index. Or it could be aerosolised and in the ventilation. Or maybe the fomites survive longer on some surfaces. Or it *is* waterborne. I mean, it probably came from the ice, after all.'

He puts down her coffee, spilling a little, unusual for such steady hands. '*We* should be OK, sealed off here in our little emergency unit and getting clean air and water piped in from the get-go. Even so, the whole research team is now confined to our glorified hamster hutch, and we'll be tested daily until we're sure. So maybe it's only *quite* bad news. At least for the original crew who may have been exposed before the lockdown. But it could also be kinda *useful* news, in other ways.'

Eloise wonders if the stark, bright fields of ice, or the separation from his family and the long, stifling hours are affecting KC as much as her. Their experiences here are adding up to an other-worldliness in which she's not always sure which way is up. Perhaps she's still asleep and KC has manifested into some hyper-real dream state?

No, she is at her desk. KC has returned from... she has no idea where and hadn't even noticed he was gone. She blinks herself back into the present moment. Fully takes in what he is saying and feels a finger of fear invade her confidence in all their protective protocols.

Is their claustrophobic little annexe safe, after all?

'OK. Well shit! That's a worry. But what do you mean by useful?'

'Sorry, I guess I'm not making much sense, huh, especially if I just disturbed your nap? Were you napping, or just zoning out? But you'll get it when I tell you that two more of the previously healthy have fevers. Two we *had* thought were safe. One of them has the rash and light aversion thing and is getting really sick, really fast. The other one has hardly any other symptoms yet. A mild sore throat. They're both being tested, so it's another chance to prove that works... But this *has* to be the new – or should I say old? – virus. And the subject who's doing relatively well is—'

'The woman.'

'Yup. You got it.'

'OK. Good. I mean, bad. For her, of course. For both of them, especially for the man if he's deteriorating so fast. And maybe for us too if we've been exposed? Shit. I guess all we can do is wait and see and get to work. So... We have their original DNA samples as a control – and I'm guessing their latest samples are underway? What about blood type and gut bacteria profiles? And we may have identified the receptors this thing binds to, but with a repeat of the gender response, we need to understand the significance of the Y chromosome... and the mitochondria...'

'The quarantine medics are sampling as we speak,' KC confirms.

'Oh no, wait! What about the Sami? Oh hell! We shouldn't have gone if there was any chance we were carriers. I know we were all sealed up, and mostly distanced except when taking the swabs... Oh fuck – and except when I did the culturally sensitive thing and shared their hospitality! Oh God, KC, I couldn't handle the guilt if-'

'They're being traced. Choppers are out there now. They'll be field quarantined and observed. It's a horrible feeling, I know, but the odds are minimal. Your respirator was off for only a moment, Eloise, and in a howling wind. But we can't let that affect us, there's no time. We'll know in a few days. Right now, we just gotta grit our teeth and plough on.'

The shock of this staggering arrival from the north has rippled through the camp, creating both excitement and unease. The men arm themselves and draw themselves tall, some of the youngest children hide behind their mothers or older siblings, but all look to The Old Woman for guidance.

She makes her status clear to their unexpected visitor. When she walks out to greet him, she has donned her deerskin headdress, its stag horns standing proud. She has bound her arms and legs with a cross hatch of ribbons, cut from the skins of so many kills – tributes from a succession of legendary hunters. Her skirt is a gift of the ones who run faster than any other living thing. Feathers are strung about her neck in a rainbow of fierce colour.

The man, or what is left of him, struggles to remain upright as a circle gathers around him at the heart of the camp, mothers now holding their more curious children in check. At her approach he lifts his head, humbly, only high enough to show her his intent, if not his eyes, which are still veiled from her by his matted locks and sunk deep into a weary skull.

As she comes closer, one young warrior puts his body between them, but she waves him away. Her inner sight may have grown sharper with the years but her outer vision has clouded. She needs to be where she can make a clear assessment of every detail. Besides, this wretched creature is unarmed, weak from thirst and helpless with hunger. Madness may be one of his many wounds but he would be a fool to reveal that to them now. She senses he is not a fool.

She reaches out and gently lifts the mane from his face then draws in her breath while inhibiting a gasp. Her grandson, the young warrior who had wanted to keep her within arm's length of the man, is unable to exert the same control. It cannot be denied, it is not a lie of the sunlight. The eyes that are revealed before them now are as rare and as fire-gifted as their own.

Could he be one of her own? One of her father's kind? Do they still live, and if so in any numbers? There is so much she wants to know about her unknown half.

The Outsider's ravenous yellow eyes have no answer for her. She attempts an offering of words. He cocks his head like a wolf pup, curious but without comprehension. He buckles, is lifted by the men gripping his wizened arms. The Old Woman sighs and nods. Decides this will go better if they can both squat. If he can eat. If the crowd is dispersed.

She turns and beckons for the hunters that hold him up to follow her towards her hut and waves for the keen young warrior of her blood to join them. Asks The Tall Girl to bring them water and a mash of pit-roasted roots.

In the cool of her den, with carvings of light falling through the cane weaving that shades her hut from the sun, her guest seems to breathe a little easier, as does she. She allows him the honour of resting opposite her and dips a shell into her stone water bowl. She then passes it to The Warrior, indicating he should lift it up to the man's lips. The young man bristles at being asked to serve in this way, but his pride can withstand a pinch or two.

Their guest sucks at the water as if it were mother's milk. His gasping mouth then pleads for more and The Warrior refills the shell for him, his compassion now stirred. He serves The Outsider until a glimmer of light returns to those impossible eyes.

There is a pause. A quiet moment as this strange new reality settles for all who are present. The Tall Girl sits cross-legged with her back to the cane, understanding that she is here to learn.

Now her grandmother takes the stick she uses to tease apart clam shells, pulls back a corner of the hide blanket that rests under her feet and begins to draw in the cool, dry dirt beneath it. The Outsider looks on eagerly, wanting to follow. She makes a circle and then a line under a generous gap below that. Points to the circle and then up above her head toward the shaded sun, then points to the line and pats the ground around them.

He nods his understanding. The Old Woman scrubs out the first circle, re-draws it at one end of the line, then traces an arc over to the other end and draws another circle. He nods again. Even attempts a smile.

She raises her chin to one of the hunters, signalling him to release one of the man's arms. She guesses which he will favour and which he will be least able to turn into a weapon. She hands him the stick. He takes it in his fist with humility, but then swiftly scratches into the dirt a torso, two legs and a head – in exactly the place she had expected. Where the sun rises. Yes. Even if he had arrived from the north, originally, he was from the east, she had known it.

The Old Woman takes back the stick and draws other figures next to his own, puts her head to one side, opens her palms. The Outsider shakes his head, reaches for the stick again. She understands that he is attempting to make his story clearer. He draws what seem to be the members of a family. A large family. Then he rubs out each member of the group, leaving only himself.

His eyes speak of pain, there can be no doubt. The Old Woman wants to believe him. She smells no hint of a lie under his overpowering reek of hunger and desperation. She wants to believe him but does not yet know whether she can. Whether she should.

For now, she will surrender, as she has learned to do so many times over the years, to the quiet pause of the unknowing.

She beckons for The Tall Girl to offer the root mash and to feed it to him, served on a small and hollowed scoop of wood, as she might for one of her crawling young cousins. Perhaps when the smell of hunger and fear fades from this mess of a man, The Old Woman's nose will be able to read his scent signals a little better.

For now she searches in a series of pouches for the ground-up leaves that will help to pull the poison from the wound on his leg. Maybe, when some of his strength returns, she will be able to see more deeply into the misted lake of those haunted eyes.

Eloise is lightheaded. Alone in her pod, she's been raking through the results from their visit to the herders and can find no active virus or antibodies in human, animal or parasite. But, remarkably, in a handful of the samples from the Sami there's evidence of resistance to it in their T cells. Somewhere, either ancestrally or in more recent history, they had encountered this virus.

But the shaman – what a warm and fascinating man, with such an open mind and heart; she smiles at the thought of him – had confirmed that none among his group had been ill recently. Nor had he any recollection of a similar set of disease symptoms, nor of learning about it during his initiation. Hopefully it would stay that way.

Meanwhile, the quarantined research staff remain clear. No signs of new illness nor any trace of live virus in any testing of the air, water, surfaces, sewage. Eloise is keeping everything crossed, including the knots in her stomach, both for her colleagues and for their indigenous hosts.

But strangely, there is more to the DNA samples taken that remarkable day on the ice. While going through the Sami genomes, she has, of course, gone looking for the 'Sarah sequence.' And there it is now, waving back at her from the readouts, even if only in some of the female samples. The first time it has been seen in an extant population, though clearly needing a pair of X chromosomes to exist naturally. *Wow*. Her head swims.

Eloise needs to digest this discovery. She also needs to actually *eat*, but settles for sweet tea from her flask instead. A short break, something different to think about before she gets back to work to triple check everything. She wants to Facetime Tom, but knows he'll be at college now, and, with a vital project to complete for his graphic design course, she doesn't want to disturb him.

So, she opens up his last email, thinking she'll reply more fully now, after the first brief coos of pleasure when it had landed. She gazes again at the pictures of Josh and Tom larking about in the park. The same North London oasis where *(how many years previously?)* she'd 'bumped' into the unexpected love of her life, courtesy of a misfired football taking the wind out of her Saturday run.

Her breath grows short. Too many neural pathways are activated by the sight of those cherished, selfie-gurning faces, so similar, so different. Nine-year-old Josh (*how could he be nine already?*) now wearing his hair shorn close like his father. A hammer to her chest. A metallic blow of love, trepidation, confusion, excitement, fullness... And the lack of access to that fullness right here, right now. Happiness once again deferred.

Eloise expands one of the images, focusing more closely on Tom. She'd asked him early on in their brief initial tryst – regretting it immediately, such inexcusable snobbery – how a street-hardened rascal had come by such an imperial nose, such lush Hollywood lips.

When he'd taken it as nothing more than a clumsy come-on, laughed his dirty laugh, preened, winked and reached for her again, she'd pushed him away with her words. Cool, clipped, clever words – always her suffocating armour. Always the wrong reflexes, defending herself needlessly from his unconditional love. She'd told him not to get too cocky, because those impish green eyes were a touch too narrow and a little too close together to make the cover of *GQ*.

'Q-what, darlin'?' Tom had rightly mocked, those same eyes now comically swivelling. And then he had rightly used those 'Hollywood lips' to stop the wasteful words. Stop the questions.

The memory of the intimate encounter that followed this awkward flirtation is sweet for her now, and somatically felt. But she's not quite ready to reply to him. More useless words, so many she might still get so wrong. All those softer feelings were tainted too, by guilt and shame. And ever-present fear.

What if she'd been right to end it the first time around, so brutally and so soon into their ecstatic three-month affair – even without his discovery of unexpected yet impending fatherhood? Won't the age gap and all those other differences ultimately cause too much tension? Worse, what if she'd been even *more wrong* than imagined by ending it before, doing so much damage by forcing Tom – and Josh's hapless mother – to 'do the right thing' and give their unplanned family a proper go, only for it all to go so dangerously wrong?

Eloise knew there were lingering triggers and sensitivities for Tom. A chunk of fear chipping away at those steel-wire shoulders, even if he suffered no insecurities about the rightness of their relationship. But she'd noticed his reactivity when he felt his place with her might yet be at risk, or at the prospect of further upheaval for his son. Worse, any distant thunder of potential violence coming their way, even if the likely culprit in Tom's case was currently serving time at His Majesty's pleasure.

Tom had been nothing less than honest with her about their years apart. But then, was the bully who'd forced his separation from Josh any worse than her own spectre? 'Madame Scarlet' – the mastermind of her hostage ordeal was still at large, after all, as Tom was fully aware. She'd been as open with him as he had been with her.

But that's just it, she realises. What you see really *is* what you get, with Tom. No pretence, no attempt to be other than who he is, even if always reaching for the best version of that. Tom feels like the first 'significant other' to simply *enjoy* her, from a deep and grounded sense of self, with no hint of competition or resentment.

Anna, her best friend from medical school, who'd been so instrumental in the realisation of what she'd given up the first time – under that damned delusion of *doing the right thing* – had noted as much in her initial appraisal of Tom, comparing him more favourably to all those 'perfect on paper types who imagine they're any different to anything else walking around with a cock and an ego.'

So, no, she won't email Tom just yet, there's another message that's easier to compose in her current mood. One full of thanks for her friend's veracity, without which her second chance with Tom might have flown by again. Would she have stopped when she saw him outside the pub after all those empty years, were it not for Anna's bullshit-free voice cutting through her hesitancy?

Eloise gets up and begins to pace the confines of her quarters, the swift turns not helping her light-headedness – and any hint of a change in body temperature or a scratchy throat gives her fearful pause as they await the final all-clear from infection – but there are thoughts she must explore and things she must express. She picks up her phone and presses the voice dictation on a draft email.

'Anna. Not quite sure if gratitude is appropriate when I find I now love this man to within an inch of my sanity, but I do have to tell you that of course you were right. As you saw in him from the outset, it's all up front and centre with Tom, take it or leave it. Well, it looks like I'm taking it. The man, his child, the long-resisted cohabitation, and all. Bloody hell!

'But we'll be fine, right? Despite a few slow-brewing if predictable issues. I know chemistry alone isn't enough, but laughter, affection and a similar taste in box sets and dance music doesn't hurt? There's an imbalance, for sure, but Tom does attempt to contribute, in his own way. He's capable of fixing pretty much anything, which I do find very sexy, but he was perhaps nurtured a little too well by his lovely if increasingly unwell mother. There's not a jot of misogyny, thanks also to his decent if overworked father, but he certainly is, shall we say, *challenged* when it comes to other household duties. So there's instant access to all kinds of bliss for us – but not so much the domestic kind!

'Ah well. We both know you can never have it all, though this really does *feel* as good as it gets. It's got to be worth my best shot, right? Because if we don't take responsibility for other humans when they need it and when we can – then what are we worth? For all the resources I've enjoyed on the planet, I need to share the good fortune of having had a loving, stable family and a quality education. And what an opportunity ahead to help a young mind like Josh's to thrive, to help all that potential to express...'

Eloise runs out of steam, and out of arguments for or against the risks to her heart and to her lifestyle. In 'talking' to Anna, she's talked herself down from the precipice of self-doubt and can now draft an easy-going, affectionate reply to Tom. She'll write something for Josh too, something to encourage his growing passion for the guitar. Something Tom can print out for him, with some newly purchased and downloaded sheet music attached.

No more holding back. Here, in this place of sickness, death and fear, she's reminded daily not to squander a single opportunity to love – or to express and celebrate that love.

⬤◁▷⬤

This is not a night for storytelling. Their guest will not understand the clan's tales, even if he senses the mood or meaning. Better to share with him some of their songs.

Such sounds are a gift understood by any who have the mouths to make them, surely? The harmony of their hummed voices may work a kind of healing within him, whether he recognises the rhythms or not. Even if their guest fails to respond, the renewed communion that rises among the clan during such celebrations will be a blessing for all.

Besides, the vibrant noise will make a potent display of their unity – to him and to any others that may be listening, unseen, in the dense forest that borders this curve of their grassland clearing – or across the wide bend of the river that, with its deep and rushing waters, guards the other side of the camp.

They seem to fear The Outsider a little less now it appears he is alone. As such, he is powerless. Or is it his intention to learn about their strengths and their weaknesses? Perhaps, but he too will be closely watched. Even by the children. Especially by the children. The Old Woman realises she must listen even more carefully to their dreams.

The night is clouded and warm, but the clan build a fire that will burn strong and high. The sparks that reach skyward will carry their sounds as an offering to every one of their ancestors and all of their sentinel spirits. As they gather in full, she begins. Slow, soft and light. Next to her, a deer's thigh bone is tapped against a skin drum to guide the rhythm. To the other side someone takes up a pair of rib bones to play. Then a deeper voice comes in to accompany her own, bringing forth the rumble of the earth. Soon many more voices take up that rounder, lower part.

Then a few of the women bring in a sweeter, brighter series of lilting chirps and one voice flies upwards, heart-thrillingly high, with an invitation to the moon to show herself through the coverings of the night. Then the rest take up whichever parts suit them and the music dips and turns, sways and sinks, lifts and soars.

Bodies rock together, shoulder caressing shoulder, knee pressing against thigh. Glistening beads of sweat shine on all these fire-facing bodies and warmth wraps the gathering in a singular embrace. The Old Woman looks over to The Outsider and into his hollowed face.

Yes, how could it be otherwise. Those kindred eyes are dampening now. His body begins to jerk with the pain of withholding, until he can bear it no longer and collapses into a pool of heaving, shaking, wailing sobs.

None among them shows surprise, none takes notice, for this would dishonour him. Bar one young child who stretches from its mother's arms in an attempt to comfort-pat his hair. Such innocence is, of course, permitted. Otherwise, The Outsider is left to his release.

⌇⬤⌇

'Eloise... Lolo...? Are you there?'

'Yes, sorry, Darius, lost you for a moment. Tricky connection. What's this about, any more news on the claw?'

She can make him out, but he keeps buffering. The video call had been most unexpected and had pulled her from her fourth check of the Sami results.

'No. Well, yes, but... Oh hell, you've frozen up again. Where the bloody hell are you, Lolo?'

'Geographically or psychologically?'

'Doesn't matter. Listen, before we get cut off again. I need to see your face when I tell you this. You know the recent quake in Yemen?'

(Did he say Yemen? Too much interference.)

'Yemen? Yes, Darius, those poor people, as if they haven't suffered enough.'

'Yes, quite. Although actually it's turned out to be something of a boon. Well, for us at least.'

Callous and self-centred as ever. Darius never failed to disappoint. Eloise thought he might at least spare more concern for his horribly betrayed regional cousins.

'What do you mean?'

'Well, archaeologically of course. One particular rockfall has exposed a cave. Probably been sealed off by an earlier fall for, well... why don't you take a guess, my dear Dr Kluft?'

'No!'

'Yes. Between 70 to 80 thousand years.'

'Bloody hell! But how deep does it go? What's inside it? Bones?'

'No. Not yet anyway, maybe somewhere deeper. But we *have* found art.'

'What?'

'Art!'

'Yes, I heard, I just can't take it in... Christ!'

'You keep calling on him like that, my love, and he may just answer. Then where would you be? But when you think about it, from the herder who found the cave to the uranium dating, and now the spectral imaging that's revealed all this ochre under the millennia of calcite, it *is* all rather miraculous, my dear.'

'Yes, I suppose it is! But what kind of art, Darius?'

'Simple, naive. Rudimentary symbols, mostly, but with an occasional attempt at the figurative. And not just hand stencils, or patterns and indentations like at Tsodilo or Blombos. In some sections it actually looks like a form of narrative. I know, my dear, I know! We've cross-checked with the French database and there are no known matches. What's more, there's a kind of geometry at work. And something else that will really float your boat, Dr Kluft. A series of carved outlines in a sequence that *almost* looks like DNA. Well, the old-style barcode readouts anyway. So yes, *Christ*, indeed.'

'Oh my word! Can you send me pictures, please?'

'On the way, my love, and encrypted, but you know the key. Your old friend and mine, the feline physicist.'

'Brilliant! Thank you so much!'

'Oh, but that's not all, Lolo. Those stripes and bars and some other symbols turn out to be an excellent match for the carvings on the Mount Kenya bear claw. Possibly made by the same hand, according to one scrimshaw expert! And get this. There's a depiction on the cave wall in Yemen of what appears to be such a claw, right after what looks like a death-battle between human and said creature!'

'You're joking? God, I'm running out of exclamations, Darius. This is extraordinary! I could almost kiss you, you bloody terrible, marvellous man!'

'Lovely thought, my sweet, but where would that get us except a time-warp's worth of trouble? And what about the toy boy? How is he, anyway?'

Now she could almost slap him

'Too far away, Darius. But needs must. What I'm doing here is important.'

'Ah, yes, the work, Eloise. Always the work. Don't give too much to it, will you? You don't want to end up a lonely old loser like me.'

'Oh I doubt you're ever lonely for long, Darius. But don't worry, I know what I've got – and what I've got to lose. That's exactly why I'm here, believe it or not.'

'Well, do whatever you must, my darling girl. But let's talk again when I know more. Email me your thoughts on the cave art, won't you?'

(His darling girl. His bloody 'girl'… Even after all these years.)

'Will do. Thanks. Bye. This is amazing. Thanks! Oh wait, what about sediment samples from the cave? You know we can get DNA from just about anything now – a few bone fragments will do, or even some ancient defecation! And we can compare protein expression even without DNA. So please, Darius, gather whatever you can. Are you still there…? Darius, can you hear me?'

He is still on screen in perfect clarity for a moment and Eloise realises it's neither the static nor the light. Darius is now completely grey, from his full head of hair to his neat and rakish goatee. A new reality that somehow diminishes whatever sting remains coiled within her memories of him.

(So. Time really does beat the crap – and maybe the grudges – out of everyone. Eventually.)

'Lolo? Can't hear you? Never mind, must go. Put it in an email? Bye, Lolo. Bye. Oh hell. Where's the bloody hang-up button on this thing…? Oh, there. Bye!'

Eloise clicks open his email, types in 'Newton' and a world of wonder is revealed behind the encryption. A series of symbols, daubed millennia ago on the rough walls of a long-hidden cave in what is now strife-riven Yemen. Not merely symbols, not merely a prayer offering to prey animals or a hand print that proclaimed 'I was here', but yes, Darius was right, these carvings and ochre markings look like an attempt to tell a story.

Whose story? Left behind for whom to read? It couldn't possibly be…

Eloise examines the various groupings of semi-circles. In some ancient indigenous cultures these might represent people. She recalls her mother's studies on such subjects, wonders briefly how that kind of anthropology would measure up now to the demand for 'decolonisation' – for all that woman's sensitivity against the prevailing cultural norms of her time.

The drawings, these groupings of people – if that's what the marks in the photographs represent – stretch along the cave wall until gradually whittled down to a series of lonely, singular marks spread out between a sprinkling of sunbursts, straight lines, waves, spirals, flames and what might be tools or weapons.

A few attempts at other shapes could represent creatures, whether predator or prey. Or perhaps something therianthropic, having the qualities of both human and animal, especially the 'death-battle' between bear and person – which looks more like a combination of both beings. If so, this suggests the artist had a sense of the supernatural. Next, there's the depiction of the carved claw that Darius mentioned – or was it merely a decorative crescent moon? Then come those bars, those DNA-like strips, finished by something that could almost be an elaborate full stop.

Eloise feels woozy and wonders for a terrible moment if she's coming down with the virus. She takes her temperature again, rules out all the other symptoms, before realising this feels more like the hallucinations she once experienced after an adverse reaction to a wasp sting. She *knows* this cave. She's seen it before. But how can that be? Her father had never dug in Yemen, nor had her mother studied its people in person. Until the earthquake, this cave had been hidden for millennia.

Eloise doesn't yet understand what any of these markings might mean and yet she knows *something*. One scrawled symbol, that strange 'full stop', makes her look again and again. It's at the end of the narrative trail and has what can only be described as a *power* to it. She feels nauseous. No – she is not, will not, cannot be sick! It passes, until she looks at the symbol again.

Then it comes to her. She takes a screenshot of the symbol on her phone, magnifies it. Brings up the electron microscope image of the new virus on her laptop. Holds the two screens side by side. There it is. They are a match – or a near enough, if crude, representation.

How can this be? How can this be?

-10-

MANCHESTER

Dear Rev Evesham

thanx for seeing me again yesterday. Sorry I did not have much to say. I am having a dificult time. I have a bad feeling I cant make out. I think the dark one has something planned for me. When can u come again?

There is something more. I kno I said I didnt want to talk about the Sarah hoax and I dont - not in person cos' I dont want to argue with u. But I really have to ask before our next meet. Do u really honestly believe she is 74 thou yrs old? How can u believe that and also believe in The Holy Bible?

Calumn B

⫷⫸

Jess knew that Max hated to disappoint. Understanding the expectations, he was good-natured about living up to national stereotype, so, weather permitting, whenever they entertained at home it had to be a barbecue. The full farmyard. He was mid-marination and she was gathering an assortment of glassware and cutlery when he belatedly asked, 'Wait, he's not a bloody veggo is he?'

'Oh? No, I don't think so. But then he did spend some formative years in India, so maybe? No. I don't think so. I think he'd consider it impolite to not mention that if he was coming to barbie?' Jess wasn't sure at all, but it had been torturous enough seducing Max into giving up a Saturday afternoon to host the 'Father, Son and Holy Ghost' as he'd taken to calling the as-yet-unmet Reverend John Evesham.

'Righto. Otherwise it's nothing but roasted corncobs and your sister's windfarm of a "superfood salad" for our honoured guest. He sounds bleeding-heart enough to be one, but eh?'

'Oh Max, please. Be nice.'

'I'm always nice!'

'I know. But be... open-minded. You'll like John. He's my friend.'

'No worries, babe. I won't start a holy war.'

Jess was nervous, nonetheless. John had invested the effort and the expense to stay over in a B&B after his visit to Calumn the day before. What's more, Manda was up for the weekend and Max had invited a good – and more relevantly, single – friend from work whom he was hoping she might connect with. But as much as Jess liked Greg, she wasn't sure how the mix would work. Especially on their tiny back patio with little room for manoeuvre, or escape. Both the warm sunshine and brisk showers of spring were predicted as possibilities, but any potential rain was skipping past them today and her mood was buoyant.

She'd made a rare sartorial effort for the occasion – while she still could – wearing a polka-dot frock with a décolletage-enhancing yet bump-forgiving empire line, which she'd unearthed with archaeological glee in the depths of her favourite charity shop. It made an uplifting – in every way – change from the twin-like uniform of jeans, hoodie and trainers in which she and Max were so often unconsciously matched.

The food was, as ever, a triumph. Jess watched as after the feast small groups settled into satisfied conversation. She was torn between keeping an eye on Max and John, who'd come together in a corner by the potted camellia, and Manda and Greg, who were deep in dialogue and smiling across the picnic table. Was her sister merely being polite? No, perhaps not. Jess saw what she alone could see, a radiation of red-pink excitement beginning to feather between them.

While she and Max may not have matched their look today, these hitherto strangers had randomly aligned their own wardrobe choices, which boded well to Jess. She left them to their tentative bonding and negotiated a spot at the end of a weathered bench, within earshot of her husband and her honoured guest.

'I do see your point,' she heard John offer, 'but perhaps God has manifested in whatever form we could relate to as we've been evolving? Whether that's an ancestor, a burning bush, a carpenter from Nazareth, a multi-limbed Goddess, or some formless, impassive, background intelligence. Whatever shape more easily allows whoever is seeking it to devote themselves to it. In that sense perhaps all Gods are true?'

'What, all of them? Even the jealous, blood-thirsty, vengeful bastards?'

'Unfortunately, Max, we humans are inclined to ascribe our own qualities and our own desires and fears to the divine.'

Jess realised Max was conscious of her proximity, even if she was switching her attention between groups, and she sensed him making an effort to moderate his tone – but she knew that he could not and would not humour John.

'So what you're saying is that God turned up to a handful of different tribes over the centuries, wearing a shop-full of different bloody hats? How the hell is that helpful? That's got to be the most destructive policy thinkable, 'cause then you've got a bunch of self-righteous religious bastards going to war under their own bloodied banners of truth! Not exactly the actions of a wise or loving deity, mate. More like some vain and bored old troublemaker. Or some desperate saddo – I mean, "Ooh, look at me, I'll be whatever you want me to be so long as you love me, please worship me".'

'No Max, what I mean is, it's not God that's choosing the forms, it's us. We call, He comes. We then mess it up.'

'Nah mate. That's too easy, too bloody wishy-washy. It lets God and his wild bunch of believers get away with anything! Like some gang of squabbling Greeks up on Mount Olympus. That kind of piss-easy relativism is almost as bad as the fundamentalist position.'

Max lit a cigarette and Jess forgave him. It was clear he needed a soulmate for his beer, and of the two or three 'real' smokes he allowed himself a week, this would have to be the fourth. She couldn't blame him. He'd tried vaping but it didn't do what he needed the occasional cigarette to do.

'So, tell me, John, what is he, transcendent or immanent? Both or neither?'

'For me, both'

'So you believe in an interventionist deity, despite all evidence to the contrary?'

'Yes.'

'But who gets intervened for and who doesn't? And who asked him to interfere in the first place? Cyanobacteria? Did a few of them suddenly turn around and say, "Hey, you! We want to be multi-celled, oh please mate, go on!"'

'Well, maybe. Why not?'

'Sorry, but that's ridiculous. Why would an intelligent creator, one that wanted us to know and worship him, design something that bore no hallmarks of that design, something that has so obviously developed of its own accord and follows its own course?'

John leaned in and smiled. That balm of a smile – Jess felt its soothing effect like a stroke of her hair. She hoped it might also work on Max, if not quite in the way that she now experienced such things.

'Yes, but who's to say that life hasn't partnered God since He first set it all in motion? Who's to say there isn't some kind of divinely inspired ambition, even in bacteria? How did Ibn Arabi put it? "God sleeps in the rock, dreams in the plant, stirs in the animal and awakens in man." Although it *is* a good question,

Max. Why doesn't he always intervene, why only sometimes? Why only when we want to believe He has, or can, or will?'

Gathering steam, John continued before Max could answer.

'...But in most cases what happens to people has nothing to do with a callous, or even an intermittent God caught looking the other way, and everything to do with our own choices in a physical environment with its own pressures and rules. Most people who die in disasters do so not because God capriciously rolled the dice. Most people who die in earthquakes do so in badly constructed buildings sitting over well-known fault lines. Or people die because they happened to get on a plane that someone else built with a problem that someone else missed or a bomb that someone else planted. Or because their governments have callously allowed them to suffer... if not actively culled them.'

'Ok, I'll give you that much, but then we're back to the old "free will" fly in the ointment, aren't we? Sorry, John, I just don't buy that. It's still not good enough.'

Max drained his beer. An empty bottle was not the ideal situation. Jess was torn between getting him another and staying to listen. The latter became more pressing, as John doubled down on his argument.

'You see, I think we're all part of an entity, a living whole, inseparably connected and all subject to a set of self-organising conditions put in place from the outset. But yes, we do have individual consciousness and choices, as subsets of the whole, if you like – and yes, we can affect outcomes. We are part of creation and so also share in some of its creative power, but we are not greater. However, perhaps if enough consciousness, purely directed and faithfully focused, is tapping into that power it can redirect it – from the tiniest scale to the largest.'

Max frowned, shook his head. 'And who decides who's worthy? Who's right and who's wrong?'

'It's not a question of worthiness. As I said, we are not greater than the creative power, and "it" may somehow know better, may see the bigger picture.'

'Ah, shit, no way mate. That's just another theological cop out. This great big bloody "mystery" that we're all too dumb or dense to really get?'

'Or just not ready yet?' countered John, 'That's why we've needed the texts, the manifestations, the prophets, laws and yes, debate such as this. But these will pass into a greater understanding in time, and many believe that time may be soon.'

Max bristled. 'So you, a priest, someone who preaches "the Word," are saying that, really, God is nothing more than a vague, interconnected, conscious life force belonging to no one and everyone? Some great universal supermarket? Take a bit of the Tao or the Holy Spirit, add a sprinkle of Buddhism, throw in some *Star Wars* and a mystical twisting of science, set up the smoke and mirrors and hey bloody presto – one size fits all?'

Jess was relieved to see John still smiling. This challenge was OK. Even so, she wished for some prosecco in her glass, rather than a virtuous mum-to-be elderflower cordial. Something she couldn't seem to get enough of these days, having developed a demanding thirst to accompany an increasingly urgent bladder. Both needs would have to wait. Jess had her own thoughts on the debate, of course, and had considered jumping in, knowing neither John nor Max would mind, but she wanted to see how this first encounter between them unfolded without interference.

Then, with a glance the other way, she realised that both Manda's and Greg's glasses were almost empty. Jess didn't want their developing rapport to be interrupted so she levered herself upward, took a few steps to Max's 'Eski' in the corner, reached into the ice-filled cooler for the fizz, then moved on to the picnic table to top up Manda and Greg.

She was happy to receive only the briefest of polite acknowledgements before their conversation resumed, with Greg raving about Orkney where his family had a home and Manda cooing about how she'd always wanted to check out the historic sites up there. Greg didn't have an obvious Scottish accent but now Jess wondered whether his distinctive colouring was indeed indicative of Caledonian ancestry. She left them to it.

Back at her vantage point near Max and John, she was relieved to hear them still deep in discussion and still with a sense of bonhomie, apart from the occasional spike of discomfort that manifested for Jess as a physical pinprick in her shoulder and the sharp smell of vinegar.

'...Yes but, Max, that does refer back to my point that many religions have hit upon similar truths – and that many of the legends have uncanny echoes in newer scientific thinking. I mean, didn't Oppenheimer say that access to the Hindu Vedas was the greatest privilege of his century? Didn't he so famously reference Shiva, the destroyer of worlds, after the first atomic detonation? It's almost as if the ancient visionaries were trying to describe something they didn't have the words for – and personally I think this will be the case more and more.'

Max exhaled his last lungful and extinguished the butt in the dregs of his empty beer bottle. 'Or we'll finally wake up and knock all that cowcrap on the head.'

John shifted his weight on the acid-green bean bag, unfamiliar with its absorbing restrictions. He'd lowered himself into it graciously, trying not to spill any of the Pinot Noir from his glass. Jess wondered if Max had put him into such an undignified position deliberately, while he sat above him in the director's chair, but didn't want to think he could be so manipulative.

'Maybe so, maybe so. But it's interesting that you say my supposition of God is "nothing more" than an interconnected conscious life force. For me that's not a reduction but a magnification! Something wonderful we could all share in rather than squabble over. Even though, yes, I do still preach from the tradition I know best to those still seeking its heart. I wholeheartedly believe in the essential message of the Christ, in the possibility of redemption. The Word is still so powerful, even if we have only what the scribes could remember – or what Constantine and all those with their own agendas decided we should have.'

'Exactly! It's less of a holy text and more of a flamin' manifesto. It's spin.'

'Perhaps, in some cases. But the story didn't stop 2,000 years ago, or with the Nicene council, or with a desert prophet, or an enlightened Indian prince. As children we're guided and kept safe by a series of threats and rewards, but when we grow up we learn to monitor our own behaviour and look outward, expand our understanding. And God hasn't stopped talking to us. The conversation isn't over. No more than for science! Isn't there so much still missing in our understanding of cosmology? Haven't we had to invent things such as inflation or dark matter to explain why the universe is the way it is... and isn't that in itself a leap of faith?'

'We didn't just invent dark matter, or dark energy, mate, we know something *like* it has to be there! We know it makes up most of the universe, we just don't fully understand its source or its nature yet. In fact, there's some suggestion that dark energy may not even be constant. But that's just what I mean, in science we admit when we don't know things for sure. Until there's a match between theory and observation. Nothing becomes "law" until it's measured, checked and proven.'

John leaned forward again. 'Yes, but why are there only four "officially" understood forces...? Why just gravity, electromagnetic, strong and weak nuclear? I know they work together in a finely-tuned equilibrium but still, how could they – or indeed life – have come from nothing? How can there really be "nothing" anyway? Something must exist outside of space, time and matter, of whatever kind, to have brought it all into being. And doesn't there need to be an "observer" for *any* of this to exist? For the wave function to collapse? Surely this astounding universe with its intricate, delicate balances cannot be coincidental. And why would a host of randomly combining elements and forces need to become sentient, need to start asking questions and making its own decisions?'

'Because that's just the way it happened. Chaos, mate. Based on chemistry and mathematical principles, but unpredictable and with a vast number of possible outcomes. Some, it seems, more likely than others, given the conditions. Set up some simple rules, let the patterns develop, add some random mutations and environmental feedback, discard what doesn't work, reproduce what does, and you have the emergence of complexity. But humanity's ancestors only got the chance to evolve because its potential competitors were wiped out in various mass extinctions, so a set of new evolutionary experiments got their shot.'

Jess could tell that Max was weary now, looking and sounding like he wanted to wind up the debate, the colours that only she could see around him drooping. But he took a breath and carried on, some final points to press home.

'Look. It's too complex to cover at a barbie, mate, but the theories do work in terms of the maths, and the maths is everywhere. And when it comes to the development of life, it's just a natural process of the right ingredients of mass and energy. Since the earliest algae started feeding off sunlight. Since the first mitochondria got munched up by an archaea microbe and became part of its host. Did you know, there are computer models that create independently "living", reproducing and evolving processes all by themselves? We've now got quantum supercomputers that will soon become verifiably sentient, we've got potentially thermodynamic law-breaking time crystals that'll tick over infinitely and give us insights into systems as complex as the human brain. We've made Xenobots from frog cells that can kinematically reproduce! *We* can synthesise bacterial life in the laboratory – *we* can create life, John, from just a few ingredients and processes...'

Jess noticed that John had sensed a window and was coming back for perhaps one final riposte. 'But how can you create what already exists? And who built the computers, Max, and the laboratories? Who pressed the "go" button? Whose thought processes wrote up the initial programmes, put those simple rules in place? Computers don't build themselves.'

'They could.'

'But not without *us* having put the first one together in the first place! By mimicking our own creator. By exercising will.'

'Christ, we could go round in circles forever with this and come to a different yet similar place each time.'

'Indeed. Isn't it wonderful?'

'Shit. It's impossible not to like you, John. And I can see that, on balance, someone like you maybe does some good, amidst all the other harm. But as far as I'm concerned, it's us mastering quantum mechanics that's going to save the world, if anything. Not the Second Coming. Or the age of bloody Aquarius. And look, no offence, but if Jess wants your hocus pocus she's welcome to it, but maybe leave me out of it, eh, if that's alright?'

'There's little more precious to me than each human's free will, Max. Of course, I fully respect your wishes.'

'Righto. Well, my will right now is for another beer. Can I top you up while I'm at it?'

WhatsApp: MandaPanda to JessicaRabbit

Home now, after some bus replacement bollox with the train but even that couldn't take the shine off a gorgeous weekend. Thanks my lovely big sis for being the best as per. Mum sends her love. Even to Max! :) I know you'll grill me about Greg but give it time. Who knows? There's defo something there but not sure what yet and there's the slight issue of geography to consider. Anyway, look after that beautiful bump for Aunty Manda, won't you? Mwah Mwah.

Jess had a good feeling. About everything. She hoped she might see more of her sister at the very least. She'd slept well the night of the barbie, even with Max snoring off the grog and she being out of sync with the usual rhythms of her night shifts, having managed to rearrange them for the weekend. Best of all, Max had mellowed about something which had become so inexplicably important to her.

Maybe it was also time to tell Max about her new 'sensitivity'?

No, perhaps not yet. She'd hinted at something to John, however, as he was leaving. She did need to tell somebody, at some point, but on the bus to the hospital she pulled out her phone and texted him with more straightforward news.

> Hi John, just to say thanks so much for coming to our bbq (and being so patient with Max.) I've spoken to him since and he's agreed that you and I and Manda (and my mother, if she'll accept a more bespoke arrangement) can baptise the baby in our own way, but he doesn't want to take any part in it. I think he's now firmly in the "I'm terrified of my pregnant wife's mood swings" place, so he's happy to take the path of least resistance! Speak soon, Jess x

Calumn's expression was one that Jess hadn't encountered before. Or perhaps she'd never really taken enough notice. She wondered whether she'd now assumed *too much* of a clinical distance, disturbed by his penetrating gazes and his odd little prophecies? There was something in his voice, too.

Could the 'enhancement' she was experiencing have some unexpected benefits when it came to her working life? She'd always been aware of Calumn's vulnerability, the melancholy beneath the religious mania, but now she could actually *see* his pain, glinting like a suit of broken glass. *Such* pain. *Such* loneliness.

She could *hear* his anguish, too, the strains of a discordant jangling. Jess wondered whether she would also feel everything that he felt, if she allowed herself, but knew that such a vortex of empathy would serve neither of them.

As was expected of him, Calumn attended the group therapy sessions but never made a contribution. Jess wasn't party to his appointments with Dr Ngoze but knew that he refused to say much to her at all, never mind allow her to delve into his deepest, most formative experiences. But everyone on his care team was conscious of his background.

The life-long type 1 diabetes. His mixed Scottish-Scandinavian parentage, the death of his father in an oil rig fire when he was 13. A sister that later skidded out of all social safety and died of an overdose. The bullying, the change of schools, the suspicious attempt to burn a bike shed that couldn't be pinned on any particular culprit, but about which Calumn had been questioned. The belated diagnosis of Marfan syndrome, the same genetic condition Abraham Lincoln had suffered, though he had taken a very different path with his impairments.

Then there was the string of cautions for possession of restricted flammable materials. A mother to whom he no longer spoke, who had remarried a man Calumn had refused to live with. His move to an unmarried uncle in another town, a man apparently also unable to cope with his own life conditions and who had since died of cirrhosis.

Then, very little of record. Until the incident with Dr Kluft and the bones.

It was all so tragically textbook. Thirty-five years in the making of an unmade man. Jess had tried to encourage Calumn to reconcile with what was left of his family but, incredibly, he was insistent that his 'true family' were those same people who'd guided him toward his crime and since abandoned him. He claimed they were merely lying low, waiting for his release, at which point he would be welcomed back into the fold. Whisked away to await the rapture.

'Good morning, Calumn. Did you sleep alright? You seem a little low, today. Is there anything I can help with?'

He roused himself to his full, emaciated height, forced some steel into his posture, tightened his jaw muscles and attempted a smile that disguised his untended teeth. 'How can I be sad when I am sustained by the Lord?'

'But doesn't God allow us to grieve, Calumn?'

'I have nothing to grieve for, Nurse Jessica. And, anyway, why grieve for what has gone to Glory?'

'There are many kinds of living loss, too, Calumn. Friends, health, innocence… freedom?'

'The love of the Lord grants me everything I need. There is no freedom without Him. And none are innocent.'

Jess knew this catechism all too well. Ached from the memory of how exhausting it was to try to be 'good' because you were commanded to, because you'd been terrified into compliance, because you wanted to be admired and accepted for your goodness – not because it felt liberating to live ethically, or that it came naturally when you opened your heart to its own beauty.

She saw now the tiny pores cracking open in Calumn's carapace. The sessions with John were having some effect, perhaps peeling away some of the crusted layers. Something which surely would be painful for one so guarded within his inner cell. Had a healing crisis of some kind begun, and if so, how would Calumn confront the realisation of any guilt? At least, under John's ministry, he might experience not so much a devastating crisis of faith but more some form of *transition*?

'Well. I'm here if you need me, Calumn, or want to talk. Or if you want me to try to contact anyone? Right then. Come on, let's get your insulin sorted.'

Calumn acquiesced. He might not willingly subscribe to interventionist medicine, he might yet be awaiting that miracle, but he did so very much need to be cared for.

⚬⚬⚬

When Max awoke he forgot for a moment that Jess was back on nights and reached over for her, to feel for the roundness in her belly that was beginning to fully bloom. Downstairs, he found her sitting in an array of discarded shoes, pregnancy books and breakfast dishes, staring past a plasma screen that had failed to connect to any channel.

'Hey babe. What's up? Why you staring at bluescreen? Is the connection playing up?'

'Do you remember when it used to be static, Max, on the old-school tellies when we were kids? It wasn't just static though, was it? Like you told me, it's the signal from the beginning of the universe. Microwave cosmic background something...'

'Radiation. Cosmic microwave background radiation.'

'Yeah, those guys, they discovered it by accident, right? And it's everywhere, all around us, light waves stretched so long they can only be picked up by radio now?'

'Yeah, that's right. What's up, babe,' Max asked with gathering concern, moving around to the front of the sofa, 'are you alright? Why don't you go to bed? You need your rest, hun. You need to tell them, Jess, like we agreed. No more nights now, not in your condition.'

'No. I'm not ready yet, Max. I'm alright. I'm fine.' But she was still staring ahead, not engaging with him, her chocolate hair falling carelessly over one eye.

'No. You're not. You keep looking off into nothing. You're exhausted.'

'But it's not nothing, Max.'

'What do you mean?'

'It's not *nothing*. I'm not looking at nothing... I'm seeing something.'

'Jess, babe, what are you talking about?'

She stood up. Looked at him.

'Something's been happening to me, Max. But I don't want you to worry, I want you to try to understand.'

His gut twisted. Whatever this was, he did not want to hear it. The pregnancy had brought changes, of course, but there was something else, something unwelcome arriving and he could handle only so much upheaval, only so much bizarre whimsy. He'd tolerated her new friendship, her demand for the baptism, but he needed his grounded, solid, sensible wife to keep holding their world together, sweet and steady. She was his tether to life as it was supposed to be, his anchor against the swell.

HERE AND THERE

At once excited and disturbed, unable to keep the revelation of the cave drawings in Yemen to herself, Eloise dashes through the corridors in search of KC. She finds him in his pod and breathlessly relays the news, the uncanny similarity of the last drawing on the cave wall to the magnified image of the virus, her conviction about its meaning. All shared more precipitously than she should have and without circumspection. She soon realises her mistake.

'Coincidence, Eloise. Nothing more. Come on now, the pace of the work, the conditions we're under, it's all having an effect on that vivid imagination of yours. All we're looking at here is some ancient graffiti! Like one of those cave paintings in the Mesa of those godlike figures wearing huge hats, which some folk *really* need to believe are ancient astronauts. I know you value your creative thinking – and so do I – but you can read anything into anything if it suits your confirmation bias. You know that.'

Deflated, Eloise admits to herself that KC is probably right. But she wants him not to be. She knows Darius would share her astonishment but she can't yet send him the image of the virus, it remains sensitive information. And Tom, with his artistic soul, would be thrilled to concur with her sense of connection. He might even choose to make a new design out of it! But she cannot share this with him either. *Tom.* The thought of him clutches at her stomach.

'Now, if you'd shown me a glyph of the Ebola virus, I might've done a double take, but our virus here is a neat and symmetrical little villain, it's not much of a stretch that a hominin capable of abstract thinking could come up with something so visually similar. In fact, wasn't there some touring exhibition of Aussie indigenous art that made visual comparisons with the microbial world, literally joining those dots?

Eloise gazes hypnotically at the screengrab on her phone again, his reminder of that exhibition only serving to illuminate the possibilities. A part of her wants KC to lean in to her way of thinking – or dreaming? – but she's also glad that he's maintaining his astute position as her devil's advocate. As ever, he is the ballast to her billowing sails.

Nevertheless?

'Yeah, but you have to admit, KC, this mark is unlike any of the others. It's almost an afterthought or a postscript. And it's unlike any petroglyph I've ever seen. For its age, I mean, and not even that amazing python in Botswana comes close to this! I really can't see any clear visual relationship with something that might have been familiar in palaeolithic life.'

'You're reaching, Eloise. The conflation is off the scale! I mean, it could be a flower, or a seed! Look, I know how the DNA mutation in our female patients has got you stimulated, and I know your sense of a "connection" with Sarah can set off these sparks of inspiration, maybe even the occasional breakthrough, but *please* don't get distracted by this. We gotta focus on the job we're doing right now – and I'm pretty sure our colleagues wouldn't be crazy about any wild conjecture. They don't know you like I do, and we really can't lose any credibility here.'

'But, when you factor in the claw, too, KC. And this, this scene near the beginning that looks like rain falling on people, but it's rain that kills them all! Couldn't that be volcanic ash? We know from the isotope analysis that Sarah was exposed to that—'

'No, no more, Eloise. Stop this now.'

Responding to her perceptible flinch, KC softens his tone.

'Hey, look, I know it's tempting to the human psyche to see random events as connected, especially if it feels like they're telling us a tantalising story of some kind, something with *meaning*. And yeah, maybe we need that sense of meaning, maybe it helps us to keep going. But you and I both know that ultimately we're all just falling through space on a spherical rock. A bit of make-believe might help the whole ride feel more exciting – and sure, it can be a bonding experience too, especially when times are tough – but it's gotta have its place and that isn't right here. Look, I get it, I do. I did so much playacting to keep the kids amused during lockdowns, I deserve a freakin' Oscar. But you know darn well, Eloise, correlation does *not* imply causation and inventing a connection across the millennia from a cave in Yemen to a set of bones in Kenya and a bunch of sick people in the Arctic really isn't gonna help us.'

'Yes. Yes, you're correct. Of course. There's no possible proof.'

Eloise decides to let go of the notion with a nod and an extended exhalation. *But not completely.* On the way to KC's pod, she'd prepared for this conversation with various references as potential ammunition. Surely he must agree to some sort of intelligence within the world of the virus? Or at least, complex behaviour such as peptide signalling?

What about the way the herpes virus travels up and down the microtubules of the nervous system? The way Covid, much like toxoplasmosis, seems to push the infected into riskier behaviour to increase the odds of them passing it on? The way HIV goes straight after the T-cell, evading interferon? That little bastard actively targets the most intelligent human immune cell, which itself can be retrained by mRNA to attack cancer cells, or work on scar tissue, or other immunological repair. *And*, she wants to shout, HIV hobbles this wonder cell with a 'brain' consisting of just nine genes!

Eloise wishes she could raise many such arguments with KC, but knows she cannot, should not. Not now. But while she hasn't entirely given up, she knows this little twist of synchronous mischief will just have to wait.

In the meantime, she decides to change the mood, repair their connection and restore KC's faith in her hunches with some unarguable news. Her extraordinary discovery of the Sarah sequence in the samples from the Sami women. *Priorities, Eloise, priorities.*

She can sense that large groups make him nervous, so she takes The Outsider for a walk along the yellow trail towards her mother's tree – but not all the way, not yet. She's not ready to share something so sacred with him.

The Old Woman has wondered whether this man may have the gift, if he has awakened to it, as any soul might. After all, she learned not only from her mother, not only from the elder men and women of the clan, not only from the unseen, but from trying, making mistakes, then trying again. It would be a comfort to find another with such understanding. There are so few among the living now able to hear the whispering of the stones, those who have earned the right to enter the hallowed cave or to climb the mountain.

A pair of hunters accompany them on this walk, one ahead, one behind. The Outsider has not yet returned to full strength and is of little threat, but they insist that she is protected. The Old Woman insists in return that she and her guest are given adequate distance. She wants to talk to him. There is so much to ask, even if she knows he will barely understand her.

The Outsider seems confused by many of her peoples' sounds, the tongue and throat clicks in particular. It seems his own tribe makes no such noises. This is no surprise to her. The Stranger, too, had been unfamiliar with such calls when she'd arrived and never learned to make them well, her attempts often becoming a source of amusement. It was easier for her daughter, arriving as she had among these people while still so young. Their songs and their sounds had soon become natural.

The Old Woman knows that she will need to gather in all her patience with this unexpected guest. Even if there is so much, too much, that she needs to know. She must learn everything she can about the people and the lands beyond.

Her mother had spoken of vast lakes, so huge the eyes of a human could not see to the other side and a person might never walk around them. With waters that could become so wild they could not be swum with any kind of safety. Had this man seen such places near his home, or on his journey here? The Old Woman cannot remember those shores, she had been too young at the time, but she longs to learn more of them now.

The Stranger had mentioned a perilous time during the long walk, when they had crossed one such world of water while it was miraculously calm and, at the lowest tide, shallow enough to take a necessary chance. Her daughter has since attempted to visualise this episode in trance, but even her most lucid dreams cannot reveal such sights in their full glory.

There is more The Old Woman needs to learn from The Outsider. Which tools and weapons do his people use? Do they mark them and if so, how? Which animals do they hunt or snare and which creatures are forbidden to them? Is the Great Snake as sacred to his people as it is to her tribe? This creature had not been revered by her mother's people. Indeed, The Stranger had both feared and loathed it.

And what of the very greatest of the beasts, what of the huge and wondrous one, so clever and terrifying, so slow and vulnerable, so wise and dangerous? Did The Outsider know this creature and honour it? She understands that some tribes hunt this giant, that its tusk is a treasure of incomparable value to them, its meat supposedly delicious, but her kind could never kill such a blessed being, nor take anything from its burial grounds, not without inviting a terrible curse.

The Old Woman had hoped that on this wandering together they might encounter the tusked one, but instead, at a distance, she sees the stretching neck of another special animal, chewing innocently from the tops of the thorny trees. She points towards it and notices his wonder at this being, a wonder that remains fresh. It appears his people have no connection with this creature, none that is bound deeply into their souls from birth.

The Old Woman makes a series of gestures, some he must surely understand, to ask if he has or would ever kill and eat such a creature, but he appears unsure of how to answer. This is wise, of course, until he is able to understand the meaning of the animal to his hosts.

She decides that she likes The Outsider for this pretence. In the same way that she admires the white-necked raven's talent for trickery, its ability to both study and teach, to watch a while before going to work. The raven for whom she will be laid out under the sky after death. It will be an honour to make a meal for such a bird and to let her essence be carried far upon their midnight feathers.

Yes, she admires the man's cautious docility, but must also remain alert to any raven-like duplicity.

∞

Rocked by her conversation with KC about the similarity between the virus and the cave drawings, Eloise is nursing a dose of remorse. He was right, of course, about reining in any tendencies to conflation – or seeing coincidence as being inevitably meaningful. Even if this had so often led to something significant in her own life.

And yet... the human mind has always thrived upon story, analogy, metaphor or the kind of visualisation that can spark cognition. The stimulation of beneficial brain waves, the arousal of the flow state, the enablement of those *Eureka* moments. Was it not the sense of *wonder* that drove our need to make manageable sense of it all in the first place?

Everything is interconnected. If only by particle, wave and field. All made of the same star stuff, instructed by fractal geometry repeating itself over and over. Eternally bound by the elusive LUCA, our last universal common ancestor. Every being, much more genetically similar than different. Those same genes acting as deep information storage in ways still only partially understood.

Perhaps 'joining the dots', as KC had described it, between ancient artefact and the knowledge emerging from new technologies might allow us to better process and synthesise all the information, or at least appreciate the symmetries? Is it really such a reckless mistake to weave together the strands of an invisible web or is KC being overly cautious?

She has often thought that scientific orthodoxy could dismiss too dogmatically any contemplation of the 'mystical' within its discourse. Rightly so, of course, in terms of measurable data or empirical evidence, but perhaps an inclusive consideration of other cultural perceptions could add to the overall construct rather than diminish it?

A particular shame to her was the brutality with which traditional psychedelic medicines had been consigned to the therapeutic wastelands and criminalised, losing decades in terms of their potential for healing the mind.

Knee-jerk dismissal by the westernised establishment could be too fiercely drilled in, too compartmentalised and almost regimental in its discipline. Such boundaries could be so suffocating, especially to inspiration. She thought of John Evesham, his core practice, discipline and behaviour so firmly founded, but his mind and heart wide open. He might have made an excellent scientist in an alternate universe.

Eloise pondered the paradox. It seemed many of her colleagues could suspend their disbelief for an engaging piece of fiction, yet all too quickly disengage with the 'what ifs' when it came to fitting in at work. Less devastating, she supposed, than the fates of those visionary scientists who'd died in poverty, exile or incarceration, only for their ideas to be vindicated centuries later.

More recently, for Eloise, the tragedy of the late James Lovelock's *Gaia hypothesis* – those misunderstood, maligned and misappropriated ideas – represented a prime example of the delays and the damage such attitudes can do.

And in returning to this thought she feels the urge to indulge her most cathartic form of diarising. Her mother had been an avid correspondent – Eloise had kept so many of her beautifully handwritten letters – and she too finds comfort and a sense of deeper connection in communicating via the written word. The process seems to soothe the staccato of an overstimulated brain, especially one firing too quickly for relaxed conversation.

She considers composing another email to John. She has enjoyed their regular exchanges. Or perhaps to Tom? No, what she needs to express right now demands a different audience. Perhaps she needs to pen one of her imaginary missives to an eminent mind no longer with us? An eccentric habit, true, but her most reliable method for working through certain quandaries or concerns.

She can resist the impulse no longer, opens up her laptop and starts typing a 'drafts-only' letter to a dear departed scientist. Her favourite addressee, poor old Charles Darwin, has had respite from her musings of late, but in thinking of *Gaia* theory, a more contemporary character has become the prime candidate to take his place. She opens her laptop.

Dear James

If they'd taken you more seriously and much sooner, would it have made a difference? If your mistake hadn't been to listen to your writer friend, William Golding, and name your ideas after a Greek Goddess? If your resolute "outsider" status hadn't diminished your credibility?

The potential for reading mysticism into *Gaia* played straight into the fantasies of a certain fringe element, while seeing it brutally dismissed by the "new atheist front" – even if it also gave focus to the emerging environmental movement. But the idea wasn't properly examined and appreciated until the proof of your *Daisy World* model, demonstrating *Gaia's* easy compatibility with natural selection.

And sadly, not before its openness to metaphysical interpretations, to the sense of some maternal power or the notion of a "divine" plan, had hijacked and thus doomed it for the scientific establishment of the time – those so influential yet not open enough. Of course, it still goes on. I was reminded the other day of the way the connections between viruses and Alzheimer's, or viruses and cancers have been ignored for so long by certain powerful parties. But the dismissal of your concerns only emboldened the greedy, the irresponsible and rapacious, while others conveniently twisted the concept into an excuse for the worst kind of *laissez faire.*

A man before your time, James? Or a man too late? And is your model of the earth as a holistic, intelligently self-regulating system now playing out in the worst possible way for humanity? Have we passed the tipping points, have we caused critical mass? I'm thinking Thwaites, I'm thinking AMOC, *Gaia* help us. This unstoppable heating of the seas that now seems beyond the ability of organisms such as algae to redress. The horror of those initially unforeseen feedback loops, rushing us toward the worst-case scenarios. All these terrifying fires and floods.

Is it all too late? Has our decimation of the natural barometers and balancers disabled the mechanism that keeps temperature, atmosphere, life in equilibrium? Have we wayward mob of matricidal children become a problem that *Gaia* must now find another way to deal with? Sometimes I can't help but wonder whether an ancient battle to dominate DNA wasn't won by the worst of us, perhaps when various plagues decimated the Neolithic monument builders in Northern Europe?

But as we enter the Anthropocene, this man-made world (gendering deliberate!) can we still mitigate the worst of it, even in controversial ways... for example, could your rethinking of nuclear energy really replace fossil fuels and their ruthless lobbyists?

My friend and colleague, KC, eased my mind a touch in the face of some dire new information the other day. He doesn't view the notion of self-regulation in quite the same way and insists that nature always has been and always will be in a state of flux and re-organisation. That we're not merely helpless drones in a system – natural or man-made – beyond our control. That we can, should and will adapt. Even if we should have done so long before now.

Oh, what we *could* have been, James, with just a few more of the right choices, the right turns. What we could have been! What we might have learned from some indigenous peoples if we hadn't so ravaged and disrespected their cultures!

But KC argues strongly against passivity or pessimism, of leaving any so-called "wiser" systems to determine our fate, whether in nature, politics or the financial markets. A firm interventionist, he insists there are still arguments to be won, still crucial action to take. Even in the light – and the spite – of the disastrous new "dictatorship" across the water!

We may be beyond preventing the worst temperature rises (and the horror of the wet bulb death sauna in certain regions!) but perhaps carbon sequestering still offers some hope? KC also mentioned an ingenious idea for protecting the ice sheets with a series of drills that pump up sea water to keep renewing the surface! More achievable and less risky than other forms of geo-engineering?

I do love that KC is such an "optimistic realist" – especially considering what's happened in his home country – and I try to draw energy from him, but I've felt so drained here. I haven't experienced a malaise like this since those last years with Darius. I very much miss the youthful levity of Tom and Josh.

Of course, it's partly this frozen world that was once home to half my ancestors. Horribly claustrophobic when stuck inside the facility, so confronting and expansive outside. And it doesn't help that we've been kept indoors for two days, first because of a polar bear sighting and then by a white-out!

I do want to share KC's optimism – even if our differences can light the touch paper to certain realisations – and I need to believe in the power of intelligent action and of ideas. In brief windows of enlightenment, we've dreamt it was possible to change our world (or at least our societies) for the better – and we've attempted to do so with vision and purpose. Even if we can get it so horribly wrong – and even if we keep falling for charismatic cultists and con men, glamorous rich boys and masters of mendacity.

But disagreements with KC or no, I can't help wondering what *you* would make of the cave art from Yemen, of my inkling that Sarah is somehow connected, that the symbolism is pointing me somewhere. That her "turning point" DNA is still at work in us and still vital, maybe even helping us survive?

I've been thinking about the mutations on the BAZ1B gene, one that distinguishes us from extinct hominins. In making our features more delicate and expressive, and thus less threatening, it may have also brought greater sociability, less fearfulness of the stranger. Becoming more welcoming and co-operative with those outside our immediate groups would have allowed crucial survival skills and knowledge to be exchanged, especially during times of crisis or change. Many such mutations long pre-date Sarah, of course, but how many of her children expressed her particular distinctions, or still have them now?

We need to get back to basics while also evolving new Anthropocene strengths – if we have any time to do so, especially with declining fertility. Perhaps we can somehow acquire new and advantageous DNA, either deliberately or just through environmental exposure, the way some fish eggs have done? Or perhaps from parasitic or other vectors... Yes, I'm thinking of the virus, not usually much of a friend but very occasionally beneficial. And what if such accidents enabled our survival in new or previously hostile environments, the way those aforementioned fish acquired a version of anti-freeze?

Then again, does our species actually deserve that chance, or can we even hang on long enough? Perhaps not without direct genetic or technological intervention in our biology, a notion both fascinating and unsettling, but which we may have to confront sooner rather than later.

Well, in fact *right here*, in the next few days, my own team might have to make just such an intervention! Less drastic but no less daunting than the futurists might envision and holding a potentially critical key to survival.

I will keep you updated on this, James (if you don't mind) but for now I am utterly exhausted.

Yours, wearily, and down, but not out.
Dr Eloise Kluft

Her walk with The Outsider has presented a challenge. The Old Woman has since wondered how she might ease his isolation and encourage him into closer contact with the clan without making either side more anxious. Without risking that he learns too much about them, too soon. How did her mother adapt to her new world, was she also this terrified? Were the tribe also as fearful of her?

For the present, their guest must spend most of his time in a hut at the outskirts of the camp, guarded by rotations of resentful people who would rather be doing other things. Hunting or carving, stick fighting, tool making or hide tanning, flirting or fermenting berries – and drinking of that mix without restraint or responsibility.

This man, this grateful man who knows he has been granted a precious chance, might easily become more useful than many currently in the camp, given the opportunity. More, perhaps, than those who must be compensated for by the stronger and more industrious, to no one's benefit but their own. The clan may not mind carrying a member or two for a while, when and if needed. Especially those among them who offer certain useful abilities while lacking other strengths. Or those who had once given much but now needed care in return.

But what of those who were hopelessly lazy, who felt simply being this man's daughter or that woman's son was enough, that having beauty or charm was sufficient? Those who believed they had little to learn and much to be granted? It had been many seasons since one such as this had been banished. Life had been bountiful enough for many years, and beauty, charm or status could be beguiling. But banishment was not unheard of.

The Old Woman had been aware as a child that her mother was graced with many gifts and skills. That she had been granted – and had also earned – much knowledge. But she knew too that her mother had been a rare creature, considered so even among her own lost tribe and even to the father of her child.

The Stranger had told her daughter that she doubted the man who had sired her would have survived for long after they had parted ways, so far from here, during the long winter of ash. That she'd needed to teach him much and give him tools and furs and dried meat before they had separated. He had been drawn inexorably northwards, despite her warnings, and had been unable to explain why.

But this same man, The Old Woman's father, must surely have had more to offer than simply his seed? There had been a softness in her mother's face when she had spoken of him, a subtle smile. There must have been a powerful bond between them, for however brief a time.

And now this tired Old Woman wishes her mother near her once more, that she might ask her about the man she never knew. She wishes she'd learned more from her, while she had the chance, about the man with the rare, bright eyes. Eyes like her own and those of her offspring. Eyes like The Outsider.

-12-

MANCHESTER

The Atacama Desert is the driest place on earth. Defined by a complex set of geological, geographical and meteorological conditions, it sees virtually no rainfall and offers a desolation almost as magnificent as the lunar landscape of Buzz Aldrin's legendary description. The sunsets are spectacular and you can admire the majesty of the Milky Way even with the naked eye...

As he prepared his lecture notes, Max wondered if this was going too far. It was only for an extra-curricular talk to first year students, after all. He was already forced to avoid the idolatrous glances of a few undergrads, to come over all romantic might be asking for trouble. But the price of his time off last year to host some links for the ABC from the Paranal observatory, high up in the Chilean wasteland, had been this series of presentations for the faculty. Worth it, though, for his dad to be able to watch him on home TV.

Poor Jess. The few escapes they'd enjoyed together had been to wherever he could get some telescope time or catch an eclipse. At least such heavenly events afforded some intimacy and Max was beginning to identify the moments when cold, hard physics were neither called for nor useful to each other's needs.

Jess had always questioned how an eclipse could be merely a cosmic happenstance. This moon of exactly the right size and distance to so perfectly cover the sun, revealing the romance of its glowing corona and calling us to a communion of stillness and awe. This all too fleeting phenomena, surely, must be some kind of intentional gift?

Sometimes Max could indulge this dreaming, he hated to see Jess crestfallen, but more often he was unable to bite back the truth. But an eclipse was a wondrous thing indeed and he too was always moved by the experience. He knew that birds and animals could be disturbed by the events, their circadian rhythms confused, and wondered at what point in human evolution we had properly marked them, even studied them? When had the first superstitions arisen? Was it when the first poor curious soul had stared too long at the transition and fried his retina?

Had his own Sarah ever seen an eclipse and what might she have made of it? Would she have cowered in fear, or celebrated, maybe even worshipped? Would she have accepted the cultural responses of her people to the event, if they'd had any in her time, bound as they were to the earth and the here and now? Or might she have questioned, even challenged them?

Archaeology suggested that humanity didn't start looking towards or mapping the heavens until agriculture and permanent settlements took hold – and with them, the emergence of a new, elite, 'priestly' caste. Or perhaps the more egalitarian early societies, for which some argued there was evidence, had enjoyed their own communal stargazing and naming sessions? But he assumed that Sarah, whoever she had been, living so long ago, would have experienced little reaction to an eclipse beyond fear.

Max had been contemplating this ancient creature more and more lately, feeling inextricably connected, wishing he could somehow *know* her. He had little doubt that she'd been something special, that bit different, if only because she'd been found so far out of the usual human comfort zone, high up on the mountain – and more to the point, alone, as far as all the evidence indicated.

Though perhaps, he also had to admit, this sense of Sarah's specialness was because *he* had found her, so fortuitously, her bones so remarkably well preserved. But was such projection any more excusable than the fevered imaginings and fantasies of his own beloved, mysterious wife?

Beyond variations in strength or intelligence, could certain people really be that *different*, that special? Could they really have greater gifts or powers – or rather, rare access to more widely unrealised cerebral potential?

His thoughts returned to Jess, to what she'd told him about her strange new extrasensory experiences, and to his fermenting fears. Maybe they needed a holiday, a proper romantic getaway, not just a tag-along for Jess on a research mission? On many such trips she would be left to her own devices with a good book, or to some solitary exploration – but he knew she'd been holding out for Arecibo in Puerto Rico, where she might also get some sun and beach time.

Too late. Arecibo was hurricane-trashed, and Hawaii was off the agenda now too, due to the cultural sensitivities. Something he was torn about, regretting the lack of access as a scientist but feeling he ought to honour such native rights, given his own mother's distant indigenous heritage. Maybe he should explore that aspect of his family, of himself, a little more on his next visit home, whenever that might be? Yes. That would please Jess.

A trip back to Australia was certainly in the works at some point, now the killer new ASKAP telescope was up and running. Perhaps even an eventual relocation? But until then, a visit to the considerably closer Teide observatory in Tenerife would more than suffice for Jess. Preferably, of course, before any volcanic activity in the Canaries could trigger the cliff collapse which would send a tsunami over the Eastern Seaboard.

Had he been too self-involved, neglected her needs? Was this the cause of her strange new symptoms, a form of attention-seeking? Jess was usually so easy to please, so tough, so willing to take on the kinds of things that others turned away from, such as long night shifts spent caring for deeply disturbed patients. But maybe she'd run out of fuel? She deserved more. She deserved everything. He must do better for her, he must be less selfish.

Max was consoled by the notion that at least she'd experienced the kind of exotic locations few others would. He knew that none of her girlfriends could post aerial sequences of the Nasca lines in the Ica desert north of Atacama as their holiday snaps! But had he ruined that for her too? Jess had been drawn by the mystery of their symbols and geometry, but naturally he'd felt compelled to debunk the alien landing strip fantasies with the more likely harsh reality. The tragedy of generations of misguided if incredibly industrious desert-dwellers begging their false gods for water and salvation.

Their pleas to the indifferent heavens hadn't been seen, of course, and now all that survived in Atacama outside the handful of irrigated oases were some extremophile organisms locked into salt crystals.

His lovely wife had not done so well with the altitude at the Paranal observatory, but had been stoic as ever and sufficiently turned on by his serenades of star talk to respond when it mattered. As usual, he'd been fine, his mountaineering experience having prepared him well.

Not so fine now, with this unexpected twist in their relationship. Their pairing had long since adjusted to nocturnal schedules, with the happy accident of her shift pattern often coinciding with his night-sky observations, thus synchronising the rhythms of their relationship. Lately, however, they'd only been passing in hallways.

And now this weird new shit on top of the baptism bollocks!

As Jess slept next door (*dreaming of what, hallucinating, imagining what?*) Max finalised the preparation for his 'show and tell' to the undergrads. It helped. The quantifiable, the observable, the comprehensible. He had a passion for anything that measured something else or could be measured. He found his inspiration in the astronomical beauty of a standard candle, the practical wonder of a cosmic distance ladder, the ticking of spinning pulsars that you could set your clock by.

Thinking of what he'd seen and experienced in Atacama through such radiant clarity, ushered in his own essential measure of calm. Enough, at least, to pull him through until his appointment with Greg at the climbing wall, when he could get to grips with some tackle and a few ropes and then scramble, swing and sweat away all this uninvited crazy.

✀

```
TO: SisterJessicaWallace@staff-secure.hmhosp.org
FROM: RevJohnEvesham@bettering.world.org
```

Dear Jessica

A reply by email as I have more to say than a text will accommodate! It was so lovely to see you last week, thanks so much for including me. Of course, I'd be delighted to baptise your baby and I'm sure we can come up with something to suit. Don't be too hard on Max, it's clear he loves you enormously and this certainly does seem to be a very considerate compromise on his part.

On another note, I've been mulling over our brief conversation at the door as I left your charming home - and if you don't mind me saying so, I picked up on a sense of anxiety from you, and some safety concerns about the hospital? I know the stolen sticky tape incident was disturbing, but if I understood correctly this was more about other inmates, apart from Calumn? You mentioned you might want to chat when I'm next at the hospital about someone coming out of maximum security? If there's anyone else there who you think might benefit from seeing me - or anyone else you'd like to discuss "anonymously" - I do have considerable expeeience of working with violent offenders.

I know you're not a naturally anxious person, but the world is a very challenging place for sensitive souls right now, and you are entering a momentous new phase of life. Although, I often say that those who do suffer from anxiety are among the most courageous people I know, because for them the whole world is on fire and yet they make themselves run through burning buildings every day!

Also, and forgive me if this is presumptuous, but I have known a few Catholics in my time (lapsed or otherwise) and empathy seems to be an extra crown of thorns to many of the faithful. May I suggest that nursing a sense of guilt, or "suffering in silence" to compensate for the suffering of others, is not the most constructive use of such a quality? Nor is the notion that if you are not suffering too, then somehow you don't care. You can care very deeply, about everything, and still allow yourself to feel joy whenever joy is available.

And you have so much to feel joyful about right now, Jessica, and in so many moments to come! Let yourself appreciate all that, make the most of every blessing and, please, don't take on too much or try to carry around other people's stuff.

Let me know if there's anything else I can help you with, personally or professionally (you also said something about some "changes" you'd been experiencing?) and let's talk further about the baptismal ceremony.

We have discussed your brief time volunteering in India as a nurse and those cherished, lingering memories (many of which I share.) I have a distant cousin who plays the sitar sublimely, I'm sure I could arrange for her to join us if you'd like to include something in the ceremony that reminds you of your travels? Almost anything is possible to make the occasion feel right for you and yours.

```
Yours faithfully
John


Oh, ps. I recall that you once mentioned a coincidence
that you might have to tell me about one day? I wonder
if that has something to do with Max? Having met him, I
felt a sense of recognition that I can't quite place.
Anyway, to be discussed…
```

The attraction was fatal. Eddie Briggs could not resist a camera, even if it was nothing more glamorous than CCTV. The very thing that had put him where he was. But a lens was a lens and what was recorded became real. Remembered.

He wanted to be famous, couldn't understand why no documentary crew had come courting, why his poetry had not been published and celebrated. He'd watched the sensational true crime shows, seen how clown pictures painted by serial killers could fetch thousands at auction.

Maybe he should have gone all the way, actually killed someone, maybe that would have upped his value. Maybe his mistake was to have no particular signature.

He would have to think about that, have a plan for when he got out. Maybe he should film himself, like the happy slappers. But he needed both hands, both feet. Teeth. To do it properly, to get the most out of the moment. Maybe an accomplice, then?

No. He trusted no one. He'd never been good at sharing. For now, he would have to make do with memory alone, the shady forms and stop-motion action filmed in the underpass, whatever he could recall from the courtroom videotape of the last battering.

He had been seduced by the grainy footage at his hearing, even while knowing it would send him down. Down among the half-wits, those who could have no appreciation of his shining distinction among them.

Now as the whirring of the surveillance camera followed his every move, as the security inspection of his seclusion room bound him corner by corner, he tried very hard not to look at the lens, not to smile, not to puff out his chest and flex. Not to grab that whitecoat by the throat and chew out his heart.

HERE AND THERE

How could she be surprised? She'd hoped it would not be so, but there are so few left who remember the arrival of her mother, remember how it was handled. All the benefits The Stranger had brought. This husk of a man has delivered only insidious fears, raised only the resentment of stolen attention, brought only the threat of a terrifying world beyond.

Her grandson tells her that some of the more restless youths plan to provoke an argument. Some flimsy excuse for conflict. Young men who believe they could be warriors of legend but have encountered few aggressors beyond the rarity of a four-legged outcast from a pack or a herd, mad with hunger or loneliness. Boys whose only victories have been in rehearsed skirmishes, or perhaps the more disruptive arguments over the favours of a girl. Those who have won only races and lost only pride.

The Old Woman can appreciate their discomfort and confusion, the sense of wanting to protect their own, or what they consider to be theirs. Young men, after all, have the most fiery sense of territory, the most urgent sense of competition. And yet, their energy is vital. Their strengths, when properly directed, are qualities of wonder, even if unpredictable.

Her grandson – having earned his Warrior title by fighting off the snarling, snub-nosed meat-stealers that were encircling his sisters as they de-fleshed a carcass – is not sure what the group are planning. Nor if any kind of plan exists at all. The boys have warned him not to interfere. They have been vocal in questioning whether anyone with eyes like The Outsider can be trusted.

This news reaches in and squeezes at her throat. It is worse than she might have imagined. Must she fear not only for the safety of their unusual guest, but also for her own bloodline? A division is being drawn, seeds are being scattered on an evil wind. They must not be permitted to take root and bear thorns. Such mischief may create a bond between those drawn together in suspicion and dangerous purpose, but ultimately it serves no one.

How can this be prevented? Must she sacrifice The Outsider? While such an impulsive action would meet an immediate need, it could only worsen their prospects by setting a perilous example.

And yet, The Old Woman wonders, is this man worth the risk?

She knows the seduction of safety is a dream spun by the most fickle of lovers. A temptation as false as the confidence of these young troublemakers, imagining they can claim or control anything for long. All things must change, all things must pass. Indeed, the whole tribe has grown too comfortable, believing its blessings to be somehow owned, somehow inherited, somehow deserved.

Her fear, however, is no such fantasy. This is not the first time her living issue has been threatened. In that long-ago spring when the hunger came, when the herd did not return, when the rains passed them over and the tribe was in great suffering, many in desperation ate of a creature best left underground. Some died and more sickened – but not those of her closest blood.

A few wretched folk, those who would bear no responsibility for choosing to stuff their stomachs so thoughtlessly, accused her of casting a spell, of somehow causing all this suffering, not asking what she might have to gain from such madness. Blame. Such a deadly, soul-shrivelling thing. It made otherwise useful people as dry and twisted as an empty river.

Once most of the clan had recovered, aided by her wisdom and care, the balance of good sense and harmony had returned, but The Old Woman could never forget the gripping of her heart, the clenching of her belly, the uncertainty of her stance and the tensing of every sinew in readiness for what might come.

Is this what The Outsider feels? Surely it must be so. A woman might have been welcomed, tolerated at least, but a man – and one still capable of siring? Capable of killing a competitor, of betrayal, of stealing another's status? Perhaps they are right to be wary.

Indeed, she must ask herself, if he did not bear those blazing eyes would she have reacted in the same way? Might she have deferred to the grumblings of the long beards and is she now risking too much? She knows that under the right conditions any human is capable of anything.

And yet... What if The Outsider can offer knowledge or skills that could become useful, even essential? Perhaps he can teach them how to survive in the face of newer and even greater dangers? And vitally, can he prepare them for whatever it is he has been running from?

The Old Woman is convinced she must learn of his ways... and of his mind. More, she must help him to understand hers.

And she must devise a new story for the campfire.

In the meantime she sets her grandson a subtle task. What these young men need is another, more compelling distraction. The Old Woman regrets the plan that takes shape because it goes against her better nature, but this intervention seems necessary and is less hazardous than doing nothing.

It means asking The Warrior, whom she knows as her own blood to be a man of honour, to set aside this quality for a while. To wound the heart of a young woman who nurtures realistic desires of winning his. A girl many of these same restless young bucks would gladly vie for, were she to become available again.

The Old Woman anticipates this proud and cunning girl would sooner create a ploy to make The Warrior jealous than abandon all hope of him to weeping and wailing.

'This is the most momentous decision you or I have ever faced, KC. The sickest patients can't really give informed consent, so unless we invoke the "compassionate clause" for something so experimental, we'd have to let their loved ones know exactly what we're dealing with and what we're thinking of trying.'

Eloise feels the constriction in her voice, and not only from the chill of their outdoor interlude. 'But this kind of intervention is as much about ethics as medicine or science. Yes, this is cutting edge stuff, but there's also a bigger question. Will this cure them or just medically nudge them to the next stage of life, changed by it one way or another? I mean, do we ever really "cure" anyone anyway? Yes, maybe we give them some extra time or quality of life but it's all such a balancing act – and is it always worth what we put people through?'

'But that's not down to us to decide, or even to really know? We just do what we can to give them that extra bit of life and they make of that what they will... and who knows, maybe one of them goes on to achieve something really important – or maybe they just say "to heck with it all" and have a whole lot more fun? I know it feels like we've been here forever already, but you do remember what fun's like don't you, Eloise?'

This smarts. She needs KC to hear her now rather than tease her – a response her bouts of contemplative gravity have too often endured.

'Yes, but it's precisely that constant urge for gratification that's got us where we are in our mad, mad world! Even the so-called "right to the pursuit of happiness" can be such a red herring when the human brain is wired primarily for survival and reproduction and anything else is just a fringe benefit. An incentive to keep us surviving, keep us running the evolutionary rat race, keep us chasing the elusive bait.'

'But we're pretty keen on chasing that, huh? I mean, right now, for me, happiness would be a decent damn cup of coffee, preferably hot for more than 10 seconds, and maybe a big fat juicy doughnut!'

'Well yes, of course, pleasure-seeking is a powerful drive but the promise of *lasting* happiness is a fantasy, no matter how persuasively it's been advertised.'

'Nice when you can get it, though, huh? Lasting or otherwise.' KC's tone carries more confusion than provocation now, but she is still smarting.

'That's just life's little carrot, though, isn't it? Waving temptingly in front of us poor pathetic donkeys.'

'Well I'll take the carrot over the stick any day! Look, I don't know where this weird tangent is coming from, and I hope you're OK, but this really isn't the time for the meaning of life, Eloise. Right now, it's all about saving lives. Come on, we gotta get back to the main event 'cause we don't have a lotta time out here. Are we gonna try this thing or not?'

Eloise looks away, gazes into a pale nothingness, then turns listlessly back to KC.

'But if we do intervene – and so dramatically – and if any of our subjects survive and then go on to reproduce... will we have manipulated evolution or are we still just its unwitting pawns?'

She rubs her mittened hands together, to little effect. Her steaming breath is all that feels fully present of her now. This momentary break outside the confines of the facility, this change of scenery – what little is available under the safety protocols – seems as good as a rest. Whatever daylight, whatever *real* light they can experience must be maximised, but the weight of decision has darkened the mood.

KC sighs and studies her with concern. He reaches out and grips her upper arms, but she is swaddled beneath her puffed-up padding and there's no eye contact through her wraparound snow-goggles which are half-hidden beneath a faux-fur-wreathed hood.

'You know, I don't think this place really suits you, Eloise, Nordic heritage or no. Where the heck is all that optimism, that drive, that ambition? It's like you're fading into the landscape, blanking out in some way, and I gotta say it has me kinda worried. Is there anything else going on? Is everything OK at home?'

'Yes. I think so.'

'Then maybe it's all these setbacks we're having – and let's face it, the deaths! I don't think either of us anticipated how tough it was gonna be to witness so much sickness and suffering? I mean, outside of the occasional field research we're at least one degree removed in the lab, but here we're more like front-line medics, getting up close and personal to all the fear and the grief. I don't know how anybody does this for a day job without PTSD. So, it's gotta be taking its toll on us too, right?'

He maintains the pressure on her arms, continues his pep talk.

'But that just means we gotta dig even deeper. Save the philosophy for a glass of something cold by the fire when you get home to Tom. Park all that self-doubt for now. The question is simple. *Could* we splice some of this new DNA from the recovered women into our sickest men? Is it doable, is it safe *enough*? Let's not go all Goldblum on ourselves here. Let's save the "should we" for the committee. It's not our decision. Not ours alone, anyway.'

Eloise allows herself to connect with him. Even through the goggles, this is easy for her, their similarity in height and slenderness of build has always made their bond feel natural. She answers him, knowing that he knows her answer already, but understanding that he needs her to be fully on side.

'We *could*. Yes. Of course. Or at least try. But even if it works, KC, getting it approved – then getting it accepted for wider use if ever needed? We're talking years – more with state of things on your home turf – and who knows what this virus will have done by then if it gets out.'

'But we're running out of options. We've tried the antibody plasma from the recovered woman, and the way some of the patients rallied was so encouraging. Then to watch them decline again so quickly, and to lose them? None of our antivirals are working the way we'd hoped and the steroids are barely touching the cytokine storm. If anything, they made Patient 6 even worse!'

'I know. I know. But that's exactly what I mean! What we're proposing could either be a miracle cure or just another time-wasting, maybe even dangerous, diversion?'

'Could be. But I'm still thinking that it *has* to be worth a try?'

'Maybe. But for me, prevention is always preferable, KC. What if we just let these infections play out in isolation, keep them as comfortable as possible and learn what we can, from both the living and the dead? We should be concentrating on a vaccine, even if we only keep it in reserve. And the way things are going, one epidemic after another, all the disabling after-effects, we really need to stay ahead of the game...'

KC seems unconvinced by her proposed *laissez faire* approach to the current cluster of disease, even if it appears to be contained – and Eloise knows he's right, but she doubles down, an uncharacteristic pessimism taking hold of her now.

'...because heaven forbid that one day we get something as asymptomatically infectious as Omicron – and the myriad offspring we've been training so well since we "let 'er rip"– but then something as acutely deadly as MERS, as aerosolised as measles and as horrific as Ebola! Even then, with people dropping like flies and bleeding from every orifice, we'd probably still encounter the same shite. Too little done too late, or so heavy-handed, panicky and badly thought out that we lose public support.'

'Yeah but that ship has long since sailed anyway, I reckon.'

She sighs in despair. 'Probably. Imagine if Western countries had enjoyed the leadership that Taiwan had! But then the "public" haven't exactly covered themselves in glory through all of this either. All those entitled, very special people who were just too sexy for their masks or whatever else might be needed, so desperately needing to cosplay 2019 and any illusion of "normal" – though who can blame them with the examples they've had? Rich countries hoarding therapies while new variants percolate in the chronically ill... long-term viral persistence and new health problems written off as *whatever* when they're just the tip of the bloody iceberg...and then your new "Turd Reich" shutting down health communications and funding altogether! I don't know how you can bear it.'

KC sighs too and nods. This is the hill that Eloise might well choose to die on and there's no point in cutting her off just yet. A further squeeze of her shoulders shows his empathy, nonetheless. Compassion that is warranted, Eloise has never felt quite so hopeless, so lacking in faith or trust in humanity.

'...But as long as people keep working and spending, eh? I mean, God forbid we should choose realistic action over toxic positivity, as electable as it is. While the powerful look after themselves with mitigations like HEPA ventilation but deny that to the wider public. Even some clear and honest information would help, like how the fact it's bloody airborne, like how effective the right kind of respirator masks are, especially in healthcare!'

'I hear ya, Eloise, but—'

His attempt to mollify misses the mark, she still has a full head of steam to discharge, and his concern now feels restrictive. It may be uncomfortable to listen to, but she feels entitled to her despair and to this spiral of sadness and rage.

'...And speaking of so-called *healthcare*, what about all the bloody gaslighting – giving psych diagnoses to long haulers with genuine pathologies. Just like they did to people with ulcers before H-pylori was identified! You know, one day Covid denial will be seen in the same tragic light as climate denial. God help our poor young people, KC. As if we haven't fucked things up for them enough.'

'And that's exactly why we gotta look into *every* potential solution whenever a new danger presents! For my kids, Eloise, and for Josh. For all of them. Look, we'll find ways to fund the work. Have a little faith.' His smile suggests a new lever into her mindset that might just lift her out of it. It fails, for now.

'But who'd even accept any novel treatment we develop anyway, KC? The bad actors have done such a good job with misinformation that science is now seriously on the backfoot.'

Eloise shivers and thinks suddenly of Sarah, as she has done so often since being here, wondering about her capacity for coping with the cold, about whatever she was doing up there on that Kenyan glacier. How had she handled the chill of her final destination, or a long migration through a volcanic winter, as the evidence implied? Indeed, how might she and anyone she'd migrated with have been treated by anyone they encountered? Could that be why she was found alone? Eloise naturally identified with anyone who chose the lonelier or more difficult path. Perhaps this was why she felt so connected to Sarah?

But the cold is in her own living bones now and she cannot stop trembling. KC moves his hands more vigorously up and down her arms, then presses his thumbs into her hunched trapezius muscles. It's the most physical he has dared to be since that *almost* encounter outside a hotel room door, what seems so long ago now, if only a few years in real time.

'I hear ya. People are real happy to distrust any advice that's hard to take. They want that promise of normal, of freedom. And it's so much easier to look down at their phones and just ignore the falling sky. Peer pressure is a powerful thing, Eloise, as any parent knows. Everyone wants to do what everyone else is doing. But then isn't that just another evolutionary paradox? That we succeeded despite the reluctance of the crowd to properly measure long term risk? Except maybe in the neurodivergent – or the 5% that step up to lead.'

'Or the other lot who are in it just to feather their own nests? Your tech-bro, big oil oligarchy is probably creaming off and privatising what healthcare funding has been stripped from government programmes as we speak.' She's intrigued by KC's question, but not ready yet to forgive every human weakness.

'Maybe so. But some things are hard wired into the herd. Like the need to believe that nothing bad's gonna happen to you... until it does. Like you said, the carrot of instant gratification is way too tempting for most people, so they feed on whatever they can and let others worry about storing the surplus, or sharing things evenly, or being inventive, or anticipating that distant rainy day. *Carpe diem* and all that.'

She shrugs, the hint of a snarl lifting her chapped, blue lips. 'Well then maybe we deserve whatever's coming. Just a shame about the rest of the ecosystem.'

Despite this wholesale dismissal of her species, she hopes KC will maintain his comforting physical connection – while also risking that her anger will push him away, as it has so many before. He doesn't let go, but he does push back.

'So, what – we just give up? Let all the shady characters keep exploiting the mess? We just abandon the frightened or the arrogant or the misinformed... and everybody they'll have a snowball effect on? Don't forget there was so much good happening, too, at least during the early days of the pandemic. So many awesome examples of community and compassion!'

'Until the empathy fatigue or the frontal lobe damage or the viral-host manipulation kicked in!'

'Aw, come on now, this is just that old negativity bias of the brain dragging you down. You're only thinking about the bad stuff. Where's all that beautiful belief you used to have in the potential of humanity? Look, I know we're in a perfect storm of climate chaos and war and tyranny and mismanaged outbreaks – and it's been hell on anyone who gives a damn. And I know how disappointing it was that more didn't change with Covid–'

'Oh, I don't know, KC,' she snaps back, 'there were about five million new millionaires, weren't there?'

'–OK, I take your point, but some people are waking up? What if we really are on the cusp of something amazing here, some real change? Darkest before dawn and all. Look at all the activists still getting active! Where's your courage to try, Eloise, your curiosity? I mean, thank God for the new sterilising nasal vaccines – and now the Japanese peptide breakthrough – and where would we be if no one had been willing to do that work or join those trials? Or without what's left of international co-operation, instead of nationalist, tribal crap. And soon we might even have more personalised, genetically informed treatments for that great bogeyman of yours, Eloise, the almighty C-word!'

She wants to hope but is so tired. 'Yes. I do get that, but—.'

'And what if our Arctic virus *has* already got out somehow – are you really prepared to risk Tom and Josh becoming collateral damage in an evolutionary war? Because I'm not,

Eloise, not where my kids are concerned. Evolution – and if it has to be an entity then I'll indulge the metaphor for your sake – but evolution has built us to love, and to love *hard*, and that makes us wanna *fight* for what we love!'

She is looking at him now, listening more attentively.

'And what about Sarah?' he persists, sensing a shift and finding a new weapon in his arsenal, 'Your beloved muse and inspiration, what do you think she would've done? The pelvic remains suggest she'd had at least one child. You think she would've given up and let your capricious *Lady Nature* take her course? Or would she have fought with every tool at her disposal? Because I've been getting the powerful impression, Dr Kluft, that you think Sarah is *still* somehow fighting for her children?'

Eloise is jolted by this intuition, an unusual admission for KC. But she needs to keep playing the planet's advocate. She can hear the strain at the higher ranges of her voice as she answers through chattering teeth. 'OK. And if we succeed, KC, not just with the potential gene therapy for our delightful new little bug, but with everything we're reaching for, and ultimately we're all healthy and we all live forever, what becomes of everything else that lives? I mean, we're already so removed from the natural world it's become something just to be selfied for likes!'

'In a lot of cultures, yes – but what if all these events, these "alterations" actually make us better somehow? Maybe we're becoming whatever it is we *can* become? Maybe it's all about that potential?' He is smiling again as the tide starts to turn. She wonders whether he'd really rather shake this out of her instead, just as she sometimes wishes she could.

'But has any of our supposed progress ever *really* changed us for the better, KC? This Darwinian "perpetual struggle" that we're in?

'Yes! Apart from some godawful holes in the road we do keep trying to get better. And we so often succeed!'

'Not often enough though. And by whose measure? We're battling a secondary epidemic these days of narcissism – or at best just the drive to fit in. I mean, most people are more afraid of social death than actual death!

KC nods, but not in complete agreement. 'Yeah, and what's new? Belonging to the in group *meant* staying alive in our early days. OK, there's always one or two exceptions, one or two brave souls who struck out and helped make a change, but probably at great personal cost. Look, it's really not that complicated, Eloise, it's really kinda simple. We're all driven to survive and we can't help that. You can't help that. You can only help *how* you survive.'

'Even if our collective survival comes at the cost of everything worth surviving for?'

'Every day is a gamble, Dr Kluft, you know that. For every living thing. A tango with the unknown. See, I can do Philosophy101 too. And with everything going down on my home turf, I'm the one who should be swimming in pessimism, but I can't afford to do that. None of us can.'

He brings his hands back up to her shoulders, keeps smiling. Does he understand its inevitable effect on her? He must. She appreciates his patience. Eloise becomes aware of how tightly her brows are drawn together with serious intent and suddenly feels ridiculous. She lets them soften and sucks as deep and slow on the icy air as she can without it hurting.

'Ah shit. Maybe you're right, KC. Humans are only what bloody *Nature* has made of us, after all. And she seems to positively welcome the arms race. So, maybe she's not quite done with us yet?' Eloise takes a breath, realigns herself. 'OK. So let's do it. Let's see if we can progress the gene therapy. And if it works, game on. But we need to do this right. We should use artificial XNA enzymes for the snip and splice, yes? They look like being a much safer and more targeted option. And inhibit gene P53 in case of cell overgrowth...'

'Hallelujah.' He punches the air. 'Yes! OK, come on, let's get as ready as we can for that green light.'

'But we do need reliable consent, KC. And complete isolation and observation – shit, probably a lifetime of observation, even *if* any of our male candidates do survive the virus. And indemnity! Personal indemnity, guaranteed. I'm doing nothing until I have that, in iron-clad writing... But, you know, you're right, KC, and that's what swung it for me. This is for Tom and Josh. For you and your son. For all the men who might be at risk. Whether they'd thank me for it or not.'

'Well, I'm thanking you for it. And you know, maybe the consent won't be so tough after all. I heard our key candidate is in a civil partnership with another scientist, some guy at the Max Planck. If he's registered as our guy's next of kin then he might be open to it – and should know whether our subject would be too?'

KC slides his other hand from her shoulder down to her wrist and begins to guide her back inside.

'Come on, you're shivering like crazy now. Let's get out of the icebox.'

The story she tells after sundown is contrived to draw some heat from the ill will rising among the young men, even as their faces flush with the warmth of fresh and leaping flames.

It is the tale of the boy who blames.

An unwanted brother had arrived in this boy's life, after his own father had been taken by a cliff fall and his lonely mother had accepted another mate. One who was different, an outcast from another tribe, one who had lost the battle to lead that tribe – and with it one eye and the full use of one hand.

The new baby brother shared none of his father's shame or sadness, however. He had been blessed with a light heart and an easy love for all he encountered. Love even for the older brother who resented how this little boy's smile had stolen so many hearts. A little boy who had not only his own living father but also far too much of their now shared mother.

So when water was spilled, when a drinking shell was broken, a bone-scraper lost in the sand, when unwatched tamarind seeds fresh from their pods were raided by the birds, it was always the fault of the little brother. Because he was taking more than his share, not only of his mother's love but of anything that might have been or should have been his older brother's.

Surely there could not be enough for both of them? And the older boy had been there first. He had the greater claim. Once, he'd had a father who belonged to this tribe.

When there were no bad things he could blame on the younger one, the older brother made things happen. Unravelled a basket, hid his mother's hammerstone for cracking nuts, pinched the little one when no one was looking, causing cries that were not merely an annoyance but a potential danger that might scare away prey... or invite a predator.

Soon his little brother's smiles were less often seen, though he never ceased loving. And he had another skill, apart from this capacity to bring joy. He was able to forgive. More, he was able to give something rare. A special gift that none of the rest of the tribe could offer. His dreams could tell them where the great herds would be. The largest of the hoofed creatures, with swaying pouches at their necks and tails of secret power, those with so much to value, from flesh to hide, from twisting horn to healing bones.

One day, when the rains had been long and heavy and the watering holes were overflowing, the little brother had seen the place where the running beasts would gather, where they would clash heads and drink and play in the mud. The whole family had joined the hunt, and when the animals were exactly where the little one had dreamed them to be they lifted him high, gave him handfuls of berries and sweet seeds, ruffled the tight curls of his hair.

His brother grew sullen and behind his angry eyes a plan had formed. He had seen the beasts run hard and fast together when scared. He knew what might happen to someone small under those hooves, someone not yet fast enough to escape. He knew how to mimic the voice of his little brother, his favourite calls. So he offered to take care of him while the adults took their place in the wide and quiet circle around the herd, to keep him back safely with the other children.

But he did no such thing. Instead, he encouraged the little one to follow him, closer to the herd, to creep along the line of scrub as close as possible so they could see their parents at work, learn how they wordlessly chose the likeliest prey and planned to separate it further from the crush at the water's edge. To clear the sight lines for the spear throwers.

He took his little brother's hand and led him toward the herd along the water's edge, out of sight of the hunters. Then he pushed him down hard and ran back along the water's edge crying out, as if he were the little one. His plan worked well enough and the beasts were startled and ran. But in many directions, including along the water's edge. The roar of their running was immense, the drumming of their frantic escape shook the earth, the smell of their musk was overpowering, the air was full of noise and fear and confusion.

In a splattering storm of red mud, the older boy slipped and fell, was kicked hard into the water, where, winded, he began to sink. His lungs were set to surrender when he felt a strong hand haul him out and push him up the bank toward his waiting mother, who sheltered him with her own body. A body battered by the flank of a running buck, but not beyond repair. Unlike the father of the younger brother, whose useless hand was now taken altogether by the jaws of a scaly belly crawler, which may have preferred a bigger meal from the drinking herd but who was happy to take a man instead.

And taken the man was, down into the silty waters to be rolled and drowned and soon digested.

The ploy to disperse the herd had not been without compensation, despite its terrible dangers, its terrible cost. Once the hunters had picked off two or three isolated stragglers from the reformed and heaving mass of fleeing creatures, they came to assist the older boy and his mother, who could not walk without help but who would mend. In body if not in heart.

And the little brother? His dreaming of the herd, of his spirit companions, had not been in vain for he had learned how they moved, learned to call in their guiding, protective spirits. He had curled into a ball, surrounded by the power that is gifted to those who know how to share their gifts, and he had survived their hooves unharmed.

He was in all ways undiminished, even in his capacity to forgive the brother whose jealousy had now left them both fatherless. A sacrifice made by that unfortunate outcast, and not even to protect his own blood, but to save what he could for the tribe who had given him a home.

The Old Woman sees that her listeners have listened well. One or two seem irritated by this tale, while another, The Outsider, is as enraptured by it as she had hoped.

-14-

MANCHESTER

As Jess abandoned the dawn and closed the door on another day she would barely see, there was no sign of Max. Usually when he heard her key in the door he would call out for her, or come to greet her with a bear hug and an exploration of the sweet spot on her neck. Sometimes he lifted her off her feet, swung her full circle and held her up like an offering to the textured ceiling.

When they'd first moved in he'd promised to strip out all the dated decoration, but that intention was as yet unfulfilled. It didn't matter to Jess, nothing mattered but being with Max, finally at home on unshifting ground.

Jess sometimes wondered whether all that exuberant affection would fade and what that might signify. Too much love was almost worse than not enough, if ever it was withdrawn. Had she gone too far, told him too much, given him too much of a burden? His reaction to her revelations about her enhanced perceptions had been met only with defensive concern and urges to seek help – though not his help, clearly. She'd hoped, at least, for curiosity.

She looked at her watch. It was too early. Max would not have left yet for the array. Probably sleeping in. She made herself some tea and found him in the spare room at the computer. She took a moment, through her post-nocturnal haze, to understand that the quivering in his muscular back was emotion. Jess had never seen Max cry.

'Baby... what's the matter?'

She put down her tea, leaned over him, but he turned away.

'It's OK, sweetheart, it's OK... tell me what's the matter? Is this about me, what I told you the other day?'

'No. Well, yeah, I'm worried about it but not enough to blub like a baby. Ah look, it's nothing. I'm sorry. Don't worry.'

'No, sweetheart, it's OK, just tell me. Here, have some of my tea.'

He swallowed. Quelled the release.

'Got a message from Brent.'

'Your brother? What's wrong? Is it your dad?'

'Nah, the family's fine. Dad's doing well, don't worry. It's about an old friend.'

'Oh dear. Who? What happened?

'Van. Van Nguyen. A mate from school. Topped himself. Overdose.'

'Oh no, that's awful. I'm so sorry. When did you last see him?'

Max laughed with bitterness. This was completely unfamiliar.

'What, darling, what's going on?'

'There are a few things you don't know about me, Jess. That you wouldn't want to know.'

'Like what?'

'Like what a bastard I really am.'

'No, Max. What do you mean? I've come across some real bastards in my time, that's not you. Trust me, I've got instincts about these things. And anyway, you might like to wear the tough guy T-shirt but *I* know what's inside. I've seen the acts of kindness when the chips are down. The way you went the extra mile for that student with Long Covid. The way you were right in there, rolling your sleeves up and helping out with that road accident. You saved the day!'

Max sucked in some air. Held it. Let it go.

'Sorry babe, but I need a smoke. Let's go outside. Put your fleece on, though, it's chilly.'

They'd made a minimal effort with the small patio at the back of the terraced two-storey red-brick. The pots and climbers, the table-and-bench combination rescued from a beer garden undergoing renovation, and assorted sun-soaking options. But neither was up to weeding between the flagstones. Max grabbed up a handful of dandelion leaves which came away without their roots. He threw them down, lit up. Looked up just in time to see a hawk chase a sparrow across their minimal patch of city sky.

'Oh, did you see that? Amazing! Never seen a raptor here before!'

'Oh? No, I must have missed it. But never mind about that, come on, talk to me, Max.'

'Ah hell. OK. Van and I were best mates, see, inseparable right up till we were thirteen. A couple of chemistry nerds, blowing things up in Dad's garage.'

'And?'

'We started getting some shit. Name-calling, you know, a few stupid or snide comments as we walked by – or a bunch of dickheads not actually letting us go by, making it... you know, difficult. They punctured the tyres on our bikes once. Oh, and some racist bollocks too, about Van. But they never actually touched us because of Brent. Big bro was exactly that – bloody big for his age. But they would have, I reckon. Van was always with me, and we usually got away with just the verbal abuse, but it wasn't much fun. Van was terrified.'

'So, what happened?'

'I put on a growth spurt, got into the rugby squad. Made new mates.'

Jess moved closer on the bench, put a hand on his.

'Oh but, Max, everyone moves on through school, changes their social circle?'

'I abandoned him, Jess. I cut him out. They bloody crucified him. I don't think he ever got over it. Well, obviously not.'

'I see... But I'm sure there's more to it than that? It's not your fault, Max, you didn't do the bullying. And it's not your fault that he killed himself. You didn't feed him the pills.'

'No. But I might as well have given him the bloody bottle.'

'No, baby. You can't blame yourself. So many other things could have happened. He could have had untreated depression, all kinds of other problems. I mean, you have no idea what course his life took after school.'

'Exactly! I didn't give a shit. Never even checked in on him. I've left everyone behind if they couldn't keep up. Onwards and upwards with the glittering career, with being Mister Popular. And you know what? I think Brent took a kind of pleasure just now in giving me this news.'

'No. Why would he?' Jess kept her voice patient-soft.

Max hadn't fully exhaled from a long draw on his cigarette and his voice was pulled back in his throat.

'Because I shafted Brent too.

'When?'

Lungs emptied now, he let the story unfold.

'When I was sixteen. Mum found a bag of weed when she was cleaning out our den. Dad was a lawyer, remember, a prosecutor, and Mum always stood right behind him. The apocalypse was coming down and right on my head. The bag was mine. Brent didn't even smoke, but he took the rap. You see, Golden Boy here was due to go on a trip to NASA and would have blown it if Dad had found out. But Brent said it didn't matter because Dad already hated him and he was a fuck-up anyway. Christ. I don't know if those two have ever really made it up.'

'Oh, I see. But you could change that, Max? You could own up? There's enough water under the bridge now. I'm sure they would both forgive you. It's not too late.'

'No. You're right. It's not too late. But it is for Van.'

⬤━⬤

Dear Calumn

I have given lots of thought to your question: do I believe that "Sarah" was truly one of our ancestors, living over 70 millennia ago, and if so, how do I reconcile that with teaching from the Bible? Well, "belief" is a very loaded word. Certain things are matters of faith, some ring true in the heart, while others are matters of evidence.

For example, having a *sense* of the divine is one thing, but *knowing* that life is better and happier when we practice kindness and forgiveness is another. While one can only be felt, the other can also be measured by our own experience.

Yet more things are indisputable facts, such as knowing that if I jump from a tall building gravity will drag me to my death - and I can't imagine even your "Scarlet Lady" being prepared to test that with her own body, can you?

And forgive me if this is too close to the bone, but in the same way that you *know* that fire burns, perhaps all too well, so science knows many things by measuring, testing and measuring again with ingenious instruments made by brilliant minds. It's unreasonable to think every one of those is out to bamboozle us. The simplest explanation is usually the right one and conspiracies require such complex weaving - so many lies maintained by so many people. Exhausting!

I do feel that most people are good and mean well. Some act badly out of fear or damage, selfishness or greed, ignorance or manipulation by others, but most people will help someone who needs it, and with little expectation of reward.

But we have more than a simple choice between faith or knowledge, Calumn. We have imagination and creativity! (Though, yes, sometimes we can let that carry us away, I mean we never outgrow a good story, do we?) We also have contemplation and meditation. We have living and evolving languages. All of which can help us access experiences we may not yet have the right words for - and then attempt to describe them in terms that we currently understand.

This is what I believe many of the prophets, teachers and priests of the past did. I'm sure you know that the Bible is drawn from different times, places and voices, and I know you believe they all speak directly for God, but even if that were true, I mean, even if *you* spoke directly for God, would you always get it right? Would you always understand correctly? Humans are so fallible!

Say if your Scarlet Lady had told you a story and you'd done your best to relay it to someone else, could you be sure you hadn't missed anything important, that you'd used the right words? What if that story was then told to a French person? Even if something did get lost in the retelling or in the translation, the chances are the *essence* of the story, its purpose, its lesson would still shine through?

Well, that's how I feel about the Bible. I gravitate to what rings true in my heart, what makes sense for more beneficial living, what would improve *my* relationship with God and make *me* a better person. Here, now, today… not as someone who lived in the Levantine desert 6,000 years ago.

I have no need to sacrifice bulls or trace my ancestry to a God-given piece of land, but I do need to be inspired, forgiven, reminded of my humility and encouraged to keep going and giving, to look after my health and to be thankful, to seek something greater than myself and to honour that in praise. The teaching is a living thing, Calum, just like language, just like science.

As for Sarah - well, yes, I have no reason to doubt that those remarkable bones, the ones you were so cruelly instructed to burn (along with poor Dr Kluft) if the claims were not retracted, are a precious gift that can teach us so much. That they, like the earth, like this magnificent universe, are as old as the evidence and our current ability to measure them suggests.

More, the thought of being among her direct line - one of Sarah's "children" - is fascinating to me. How joyful to call any stranger I meet, anywhere on this earth, "sister" or "brother" and not only metaphorically or spiritually, but as interwoven in my cells?

Perhaps Eve was not merely one woman, Calumn, one poor woman whom we blame for her man's choices. Maybe there have been many Eves, many mothers - and just as many Adams? For me, God simply never stops creating. How wonderful is that?

Some say time is meaningless anyway. An illusion spun by our brains to make sense of the physical world as we experience it. Some say there's only an eternal field of *now*, and if you consider God to be infinite then his true kingdom must be so too. In which case Sarah and all the ancestors, prophets and teachers exist alongside us somewhere, as do all our descendants.

Whatever the truth may be, I don't think it hurts to live more fully in the moment and not worry so much about *before* or *after*, other than the essential planning that keeps our bodies safe and well. I'm sorry if this is all getting a little too fantastical, but I think the key thing is to worry less about what we cannot control, and the mysteries we don't yet understand, and just be the kindest, best and happiest people we can.

So, if you ask me why I practice Christianity as my
faith, it's because my heart soars whenever I hear those
teachings, or when I speak of or sing about the example
of the Christ. For me there is little more beautiful or
poetic than the beatitudes. Few more lovely hymns than
a version sung in descant of the prayer of St Francis,
as my mother and her sisters used to bless me with in
lullaby. From such deeply personal joys and openings
of the heart, Calumn, faith flowers.

With my kindest regards,
John Evesham

(PS thinking of the beatitudes, blessed are *you*, dear
Calumn! Please know that you are loved, not for what
you are prepared to sacrifice to a cause, but simply
for being.)

It was quite a find. Jess had been unaware of this little gem
tucked behind a shopping centre she'd rarely bothered with,
until impending motherhood. She didn't care what name they
gave to any church and felt those who had devotedly carved out
the stones would have found it irrelevant too. But it was so rare
for Catholics in this country to call anything other than blocks
of brick and concrete their own, after greedy old Henry and all
the others had had their way. All that blood, all that burning, for
what? Not for Him, not in His name.

Jess looked around. Toured the stations of the cross. Some
might call it idolatry, all these elaborate visual reminders of
the Passion. To Jess they were just expression. Perhaps too
concentrated on the violence, instead of how he had risen above
it all, but it was only a matter of taste. The costumes, the rituals
may be a little ridiculous, no better than the incantations of
superstition to some. To Max. For Jess, over time, they had

indeed become empty repetition. In her teens she'd felt guilty for being so bored. But sometimes you had to put something aside in order to come back to its power.

Do this in memory of me. Jess contemplated those words, the inspiration for the heart of the Mass. The invitation to become one again with the body of God. So simple, this instruction to remember, to believe. It had entered her heart so early, never really left, despite her 'transgressions'. For one brief year, as the careers counsellors doled out their advice to uninterested thirteen-year-olds, Jess had seriously considered the spiritual life. The purity of it, the peace, the singular dedication to the ultimate in communion. Sainthood seemed so much more satisfying than, say, sales and marketing.

The fantasy had fallen away piece by piece. Discovering sex was thrilling and terrifying in equal measure, even if it wasn't until Max, until commitment, that she'd felt completely at one with that part of herself. But she could have lived without it. Chastity would not have been the spoiler. Nor the vow of poverty. Jess wanted and needed very little in material terms.

Obedience had been the ghost in the machine. Although she had always been the 'good girl' and had so often measured her own worth by her ability to please, Jess had found that she simply could not agree with so much of the dogma.

I am not worthy to receive you, but only say the word and I shall be healed. Around such incandescent sparks of faith, so much had been built, so much had been done. Here before this beautiful old altar, Jess was swept back to all the prayers and hymns she had loved. The simple calls to surrender to love had resonated the most.

And then to all those other words, those contradictions, those tacked-on teachings and interpretations that would not, could not resonate. The suffocating control. Onward Christian Soldiers. All the battle cries. All the divisions, the castings out of those who could not follow.

Faith of our Fathers, living still, we will be true to thee till death...

No wonder so many had turned away, for all their different reasons. For Jess it had not been the pomp and ceremony. She'd actually enjoyed all that, found it as 'joyful and triumphant' as she supposed it was intended to be, at once calming and uplifting. It hadn't been the fiery admonishments in the sermons of old Father O'Rafferty, the unintended effects of which had led to two young sisters receiving a pinch for their giggling.

It was simply how wrong they had been and still were about so many things. Jess had become unable to say the Creed, or at least parts of it. There was not only one church. His church was everywhere, all around us. Not only one separate, special Son, in a holy state of grace demanded of all the lesser children, yet made to seem so unattainable for his fallible, unworthy siblings. Too many were asked to live impossible lives, too many were so blinded. Too many killed, displaced or traumatised. All the stolen children, the stolen cultures.

And those prostitutes in some church-bound countries, rife with HIV, who would not use condoms because it was a form of birth control and *that* was prohibited! Even more hazardous to the soul, apparently, than the desperation – or the bastards – that had forced them into selling themselves. Yet prophylactics were somehow the one sin they had the power to refuse.

Jess had done a training rotation in a sexual health clinic in Plymouth as part of her studies. She'd got to know a few working girls – and couldn't help wondering whether any of them had 'known' her father. Love the sinner, hate the sin, and all that – but how many of their customers were church goers, or churchmen?

And what about the political grifters feigning their religious feelings, dangling that one elusive victory over reproductive freedom, a one-ticket election winner that meant any other destructive policy or quality went unquestioned? Because for the controlling or the controlled, for the judgmental or the simply terrified, some kind of moral *certainty* felt essential.

All the self-delusion, all the secrets, all the lies. So many small and so many huge things.

Some so terrible. Yet some so beautiful. All those believers who had given themselves over to changing the world, fighting cruelty, injustice, ending the slave trade. Jess wondered whether if we all still believed as much today we might be more successful at changing things, less selfish? Would we respect each other more, respect the environment more? And were all these academic arguments over belief only the luxury of the comfortable, of those with too much time on their hands?

Max had once quoted something about religion being 'true to the poor, untrue to the wise and useful to the powerful', and Jess had understood the point, but she had also seen the lives of those poor at first hand.

After completing training she'd volunteered for medical charities in India and South America. Nursing was a great way to travel – and an uncompromising way to experience the crushing reality of other people's lives. She had seen and understood that most of the world was so desperately deprived – and that poverty was also right on the doorstep of the supposedly richer nations, in an ever-growing wealth divide.

But at the most brutal end of that scale, how do you tell people who are grinding out an existence day to day, who are losing, even selling their own children, who are dying of diseases that should be so easy to prevent, that their sufferings are pointless and that *this* is it, there's nothing better for them on the other side? That neither God nor Karma will save them nor bring them any comfort? Yes, we needed to change it all, but she knew this wasn't going to happen in most of those people's lifetimes.

Jess had seen the way many of those who truly believed and understood their belief, who put that belief into practice, seemed to be coping so much better, seemed to be trying not to pass their pain along.

Of course it was possible to do all of that without religion, but she had worked alongside nuns and monks whose ability to keep working stoically in the face of such daily misery, with an extraordinary kind of peace and commitment, had made her almost regret abandoning her own religious path. If she hadn't been having an affair with a French doctor at the time she might well have thrown in her lot with them and joined one of their orders, Catholic, Buddhist or otherwise.

Jess thought it was all very well if you had education or ambition, or a secular vocation such as her own, or Max's, and the lifestyle that went with it – but what if purpose or passion could not fill in the gaps? She knew that in some countries they'd tried to replace God with the State. But it hadn't worked, and now that those ideals had proven as corruptible as what had gone before, so many were turning back to their old churches, or to opportunistic new ones.

And in the West, what were we replacing God with? Some with new and perhaps more enlightened philosophies, others with the psychodramas of tribal patriotism stoked by hypocrites whose only true allegiance was to wealth and power – no matter which flags they so furiously waved. But so many were replacing the old religions with nothing at all, with a meaningless vacancy – or with the fleeting, sugary highs of money, celebrity, sex or whatever other sport. Where was the *beauty*?

Beauty, the breathtaking light she saw around John, though she had not told him for fear of embarrassing him. Some of the fundamentalists might call him a 'false prophet', a diluter of the total surrender to the truth that was required for salvation. The atheists (Max, again) might call him 'just another charlatan selling snake oil in different packaging'. Jess saw only his goodness.

She had told John little yet of her new experiences, her new vision. But he had counselled her about her problems with Max, their differences, the ones they both tried to ignore but which were slowly unpicking the threads of their connection. John had given her back such hope for their life together, their child, in spite of her creeping fears.

She had argued angrily with Max about such silly things... Whether or not they should encourage their children to believe in Father Christmas, or celebrate Christmas at all. Jess could not imagine a childhood separated from such joys, but also remembered the trauma to her trusting nine-year-old nature on learning the truth about Saint Nick. How much more painful had it been as an adult to outgrow God?

Jess had protected Manda from a life without magic chimneys and flying reindeer and happy, generous old men for another couple of years and then comforted her as best she could when the myth was demolished. But the desolation had opened up a waiting chasm of confusion for both of them.

It was John who had brought her back. Back here. To the *simplicity*. To the realisation of how much she'd missed being in a church. Lately, she would drop into one when passing, as now, just to *be*, and was often surprised by how she was affected, how water prickled at the corners of her eyes, how she found herself hunting in her handbag for a rag of tissue. In the silence of this sanctuary, she could not help but reflect on the opposing pull of all the bliss and the sorrow that weaved through life.

All the love, drawing her back to the sacred. All that was so fragile, so frightening. The irony that her love for Max, for this coming child, had re-opened her heart to something that risked pushing him away. She shivered. Hadn't he recently told her that his direction could only be 'onwards and upwards' in spite of his remorse about his friend Van? So shouldn't she just stick close to him on that ride, putting aside her own 'evolution'? Putting aside her friendship with John, however different that man was to everything she'd once rejected?

She thought of Calumn, someone to whom faith *should* have been a comfort, might have been a preventative to the wrong path, if only he hadn't been so exploited. Or so isolated and fatherless. So desperate for any kind of family or in-group. So attached to a sense of belonging that he would believe whatever was asked of him. A belonging that indulged his worst instincts in the name of God and relieved him of guilt or responsibility.

And Briggs. The cold, dark, lonely terror within him that she could not explain but wished she had the power to dispel with a sign of the cross and some holy water. The broken mind in a monstrously powerful body that she wished she could mend, bidding him to 'take up his bed and walk', but knew she could not. The mangled family that had made him, and was perhaps still making others in his image?

Her own family was hardly a model of functionality. Her father had been so often absent, so flawed, and yet she'd been in no doubt of his love. If only through passing moments. He possessed a kind of workable compassion when stirred, and perhaps an all too painful self-awareness – was Max developing something like this too? – whereas her mother, once overflowing with voluble pride about her girls, could now barely summon any interest in them at all. Certainly not if that competed with her own emotional needs.

And all at once, the well of empathy that so many in her life and in the world around her seemed unable to access, came flooding over her. Jess gave herself up to it, released herself in prostration to a lovingly polished pew, and wept.

How many paces? Heel to toe. Across and around, how many has he done now? From bunk to latrine takes a deep lunge. He can hold it for at least four, maybe five minutes. How many press ups, one handed, if he did fifty a day? Fuck. He's lost count of the days. How did he let that happen? He could ask someone, but he won't. Definitely not the fucker that gets hard from pinning him down. Not a chance if he was alone, not a chance.

They won't get any satisfaction from Eddie Briggs.

He won't let them know he's counting. Or thinking about anything he doesn't want them to know he's thinking about. He's too wise for them. Just keep moving. The more he moves, the more he sweats out the medication. And stinks up the dripping walls and watches their noses wrinkle in disgust. He likes that. Maybe he will write about that. What will those tossers want to hear?

15

HERE AND THERE

TO: dreloisekluft@children.of.sarah.org
FROM: tom2tattoo@finte.mail.com

Hey Gorgeous,

Hope all good. Just a quick one, got a favour to ask. What do you think of the attached? Recognise it? Well, of course you do, d'oh! How could I forget that I'm the lucky bastard who scored a brainbox. I was always good at numbers and stuff, but never took maths (or anything really) seriously enough in school, so I'd never heard of the Mandelbrot set until it turned up in some web research.

I found some really cool pictures on the net, and fuck, this fractal shit is amazing! It's got me thinking it could become my signature, you know, give me a bit of a creative edge?

From fractals I went down a few wormholes and dug up all kinds of "sacred geometry" and then I thought, what if I personalised the geometry? What if I created designs based on people's own numbers, like birthdates, or whatever else matters to them?

So here comes the favour. You being connected to loads of clever people and all, I wondered if you knew some genius who could write a programme for me where I feed in all this info and out the other end come patterns I could work into my final project? Maybe even into actual tattoos or graphic logos. How cool would that be? It's mind blowing what you can communicate with a few simple symbols. Thanx again for supporting me to do this course, it's a game changer.

Anyway, have a think or a head-hunt for me, will ya? Cheers.

Big love xtxtxtxtx.

He flinches at the sound of her footsteps but breathes more easily when he sees who approaches. The Old Woman wonders whether he is conscious of the threat from that gaggle of restless – but now successfully distracted – youths?

She knows most women can tell when a man, or gang of men, is dangerous. Without word or action, merely by a hardening of the eyes, a stiffening of their spines, the faintest scent of separation from good sense or good will. Might it be the same for men – for a man alone? Are the signals as clear?

But The Outsider's reactions are permanently primed, he is always alert, even if exhausted by it. She remembers that her mother had something of this ever-present vigilance about her, even if the long years with her new tribe and the loving care of her daughter had soothed her with the gift of contentment. Could this new stranger be comforted in the same way?

Perhaps. But there is something else that haunts him, something far worse than too many days of solitude or a journey fraught with dangers. Something born of darkness is scratching at his soul. The Old Woman sees that now. Even as the hunger leaves his body, a chasm within is exposed.

Something terrible has been done – but to him, or by him? It is imperative that she discovers which.

He rises from his squat in respect of her approach, or perhaps to feel less vulnerable, but she signals for him to rest again. She has shown him a cherished spot of shade under a thick and generous tree, within sight of the river and within hearing of the camp, but not immediately visible to it. She thought he might appreciate somewhere unseen to listen to the water, to watch the river grow, fall and flow. To remember that change, for good or bad, is both possible and inevitable.

The Old Woman squats beside him and smiles. Places a hand of comfort on his withered shoulder. The Outsider withdraws at first, though not completely, and then relaxes to her touch. She passes him the firm flesh of the spiky fruit, which she has already peeled and stoned as he is not permitted to carry anything sharp. He takes it gratefully but soon abandons all courtesy and gobbles it down. This starving creature has no faith yet in the blessing that food is now readily available to him.

At least all that sun-scorched and matted hair has been cut from his eyes. He may not have enjoyed the closeness of a fine flint blade, but submitted while her grandson completed another reluctantly accepted task. Now he can no longer hide from eye contact, except by looking away.

Once he has swallowed the last morsel of fruit and licked his fingers of its juice, she begins the lesson. Using her stick, the sand and her words she tries to untangle his more unfamiliar sounds. She attempts some of the clear and simple shapes she sees in her mind, even if these are not as distinct as the rocks or trees or living things around her. He responds to some of these marks and words with a kind of recognition or interest, though they seem to hold no special meaning for him.

Hand signals are used when the drawing does not work. Frustration is resisted when the signals fail. Patience, repetition, rest, new ideas, repetition, patience. Smiles of encouragement when he feels his failures too sharply, wider smiles when they both succeed.

The Old Woman asks again in sound, in signal and in sand about his family. The Outsider shakes his head, turns away. His pain is palpable. But there is more. What is it? Ah. Yes. Guilt. For what? Failing them? He will not – cannot – look at her again. She nods, sighs, rises tenderly against the stiffness that has settled into her hips.

Enough for today. She leaves him to return to the camp in his own time. Exploring that chasm he protects so carefully may take more than simply learning each other's meaning. It may demand a more soul-searching form of medicine. The Old Woman decides that in the morning she will go foraging for a particular fungus. She needs a certain tree, at a certain time, so will follow the flightline from her last guided dreaming.

⚕

'Look, look, KC... a hawk! Oh wow. Oh, it's gorgeous! You know, I think that's the first wild thing I've seen since we got here?'

Now they are both more acclimatised, their ritual of outdoor 'coffee breaks' – which involve holding sealed go-cups near the door before heading back inside to actually drink them – have become longer and more frequent, weather and workload permitting. A necessary distraction while waiting for any significant results from the splicing in of the 'Sarah sequence' to the volunteer candidate. Too much time in pod-like seclusion working through the variables is suffocating.

'Oh! Hey, yeah, I see him. Wow, that is a beautiful thing, for sure. I guess he's back up here for the spring and summer?'

'How do you know it's a him?'

'Well, I could just as easily ask why "Nature" always has to be a *she*? I mean, doesn't that just separate *us* from *her* even more – 'cause like you said the other day, we're nothing if we're not nature too?'

KC's black fringe flops out from under his hood, flirting with his mirrored goggles, as his lopsided smile curls upward to the left. Eloise can hear the opprobrium in his voice, but sees a playfully arched brow and assumes she'd see affection in his dark eyes if they weren't shielded from her.

She cocks her head. 'Yeah, but apart from the whole figure of speech thing, it's the women who are beating this, right?

So maybe that's what *she* wants in the end. Maybe this new DNA eventually makes us all hermaphrodites, or self-replicating. Maybe *she*'s finally done with your lot? Another great leap forward in reproductive evolution! Hey, you know it was probably a virus that gave us the placenta, right?'

'No surprise there. That is one weird alien of an organ.'

'Yup, the only one that's disposable! And before that piece of the puzzle we were still laying eggs like the platypus. Until some archaic virus infected one of those eggs and somehow fused with it... a few generations later and mammals have a wall of cells from which a baby can draw nutrition and yet remain separate from its mother's blood supply and safe from immune rejection.' Eloise raises her coffee cup in a toast. 'So, hey, thanks evolution! Women not only get the hormonal hell ride, we get to endure the agony of live births too. Woo hoo! All down to some mammalian great-grandma who absorbed a new bit of DNA then domesticated a separate organism. Well, in molecular terms, anyway. Lucky bloody us!'

'Yeah, but have we been domesticating the virus all these years, or has the virus been domesticating us?'

'I suppose it's a human and egg kind of thing?'

'Cute. But it's good to see you smiling again and out of that abyss of doom and gloom. I mean, Good Lord, Eloise, you find ways to worry about *everything*! It's gotta be exhausting living inside your head, even with all the imaginative fun stuff. Here, hand me that coffee and I'll go zap it back to life. Should I bring it to your pod, or will I see you back at the coalface?'

'Pod please. I need to shower first and to warm up. But, hey, wait a minute, it's not just me with a soft spot for nature, Mr Serious. Weren't you the post-grad who chained himself to a bulldozer to stop them cutting down the forest you were researching? And you call me a tree hugger! Although there is something to that, I must admit. And that's something else I really miss up here. My old arboreal chums on Hampstead Heath. A bit of forest bathing does a body the world of good, you know, especially the immune system.'

Free of her coffee, Eloise performs a closed-eyes, head-raised spin as if luxuriating under a crown of greenery, even if in slow motion to avoid freezing her lungs.

'Yeah, but I nearly lost my scholarship and got a criminal record over that protest! Never mind nearly freezing my ass. What on earth are you doing now? Oh, never mind, don't tell me. You know despite the occasional weirdness, Eloise, I do get you, and I appreciate those sparks of intuition, wherever the hell they come from. I mean, you do have a pretty intense inner life, don't you? I guess that's down to all your exotic childhood travels and all that time spent alone, huh? I've always been a little envious of that. The digs and the expeditions, I mean, not the only child thing.'

He opens the door, juggling both coffee cups in one hand. 'Even so, Dr Kluft, we need the work we're doing here to be taken deadly seriously. So just make sure you save your rants and flights of fancy – and this weird new twirling thing – for yours truly, OK? Or else go write one of those letters to Darwin you once told me about after a couple of pints. Or make up some spooky campfire tales for Josh – 'cause I can't help thinking that in another life you would've made a great storyteller...'

'Maybe so! Maybe so. But it's James Lovelock now, by the way. For the letters. And, yes, I know I need to stop putting my inner life "out there" quite so much, but this place is affecting me in some powerful ways. Though, I do appreciate your patience, KC, and I thank you for "getting" me. Weirdness and all. And for listening. But mostly I'm thankful that you trust me to honour the science, because you know that I'm all about the method when it comes down to it.'

She smiles, knowing it will help them both.

'Well, you're welcome, Dr Kluft. So, Lovelock, huh? Sounds about right. Anyway, let's get inside before both our immune systems go into shock. Especially as we have no forests to go bathe in.'

'Ha, ha. But wait, before I forget... I really wish you would consider my offer of talking to Eugene about a role for you at the institute – and a visa to get you and the family over to the UK, away from all that horror and anti-science mess, especially with the way they've gone after John Hopkins, I mean how long can you hang on? But America's brain drain really would be our gain. My gain, too, that's for sure.'

It is time. There are enough words, enough signals, enough symbols. They understand one another. She asks him about his eyes.

Mother, father, both?

Father.

Others in his clan, before his father?

No. Father first and only.

Father grew up with the clan?

No. Somewhere else. Came hungry to them, like him to her now.

Where from?

Not known.

Father had other sons, daughters?

Yes.

In the other place?

Yes. But dead. Like everyone. But maybe there was also another. Made along the way, maybe one that lived?

How?

Father told a story, of a journey, of a woman, fierce and strong, who helped him.

They were mated?

Yes, maybe, probably.

Where is she?

She went another way. Towards here. Wise in her choice. All father's clan, all my family now gone... but hers, the fierce woman's?

You think we are kin?

Maybe. Never saw another but my own children with these eyes. You?

No. Not until now.

Is it possible this man is her brother? Or is this a clever tale devised to ensure her continued protection? But how could he know about the two that met on separate journeys and then parted? One with eyes of fire, one with the courage and the gifts and the faith to follow a vision as far – so very far – as it would take her. And alone. The Old Woman has seen The Outsider talk to no other here. How could he know?

And yet she still cannot trust him, blood or no blood. She must know what he continues to withhold, what she senses of him in her stomach.

She begins preparations for the ceremony, gathers and brews the fungus, brings it to full power over the coming days, lets it commune with its spirit family.

The wind chill today is too intense for anything but the indoors, the burden of the waiting is too heavy for anything but attempted rest. Even if this amounts to nothing more than lightly closed eyes in an empty, makeshift canteen. Rest that is too soon disturbed.

'Bad news, Eloise.'

She snaps her eyes open and upwards to KC.

'What... an adverse reaction?'

'No, our patient's still doing well. But he's going to have to do a whole lot better very soon if his participation is gonna to help. It's out. Maybe.'

'They broke the news? Have you just had another call with "The Suit"?'

'No, the bug. It's out. Don't worry, the Sami are still clear, but there's a couple of suspected cases at a hunting lodge about 100 miles south of here. Some miners on a break, though it's not clear what their exposure might have been. And a possible case connected to the lab in Manchester where Patient Zero sent some of the ice core samples.'

'Oh hell.'

'Yeah, could be.'

'Right. When are they going live with what we know?'

'I don't know. It's out of our hands, but I'm gonna talk to Mary Jo. Tell her to put the protocol we discussed in place. Give her the code word.'

Eloise is up on her feet now, wiggling her toes inside her boots to bring them back to life.

'Christ, you have a code word? And a "protocol"! Smart. But I guess you have to be ready for anything over there now? What shall I do about Tom and Josh?'

'They should be fine. Every chance it can be contained. But I can get MJ to call them if you give me his number. Can you trust him to be discreet?'

'Yes. I think so. God, I don't know. Something like this has never come up. Makes me realise there's still a lot we don't know about each other yet.'

'What does your gut say?'

'Yes. Yes.'

'OK. Good. Keep all your communications with him normal otherwise.'

16

MANCHESTER

'Jessica, please don't fret. Calumn is on his own journey, a necessary one. And yes, such a crisis can be risky, but I really don't believe he's a threat – to himself, or to you. I know you worry that he doesn't socialise, but he's had too many difficult experiences, he's been exposed to too much mockery. And how the fragile ego collapses under the featherweight of ridicule! He's a sensitive soul and like you he picks up on things, but he's also very easily manipulated. He soaks things up. I think what he feels for you is actually his own peculiar kind of concern.'

Jess was consoled both by John's company and by weather fair enough for a walk in the small wooded area outside the walls of the hospital, but it wasn't just Calumn that she wanted to discuss. Her experience in that church resounded from deep within a conditioned conscience she'd thought she'd long since set aside. And yet here it was, chanting like a muezzin from an inner minaret.

It certainly felt like the call to *some* kind of prayer, but she couldn't process it. What's more, she wondered, would she – or her marriage to Max – be able to stomach such an uninvited renaissance of faith? What if that made her just another person who couldn't 'keep up' with him? Whether that be his intellectual rigour and ultra-rational world view or his particular needs and ambitions. Might he then decide to leave *her* behind as well – like the others he'd admitted to abandoning?

There had been a few positive changes since the news of his friend's suicide. After a painful heart-to-heart over Zoom he'd begun to reconcile with his brother, Brent, but this was difficult to nurture at a distance and considering the time difference. Max had also mentioned bringing forward their long-planned trip back to Australia, as soon as Jess felt she and the baby were ready to travel. So things were shifting in her husband's inner world as well.

He'd even been in touch with Van's parents, though it hadn't brought him much peace, especially after an excruciating request that he pray for their poor boy's soul. Max had made a small donation to the Samaritans in his name instead, which although started by a man of the cloth seemed a sufficiently secular organisation to warrant his support. But he remained adamant in his rejection of any religious comfort. Van was neither in heaven nor hell for his act of despair. As far as Max was concerned, he was simply no more, and all that anyone left behind could do was suffer his absence.

So no, Jess knew she couldn't discuss these resurgent inclinations with him, not yet, not so soon after telling him about her extra-sensory experiences. While she knew they were coincidental and unconnected, Max might only dismiss this new 'dimension' as part of some weird religious mania. Then again, maybe she was overreacting? The pull of spirituality was one thing, but she shuddered at the thought of any form of fundamentalism.

Jess answered John, hoping his wisdom might calm the stormy waters.

'Well maybe it *is* that simple with Calumn, and yes, maybe his feelings and intentions are benign, but it's all that grandiose religiousness that gets under my skin. All that "guided by His hand" business... the sermonising, the dogma, the rigid conviction. You say Calumn has empathy but it's exactly that sort of righteousness, that sort of separatism and misplaced ideas of "specialness", that sent me fleeing from the church in the first place. It reminds me too much of my mother.'

'But there are many paths to the same sea, Jessica. That sea of greater love that I think you're now seeking. Calumn, and even your mother – their faith and their way of expressing it – that's their business and they're best left to find their own ways to live with it. Tell me, Jessica, have you ever meditated?'

She felt calmed by John's fluid and expressive hand gestures, but also noticed how he matched his pace to hers, with a focussed yet gentle attention that allowed for a free flow of movement, thought and word. The subtle aroma of the dark soil along their path, the fresh shoots and blossoms of a riotous spring, were also having a comforting effect, as the dry twigs of winter snapped with satisfaction under her 'sensible' work shoes. She took an easier breath and replied.

'No, not really. I mean, I've chilled out and "ommmed" a bit after a yoga class. And I do tend to zone out very nicely during a massage. But no, I haven't ever really meditated. Not in any disciplined way.'

'Well, I can highly recommend it, Jessica, and you know there are several forms? Not too hard to find one that suits. Especially for a rationalist – and I can't help wondering whether some kind of secular practice might work for you?'

'Well, now you mention it, there's a mindfulness class starting here soon. It's for the patients, but there's been a request to set one up for the staff too.'

John smiled, cocked his grizzled head with its well-tended quiff, then brought his hands together in front of his heart and bowed his head to meet them.

'That's marvellous news, Jessica. I highly recommend that you give it a try. And if the form fits, then maybe take a closer look at where it comes from? In many ways "mindfulness" has been spiritually denatured for Western tastes, and while most traditions involve some silent contemplation and insight, the original philosophy – and its very useful tools – is rooted in Buddhism. And there once walked a wise and wonderful teacher!'

John's smile was easy, his grey eyes brightened by what he felt able to offer her, and Jess was glad of his openness to various schools of wisdom. Such broad-mindedness seemed a rare quality.

'You know, Jessica, it's not surprising that all these questions are coming up for you now. You're on the verge of one of the purest and most powerful experiences among those many "paths to sea" I mentioned – the unconditional love tsunami of parenthood! I mean, romantic love may be the first to explode open our hearts again, once we've navigated the rough and tumble path to adulthood, but there's nothing like caring for a helpless little piece of yourself to take that heart to a new and very special place. Or so I'm told!'

He shrugged in acknowledgement of his innocence of both the former and the latter 'love' experiences. Or so Jess presumed, but who knew what encounters John may have had either before or since taking the collar? He wore no ring and gave no clear signals of an active sex life or orientation, but she guessed he was in his fifties somewhere, so surely he had some kind of personal history?

'But I *am* very familiar with platonic love,' John continued, wagging a finger. 'Or the concept of Anam Cara in Celtic, and a soulful friendship is a greatly underrated path to a peaceful and lasting kind of love – as is a deep affection for nature – and *all* these loving experiences are capable of opening the heart. The trouble is, it can then so easily tire and bruise and close up again, at least without regular exercise. Without some kind of *practice*. Now of course I'm biased, but the most reliable route to awakening is always spiritual work of some kind, and the key to that is in the word "work" because the process never stops. There's no end point, no finish line where we can pat ourselves on the back. We need to keep finding ways to come back to the heart as a compassionate doorway to true communion. Which is why some kind of practice or devotion does matter. Even if it's... I don't know... conscious gardening! Or secular volunteering, or singing in a choir!'

'Oh yes, thank you, John. That does make complete sense to me. I'll look into it, I really will! And I feel much better already, you know. I always do after one of our chats.'

'Well, that's lovely to hear! But I get the feeling there's something else, Jessica?'

'Yes. Actually, there is something else. Something... well. I *have* talked about it with Max, but not with anyone else yet.'

The array was flooded with new data. A satellite had picked up a massive gamma ray burst and Max had received an automated text just as he was contemplating an early night. Messages were shooting out to every observatory that could turn their telescopes toward its coordinates, in the hope of catching a supernova as it fireworked in some distant galaxy of the sky.

Dying stars. How could you not love them? Pulsars flashing out their last farewells. Huge supernovae creating Swiss-cheese bubbles in the galaxy, of the kind our own solar system inhabited. Kilanova forming vast burning orbs. Mira speeding through space with whirlpools of debris from her bow shock, revealing how our own sun might give itself back to the galaxy in another five billion years, leaving the ingredients for a whole new cycle of stellar and planetary formation. Order out of chaos and back around again. Spectacular.

It was dark when he'd received the text alert but Max wanted to be there. He raced toward the telescope on his bike, came off on a greasy corner, but flew left into a grassy bank instead of right into traffic. *Lucky, silly bastard.* He waved away the anxious young driver who had driven over the back wheel of his bike, and who was only too happy to roll up his window and leave him to it. Max took a minute to lay there and look upwards before assessing the damage. Nothing to see, too much light pollution. Light fighting light.

All those tiny units of illumination. But why did the very small look so similar and yet behave so differently to the very big? Particle physics versus massive cosmology. The chaotic electron with no recognisable or predictable orbit. Ghostly photons running interference in defiance of their logical solar source. Nothing really even *existing* except in relationship to something else. And what, *exactly,* was holding together whatever could be observed or experienced? And pushing it all apart? Bending space this way or that, stretching it way beyond predictions. And what of the impossibly large void which our galaxy seemed to inhabit?

All these apparitions and anomalies... Would he see any unifying satisfaction in his lifetime?

If some biohacker succeeded in defusing the degenerative time bomb and turning on the fountain of youth, Max would drink from it, greedily and without hesitation. Even if Jess would not. He wanted, needed, to take that ride. *Out there,* all the way, with a slingshot around the gravity of each passing planet. Threading the asteroid field, then through the Kuiper belt and onward to leave the last, dark ball of rock behind. Escaping the far reaches of the sun's grip to emerge from the icy Oort cloud and sail the interstellar wind, surfing the spiral arm of this galactic outpost right to the shores of its spinning, supermassive core.

'Apollo's Children' – all drunk on their space dreams, never really growing up. Always, always, the *wonder*. For Max it had begun with his first meteor shower over Uluru, as ten-year-old eyes gazed backward thirteen billion years, then forward into a brilliant future.

He had never wanted to acknowledge his wife's worst fears about the planet, or even about his own species. He was a natural optimist, but the relentless waves of bad news were turning that gift into something of a poisoned chalice. Well before the climate emergency had been driven up the popular agenda, he'd studied the startling images from the space station showing exactly how much damage we were doing. The deforestation, the top soil run-off into the sea, the dying coral, the shrinking ice.

And yet he'd also felt the unity, the strength, the wholeness and indescribable beauty of our 'pale blue dot'. Even if it was obvious, as so many astronauts had said before, that from space you simply cannot see the hand-drawn divisions, the trivia-driven insanities, Max thought that it really *should* be, could be that simple, despite how daily life sucked you back into myopia.

There was plenty more trouble coming, for sure, but the earth was tough, forged in a furnace, and so was humanity. Eminently adaptable. It was endurance as much as intelligence that had made us so successful. Max could not contemplate that we – or rather that he, or his descendants – would not be around to see it all, to *go there*. We were smart (*well, some of us*) and science would find a way. To imagine anything less was beyond his capacity to bear.

His progeny, if not him, *would* walk on other worlds. Only now, he had to limp. Alongside his mangled bike. Shit. The same ankle he'd weakened on the mountain when he'd tumbled into that crevasse and stumbled upon the skull of Sarah. His wrist too. *Bugger.* He'd have to hide it from Jess somehow. Or could he? Could she look right past his dissembling and actually see it now, the sprain taking shape, his fear taking form?

He'd googled her symptoms and then confronted her, hopefully convinced that her jumbling up of the senses was something as harmless as synaesthesia. She'd shot him down. Synaesthesia rarely came on suddenly, it was usually present from childhood, Jess had calmly informed him. She had done her research too, it seemed. It was probably present in our earliest ancestors and possibly the inspiration for our first attempts at language, which had then, ironically, negated other senses and abilities. Only the need to order and compartmentalise, to manage so much conflicting stimulus, only the draining away of our childish immersion in the sensory world had boxed away each response and deprived most of us of its perplexing richness.

Furthermore, she'd so formally insisted, for her this 'manifestation' was not confined to the five physical senses. It wasn't about tasting names or smelling words or seeing numbers written out in colour. It delved deeper, went wider. It was a more searching and complete experience, empathetic and powerfully connecting. Sometimes, she'd even thought she could actually *hear* the stars...something about which Max, in spite of his incredulity, had felt a powerful twinge of envy. But, she'd claimed, none of this was *just* her imagination.

'And even if it was, what would be wrong with that?' Jess had demanded of him, 'Imagination is what distinguishes us as a species. It's what named the shapes of the heavens, called us to creativity and invention. Imagination goes far beyond the drives of reproduction and survival, so why do we have it, where does it come from?'

Max had said nothing at the time, though he'd heard the unmistakable voice of John Evesham in her words. He wondered now whether Jess had talked to her pet priest about all this. He was raging. Was John encouraging her in this insanity?

He decided he needed his own 'confessor' – needed to talk to *somebody* about this crazy turn that his couplehood had taken. It was too soon to bring it up with Brent, who really wouldn't get it either, even if his brother had more natural sensitivity than he and took more after their mother. But Max didn't want to burden her either. She had enough to juggle – and he certainly couldn't bother his sick father.

Greg, then? They hadn't socialised much since the barbie, but he'd arranged another play date at the climbing wall. Maybe his colleague's developing relationship with Manda might make him more sympathetic – and less likely to betray his confidence at work? Any whispers about a wife who'd gone whacko would be unbearable for Max. Those of his peers who'd met Jess had called him a lucky bastard, had commented on what a great couple they were. And they were! He had to find a way back to that. Had to find a way to help Jess come back to herself.

But first he had to get to the telescope as quickly as he could, on only one good foot, and under a beckoning night sky. The bigger picture for him was always the siren song of the stars. That, he could never resist.

❧

```
TO: Revjohnevesham@bettering.world.org
FROM: JessWallaceMichaelson@finte.mail.co.uk
```

```
Hi John
```

```
I hope you don't mind a private email but I wanted to
share some thoughts, or worries really. It's to do with
those new experiences I mentioned, but in reference to a
particular patient (I think I've mentioned him before,
Eddie Briggs?) though I must be careful obviously.
```

But it was something you said in our conversation about mindfulness, about how the Buddha isn't seen as a god or worshipped as such. All those statues are not idolatry but visual reminders about an "attitude of practice" – and that his "hand down" gesture was to receive but his "hand up" was to protect? That surprised me! I love the idea that compassion should be practised with both wisdom and discernment. That true compassion isn't the same as blind empathy and that even the most pacifist of devotees need to protect themselves and others!

Thank you, too, for agreeing with me that it's important to listen to your gut. The thing is, I feel so strongly about Eddie Briggs but I really can't say so at the hospital. I especially can't mention my "intuitions" because that would only land me in hot water and might even get me signed off sick and I'm not ready for that. I don't think my patients are either and I feel we are so close to a breakthrough with Calumn.

It's kind of crazy but I get this weird, moustache-twirling "pantomime villain" image whenever I think of Briggs, only more sinister, more "Child Catcher" in its effect. And it's ridiculous because I know that nothing about human psychology or neurology is that simple, or painted with such broad brushstrokes, there are always nuances, and explanations, if not excuses.

And I *do* feel a kind of compassion for him, I do – just not a jot of leeway, for want of a better word. He really can't be allowed back into the general population – of the hospital for sure and of wider society absolutely. Spiritually, I do believe in redemption and there's never any benefit in cruel punishments except to satisfy some ugly hunger for revenge. But some people really

are more like a black and white pencil sketch, in terms
of their threat level, at least.

Briggs is even more dangerous due to his size and
pugilistic abilities. I understand he had some boxing
training as a youth and that his father was a
back-alley, black-books fighter, which may explain the
brain damage Briggs sustained as a boy (and which
I feel I can actually see, even if his scans are
inconclusive.)

His official diagnosis is "antisocial personality
disorder" but to me the way his slightly diminished
prefrontal cortex probably communicates with reward
centres like the nucleus accumbens, and areas deep
within the hypothalamus, makes his aggression merely
a hair trigger away. And while this also brings
up considerations about free will and personal
responsibility etc., it makes him no less dangerous!

I feel duty bound to make sure all the other patients and
staff will be protected when he is let out of seclusion.
I'm so afraid that something will go wrong and will set
us all back - because there are so many people who *should*
get the benefit of the doubt, who *can* improve, even if
I can't rationally explain my conviction that Briggs
just isn't one of them. Not when he's so convincing in
his portrayal of the model patient.

I know you don't have an answer to any of this, John. I
suppose I just needed to be able to tell someone. And
all this would only worry Max even more. He's already
been a bit withheld from me, probably because of what
I've told him about my enhanced senses, but I also feel
like something else is going on with him, I just can't
put my finger on it. Thanks for listening, anyway!

Best, Jess x

17

HERE AND THERE

I t is ready. The stench of the concoction is such that she will
be unable to pretend it is some kind of delicacy. She will tell
The Outsider it is a remedy, like the others, to make him strong,
to heal his wounds. But this one must be drunk down quickly.

The Old Woman knows that it will come back up again,
soon enough.

She will make them a fire, near their tree, away from the
camp. Set her grandson and his cousin, The Tall Girl, to keep it
burning and to keep watch.

She will bring furs to keep him warm, straw bedding to
soak up his sweats. She will smother his skin with ash to keep the
insects away. She will bring a full gourd of sweet water and food
to settle him when it is done.

How can he refuse?

It is not how The Old Woman would normally minister, by
subterfuge, by a kind of force. A soul must choose its own repair.
The spirits of the living plant may punish this transgression
but she *must* reach his truth. And she knows that sometimes a
healer must inhabit the skin of the one in her care, be with every
moment of their suffering, allowing a layer of her own skin to be
flayed away in the process. It will grow back. Scarred, but stronger
and wiser.

She prepares as well as she can and now the young Warrior
delivers his terrified charge. The Outsider senses something is
afoot but he does not shy from it. He is too tired, too weighed
down by his burdens to resist. He is ready to put those burdens
down, come what may.

The Tall Girl offers him the hollowed out old shell, the former home of a walking creature, the precious remainder of a tiny companion that her grandmother had carried here as a child. This is now The Old Woman's most treasured vessel. The Tall Girl encourages The Outsider to drink of its reeking contents with a kind and curious smile and his eyes water as they meet the hope in hers.

Now her grandmother invites him to lie, places a rolled fur under his head, scoops out a bowl in the dirt beside him to catch what will come up and draw it away from him. She beats two stones together and sings a song of comfort, to call in the power of the plant. She takes a little herself and prepares for everything to come apart that it may be put back together again. Like the hard layers of a nut crumbling to the ground, only for new growth to work its way up through the soil and stone around the broken pieces.

He writhes with the first spasm in his guts. It takes only two more for them to empty. Too soon? She looks into his eyes. They have widened to the wonder. It has begun.

☡

In the isolation of her sleeping pod, the Arctic wind drumming its determination against the prefab walls of their emergency structure, Eloise is thrilled to awaken from a fractious sleep to the cymbal crash of a 'VIP' email, but then is immediately churned by its content.

```
TO: dreloisekluft@children.of.sarah.org
FROM: tom2tattoo@finte.mail.com


Hi Hun


Look, I'll come straight to it, don't want to worry you,
but Rev John said you should know. Had to bell the 5-0.
Some woman was watching our gaff. Wouldn't have given
```

it much thought but then there was something through the letterbox. Red cross on white paper. Nothing more. Thought wtf either an England fan or a godsquadder! Coppers took a description of the watcher (fuck, it's never a good feeling to snitch, but I've got the boy to think about) and they suggested redirecting the post to the farmhouse and sealing up the letterbox for now. Maybe even rig a camera! Bloody Nora as my gran would say, it's all gone a bit Crimewatch! I mean I know that nutter firebug is banged up but we can't be too careful right?

Bit nervous about what the social might make of it if they come round for a check but fingers crossed. I was thinking though, maybe we should go to the farmhouse even if the solar etc isn't fully cranked up yet?

Our case worker knows we plan to move there soon anyway and that Josh is on the list for the local school, plus its Easter break next week and I've got him for all of that. I could clear it with her as a holiday? We'd be roughing it but that could be a laugh! I could even start work on reopening the well. Let me know what you think.

Don't freak out though. Don't get too vexed either. I remember the first time I saw you lose your shit. Well, I heard you first, exploding at your computer, never knew a posh bird was capable of such colourful cursing! It completely cracked me up (sorry it's not that I don't sympathise) but anyone else might have had a wobble. Eloise in full battle gear is not for the fainthearted! So don't go chucking any test tubes about will ya? We'll be fine. Really.

Big juicy hugs. Miss you like effing crazy xxx

The flashback is insistent, a burglar breaking and entering her consciousness at will. A physical and emotional re-inhabiting of that moment she turned away from her poignant farewell to Sarah's remains, before they were shipped off to the museum in Nairobi, and realised Calumn was there. Not with benign intentions. The taciturn new caretaker – or rather the stooge for a dangerous creationist cult – had locked them both inside the glass box of the laboratory's 'clean room'.

The smell of the kerosene as he poured it over the floor, the flash of the Zippo lighter as he held it aloft. Then the sight of that woman, her red beret crowning a bitter face with its icy smile, her red-gloved hands on the outside of the glass, the steam of her exhalation as she watched her plot come to fruition and then walked away to let it unfold.

Breath falling short now, Eloise seeks out her psychological first-aid kit. She rarely needs to pop a propranolol these days. The trial CBT/MDMA combination therapy had been so successful after the hostage trauma, she often feels better than ever. Unless triggered by a memory. Or a vivid enough sense of threat.

She swallows the tiny pink beta blocker then starts her tapping and breathing practice. But soon something else takes over, something more incendiary than the acid reflex of fear. Every neuron of her protective instinct sparks – and she knows she'll do whatever it takes to keep Tom and Josh safe.

Sick at the thought of the scarlet psycho's reappearance – and setting aside her Hippocratic ethics to fantasise about calling in a drone strike – Eloise acknowledges a silver lining to her stalker showing up. The ideal stratagem for spiriting Tom and Josh out of the city – and away from any potential viral cauldron. Yes, they should definitely go to the farmhouse! Perhaps take his parents along for a country break? Maybe even Anna and her daughter too?

She'll wire whatever funds might be needed to get the place comfortable and stocked up in a hurry. Tom should leave her old Golf in London as a decoy and buy a second-hand van. There'll be a mountain of stuff to move anyway, in due course. While Eloise wouldn't describe herself as a hoarder, she will admit to an only child's weakness for anything sentimental – and a worrier's attachment to whatever might prove useful 'one day'.

Questions begin to percolate and she makes mental notes for her next letter to Lovelock. *Why do we gather so much stuff around ourselves? Is it because humans have no scales or exoskeletons, no horns or claws or beaks? Only the pared-away remnants of canine teeth. Only bone-fragile fists. Do we grow our shells of paraphernalia because our jaws are so weak, our flesh so exposed, our morphology so comparatively feeble?*

Vulnerability. Such a deeply uncomfortable experience, especially for the fiercely independent soul. It demanded the acquisition of *any* form of armour, physical or psychological, especially when one might be lacking the protection of the herd, the crowd, or the in-group. Eloise realises this is another reason Madame Scarlet's return is so unsettling. She cannot abide a bully. And recent years had thrown so many out of hibernation, offering sly opportunities to gather their own malevolent mobs, to stalk.

How she had sympathised with colleagues in epidemiology who'd suffered such revolting abuse throughout the lingering Covid pandemic. Delivered from hive minds so threatened by the neo-bogeyman of 'control' – a fear apparently more effective than the immediate reality of a deadly and damaging virus – they became the 'controllers' themselves. Bonding with glee over the harassment of private person or professional alike, while their victims tried only to protect their own health, or their families', or that of the general population. Ultimately those perpetrators were only dehumanising themselves in the impulse to dehumanise others, perhaps to shrink with guilt and shame if ever awakened to their actions? Probably not.

How so many keen minds remained so courageous and committed, kept sticking their heads above the parapet, kept contributing, seemed miraculous to Eloise and she would have blamed none of them for withdrawing their good will or going to ground.

But now she realises there may be another benefit to Tom's news about her own poison 'troll' resurfacing. *Maybe now that bitch has broken cover, the authorities can identify and round her up, at last?* This idea delivers a much-needed dose of optimism, even if she's not ready yet to compose a measured reply to Tom. There's the fuel of pure fury to burn off first.

Eloise springs up, finds her headphones and begins her new exercise regime for confined spaces, adopted after realising that her Arctic malaise was partly down to a lack of physical exhaustion to balance the mental fatigue. She's never experienced such deprivation before, but here, outdoor exercise is out of the question and the tiny gym has been quarantined since their arrival.

Sarah had been striding through her dreams again when this notion of the need to get moving had arrived in the hot flush of a sleepless night. Once fully awake, she'd googled 'exercises for confined spaces' and found a clever system devised by a political prisoner. As a lifelong contributor to Amnesty, it seemed appropriate.

Now she presses her motivational playlist and begins, understanding its necessity. Exertion has always been such a primal human need.

Once, Dear James, we walked across continents, but now we spend hours in hunched inertia, operating one type of addictive device or another.

As she pushes through the initial resistance to motion a sweat begins to break and Eloise moves deeper into the routine. Recognising the irony that the propulsive beats of *Blue Monday* now driving her determination emanate from one of the very devices she blames for encouraging human indolence, she welcomes the visions of forgotten wildness that now dance furiously around her mind.

All that unspent energy we're left with today, all that boredom, seeking relief in manufactured excitement, feeding an infectious narcissism that's so easily manipulated and exploited.

Eloise imagines gladiators in virtual conflict, thinks perhaps the 'bread and circuses' of Roman times were little different to the dopamine-sucking, algorithmic enslavement of today.

Yes! The emperors are still making us look the other way, only now with hi-tech sleight of hand, keeping us distracted by our daydreams or caged in electronic worlds of rage, resentment and desperate groupthink.

The kind of rage that Eloise must also accept as her own, as determined as she is to burn it out of her body. A few more skip steps, a few more planks, a few more press ups.

That's better.

Her routine is coming to a close and she feels satisfied with both the effort and the result. One particular form of exercise is missed more than she cares to admit, however. The thought of Tom leaping once more from her thumping heart. The ache for him, for that vigorous, football-in-the-park form, the close-cropped hair around sensuous features, the warm hazelnut eyes that narrow when they feel desire, or humour, or contempt for a world driven by class, cash and callousness. The sound of his passion for her, his guttural and ecstatic disbelief to have found her again when convinced he had lost her to the very world he loathed.

Time now to steady her breathing and monitor her pulse. Time to sit and type her reply to Tom, transfer the money, email an instruction to the agent to drop the price on the London house. She's prepared to take a hit so long as they clear the mortgage on the farmhouse and can still achieve all the self-sufficient upgrades over time. With Madame Scarlet and her unknowable threats now banished to the frozen wastes beyond her close and percussive walls, Dr Kluft gets back to work.

⚭

It is a shock but not a surprise. She has seen it among certain beasts – and occasionally among the men of fur, the men of the trees. It is not unnatural to the world of flesh, a world in which nothing is wasted, where one creature may live only because another dies.

Even so, this forbidden act strikes horror into the human heart. Now she understands the damage that has been done to this man. To have seen such things. To have been forced into a form of it himself.

She has learned from his journey with the sacred fungus that the straggling remains of The Outsider's clan had set out to follow a certain trail. The trail described by his flame-eyed father, who had remembered well what he'd learned from the woman he'd coupled with on his own journey of survival through the ash. He'd remembered everything she had told him about her visions, and all the other knowledge she had shared.

The Outsider had kept his father's stories close to his heart and had been confident he could follow that inner guidance when his own diminished band had first set out.

Over many seasons, over lengths of land there are no words for, his group had lost numbers to hunger, to goring wounds from hunts gone wrong, to bad water and sickness – and ultimately to predators. The last of which were the worst imaginable.

Those with a taste for their own kind.

As The Outsider had re-lived what had brought him here, his screams had split the night air, terrifying The Tall Girl. Even the young Warrior had never known such a sound and shivered in rejection of the chill they offered to his soul. The shrieks of memory from within The Outsider's fungus-induced fever were as real as they might have been when the horror was experienced.

In her own milder trance The Old Woman had accompanied his journey and she too had received a memory not so far removed, but with a different outcome. As real to her as when it had been formed. She is strapped to her mother's back, it is a moonless night, they are running beside some water. Her mother stops to soothe her, stifle her cries, urge her silently back to sleep – and understanding something sharper than a normal fear, the child obeys.

Her mother is crouched now and quiet, then all at once is leaping, slashing, gouging. The child sees an arc of what she now knows to be blood and then hears the sound of her mother's footsteps splashing across shallow water. The Old Woman recalls the speed of that run, so fast, even though once she was tall enough she could easily outrun her mother.

The Outsider had run too – and he too was fast. Even with a child under each arm, clinging to his sides. He'd left all the others behind. His weakened mate, his starving friends. But he had heard them. His children had heard. And one of those little ones was unable to recover from the loss or terror. There were fewer mouths for him to feed in the following days, but his little girl would take nothing from his small kills or his gathered morsels.

When she had faded to a breathless shadow in his arms he could not leave her, carried her still. Until it was clear. The other one, his son, would die too if he did not do what he must. The very thing they had run from, so far and so fast.

The Old Woman senses that this man could never make peace with such a thing, even if it had been an act of unthinkable desperation. Perhaps because, ultimately, it was not enough. His young son had soon followed his tiny sister. And then, in the tragedy of deathly necessity, the boy had served the same form of inescapable, agonising desperation for his father.

The Old Woman cannot blame him. She knows that terrible hunger can open up the entrance to another world. She knows that living things will fight with every breath to keep on breathing.

The fever of the fungus has subsided now, but it leaves a quivering sickness in its place. She sends The Tall Girl home to sleep, while resolving to watch over any disturbance in that child's dreams. She decides to keep The Outsider separate from the clan for a while, not only for his recovery, but in case the sickness he suffers now is something they could catch. Illness is rare amongst the tribe but she remembers her mother's story – and her own deep echoes – of the time when they were both nearly taken by a shivering spirit in a faraway cave.

Something caught from a dead thing her mother had found and burned there. Or perhaps some serpentine punishment from a creature her mother had refused to ever eat again. Or maybe, as her mother had admitted, the dangerous illness had been inflicted because of her marking that same cave with symbols that had come to her in a trance. A task she'd felt compelled to complete, despite not fully understanding all that she was creating.

Afterwards, the two had spent days recovering. The Stranger was never sure of the dreadful fever's cause, but both mother and child remembered the suffering. And yet, even once fit enough to leave, her mother had left intact the marks she'd made upon the rocky walls.

For this reason The Old Woman remains cautious about making real what she sees within her mind. She always ensures that certain marks, certain shapes are drawn only in the sand – and always brushed away once their purpose has been served, lest they draw their own unguided life once more from the nourishing earth.

18

MANCHESTER

TO: RevJohnEvesham@bettering.world.org
FROM: calumnberryman@patient-secure.hmhosp.org

Dear Rev John

Thank you for ur reply about what u believe, about time
and history and how u make it work with ur faith. But
I still cannot aggree. You can still visit, but please
dont talk anymore of Dr Kluft, the so called bones of
Sarah or my congregation (and yes they mite all of been
white, but that does not mean our Mother, the Scarlet
Lady as you call her, is a racialist and we dont deny
we all come from africa becuase of that - or that we
must keep our land and our ways cos God says so. Your
twisting it all.) Anyway, I dont want to talk about
my church or its people anymore with u, or with the
police, the fake news press, or anyone.

I take full responsibillitty for my actions. God will
be my Judge, but I have to axept the rules of human law.
I will axept ur company too, as there is no one else
hear that I can relate to even a bit. Nobody with any
real faith and tho we do not aggree on some matters, I
think ur faith is real. Wrong on some things yes but
maybe I can help u more than u think u can help me.

The only other person who mite be able to is Nurse
Jessica. She has God in her heart too, tho she does

not proclaim it. And in her eyes I can see the fire of
The Holy Spirit. You see it too don't you, those little
flames of gold? My grandmother had a touch of that and
she was good to me. But I do worry that Jessica might
be in danger, Rev John. (NOT from me.)

See u soon. Calumn.

⚮

The practice wall at the recreation centre was no substitute for
the real thing, for the sensation of axe into ice, but it was a start.

For a sun-ripened beach brat, Max's fondness for ice was a
mystery to most, but he revered the compound in all its forms
– frozen, vaporous or liquid, and especially when basking in the
'goldilocks' zone of a solar system, the first thing to look for when
seeking signs of complex life.

But *ice*, ice was special. So promising, so perilous. So
precious and fragile and being lost at an alarming rate. Max had
been captivated by the part it played in the story of Shackleton,
the frozen anvil against which his boyhood hero had hammered
out an inspirational will to live, and to keep others alive.

Ice was the great reflector, the once-protector against
overheated oceans, the keeper of so many secrets. It had, after all,
been the source of his own heroic tale on the shrinking glacier
of Mount Kenya. How many more discoveries were waiting in
whatever ice was left, how many more Sarahs?

What lay deep beneath the polar caps? Did they lock away
clues to the 'genesis' liquid supposedly delivered three billion
years ago by the glacial comet storm? There was research going
on right now in the far north of Norway to find out, a project
he'd have loved to join in another, freer life. Ice was irresistible,
whether on a Himalayan peak or in the illustrious rings of
Saturn and the glistening crust of Europa. He longed to see
such wonders up close, but any such extreme expeditions were
confined to fantasy for the foreseeable.

In the meantime he'd promised Greg a climbing trip to the Alps as soon as his protégée was ready. After just a couple of sessions, however, with a less than enthusiastic pupil at the practice wall, Max was questioning the wisdom of that pledge. Besides, with the baby on the way – and this insane new drama with Jess – such ambitions would have to simmer on a backburner.

Max reached for the highest handhold on the wall but missed his footing, stumbled and spun. He was irritated. Were those fleeting thoughts about the fall that had uncovered Sarah messing with his equilibrium now, or was it simply a lack of focus and too many distractions? Such instability wasn't normal and it didn't feel good.

'Max! Are you alright?' asked Greg with unease.

'No worries, mate. Just showing you how safe it is... even if you spill!'

'If you say so. Look, why don't we call it a day? Neither of us is really up to it. Let's get down and go to the pub?'

His friend had made the admission that Max would not.

'Righto. But it's your shout.'

Dutifully, Greg had then braved the crowded bar, on the unspoken understanding that it was a Guinness kind of night. The place was a dive, but at least the bartender knew how to draw a decent top. Pint received, Max toasted his friend – and a not yet completely abandoned dream. 'To the north face of the Eiger, mate. You and me.'

'Yeah, sure, 'cause that'll happen.' Greg leaned back, settling his slight frame into the grimy upholstery. He ran a freckled hand through strawberry blonde hair and looked at Max with clear green eyes, in a way that indicated he was about to ask an uncomfortable question.

'Max, are you OK? You seem a bit... subdued."

It took a beat and a sip of creamy froth, but Max decided to forego any attempt at a front.

'No, not really, mate. Not at all to be honest. It's Jess. I'm really spooked.'

'Oh no, are there problems with the pregnancy?'

'Not exactly. I mean she's got to watch her asthma but that's mostly under control, and there's some blood sugar stuff going on, but she had a full checkup the other day and apart from managing all that she's supposedly in pretty good physical shape.'

'Well, what's worrying you then?'

'Mate...' Max grimaced, 'She's seeing things!'

'What do you mean?'

'She's hallucinating, Greg, she's losing the bloody plot.'

'What? No, come on, there has to be a good explanation. What's she seeing?'

There. It was out. He was committed. Max knew he might as well go all in.

'I dunno. All kinds of trippy stuff, and I'm honestly freaked. I've tried to get her to see a head doctor. I mean, she knows enough of them. But she won't, swears there's nothing wrong with her. I told her it could be a bloody brain tumour or something but she laughed, said she was fine and there was nothing to worry about.'

Was the look on Greg's face concern or incredulity?

'Is she having any other symptoms?' he asked.

'Not really. Just says she sees things. Lights, colours, feelings, sounds... oh, and these luminous rays threading through and all around us.'

'Feck. That's pretty intense. Has she always... I mean, has anything like this happened before?'

'No way. Not since we've been together anyway. Though, she did tell me ages ago about some imaginary friend when she was a kid, but she supposedly grew out of that. No mate, this isn't normal and it all seems to have come on pretty recently.'

'Just since she's been pregnant, then? Well, maybe it's got something to do with that? Hormones or something?'

'Nah. That's not it. I mean it's not exactly a common symptom of anything other than flaming hysteria.'

'You do know that hysteria means "of the womb" don't you?'

'Look, it's more serious than hormones, mate.'

Max was discomfited by the pause as he watched Greg take a breath, a slug of Guinness, and then a risk.

'Well, maybe there is nothing actually *wrong* with her, Max... Maybe this is something... somehow right? For Jess, anyway.'

'How could it be right? My wife's going mental mate – or she's seriously sick or something. And I really don't know what to do. Ah shit, Greg.' Max put his hands on his head in despair. 'I love her so bloody much, and for all our differences we seem to somehow fit each other, like a couple of lost pieces in a jigsaw. And I do want to *try* to understand it all, but it honestly scares the shit out of me.'

'Yeah, well that's understandable. But is anything else wrong? I mean, is she acting weirdly or anything?'

'Apart from having bloody visions you mean? Christ, mate, isn't that bad enough?'

'But *are* they necessarily bad?'

'They're not *real*, Greg. They're not anything – other than a symptom of something she needs to get sorted. And she's a bloody psychiatric nurse but she refuses to deal with it!'

'Well, do you blame her? I mean, she knows exactly how the world treats anything a bit different. And to be fair, look at the way you're handling this now. If I didn't know you, or Jess – or Manda now as well – I might really wonder what she sees in you. Glamour boy or no. You two are so different in so many ways. And Manda's admitted that it took her a while to see it too, and to really *get* you guys as a couple.

'But all you have to remember, Max, is what an amazing woman you have in Jess. Someone who truly, deeply loves you – even if that seems beyond reason sometimes. Someone who still has such faith in you and your relationship, even if yours is having a bit of a wobble right now. So, I don't know, maybe just take a breath and check in with yourself, Max. I mean, what are you risking by not seeing her point of view in this?'

'Christ. Don't hold back, will you!'

Greg took another tight inhalation and moved forward. Max could see his friend was now emboldened and he shrank in response.

'Look, maybe, just maybe, there really is nothing *wrong*, Max. Maybe Jess is… developing something. There's still so much we don't know, about so much. And the brain is an extraordinary organ, we still understand so little about it. Some say it might even process stuff in eleven dimensions! Then you have to consider the bigger questions, Max. I mean what is "reality" anyway, other than a quantum collapsing into a consensus that's then agreed upon by the observers? What if there's more we can access beyond the current consensus? I mean, quantum entanglement might even be the source for consciousness itself.'

Max had been hoping that his expression might halt this bizarre tangent in its tracks, but Greg seemed unperturbed by the kind of death stare that could wither a door-step evangelist. Max's only recourse now was to banter it away.

'Ah shit, you're joking right? You're a bloody scientist, Greg, please don't *you* start with the metaphysical bullshit. Christ, I feel like I've flipped over into a parallel universe as it is! Next thing you'll be telling me the Hadron Collider is going to swallow up the solar system. Or that the speed of light really isn't constant at all…'

'OK, maybe I've taken that a bit too far for now, but please chill out, Max, and listen. Seriously, maybe this is actually a part of who Jess is and who she's meant to be, or one version of it anyway… or maybe even the baby? Or something else in her makeup or background. You mentioned "trippy stuff" – what if this is an emergence of something she could have accessed before with psychedelics? I mean, you've said you've smoked a spliff or two in your youth – maybe Jess experimented even more on her travels?'

'Nah. I can't see that, mate. Jess has always been too much of a good girl. I think?'

'So what if it really is something spontaneously *natural*? Even evolutionary? Everything's speeding up Max, everything's expanding. What if we are too? Maybe some people are getting better radar. Or maybe we've all had it all along...'

'I can't believe this! I thought you of all people, Greg... Wait, is this something to do with Manda? Does she know about this new stuff with Jess?'

'Not as far as I'm aware. Hey, look, take it easy, bro. Try to keep an open mind, that's all. This is Jess we're talking about. She's not stupid. Maybe you just have to trust her. Look, I'm sure everything will be alright. Though maybe I *should* mention it to Manda?'

On a good day, Max could have lifted Greg in an effortless bench press. Now he was wilting under the weight of his own confusion.

'Ah hell. I don't know mate. Maybe. Maybe she already knows? I suppose I've just got to get my stubborn head around it one way or another. But, eh, please don't breathe a bloody word of this to anyone else!'

'God, of course not. I think you just have to man up, Max, and talk to Jess? But just make sure you also take care of her no matter what. Anyway, we might have more pressing issues. Those knuckle-draggers over there have been giving you the evils ever since we walked in. Have you got some kind of history in this place? I mean, not *everyone* falls for the Michaelson charm, after all.'

'I doubt it. I've only been in here once or twice'

Max looked over. Felt the vibe but had more serious stuff to worry about. They were probably just waiting to call him Crocodile Dundee and feel a bit clever. He'd brushed off worse before. And he had the metaphorical 'bigger knife' in the form of his killer smile.

'Bah, they're no problem. They probably just recognise me from TV.'

'Hm. Not so sure they'd be the documentary watching types?'

'Bit of an assumption, eh Greggo! I thought we were supposed to be keeping open bloody minds?'

'Yeah, but the thing is, I don't much fancy an opened-up face, thanks very much. Come on. Let's drink up.'

⟢⟡⟣

```
FROM: RevJohnEvesham@bettering.world.org
TO: calumnberryman@patient-secure.hmhosp.org


Dear Calumn


I will of course respect your wishes with regards to
discussing your church or the bones, or Dr Kluft, but
I must ask what you mean by Sister Wallace possibly
being in danger? Yes, I do also see a wonderful spirit
in her, she has such care and dedication - and yes, her
eyes are lovely, a relative of mine on my father's side
had a similar golden sparkle that was quite hypnotic -
but I'm concerned that you're becoming too attached to
Jessica. You must remember that she'll be taking her
maternity leave before too long, so it's important that
you also build relationships with other members of the
staff.


More urgently, if you say she is in no danger from you
(which I choose to believe, despite your attraction to
the "fire" in her eyes) then I must ask whether you
know from whom or what she is at risk? Or is this your
sense of "prophecy" at work again, do you believe you're
seeing a spiritual danger of some kind? Or perhaps you
have concerns for her health, or that of the baby?


If you don't want to talk about this by email (although
you do seem able to express so much more this way) then
I can try to set up a call or maybe get up to see you
sooner than planned.


You must also realise that your care team see our
```

correspondence as well and will be aware of what you have said about Sister Wallace, as will she.

I very much look forward to hearing from you soon, Calumn.

Sincerely, John.

19

HERE & THERE

Patient 6, the first gene therapy volunteer, is doing gratifyingly well, but it's Patient 7 who is worrying Eloise now. Something isn't right. Something in his eyes.

As she continues to observe him, it dawns on her that she's seen this before. The sense that the person who is (almost) looking back at you isn't seeing *you* at all, but rather experiencing an alternate perception of existence. Eloise had once been part of a project seeking genetic indicators for schizophrenia and had spent time acquiring both samples and a better understanding of the condition.

A keen interest in neuroscience – so nearly her post-grad speciality before the bright lights of genetic medicine had caught her in their glare – was preceded by a childhood fascination for the atypical. Having witnessed the ways in which other cultures handled, even revered, diverse conditions of consciousness or alternative ways of being, young Eloise had been exposed to unconventional perspectives. Travels with an anthropologist for a mother and an archaeologist for a father had broadened more than her horizons.

But what Patient 7 is presenting appears neither as harmless as 'difference' or eccentricity, nor as familiar if worrisome as hypoxia or the delirium of fever. It feels as though something else is brewing. She texts KC, asks him to suit up and come to the observation room. Doesn't say why. This remains only a feeling.

Eloise understands that people can occupy moveable degrees along the scale of mental health during their lives, and has often wondered what it might take to tip the balance of her own psyche by unlocking a predisposition, or from relentless stress upon her neural chemistry. She knows that any human might be only a trauma away from a mood disorder, such as depression or anxiety – but at what point are the red lines crossed, and when does someone become a danger to themselves or others? Indeed, what constitutes danger, when it could range from self-harm to violent acting out, or simply narcissistic gaslighting and coercion?

A psychiatry rotation as a med student had taught her that the trickiest conditions were personality disorders. Harder to diagnose, harder to understand, harder to treat – and with their higher functionality and often discreet expression, perhaps in their own way more insidiously damaging than the upfront drama of a psychosis or a dissociative illness. Or the paranoia, delusions and disordered thinking of an untreated schizophrenic episode.

A schizophrenic episode. So is this what she's seeing now? Maybe... but she needs another opinion.

This is unlike anything encountered so far with the new virus, even in the most unwell of the infected. Patient 7 had appeared to be responding well to the antibody plasma, the first step before more pioneering interventions. He remains weak and disoriented but he's up and about, trailing an IV drip attached to a cannula at his inner elbow, at which he keeps staring. Which he is now fingering, without comprehension. He approaches the window again and appears to look at her.

The sudden spray of rehydration fluids cannot reach Eloise through the tempered glass, but she flinches within her helmet even so, shrinking into the synthetic shell of her second skin. Surely there shouldn't be so much blood. The cannula and its aperture in the vein must have been larger than usual. The scarlet flow that he is now painting, Pollock-like, over the blank canvas of the floor is soon staunched when he's restrained by a pair of hazmatted medics, but it's a disturbing sight nonetheless.

Patient 7 has no strength to fight his carers, but the eyes that veer upwards to graze the glass and gaze without seeing tell the story of an unwelcome new morbidity to this ghastly disease.

Eloise realises she's been half expecting one of their number to lose the plot at some point, but imagined it would be one of the staff, a colleague rendered into a breakdown by exhaustion, sensory deprivation, or separation from every touchstone of grounding normality. But to witness it among the infected is as unforeseen as it is devastating.

KC arrives and something cracks in Eloise. She briefs him in calm, numb tones, but once they are changed again, showered and sipping soup in her pod, the tears break through. The shaking takes over. She is soothed by a kind hand on her shoulder.

'Hey... hey...?'

'Oh Christ, I'm sorry, KC. I'm so sorry. I mean, we got into this field because we wanted to help people and because we give a shit, but then of course we have to develop some kind of professional detachment – oh thanks, but I think I'll need a few more tissues than that – and we accept that we're going to see a certain amount of suffering, but nothing truly hardens your heart to it. At some point, I suppose, it all becomes too much.'

She feels herself crumpling.

'This is that point for me, KC. It's now and it's all a bit too much. Oh God, I'm sorry to snivel in front of you. I mean, I know you're used to my rants and my weird "what if" tangents but you haven't seen this before. Well, to be fair, not many have.'

She looks down at the tissues in her hands and wonders what KC can be thinking of all this.

'It's OK, Eloise. I get it. I do. It'll be OK.'

'Will it, though? I mean, all I really want to do is walk past that glass and look right into his faraway eyes and steady them. I want to be able to hold that poor man – Ricardo, yes, I think his name's Ricardo – and tell him that it's going to be OK. But I can't, can I? Not only because of the risk but because I can't *know* that. We don't really know anything yet. It's not just that we can't save everyone or that we'll never know what more they might have had to live or give – it's that we don't even know whether we *can* save any of them. And we don't know how "recovered" any of the survivors really are... or for how long they will be. We have no idea what their changed DNA will do in the long term, whether they got it naturally from the virus, or with our intervention. And we have no idea when, or even if, they can go home.'

She takes a breath to wipe and blow.

'And let's face it, we don't know when *we* can go home, or what we'll find when we get there... Oh I'm sorry, KC. Well, I'm not *that* sorry. I don't believe that letting out a bit of emotion weakens anyone – quite the opposite really. It's just that I've never been much good at showing mine. More of that only child stuff, I suppose. Not wanting to worry anyone. Or all that moving around and having to fit in and adapt. You can never show vulnerability as a newcomer.'

Eloise shivers internally, still so uncomfortable with this display. As a youngster changing schools she'd known instinctively not to reveal too much too soon, always feeling she had to stay *useful* in order to be accepted. She is comforted by KC's smile, however, which is warm and genuine.

'But I'm so bloody worn down now that all the barriers are breaking. And it's your fault too, you know,' she gives him a gentle, playful arm punch. 'You're just being too damn nice!'

'Well, that's a first! Hey, it's OK, you know. Just let it all out, Eloise, let it all out. We all gotta let go sometime. And yeah, for sure I'm nice... *but*... I also know that when we're done here with all the letting go, we're gonna have to get right back in the saddle. So when you're ready, and only when, you take a big breath and dig down into all that strength and intuition that I know you have. Get into that weird, time-travelling conversation you seem to have with Sarah. Which, to be honest, I've always been kinda envious about. Here...'

KC hands her another tissue and carries on. 'So... you said you had a "sense" that something was wrong right before our guy went into a full psychotic break? And you know, as much as I might test those perceptions or need to rein them in from time to time, I do actually trust them. Because you gotta have some kind of trust in something and I have faith in you, Eloise, and in our partnership. That's why you're here. Even if it turns out that really you're just some whacked out hippy who woke up in the body of a scientist. Even if you're really a big old girly-cry-baby, after all... Ouch! But, hey, that's better. A bit of fighting spirit. Anyway, get some rest now. Then we'll figure out the next move. You got this, Eloise. *We* got this. We'll be OK.'

The moon has grown from a sliver to a smile since she acted on what she'd learned from The Outsider. One of those to whom she had assigned a quiet task has now returned, breathless and filthy. One of a skilful pair she had sent out far along the path by which their guest had arrived.

There is terror in The Outsider's eyes now as The Scout re-enters the camp, and as he imagines what she might have seen – or what has happened to the one she had left the camp with. The Old Woman had told the pair what to look for, what to be wary of, and whatever The Outsider had been able to tell her about the predators he'd evaded on his journey here.

She has so many questions to ask of The Scout. What did this nimble, quiet young woman see? What did she sense as she let her nose guide her way? Most vitally, what has become of her brother? And if this turns out to be the worst that she can imagine, how long might they all be safe here?

But The Scout must recover some strength first. She drinks and then refuses all other care until she has shared her news. There is some relief when it seems that neither of the pair The Old Woman sent out on this task had been noticed by the char-painted and bone-bedecked gang they'd sighted, exactly where she had expected them to be.

In fact, The Scout's brother, a stealthy tracker, had found the courage to voluntarily stay behind and discreetly follow the group, while his sister fled home in warning. It seemed they could be careless, these raiders, too confident in the consumed flesh of others to worry about any souls that still walked. The Tracker believed he could pick off one or two and reduce their numbers – which it turned out were not so many, after all. But they were brutal, yes. Unburdened by children, or the elderly, or by women they kept alive for only so long.

The Scout and her brother had argued about his plan. She felt that this tactic, if he were to be discovered, risked alerting these roving brutes to a new source of prey. She felt the gang could not yet know about her clan and their river valley of refuge. But she had been unable to convince The Tracker, who was determined to stay behind.

The Old Woman wonders, as she hears this report, should they all now flee? The whole tribe together, abandon this blessed place? Maybe only to be pursued and left exposed on open and unfamiliar ground? Better, surely, to stand and fight? They had the advantage of knowledge now but were inexperienced in the ruthless bloodshed that could be coming their way. At least they knew this place, knew its weaknesses, knew how to defend it.

Better, perhaps, not to have to defend it at all? Better to take the fight out to the predators? Use the advantage of surprise against them – but at what risk?

The Old Woman longs with a deep ache for the wisdom and the counsel of her mother. The fierce one, The Stranger, would have known what to do. She decides she must go into the quiet place and find her. Walk with her for a while in the light.

But it is not her mother she sees in the stillness behind her waking eyes. It is another old friend. Grandmother to the little boy who dreamed of flying like a hawk over cold white ground. This boy must dream again, it seems.

⬿⬾

She rubs her eyes, leans back from the magnified cells onscreen. Receives a sudden flashback to her lab in London, to Sarah's beautiful bones. To another late working night and the (now) menacing memory of Calumn, the imposter caretaker emptying the bins behind her. An involuntary twitch does its best to reject the image, but at the same time triggers an epiphany.

'Fossils.'

'Huh?'

'You know. The things that drive creationists bonkers. The long-buried stuff that almost got me burnt at the ideological stake.'

'Yeah? And? You haven't been Zooming with your ex again, have you? What's his name, Indiana Rockefeller?'

'Darius? No. And he's not *that* rich, KC. And, sadly, nowhere near as *Harrison*. No, don't worry, my head is entirely back in the game. Come on, keep up with me... viruses can be fossils too.'

'Yeah, I suppose, in a way. Oh, wait! I see where you're going. To Africa, the HIV project we never got around to. A spot of viral archaeology, what ho!'

Eloise winces. 'Don't try the accent, KC. Really, please don't. But yes, in a way. Consider this – what if our new-but-old virus, or rather the illness it causes, has activated something else? Say an ancestral retrovirus buried for who-knows-how-long in the DNA of our subject?'

KC rolls his chair closer. 'And it's the retrovirus that's causing Patient 7's unique symptoms? Wow. OK. Which would mean it's not only that he didn't develop the new DNA sequence, like the recovered women, but that he's become so much sicker because of something opportunistic, something hitching a ride through his system. I like your thinking, Dr Kluft.'

That wink of approval. It could always raise her spirits. 'Well to me it would explain why he briefly rallied with the antibodies, in terms of all the typical symptoms we've been seeing, but then randomly developed what looks like schizophrenia.'

'Which in turn could be an autoimmune response to the second infection, to our hypothetical retrovirus? And, you know what, there's a precedent! You're right, Eloise. Some patients with HIV have developed symptoms that look like diabetes or schizophrenia – which then abated with antiviral treatment.' KC rolls back to his own screen and keyboard. 'OK, so what are we waiting for? Let's get our guy on some of those specific meds as soon as we can. See if they affect these new symptoms. Because the sedatives they've got him on now are only increasing the risk of respiratory failure and he really isn't in good shape. But maybe we should also look for some ancient stowaways in his cells, like you said, some sneaky little retroviral fossil. Because if we *could* identify anything then we could maybe tailor his treatment.'

Eloise thinks of the gift that Tom presented to her before she left, insisting she open it only on arrival. She couldn't wear it here, but it hung from a hook in her pod. A pendant with a butterfly caught in resin. Too neat, too perfect, too faux to be a natural find, and she pitied the poor butterfly sacrificed to fabricate it – but a sweet and thoughtful gesture nevertheless, and one which now gives rise to a wistful notion.

'Like a relic trapped in amber.'

'Kinda. Yeah. Only not quite so pretty and, unfortunately, a lot less dead.'

Will this be enough though, she worries, and why does *this* patient's survival matter to her so much? Something has reached in and connected them. She can no longer refer to him only as Patient 7.

'But we also need consent from Ricardo to splice in the new DNA. Somehow. Then hopefully the Sarah sequence can fight the original infection as well. Wait... what if *that's* what's protecting the others from similar retroviral activation?'

'Could be, but only if they were already predisposed, which would be a needle and haystack hunt to figure out. And we don't have time for that, especially when we don't know exactly what we're looking for. Having said that, while we're doing all this archaeology stuff, why don't we also run through his genome for Neanderthal markers?'

'Yes. Good thinking, KC. That might reveal even more about genetic susceptibility. Plus, we should look at chromosome region 3 – and at TYK2...'

'Man, I wish we could open source this! Then the whole epidemiology community could be exploring personalised treatments for this thing, based on genetic and other profiles, just in case we can't suppress it. Or before we can safely roll out a vax... Hey, where you going?'

'Coffee. I'm going to need a shedload more caffeine for what we have ahead. This could well be an all-nighter. Do you want anything?'

-20-

MANCHESTER

Dear Rev John

Your right, I must be less attached. I kno she will leave. And I dont kno why she is in danger, its just something the Holy Spirit is moving in me, in my mind. This place always feels like not a good place to be anyway. It will be better for her when she is gone from here. But we are ALL in spiritual danger from temptation, Rev John, everywhere we are, all the time. We must be ready.

C.B

He was withdrawing from her. Jess could feel it and it became a dull ache behind her diaphragm. Perhaps she shouldn't have told him what was happening to her. She'd wondered whether the sceptic (or the coward?) in Max might turn away.

She felt for him, even so. He had enough to process, what with a sick father in another hemisphere, a blossoming career and a baby on the way. A wife going doolally, from his perspective, might well push the outer limits of his coping system.

But how could she not have told him?

He was her partner, for better or worse. She was going to be the mother of his child. Could he really just cut himself off from everything he'd once felt for her? What sort of person could shut down from their own heart like that? No one she could think of, except a few of her patients, she supposed. And her mother, in her own self-involved, navel-gazing, hard-done-by way.

Maybe he was depressed? That could account for the numbing of his emotions, but she could see no other clear signs of the condition; no withdrawal from any other part of his life, and none of the anhedonia that her mother expressed. On the contrary, Max still seemed to enjoy everything he'd always loved doing.

Yes, OK, he could be something of a narcissist, and in that way was more like his mother-in-law than he'd ever care to admit. But it was nowhere near a 'disorder' and he was neither notably manipulative nor lacking in empathy, no matter how well his tough exterior and dodgy sense of humour managed to downplay his softer side.

Ultimately, Jess knew that there was no use in ruminating. The only way to know for sure was to confront the problem. Denial would serve neither of them. Indeed, she'd finally had to admit that her own fatigue and too frequent need to drink and pee were beyond reasonable levels for this stage of the pregnancy. So she'd been to her GP, had some tests – one medical intervention, at least, to appease Max – and now a diagnosis of mild gestational diabetes meant a different kind of denial. *Though surely an occasional carb or two wouldn't be the end of the world?* Even thinking about what she wasn't allowed to eat made Jess ravenous.

As she pulled herself out of bed, she was glad that Max was still home, even if much of the day was lost to her. She could feel his energy, light and fizzing, from the corner of the dining area that was now his study, as their second bedroom was becoming a nursery. Shrouded in a faux-fur turquoise onesie, hood up over her messy hair, she flopped downstairs in her bunny-faced slippers, a comedy birthday present from her 'no-bloody-idea-what-to-get-her' husband.

He must have heard her approach and she sensed a change in his smell. From the buttery popcorn of bursting ideas to the astringent citrus of his hidden fears. Her diaphragm dragged even further on her sinking heart. But the weight of the baby added to both the gravity and the caution of her descent, reminding Jess of her purpose in this approach. Her courage did not fail.

'Hey...you're up!' His breeziness was unconvincing.

'Yup. Just about. Tea?'

'Sounds good, babe.'

Jess foraged through the assorted snacking options in the nearest kitchen cupboard. The cravings, she had discovered, were real.

'Do we have any ginger biscuits left?'

'Not unless you replaced the last packet you inhaled. But I thought you weren't supposed to be eating any carbs? Why not have some real nuts or something instead, eh? A bit of protein.'

He could have offered to go to the corner shop and get some more biscuits or nuts – yes, he was right, she must stifle those sugary temptations. Or he could have offered to cook her breakfast, as he might once have done. Instead, he returned to the sanctuary of his screen. Straight out with it then, that was the only way. She rested her shoulder against the kitchen door jamb, the door itself long gone as part of an attempt to be open-plan, as she dipped her herbal tea bag in and out of a stained, free-from-a-conference mug, having forgotten about making a cup for him.

'Max... what's wrong? With you, with us? You've been so weird with me recently. So distant.'

'Have I?'

He kept working but couldn't pretend. His back tensed, his chin jutted. He turned to her briefly, but the face the camera so flattered – structured around a smile of mesmeric ferocity – seemed utterly lost and childlike. He turned back to the screen.

'Please don't deny it, hun. We've got a kid on the way, so let's be the grown-ups, OK? Or is that it? Maybe you don't want to be forced into growing up?'

He turned to her with a snapping velocity and her solar plexus felt as though it had been punched. Was he angry?

'*What?* Nah. Nah, that's not it, Jess. Not bloody remotely. Is that really what you think of me?'

'No... but... there *is* something?'

'Yeah, there's bloody something! You talk about being grown-ups, Jess, but you're the one who's maybe sick with something, only you've gone and stuck your head in the sand about it. Or it's away with the fairies! What if this ESP stuff is connected to the gestational diabetes after all? I've googled it and you know, it *can* be associated with mental health stuff. But did you mention any of that to your GP? Did you fuck. You're the one living in a la-la land of altered consciousness, Jess! How am I supposed to know what to do? Or what's going to happen... to you, to the kid...'

'No one knows what's going to happen, Max.'

'Oh, so you don't have the gift of prophecy as well then, as part of your flamin' new superpowers?'

She wanted to tell him to fuck off, to *fuck right off*, but knew it wouldn't serve her agenda right now. Knew through all her de-escalation training and experience that confrontation or reactivity wouldn't achieve anything useful.

She knew it was her husband's fear at work here. The fear of a small boy once bullied for being clever, now in the body of a huge, strong man but feeling nothing of that power, or ability to protect himself – or anyone else. She was stung, nonetheless.

'Oh, come on, Max. There's no need to be nasty. This isn't about my enhanced senses. This is something else.'

'Which, I suppose, is something that you just "know"?'

'Yes, actually. But because I love you and I *know* you, not because I'm whatsername, Wonder Woman... more's the pity.'

Max exhaled and released something. Half smiled in apology. 'Yeah, she's alright I suppose. But that Gal's got nothing on you, babe.'

The compliment fell flat.

'Yeah, whatever. But seriously, we have to deal with this, Max. We've created a new life in here and everything's changing. And, yes, that's scary. For me too.'

'But it's not the new life that scares me, Jess. It's *losing* that. Any part of it. Because it's all so fucking fragile. And the ground's constantly shifting. There's so much that's completely beyond our control. And in your case, beyond my understanding, doctorate or no.'

'OK. I think I'm beginning to get it now,' she exhaled.

'Are you? I don't know. Maybe it's my fault, maybe I don't tell you enough about what I'm really feeling. Typical bloke, eh? Just trying to tough it out. But the real problem is that it's all *too* bloody beautiful. You, I mean. Just looking at you standing there, growing our baby, practically destroys me with its beauty.'

Were those tears forming? Was that why he looked away again? Something in him was releasing.

'But then it all flips over and it's all *so* fucked up again. *Life*, I mean. There's so much beauty and wonder and we get so attached to everything, but then it's all so flawed and fragile, so bloody ephemeral...'

Max paused, stood up as he gestured to his laptop, now displaying its screen saver, an optical illusion of geometric emergence. 'So maybe *that's* why I'm burying my head in all the tech, getting into all the new cyber potential. Which really *is* mind-blowing, babe, even if in a different way to your new psychic programming. But everything I'm exploring only makes me think about other ways of holding on to what we love. Because everything can change or disappear in an instant. So, who knows, maybe AI will turn out to be the perfect revenge of human against nature after all.'

'Revenge? What for?'

'For making us so damn disposable! For trapping us in these meat suits that are just moved around by information and energy... and all of it entirely at the mercy of damage or decay. I mean, the amount of things that can go wrong with a human!'

Max left the comfort of his tech behind and walked over to the sofa, gave in to its misshapen imperfections, but held onto his theme.

'Look, we've developed this consciousness, right – and in your case apparently a pretty advanced one – but it's all so impermanent. Even if our emerging sentience then fucks itself up so perversely by starting to dream about eternity! But we can't stick around here for more than the blink of an eye. So, maybe designing a system of machines that are imprinted with our own consciousness is the smartest move we can make? Or, ironically, the most "natural" progression for humanity in the end. A final blast of rebellion against the divine powers that some people still fantasise about – or against this evolutionary rat race that wants us to fight for a life we can never keep! A life that gives us rope burns if we try to hold on to anything at all.'

Jess joined him on the sofa but kept to the opposite corner, knowing Max still needed his space. She let him continue.

'Because all we're allowed to do apparently is *pass on* all that information, one way or another, whether genetically or recorded in another way. But the truth is, Jess, despite my natural optimism, I'm completely bloody terrified for the little being in that beautiful belly, and everything we keep fucking up for it to inherit. And I can't help wondering whether little Wallace-Michaelson's only reasonable future isn't some kind of augmented reality or a few transhuman upgrades? Maybe that really will be the only way we can live as long or as well as we want.'

Jess took a deep breath, hoping it might be as empathetically infectious as a yawn. It was time to start talking him down. She'd never seen him like this.

'Maybe so. But then, would any of it actually be worth it? I mean, would we still really *love*, after all? If you take away the doubt, take away the vulnerability, replace it all with certainty, would we still love in the same way as we do now? And would any of it still matter? If beauty became permanent, would it still be beautiful? It's like with a stunning sunrise or a sunset, you don't expect it to crystallise, you don't expect it to last, and it wouldn't be the same if it did.'

'But maybe it's worth finding out? OK, so we probably can't fix what we've done to the ecosystem now – but I'm buggered if I'm just going to give in. We're the result of an amazing *natural* process, yes, but it's an imperfect one. I mean, watching my dad's health fail from afar and feeling so helpless, seeing a once vigorous man slowly wither away...'

'But *he* seems to have accepted it, Max, he seems to have made his peace.'

'Or he's just bloody given up.'

'But he's had a good life?'

'Yeah, but he could have and *should* have a whole lot more! If it was me, I'd be so fucking furious. Christ, even when I buggered my ankle in the glacier, remember, I was like a bear with a sore head – or foot. You hated me! I wouldn't be able to stand being held back like that. And it makes me worry about anything either me or the kid may have inherited from Dad. I tell you, if *my* body ever betrayed me like that, especially in a way destined for some long-drawn-out suffering, I'd probably want to punish the bastard thing. Either by saying "fuck you" and finishing it quickly or by hacking into it by any means possible. Like that guy back home with ALS who can now communicate via a brain implant!'

Jess nodded, even if disturbed by all this. 'OK, look, from a mental health point of view I can see some advantages to "bio-hacking", if you like. There's already some amazing work being done with optogenetics and stuff like that. And maybe some quality of life could be regained if we really *could* rewire some parts of the brain – some of those tangled up shortcuts to uncontrollable anxiety, or despair, or rage. Yeah, it might be all a bit *Brave New World* to try to level out normal emotional states, but I doubt it would get that far, and it's the tipping point into illness that matters, not having a good old cathartic cry after a sad movie or bonding over the birth of a child. But I'm talking about *healing*, Max, not rebuilding humans for eternal life! Because if we all did that, what would be the point in having children at all?

What room, what resources could we leave? *They* are how we live on Max, not by machinery. Or by reanimating dead organs like they did with that pig brain. I mean imagine a world of eternal tech-bro billionaires!'

'Yeah, I see your point babe, but that doesn't change the fact that *I* want to live on to see *my* child fulfil every bit of their potential. I want to see my kid, if not me, break the bonds of this planet and go all the way out there!'

'I know, hun, I know. But that's way in the future. Right here, right now, all we can do is deal with what's right in front of us. Look. It's OK, Max. It'll all be OK. Us. The baby. Life...'

'And if it's not?'

'Then it's not. But all we've got is *each other*. So let's not spoil it. Let's just stop and breathe and make the most of it?'

Enough talking. Jess understood that his self-imposed isolation was coming from the fear of *too much* love, not his lack of it. She shuffled over from her corner of the sofa and moved into his lap, slipping into a place that might have been moulded for her, melting into its depth of wordless meaning. She caught up and wound one of his surf locks around her ring finger.

'I get it, you know, I do. I'm terrified too sometimes, though it might not show. But all we can do is take it day-by-day and we do that so much better together. Please don't pull away from me, Max.' She guided his hand onto her belly. 'From us. And hey, what about this... what if these new gifts aren't really *mine* at all, what if they come from the baby? And if that's the case, then maybe they're partly *yours* in some way too? Or at least half? So maybe we are becoming "transhuman" after all, even without the machinery?'

He smiled at last. 'Well maybe so, babe, maybe so. Look, I may not ever really get it, all this stuff you've told me about – and if it ever looks like putting you or the baby in danger, then I'll have to put my foot down – but I suppose I'm just going to have to trust you, aren't I? And I do love you, babe, you know that, right? *So bloody much.* So I suppose I'll just surf the benefit of the doubt for a while and see where it takes us, eh?'

She kissed him. 'Thank you, my love. But we do have to keep talking, yes? Because that's *our* superpower. Our affinity for each other, in spite of everything. And you know we'll *always* be connected, don't you? No matter what.'

It's good to be back on the block. He's worked hard, been a good boy, given them what they wanted. But he shouldn't be in this shithouse at all. Hadn't killed anyone, hadn't even tried, not really, not yet. He knew how to do just enough destruction without taking it too far, if he couldn't be sure he'd get away with it. He likes the sight of blood, that's all, likes the feeling, likes being the bad-ass bastard that everyone fears. A bit different, a bit special.

They said he was probably brain damaged, maybe from a childhood beating he doesn't even remember, but to him everything is clear. He isn't held back by the bullshit that pens in all the sheep, can't feel what they feel and doesn't care, not at all. You can't miss something you've never known.

They're watching him, oh yes, every moment out of his cell. He can't go anywhere without eyes on him. One foot wrong and it's back in the box. That nurse, the one he'd had an itch for before solitary, all big and bloated now with a brat on the way, not so sexy anymore. Even if those eyes with the little bonfire-night sparklers in them could still ignite an urge or two in all the right places.

Not a jot of warmth from her anymore though. She should have been easy. Used to smile at him. But not now, something's changed. It's like she's looking right into him, right through him. Gives him the creeps. Those sparkles are not so enticing anymore. But maybe he should write a poem about them. She's never seemed much impressed by his talent, so yeah, that'll wind up the little witch for sure!

Still, having women like her around is the one thing that makes this madhouse any better than normal bird. Next time he sees her on her rounds he'll think of something to get under her skin. Whistle that tune from *Kill Bill* or something.

Some of the common areas, the places that are supposed to keep them socialised, are still out of bounds but never mind. There's enough new prey about since his confinement. This time, though, he has to play the game just right.

There's one new mark who might be fun to toy with. Found his new target in the chapel, one of the few places other than the library they'll let him go, let him be. There, all alone on a bench up at the front, a long, thin strip of a thing. A weaselly godbotherer, always lugging a bible about. Firebug too, apparently. A loser for sure. Cal... something or other. Should be easy enough to wind up. Maybe he can score a lighter somewhere, set off some naughty little fireworks in the bible-basher's head?

Either way, he needs to stay sharp. The crap they're pumping into him since he came out of seclusion isn't helping, though. A fuzzy fog that slows him down. They've promised to reduce the dose if he shows them he's serious. But now he's got an idea about how to work them, keep them off his back. How to make them think he's replacing their chemical cosh with something else, some other kind of drug... a bit of religion! Now he's found the perfect stooge, it should be easy enough to put up that front.

❧

'Sister Wallace?'

'Yes?'

'It's Colin, the duty nurse. Sorry to disturb you at home, but Dr Ngoze thought you ought to be kept in the loop. It's about Calumn Berryman?'

Jess roused herself from a catnap curtailed.

'Oh, what is it?'

'We've had to intercept some mail and will have to refer it to the police. It was really strange, just a red cross on a single sheet of white paper, but more like a crucifix than a St George flag, and with the words "BE READY" in capitals cut out from the paper. It was postmarked London but there was nothing else to identify it.'

'Right. OK. What's the plan?'

'Once it's been processed by the police the board will meet to decide whether it should be passed on to him or not. Though probably not, I expect? It doesn't sound like something that's going to do him, or us, any good.'

'No, probably not. Alright, thanks, Colin. I'll wait for any further briefings.'

Somewhere from her memory banks, as hazy as they were through the hormones, Jess retrieved a notion that the colour red was associated with Calumn's former cult in some way, so perhaps the group were not as defunct as it had seemed, even if they'd been quiet all these years.

She thought about the two words on the letter. What exactly would Calumn need to be ready for? Then again, surely whoever sent it would expect it to be intercepted, so who was the message *really* for? Jess prepared herself for a call from the detectives who'd investigated Calumn's case, cold as it had been up to now. She'd had no contact with them previously, though she understood MI5 had been involved at some point to assess any threat of domestic terrorism.

No chance of napping again now. No sugary comforts permitted either. With some effort, a few groans and puffs she got up to make tea.

As the brew deepened, she wondered whether she should mention anything to John. He might have a better idea what the letter was about, especially with his knowledge of the original case, but he would also be in a difficult position when it came to sharing anything Calumn had since imparted in confidence. Either way, she'd have to ask permission to involve John.

The news was disturbing, but Jess found her feelings shifting from curiosity and concern to a protective kind of anger. Whoever had sent the mysterious mail, those manipulative bastards needed to leave poor Calumn alone.

HERE AND THERE

Eloise ignores the urge to peel off her hazmat suit. It's enough that she's been allowed into the recovery ward, enough that she can take this man's pale hand into her thick glove and make eye contact through her sealed visor without a toughened window in between. KC has arranged this. The ventilation is functioning at optimum, HEPA filters are scrubbing the air, all tests indicate she will be safe. Dr Kluft will of course observe all the extra measures afterwards, but this now, this moment of contact for *Eloise*, is crucial.

It is the first time any of the research team has been allowed as near to the patients as the ICU medics, but the more they learn about the virus, the more they hope to learn about what will help not only those suffering – but also those battling to save them. This particular researcher needed distance from the petri dish, from the screen, the sequencer and the machine learning algorithm. She needed a close encounter with the flesh and blood crucible at the heart of their quest. She needed to know the person, not the number. And as that person returns a gentle squeeze of the hand, Eloise also knows that Ricardo – Patient 7 – is back. As is her conviction, both in the work and in her own approach to it. In what she has to offer.

Even more encouraging, Ricardo is conscious and lucid enough to be asked for his consent to the DNA trial and to understand what they are asking of him. To see how it has affected – only positively, so far – the others who had agreed to and received the insertion of the new sequence.

The team has scanned for lasting changes in his brain structure resulting from the illness-induced schizophrenic episode, but found no larger ventricles, no loss of brain volume, nor any reduction in the hippocampus. No alterations in the frontal amygdala or the prefrontal cortex.

Despite the recovery in his mental health, however, the team don't know for how long the repurposed HIV medication will suppress the secondary retroviral infection which had been unleashed by the new virus. The antibody plasma has not yet produced a prolonged immune response in any of the patients and it's unlikely it will do so in Ricardo. It can only buy them time. If either infection, original or opportunistic, rebounds then they may be out of luck and conventional treatments. The prognosis is unclear.

So far the only effective remedy appears to be the altered DNA sequence, whether acquired spontaneously by the women or with intervention for the men.

Patient 7 understands this. Ricardo is exhausted by his experience as an unwilling psychonaut, even if he has little memory of it, but he'd chosen his assignment at this facility to ride the cusp of scientific endeavour. To see if there be dragons at its waterfall edge, or preferably another wide ocean to explore. And if this now means joining his other surviving colleagues on a genetic adventure to stay alive, he asks her: 'Fuck it, where's my ticket?'

Eloise smiles. Another of Sarah's children determined and hopefully destined to push the boundaries of her species.

⚛

The boy has encountered what The Old Woman hoped he might in his dreams. He has flown high and far with his hawk, finally discovering a winding narrow valley between a set of steep sharp cliffs. It takes a moment of listening, eyes closed – and expressionless, so he is not tempted to please her with this unprompted divination – but soon The Old Woman recognises the valley of which the boy speaks. The place she has in mind is more of a fertile canyon, somewhere useful to stop when roaming afar or when the bounty of a favoured camp grows thin.

The Old Woman can picture this place, remembers how to find it, even if it is many years since she has seen it. Why does the boy dream of this valley? Who has shared this vision with him from the world behind the stars? The vital question – does this place yet lie between current safety and the oncoming danger?

She consults The Scout, who believes the lazy and slow-moving gang cannot yet be near this place. The canyon is known to the girl, although she did not return this way despite its gentler trails and access to running water. She feared it could be too easy to become trapped there, especially alone.

The Scout says she came close to taking this route, but after a rare rainfall for the season she'd noticed tracks made by the great yellow beasts and surmised these creatures had now claimed the canyon as their own, growing many and strong from its resources.

So she'd sped home the more direct way, scrambling up over treacherous rocks. A more testing path, but as one of the best climbers in the clan, often drawing gasps of admiration for her agility, this seemed the wiser choice than walking blindly into a den. Even more so with deadly urgency snapping at her heels.

The Old Woman looks closely at The Scout, considers her report and her reasoning. This slight but strong girl is quick-eyed, intense and determined. A young woman with no patience for pretence, no time for games. All her thrills come from the hunt, from the joy of scaling and swinging from heights that few others would attempt, from seeing far into the distance and noticing everything, from being uniquely useful.

The wise one rests a while now to contemplate all the information she has gained from both the dreaming boy and this waking wanderer. And then it comes together. A steep-sided valley, an attractive place with water and abundant life – and an easier route, if time is no concern and the inclination of those travelling is towards ease – but also perhaps a route into the red mouth of danger.

The apparent signs of other predators intrigue her. These beasts are far enough away to be of no immediate threat to her clan – and likely to remain in the rich territory they have claimed for as long as it feeds them. These many-clawed, cunning, well-organised hunters can blend into the rocky cliffs, which surely they will know well by now.

And yet the approach of the worst kind of predator is still to be reckoned with – the two-legged beasts who have abandoned their souls, who hunger not only for flesh but for power over the suffering of their own kind. A different kind of pack, but one that may also have become complacent in its power?

So could The Scout's four-legged creatures of the canyon be a portent? Perhaps a gift and a precious chance? Or are they merely a distraction, some useful knowledge for the future? Then again, could they somehow help secure that future?

Now comes a vision. Without inviting this painful intrusion from the past, suddenly The Old Woman sees her beloved's blood raining over the waving grass, her mauled mate lying helpless in her wretched arms.

She shakes off this memory, as she must. Unless its return might carry a meaning?

The mighty yellow beasts had once taken so much from her. Perhaps it is time for them to give something back? A plan is forming, even if she knows it to be a wild conceit. How could she be sure the murderous gang would choose this route, would take its appealing bait?

Bait. Yes! That's it. But of what kind?

Then it comes to her. She will offer a different temptation to each group of stalkers. Something for the men, something for the beasts.

Yes! This could be their best chance, perhaps their only chance. The memories shared by her mother had taught her that such beasted men have a knack for seeking out the vulnerable, the innocent, the flourishing. For razing all before them, burning all behind.

It could be that not all of this gang are so wicked. Maybe some are as much victims as the roasted dead, but have borrowed such rotten skin in order to belong, in order to keep living? Could any be helped, could they be healed and absorbed amongst their own?

No. She cannot afford such contemplation. There is no time to tell the difference, they have not enough strength nor resources to make this worth the risk.

Nevertheless, The Old Woman wonders what fables these ruined people might tell each other, if they tell each other tales at all? Dark and dangerous ones no doubt. Lies that can make heroes out of villains and aim a spreading poison from the scorpion's sting straight towards the heart. Those who are far enough along a certain path that they must be convinced that night is day if one among them claims it so. Though she imagines, inevitably over time, how each one will come to fear the other and never know who among them is to be trusted.

She must act. Now.

The Old Woman asks if The Scout feels strong enough to go back out again, and how soon? The girl need not go alone, she will send her own grandson with her. Can the girl find her own brave brother again, quietly and unseen?

Yes, she believes so.

Could the three of them together then manage to snare one of these overconfident stragglers, one who smells and tastes of his terrible companions? The Old Woman feels that those who feed from their own must be changed in this way forever. Maybe this way the yellow beasts of the canyon can be teased with a taste, a morsel of the possible feast to come?

The Scout is shocked but soon impressed by the idea. She understands now her own clan must do almost what these marauders might do in order to defeat them. Almost. The girl confirms she will take a night's rest – for many days she has slept only in the right kind of tree, when she could find one – but then she will go out again to bait the trap.

This is good. The Old Woman is pleased. But there is other bait still needed. One other person must now do his part. His crucial part. But that man must offer to do so. She cannot compel him.

TO: tom2tattoo@finte.mail.com
FROM: dreloisekluft@children.of.sarah.org
Subject: Another letter for Josh as promised

Hi my love, please print and read to him from below. I'm still so furious and upset on his behalf! Glad you managed to get a snap on your phone of this culprit. You said "a paunchy man in a red sweatshirt and a red beanie" - could be a coincidence but I think it *has* to be connected to her? Have the police responded? Brings up some difficult stuff for me, as you can imagine.

I could really do with one of your healing bear hugs right now (and all the rest.) Feeling so deprived! You've always known just what to do, or not to do, when I hit an emotional speed bump. And God how I need to hear your infectious laugh. I keep thinking of that day trip to Brighton, walking on the pier, how we were doubled over in hilarity about something and incapable for about ten minutes! I can't even remember what it was about, something randomly silly, but I do remember being so deliriously happy. Soon, my darling, soon.

****

Dear Josh,

I have asked your dad to print this out for you and read it with you, maybe helping to explain anything you don't understand?

Firstly, I miss you so much! I'm sorry I've been away so long, but as you know I have quite important work to do keeping people safe and well. I wish I could tell you more about where I am, but for now it's a secret, which might seem weird or like something out of a spy film, but sometimes science has to be like that.

I know you're really interested in science as well as your music, so hopefully when I'm back we can talk more about what I do? One day I'll be able to show you some very cool stuff, but mostly I'm just working really hard and against the clock.

You know my job means studying very small but very powerful things, like the genes that make us who we are, but we've also talked about the other ways people become who they are. Like the way you're naturally so good at music but after the guitar lessons for your last birthday, you're also learning that you get so much better with practice? But people can also "learn" things that are not so positive.

Your dad told me some scary person called you a "lab rat" the other day when you went for your new nasal spray flu and covid vaccinations? I'm so sorry that happened, but I'm also sorry for that person, they must be very scared themselves to try to frighten little kids. I don't think anyone should be forced into anything, and they (or their parents) should be able to make proper choices based on clear information. But shouting and name-calling doesn't help anyone!

I know the way people act can seem confusing sometimes, but we've also talked about why we all need to work together for the greater good. Because, my lovely Josh, that's not only how we survive, but how we thrive - and how human beings always have done!

You remember the story of Sarah, the lady who lived a very long time ago? We don't know who her "children" might be today, but we do know that if our own ancestors hadn't worked together, then we probably wouldn't be here at all.

You see, they learned to trade not only things but also *ideas* about new things that might make life easier, or better, or safer. And if they hadn't been curious about the latest bow and arrow, or a plant that another tribe knew could clean a wound, if they hadn't learned to co-operate and look out for the wellbeing of <u>all</u> their group, we might never have made it this far.

My mother really admired a lady called Margaret Mead who studied the different peoples of the world. She said that something important in our development, maybe even the start of what we call "civilisation", was revealed by an archaeological discovery that showed how some ancient humans had learned to mend a broken bone.

This was important not just because they had set the bone successfully, but also because it would have taken time for that person to heal and they'd need to be looked after while they couldn't hunt or forage (Dad can explain that word and maybe even show you!)

So, the fact that people with so little who were living with so much risk were willing to "carry" and care for someone else shows that we'd become more than just apes who walked on two legs. Maybe we'd also realised that we needed to look after each other and were thinking ahead, hoping *we* could rely on other people, too, if we needed it.

That's why I wanted to be a doctor in the first place – to help not only the people I love but anyone else who might need it. Because when people are healthier then they are usually happier and more able to do their part, which helps all of us. It gives us all *more* freedom, which is maybe what selfish people don't realise.

But you know what else? That person who frightened you was strangely kind of right. The thing is, all of us really are "lab rats" - but in the best possible way!

Anyone who walks the earth - and all life anywhere in the universe - is part of this great experiment called evolution. We are all the result of nature trying something new, or taking an "accident" and making it work - and then trying and trying again. In the same way science is learning and adapting all the time.

Being as naturally kind as you are, Josh, and making the most of all your gifts, is probably the best use of our incredible opportunity to be here at all, and part of this huge science experiment! It's also a way to thank our ancestors for all their struggles and everything they learned.

Yes, some people might treat badly anything that seems different from them, but that's just fear. Then other people might try to benefit from that in some way, but that's just greed.

For me, the main thing is to stay curious. It's what keeps me going when the going gets tough. So don't be afraid to keep asking those questions, Josh, to keep looking closely and wondering about everything there is to wonder about.

I really admire how you've handled all the tough stuff you've had to deal with, yet also stayed so generous and keen and full of hope. But we don't always have to be strong or brave or get it right. I sometimes cry and worry about things and need my friends and family to lift me up. I mentioned in another letter a work friend who'd really cheered me up when I needed it? And recently, another very brave scientist, someone who needed to get well so he could help others get better too, has been a huge inspiration.

So, if you ever want to talk, please let Dad or me know, won't you? Anytime. We are all in this together! I'm signing off now but sending you loads of love. Your Dad and I are so proud of you and really looking forward to moving to the farmhouse - what a world of fantastic new experiments we can all do there! Hey, maybe we can set up a lab in the old barn?

Big hugs, Elly x

(Oh, and please give Dasha a big furry hug for me too, I really miss her too, even her naughtiness like chewing up the skirting boards! But I'm so glad she's settled down since being in daycare and making friends with all those other dogs. And here's another idea! Maybe when we're all settled on the farm we can rescue some more animals?)

-22-

MANCHESTER

'Max, have you seen my umbrella?'

'Er... no, that would be wherever you last left it, babe. Like everything else that's just left wherever.'

'Oh, no, it's OK, here it is.'

Jess had a date for the cinema. Not with her husband – Max was dog-housed. He'd broken her confidence, told Greg about her 'hallucinations' (which they weren't) who'd discussed it with Manda, and then her sister was nearly on the next train up.

Jess hadn't been ready for that conversation, had to beg Manda to keep it from their mother, knowing it would worry her to distraction. In her particular way of catastrophising, the poor woman might imagine her daughter to be possessed or something of that nature. Pull out her rosary, have Masses said, try to fix up an exorcism. Even an anxious phone call was more than Jess could cope with right now.

Max had been contrite at the time but didn't seem too perturbed by the frosty shoulder this evening. There was a Liverpool game on and he was scarfed up and ready to go full-throated tribal by drawing on some distant scouse DNA – a grandfather who'd emigrated to Australia as a 'ten-pound-pom'. Any further conversations on this sorest of subjects between them would have to wait. Jess knew they would come together again, in that sublime, often inexplicable place where they found their communion. Was she a fool for love? Maybe, but when it was good between them it was better than anything she'd ever known. Once the baby was here it would mellow him, she was sure of it, awaken his softer soul and shave away the selfish edges.

'Alright then, I'm off. Don't get too excited or scare the neighbours. I know Mr Shankly said football was not a matter of life and death, it was more important than that, but a little perspective won't hurt.'

'Ah yeah, but the great man was bang on, babe, the human race has always needed competition. We might not like it much, but life itself has always needed some kind of conflict. It's the battle between hunter and hunted that pushed everything forward. It's how we all got here, for better or worse.'

'Oh, here we go… Just as well I'm off out or I'd be in for some mansplaining Max-style.'

'But you know it's true! When one creature develops speed, the other gets better agility. One gets sharper teeth, the other grows a harder shell. And we might get all sentimental when a lion chomps down on a baby zebra – well, *you* do my sweet-natured softie because we can't even watch good ol' Dave together anymore without you blubbing – but as our Lord who is Attenborough would "mansplain" it to you himself, competition is the drive that made life on earth what it is.'

'Well, if that's your excuse for hooligans turning over inner-city squares after a game, sorry, but I'm not buying it.'

Jess was wrapped up for the rain now, keys in hand, but not quite ready to let Max have his way.

'Nah, I'm not excusing any of that, but Shankly was right on the money. The beautiful game embodies all the conditions of survival… of bloody everything! You've got a set of rules, potentials and probabilities in place but within that anything can happen. The slightest chance, a moment of genius, fluke or madness, the smallest decision and everything changes for better or worse. And you'll never know what else might have happened or what effect all those other ripples will have.'

'That's all very well if it stays on the pitch, Max, or as some kind of intellectual exercise, but not when young men get sent off to die in pointless wars just to appease nationalism or dodgy economics… or to win an election.'

'Yeah, but maybe there's a part of us that goes to war because we *love* it, babe? Maybe even need it? And it might be an uncomfortable truth, but wars have actually stimulated some of our greatest advances in technology! A lot of what NASA uses today came originally from weapons research you know. Look, I don't like it any more than you and most of it *is* avoidable bullshit, but not always. Sometimes you simply have to fight. I mean, it's only now I'm really feeling it, but if anyone came after you or the kid? Turning the other cheek is all very well, my angel, but we can't stand by while madmen slaughter.'

'But who are the madmen, Max? It's not always that simple, is it?'

The kick-off whistle blew and Jess knew the conversation was effectively over, and that the oversized screen would demand all of him now. He'd be on his feet, prowling the sisal rug like a tiger, and then either leaping for joy or complaining in fury, hands on his head.

'It *can* be that simple. Especially when you look at the Pol Pots and the Putins and the Bibis of the planet. Oh yes... what a start! Come on... that's it.... go on, skin him.... shoot, shoot! OH YES, YOU BEAUTY!'

'Right. I'll leave you to your beer and some chaos then.'

'Look who's talking about chaos! I don't know anyone who embodies that state better than you, my beautiful, messy beloved.'

'Oh I see. A compliment and an insult all wrapped up in one? Sorry, but I'm not playing *that* game. Byeee!'

WhatsAppWorkGroup: From Dr Ngoze to Sister Jessica Wallace

> Sister Wallace, hope you are enjoying a few days off? To keep you in the loop, it's been decided to withhold the recent mail for Mr Berryman. He is making progress, especially in your care and with the visits from Reverend Evesham, and it's felt this would only set him back.

> Oh, and btw, the police and MI5 were in favour of letting him see it in case he attempted to make any contact with the cult, but as you know, we don't think he even knows how to find any of them. And if he thinks some kind of "rescue" is coming, physical or spiritual, this may only encourage him to take risks that could endanger himself or other patients. There were no significant forensic results from the letter or envelope, but there has been a request to covertly observe his meetings with any visitors, including the Rev Evesham, which of course we are resisting. There may be a court order on security grounds, however, as we have been informed that the cult seems to have resurfaced in other menacing ways. I will update accordingly.

'Calumn, good to see you. May I sit?'

'Please.'

'You look a little tired, are you alright? But then, the light in these tiny rooms is not particularly kind, is it?'

'Being well enough to pray is well enough for me, thank you.'

'Gosh, these chairs don't get any more comfortable, do they? Well, I do admire your stoicism, Calumn, and putting up with the conditions here with such grace. I'm not sure I'd be so sanguine. But first let me thank you for your last email – and especially your reassurance that you pose no threat to Sister Wallace. I'm choosing to trust you on that because I know how much you value loyalty... and I can't help feeling that's better placed with those who care for you now than with those who were willing to put you – and anyone else for that matter – at such risk.'

'I'm glad that you trust me, Reverend. That's very important.'

'Good. Good. And I'm glad you understand the transition that's coming, Calumn. I'm sure you wish Jessica all the best with her maternity leave and the big change in her life, too? But I do appreciate that change is challenging, even if inevitable, so please trust in return that I'll do my best to stay available to you and help you however I can? On the other hand, change can also bring good things, and new opportunities, no? With enough time and patience we can all adapt when necessary. It's part of what makes us human, isn't it, what makes us strong?'

'Oh, but we are weak, Reverend John. We are the fallen. Only faith can lift us up. Only faith makes us strong. And following the path that He has written for us.'

'Well, yes, some say that everything is predestined. Even the neuroscientists claim that our brains make decisions before we're even consciously aware of them. But I think we *do* have choices, Calumn, as limited as they may appear sometimes. And speaking of adapting, there's been something on my mind ever since you mentioned Darwin in one of our email exchanges.'

'I'd rather not...'

'No, please bear with me, Calumn, because there's something I need to understand. You proclaimed that while Darwin may have been clever and dedicated, he could only have been driven by the devil, and that's been bothering me because I find that judgement rather ironic. It strikes me that many biblical fundamentalists – and their political counterparts – are quite happy to practise their own form of "social Darwinism" if you like, and to abandon the vulnerable to such a reductive interpretation of survival of the fittest?'

'That's because we trust that God will take care of His own.'

'But we must also take care of each other, Calumn, and follow the example of the Christ. For me, those who manipulate people into serving this "sink or swim" ideology are simply capitalising on one of our greatest human fears. Other than death, that is. And I think that's our fear of the "other" – or worse, the fear of *becoming* the other! The fear of being perceived as the weakest link and then cast out of the clan. I mean, let's face it, Calumn – you were nothing but loyal to your group, but their "devil take the hindmost" philosophy left you utterly out in the cold. So I must ask, does that way of thinking mean that *any* collateral damage is acceptable in this quest to hasten the rapture? Because, you know, the Second Coming cannot be forced, Calumn... nor may it turn out to be quite what some people seem to expect.'

'Well, naturally, we cannot know His mind or timing, but we *can* prepare the way.'

'Indeed! Indeed. So to my mind, Calumn, all these master manipulators – whether in politics or religion – can't have it both ways. Are we God's children after all, or will nature simply have its way in terms of who gets to survive? Either we are all entirely subject to nature's laws and the requirement to care for it in return, or we're not! But *certain people* want to cherry pick from the notion of natural selection and seem quite happy to sacrifice "lesser" beings while considering themselves above it all! The paradox completely passes them by in their rush to be at the head of the race, but eventually the tortoise may well overtake the hare. But most dangerous to me it seems, is the temptation to imagine you are party to some kind of "secret" gift or knowledge, and that being so graced, you are somehow exceptional. Which means you can never be wrong and any arguments against you are the work of the wicked. Those who are not worthy.'

'I have no love for leaders who pay only lip service to God, you know. For they cannot pass through the needle and the meek *shall* inherit the earth.'

'Ah! But was your group or its leader truly meek, Calumn? I mean, was it meek to threaten Dr Kluft in that way?'

'No, please. I have told you that I will not speak of her or of my special family, or of that action. You may very well nod and sigh, Reverend John, but as you say we must have trust. And we must honour our agreements?'

'Yes, Calumn, of course. I'm sorry. And I notice you seeking the protection of your bible there, but you have nothing to fear from me. What's more I do understand your need to belong, you know. We are pack animals by nature and most of us are terrified of being alone, although I've known some exceptions. But I imagine the worst kind of loneliness must be the inability to trust even those closest to you? And when I look at many so-called "leaders" all *I* see is abject terror! This nagging fear that they're not so special at all, that they understand deep down the fragility of power. But then they refuse to see the *beauty* of that very humility that comes with our interdependence, of being in communion with all that is, they see only a terrifying destruction of the ego. So instead of valuing nature and a co-operative world, they'd rather tear it all down and scrabble for the spoils, deluded that they are somehow insulated from the devastation. Such narcissism. Which is such a problem in today's world and which comes at such a cost.'

'Well I do agree that we should care for nature, Rev John. It is His creation, after all. And I have to admit that I do have a fondness for trees and I miss them in here. I used to like to go to Hampstead Heath and I could name every single one that I saw, before...Well. I can see some trees from my window in here, ash and birch at least, but sadly we are not allowed into those woods beyond the fence.'

'Well it's very good to hear you speak of your love for nature, Calumn! I haven't heard that from you before. Now I wonder if I could get permission for an excursion into those woods for you and I? I can't promise anything and we'd have to be under guard, but yes, Calumn, trees are very special indeed, so very precious. Which brings me back to Darwin. The tree of life and all. No please don't wince, Calumn. This is about your claim that scientists such as him are under the control of "The Devil", but I wonder what guise you see that in? Not hooves and horns, I hope? I mean, what on earth is threatening about a classic prey animal, like a gazelle or a deer? I do find it fascinating how we are driven to give shape to abstract ideas such as good and evil.'

'The fallen one can take whatever shape he wishes. He could be wearing your clothes right now.'

'Well, I certainly hope not. Not sure how I'd ever get the smell of brimstone out! Apologies for a rather poor joke, Calumn, but you don't *really* believe that of me, do you? I don't mean to mock your fears, you know, and I am not so progressive as to deny the existence of evil! But as Hannah Arendt once famously remarked, it's the *banality of evil* that's often most terrible and tragic. It's the everyday ease with which evil can be encouraged among ordinary people desperate to belong, or to have a little more of what they think they deserve. It's how this is then exploited by the unscrupulous in their hunger for power. Those who believe themselves destined for greatness.'

'But some *are* chosen, Reverend. He has a plan for them.'

'Perhaps, but believing that about yourself, or your group or leader, could also be a classic trap for the ego, couldn't it? Look, it's not that I don't think some people have particular gifts or talents to be nurtured, but these can be found throughout society and even arise latently or spontaneously. Even if so many people seem to believe they were just born special. But we are *all* capable of wonderful things and I do really hope that humanity *is* still evolving. There's still so much more right with us than wrong! And I hope with all my heart that we keep developing more compassion. Not only for our own "in-groups" – because it's easy to love those closest to you, isn't it? But the real spiritual challenge is to love *everyone*, is it not?'

'Forgive me for yawning, Reverend. I'm not sleeping well.'

'Oh dear, I do go on a bit sometimes, don't I? Just as well I chose a vocation that lets me talk a lot, hey? It's you who should forgive me, Calumn. Your care team have wondered whether I'm overtaxing you sometimes with all the philosophy and with my choice of language. I do hope not, but then I don't want to patronise you either, Calumn, nor assume you can't follow our more complex discussions.'

'That's alright, Reverend John. It's not you, I really am just very tired. The fact is, I quite like your way of speaking. I like listening to you, even if I don't always agree or understand.'

'Well that's a relief! Anyway, enough from me. Do you have anything you'd like to say or ask or share, Calumn... or would you rather we read together again?'

'Can you read please? And then can we pray?'

'Yes, of course, my friend. And *I* for one should certainly pray to be spared the sin of intellectual pride, should I not! Shall we start with the good book? Though I've also brought along some other spiritual writings that I'd like to share with you too, if you don't mind?'

The box office queue was long, but Jess didn't mind. It was a chance to catch up with Lisa, a fellow graduate from nursing school who was now at the Royal Infirmary. And in compensation, the rain was purple and sparkling. She might have lowered her umbrella and bathed under it, but couldn't risk a cold or worse, not with the lowered immunity brought on by the pregnancy. She had her nasal spray and a high-quality mask. But what was life without a little risk and doing the things you love with the people you love?

Then the movement, unmistakable. *Oh God.* Why wasn't she with Max now after all? He still hadn't experienced this with her.

'Jess?'

'Oh! It's kicking.'

'Wow, can I feel?'

'Oh. It's stopped now.'

'God, how exciting. I can't wait. Might have to settle for whoever looks half ready, though. I mean, let's face it, I don't think Mr Right is coming my way anytime soon... unless I go for a donor and a test tube!"

'I could always lend you Max. Sometimes I think I'd like to give him away for good.'

'Yeah, right. You two were made for each other. But the path of true love and all that. Anyway, come on, looks like we're on our way in... fancy some popcorn?'

It was impossible to concentrate on the film. The movie wasn't made in 3D but that's how Jess was experiencing it. Too many people in the auditorium. Too many of their thoughts and feelings, hopes and fears. Jess gathered her things, reaching with difficulty over her belly to beneath her feet, and whispered to Lisa, aware of the looks and sighs and grunts of disapproval as they disturbed those around them.

'Leese... I'm so sorry, I don't feel well. I have to go.'

'Ok hun, no worries. Come on... Sorry, sorry, coming through...'

That's what she loved about Lisa. There were never any worries. She was as loyal a friend as she was easy going.

The rain had stopped once they got outside again, but the wet streets glowed orange and Jess wasn't sure whether that was real or not.

'Come on, angel, let's get you home.'

'No, not yet. The game will still be on. It's nothing, really, and I don't want to worry Max. I just needed some fresh air, I think.'

'Alright then, let's walk.'

'Yes. That sounds good.'

'You've got to look after yourself, you know. Especially now with the diabetes. Didn't I tell you to lay off those bloody ginger nuts! God, I remember you could wolf down a pack a day when we were in those student flats. Or broom cupboards, more like. But seriously, Jess, I mean it. You're really good at taking care of other people but you've got to do the same for yourself now.'

'God, you sound just like Max! But yeah, I know. Even if it all feels so boring and restricting sometimes. I mean, I'm doing all the right things now with the diet and stuff, but life's too short for too much fuss. And there's one hell of a speed bump coming my way soon enough. With one hell of a right foot, it seems. Which will certainly please its father! But I'm fine, Leese. Really. I'll be fine.'

TO: RevJohnEvesham@bettering.world.org
FROM: calumnberryman@patient-secure.hmhosp.org

Dear Rev John

It was nice to see u. After u read to me from John
ODonohue (did I get that rite?) u asked me if my mother
had read to me, stories and poems and stuff. I did
not answer cos I dont like to talk about my so called
family before the real one, before my church. But I was
wondering why u asked? The only "story" that matters is
the life of Our Lord and the Prophets, wich I am still
trying to share with others, as we are commanded, even
here. But its impossible to believe anything else, the
world is made of lies. So many liars, too, it can be
v hard to tell who is true or not. I can get quite
confused, but we must keep trying to spread the Word?

The stories you talk about tho are just another kind of
lie. I remember some from school. I never liked them. I
never liked films or that sort of thing either. Or sport
because of my condition. I did like drawing but only
to see how real I could make it look. But nothing here
is real so I dont draw anymore. I only like to clean
and fix things when they need it. And I used to like
to grow things and learn the names of plants. Anyway,
my church says u have to choose between the world here
and the world beyond which passeth all understanding.
I dont need to "imagine" as u say or to question. Only
to beleive. And Pls dont ask about when I was a bairn
anymore. That boy is gone and he has been reborn in
His Blood. As we all must be. For He is coming again
soon.

CB

Max was still merry from a 5-2 win and the mood between them was already finding its sweet spot again. Jess was stretched out on the bed, a pillow under her rump to support her lower back, but even after the long, scented soak in the bath that her repentant husband had drawn for her, her feet still hurt after the walk with Lisa. Always her weakest point and the wear and tear of nursing didn't help. The pain often brought to mind the little mermaid, sacrificing her tail fin for the sake of love, cursed to walk forever on broken glass.

Jess wondered if she would have abandoned her waterworld for Max. Yes, probably. Especially as he gave the most amazing foot massage. One of several talents well worth a necklace of shells and a contract with the sea witch. She would forgive her husband (almost) anything and believed this to be more of a strength than a weakness.

'Better, babe?'

'Mmm. Yes, thank you my love. Don't stop though. Don't ever stop.'

'Well I might need to take a slash in a minute. But promise to tell me if the kicking kicks off again. I can't believe I keep missing it!'

'I will. Oh thanks, hun, that's so good. Oooh yes, that's it, right there. There. Aaah.'

'You need to stop making those noises or I'm going to have to do something about it.

'Promises, promises! But not just yet. More of the foot thing first please.'

He obliged.

'Max,' she asked, hand on her tummy, 'what shall we call it?'

'Thought we didn't want to choose a name yet, like how you don't want to know the sex. We're going to wait and see, right?'

'I know, but I'm having a few ideas.'

'Like what?'

'How about Neil if it's a boy, after Armstrong?'

'Or how about Keegan, after the Messiah?'

'Max.'

'What if it's a girl?'

'How about Aurora, after the northern lights? I can't believe we both missed that time you could see it right here in the solar storm. And when we're so often up at night anyway! But we must go to Iceland or Norway sometime, promise me. Why are you laughing?'

'Ah shit, babe! *Aurora*, are you serious? Do you want to scar her for life?'

'Ok. Maybe not, then. But I *am* serious. I want *you* to see them, at least. The lights, whenever you get the chance. And everything else in those amazing places.'

'We will. We'll all go, promise. OK. Here's an idea – how about Amber? After that gorgeous glint in your eyes. That's if the kid turns out to have it too.'

He moved his hands upward from her feet along her inner thighs, and gently apart.

'Hmm. That's nice... mmm... No, wait, Max...'

'What now? Copernicus? Kepler? James W... or no, how about Artemis after the girl-power moon mission?'

His lips took over. His tongue.

'Oh, come on, don't be silly...'

Then that sudden, gasping sip of breath. And another interruption.

'No wait, wait a minute Max, not yet. There's something else I need to talk to you about. I've been thinking. We should both take out a life insurance policy.'

'What? Christ, well that's a bloody downer. In every way.'

'I know, I'm sorry, but we have to start thinking about all that sensible stuff now. I'm serious. I'm going to get some quotes.'

'There's only one thing we need to be thinking about right now, sweetness. Sshh....'

HERE AND THERE

T he Outsider listens, looks long at the scribblings she has made in the dry earth, but he shows no readable reaction. The Old Woman has noticed how much calmer he's been since his journey through and out of the shadows. Since receiving the forgiveness of a pair of tiny spirits. The racing of his ravaged heart has slowed, the sharper edges of the world have receded for him. But The Old Woman knows he can never be truly whole again. Not while captive in the cruel skin of a life that cannot be reimagined – but which perhaps can be redeemed?

It seems he understands what she is asking of him. He must find what he has fled from and then run again. First towards and then away from it, to lead the horror somewhere else. The body he loathes, the meat that cloaks him, must now be offered up. It may be taken by spear or by claw – or perhaps, with the blessing of some merciful spirit, he may yet walk through the valley untouched. The Old Woman cannot know his fate. He is fast enough, however, and through her care, through the grace of her clan, he has grown strong again.

She assures him that her own hunters will be hidden at the other end of the canyon, in the hope they can gather him up again unscathed and then finish off any marauders who have escaped more violent mouths than their own. Even so, it is a lonely and dreadful risk that most men would never take. But one trapped in a half-life?

She can only hope.

He allows a flicker of terror and a sharp intake of air, but then seems almost relieved when he turns to her, slowly releasing that breath. With a single silent but grave nod, his eyes engage hers in gratitude and she knows he understands.

Here is his chance.

Live or die, fail or succeed. *This* is his way home.

Eloise had wanted to make the return trip by snowmobile at least, huskies at best. To hear their primal howls, feel the ice crunch and melt under glinting, gliding blades. But there is no time for such romance. A monster of a military helicopter bears her more prosaically and expediently away. The cushioned headphones grant her some temporary refuge from the all-too-soon encroachments of the 'real' world. Much as she has longed for it.

She bids farewell to the ice and snow as it recedes rapidly beneath her and thinks suddenly of that Led Zeppelin song, feels its euphoric wail at the centre of her chest, wishing she could match its war-cry chorus with her own hidden voice, her own atavistic Viking heritage. *Immigrant Song.*

We were all so, once upon a time. Don't we all live now because someone, an age ago, had made that long and hopeful march?

But then a crackling, too modern voice invades her reverie. He is right beside her, though they may as well be a continent apart.

'Whatcha thinking 'bout, Eloise? You're miles away again. Where now?'

She smiles. 'Not so much where, as when.'

'Ah. Sarah?

'As ever. She spends so much time inside my head, she ought to pay rent.'

Eloise accepts this diversion and turns fully to KC now, not knowing when she might be this close to him again. As close as they have ever been. And as they can ever be. *Perhaps some things are all the sweeter for never being tasted?*

'So where is your best ancient friend pointing you now?'

'Home, I suppose, thankfully. But then, where's true home for any of us? Where was "home" for Sarah? I mean, we established that she lived at a time of environmental upheaval, with likely huge changes and population reduction, and that she seems to have made some kind of marathon journey of migration. And you know how I feel she was somehow distinctive, found all alone up there on the mountain... not to mention the artefacts that have been discovered since which might have been hers. And all the hours spent wondering how she survived, what she may have passed on to any descendants and how *they* survived, where they migrated.'

'Yeah?'

'So, what if we're in a different-yet-similar time of cataclysm now? What genetic effects might a *new* bottleneck of survivors result in, for better or worse? If our virus gets out and spreads unchecked... if it decimates the male population and those with vulnerable immune systems – would the post-viral DNA sequence, our own Sarah's sequence or something else like it, become globally dominant? And if so, would that bring any advantages after all the devastation? I mean, would any survivors who'd naturally acquired the sequence, or any men voluntarily acquiring it, *experience* those changes as advantageous? Would anything else in our world change, as much as we keep promising the next generations that change is coming? I mean would we actually *be* any better? Or would we just be clinging to survival in an even more imbalanced world?'

'I guess that depends who you mean by "we"?'

'Well, of course some cultures and persuasions have been trying to get it right – or put it right again – all along. But everything's been moving way too slowly. So many setbacks.'

'For someone who appreciates the incremental but magnificent turning of the cogs of evolution, you don't have much patience, do you?'

'I don't have the time, KC. None of us have the time.'

'Well if that's the case, something else will take our place. Eventually.'

'But at what cost? A whole spectacular ecosystem?'

'You can't bring human perspectives or value judgements to ecosystems, Eloise. They are what they are and only thrive if they work. That's the only criteria. Does any system function well enough that enough of its components thrive? That its checks and balances keep it all ticking over as a healthy whole, but that it also keeps evolving?'

Eloise turns to the window again. Watches the irreplaceable system below her begin to fade into the monoculture of commercial forest. Or perhaps this is one of those genetic conservation zones, maybe a preservation of biodiversity after all? Hard to tell from this height. Ah well. She shouldn't complain, she'd been craving the company of trees. Any trees.

'*The centre cannot hold.*' Eloise is aware she's thinking out loud, but assumes KC is accustomed to such quirks by now. 'Well I wonder what slouches towards Bethlehem now?'

'Say what?'

She sighs. Lets go of the trees, lets go of the ice. Pushes her shoulder against that of her cherished companion. For as long as she still can. The crush of civilisation will welcome them both soon enough.

'*The Second Coming,*' she explains. 'It's a poem by Yeats. Look it up, you might like it. It's about entropy. Kind of. And cycles. Kind of. Well I suppose, like most poems and stories, it's about whatever you want it to be. The limits and prejudices of human perspectives, as you say.'

❦

Each party she has sent out to fulfil her strategy must now be in place. No part of this works without all of it working. Accompanied by her own beloved grandson, The Scout has hopefully found her brother by now, the one tailing the marauders and hoping to pick off a straggler or two. Now these three, when and if joined together, have a new mission.

Any such straggler target, perhaps one too proud or foolish enough to defecate out of sight, must surrender himself unknowingly to their silent blades and then become bait to tease the beasts of the valley.

Then the rest of this brutal gang must believe that by their own good fortune they have discovered The Outsider, who must then lure them into the canyon at a ceaseless run. At a pace that should both tire his pursuers and distract them from thoughts of any predators even worse than they.

The Warrior, The Scout and her brother will hopefully have baited the valley by then and found somewhere to watch from safety, both to ensure the marauders have fallen for the trap or report back speedily if not. But if all unfolds as she hopes, the three souls she has entrusted with this vital task must maintain a hidden watch in case any of those entrapped become aware of the feeding frenzy ahead of them and attempt to escape by doubling back.

A small party of her best hunters, men and women, will be positioned safely at the opposite mouth of the narrow, rocky valley, keeping all senses alert for both the cunning stealth of the yellow beasts, and for whichever of the murderous gang might make it through. Some would surely make it through – those huge creatures can become lazy once a sufficient kill is made and will not waste energy without enough demand.

The rest of the tribe will stay behind to defend the camp, should this daring – some say foolish – plan fail. They will form the circles within circles as taught by The Stranger and practised since by each generation, if thankfully without cause until now.

The youngest children will be huddled by the oldest women at its centre, the young women in the next circle, armed with whatever they have been able to make and learn to use in time. The younger men will be next, armed with the best weapons. Lastly, the oldest men, well-armed too, but ready to sacrifice themselves if need be, at the outer edge.

The children are prepared, they know how and where to run if each circle succumbs. But the older women, with finely flaked and well concealed boning flints, are also prepared – in ways they alone can know. Ready to dispatch the little ones mercifully and spare them unthinkable horror should the worst outcome prove inescapable.

The Old Woman will take her own place alone under her tree by the river, near the secret cave. Seeing through the eyes of any creature that will assist her and into all the places she needs to see. Calling on the help of others too. Begging for the intervention of those who have gone through the cave ahead of her, those with no blood left to shed.

Such intervention may be needed. She nurses a nagging fear raised by one of the rebellious youths who has never trusted The Outsider and supported by the boy's grandfather, an elder of the clan whose voice she must respect. What if this man they barely know, The Outsider, should betray them? Not only by the failure of his courage or strength.

What if something like this has always been his plan? *Their* plan? To gain both trust and knowledge, to split the tribe, drawing the best fighters along some false trail and leaving the most vulnerable exposed? What if the enemy is as clever as The Old Woman imagines herself to be?

These words had been a spear to her soul. It seems she may not be so wise, after all. She had not considered this possibility. She so completely believed and wanted to have faith in the one who might be her kin. One whose eyes, whose familiar eyes, could surely not be lying? One who had accepted her kindness and her healing. All the work it had taken to connect with him, work she needed to believe was a success, a special kind of achievement. Such pride! Such foolishness.

And yet. Her faith, her hope remains. What other choice is there? What other workable plan? She had assured the doubters that she would send the tribe's best spear arm to accompany The Outsider at a distance, one of their best bow hands, the most skilled with a slingshot. One capable of besting even her own grandson on occasion with the reach and accuracy of a throw. One even more precise in the direction of an arrowhead than The Scout or her brother. At the first sign that The Outsider might be looking to rejoin or communicate with the gang, those weapons would fly.

Even so, the final decision had been put to silent agreement among the adults of the clan. If enough stones appeared outside her hut overnight the strategy would proceed. If not, they would all leave together, staying ahead of the coming foe, the coming woe, for as long as they could. She had considered hiding them all in the sacred cave, but it was neither large enough nor could it sustain them all for long. And if discovered? They would be trapped.

The dawn brings her answer from the tribe in the form of an abundance of stones outside her hut. She has their confidence. All will go ahead as planned.

The Old Woman leaves the remainder of the clan to walk to her chosen place, closes her eyes to begin her watch, and waits.

-24-

MANCHESTER

Max was in a bad way and not even a lie-in was improving the situation. Rutherford might well have been splitting that first atom inside his head. A small city could have been powered from the throbbing shockwaves. The primordial soup churning in his guts was producing enough acid to fry right through to his heart. And that was pumping way too fast. Regret, he acknowledged, was a terrible thing. So was displeasing Jess.

'I have absolutely no sympathy, you know, not when it's self-inflicted. You're old and wise enough to know better, Max Michaelson.'

Shit. She wasn't even smiling or giving him a gentle eyeroll of kindly disapproval. Jess was not happy. A play for sympathy felt like his best shot.

'Ah babe, please, don't. I can feel an evil chunder coming on. Please can you bring me some head pills... and some antacids... oh and some tea. Please. I'm seriously crook.'

'Ah yes, that'll be the deadly detox flu then, will it? At least you were compos mentis enough to do a saline nasal rinse and a CPC gargle when you got in, so thanks for *that* much. But you know I'm not happy that you went out at all, for all kinds of reasons, not least because we still don't know if the new sterilising vaccines will really work, especially if there's a stupidly low uptake, and there's quite enough other germy crap out there for a pregnant woman to worry about. *And* there's more saline on the floor than up your nose *and* you left the lid off the mouthwash. I practically slipped and spilled my way through all my necessities this morning. Not to mention the fact that the bloody loo seat was up. Though I suppose that's better than not, if you really *are* going to throw up?'

His head hurt more than ever now. 'Yeah, but I've been poisoned, babe. It's not my fault.'

Jess was rummaging for whatever it was she couldn't find, but that distraction did nothing to blunt the edge in her voice. 'Oh, no? Whose fault is it, then? Was there some mariachi in a sombrero and a poncho pouring tequila down your throat at the barrel of a gun?'

'More or less, yeah...' He tried a flash of the smile that rarely failed, even if an appealing toss of his locks was out of the question in his current condition. No joy.

'How many cigarettes did you smoke?'

'Heaps. Way too many. Oh God...'

'Don't go calling on him in your hour of need, you hypocrite.'

'Just a figure of speech, babe. Please, don't be mean to me.'

'Well, wave goodbye to a few thousand brain cells, you idiot. You won't be much use to anyone today.'

'Actually, that's an urban myth, babe. My brain is fine. Ish. My liver, on the other hand...'

Despite his latent contrition, Max would have regretted declining last night's invitation even more than the hangover. Jess would be finishing work soon and she would need him around. There might not be too many more opportunities to get so thoroughly trashed once the baby was here. Last chance saloon.

He hadn't seen his climbing club since Kenya and they were gearing up for an assault on Aconcagua in the Andes, an adventure he would have signed up for, if life hadn't been changing for him so fast. The entire crew had more or less taken over that crazy Tex-Mex place and kept it open way later than the staff seemed thrilled about.

'Oh God. Call in for me, babe, get Greg to do my lectures. Tell them I've got food poisoning, Montezuma's revenge or something. Anything. I'm not going anywhere today.'

'Oh bloody hell, Max! Alright. But only because I wouldn't want to see you anywhere near a bicycle today. You know how lucky you are to have a friend like Greg, don't you?'

'I'm just lucky full stop, babes. Otherwise, how could I have you? Born under a blessed star...'

'Oh, so it's astrology now too, is it? Blimey, you must have had a good night. It's no good trying to butter me up, Max.'

'No chance of brekkie then?'

'None. I've got to get to work. Now that I'm actually on days, as you requested, I can't exactly show my gratitude by being late, can I? And I've got to talk to Manda about her visit next week. Don't forget she's coming up, will you? Though I must give you this much, your intuition about her and Greg was bang on – "Mr I-don't-believe-in-intuition" – and it *is* all rather exciting, so I suppose I do owe you one. But not breakfast and not now. And not dinner because I need to go check out Mothercare on the way home. We've still got to get a buggy, remember. See you later...'

The coldest goodbye he'd experienced since that time he stuffed up a big date they'd been planning in the early days.

'OK, but don't go carrying anything heavy like that home on the bus, babe, will you? Just choose one and then I'll go pick it up. No lifting or bending, right? Have you got your inhaler? In case the traffic fumes set you off again... did you hear me? Love you!'

By noon Max had recovered enough to sit at his computer, but five minutes in, the power went out, and he'd forgotten to charge his laptop the night before. *Shit.* He couldn't even make a cup of bloody tea. A ciggie outside would have to do, even if it brought back the nausea he'd only recently subdued with an egg and bacon sandwich.

Max smoked and wondered how long until he was powered up again, in every way. *Better get used to it, but eh?* Blackouts. Until they mastered fusion – maybe closer than anyone had hoped? – and its clean, endless energy, until Solaris was beaming back energy from its panels in space, or until hydrogen was running more vehicle engines, blackouts might well become the norm. Especially while despots had their wicked ways or while we were still catching up from failures to properly invest the public purse.

Back to pen and paper then. The smoke break had given him an idea. Something Jess had said about 'a bloke in a sombrero' suddenly brought to mind the Mexican Hat graph of wavelet function. And from there to the Higgs Boson, super symmetry in the Standard Model, and all the sticky, superfluid molasses of space.

Still so much out there as yet unknown, unseen, unproven. All the problems, theoretical, mathematical, predictive. All that elusive dark matter awaiting *measurable* discovery. Max regretted not admitting to Reverend John that, of course, we didn't know quite what it was *yet*, or even that it was really there *for sure*. He could have told him about the idea that dark matter was able to replicate itself from other matter – which would solve quite a few problems – but he hadn't the energy or the inclination at the barbie to debate the alternatives, never mind get into the kind of tweaking of Newtonian equations which could dispel the troublesome 'darkness' altogether.

No. He hadn't wanted to give John Evesham an inch, nice enough as the old bastard was. Not a single piece of potential ammunition. He definitely wasn't going to bring up all those wonderful if uninvited wobbly muons, hinting at another force of nature, after all. The fact that science was constantly repositioning itself with each new discovery was integral to both its beauty and necessity... but perhaps also the reason so many felt justified in being so suspicious of it?

Max would, of course, surrender any cherished notions if need be, just like every sensible scientist who'd ever had to let go of something once disproven, or replaced with something better – even their own professional 'babies'. Nevertheless, despite its piecemeal development since Emmy Noether's seminal theorem, despite its convoluted nature, its inability to explain dark matter, Max really *liked* the Standard Model. He'd been nurtured on its structure. Regardless of its complexity, it allowed for a convenient tidiness amidst all the unknowing. An attempt at order. And in recent years, there'd been enough untidiness and disorder, in both his working and domestic life.

Unable to keep focus, distracted by the elusive appeal of symmetry, his mind switched back to Jess, to *them*, to their discovery of each other. Pairing up like fermions to absorb mass from the condensate, to become something new, to create something *other*. So beautiful.

Or to collide and obliterate each other like matter/anti-matter in the constant fizz of space? There were still so many little niggles between them. In the end, were they just too different? No. He couldn't accept that. Their differences had created their chemistry as much as caused the tension within it. He must try harder to see things from her point of view. He must have faith in all the natural wisdom and empathy that he'd been drawn to in the first place – soon after his instant appreciation of the way she could fill a bikini and his enchantment with its surf-unsuitable malfunctions.

His head throbbed. His mind was wandering, mixing everything up. He wouldn't make any progress in terms of work or smoothing out his domestic life today. Though things had been a bit better – at least they'd connected again in terms of intimacy, the bedrock of their bond. But he needed to park his thinking until *all* the lights came back on, along with his battery-drained laptop. Even if sometimes being worse-for-wear could actually benefit certain mental processes, perhaps by blotting out any other busyness in the brain?

Weird, he mused, how it could take a state of vulnerability to bring on the *eureka* moments. The brain waves induced by defecating were the most amusing source of inspiration to Max. He often wondered how many of the great ideas had in fact been born on the dunny. Was old Newton really sitting under an apple tree? Was Archimedes really in the bath?

Brainwaves. Rippling out, displacing ignorance, arising from even the most banal of situations. The pattern of nature, even in matter. Everything came through in waves. Diffracting when they encountered an obstacle, creating phenomena that freed itself space, from surf to sound to light. Was love the same? Would he feel it for the child, instantly, constantly?

There were moments when Max worried he might not love anyone enough to make the ultimate sacrifice. Yes, he could admit that to himself. But these were only tiny wormholes in the fabric of his world that disappeared as quickly as they manifested. Were the particles of love that had leaked through them to the other side still there somewhere, re-charged and waiting?

Enough. Really, enough now. Particles and poetic thinking didn't mix with a hangover. Action was always the best way out of a mental quagmire. But the weather was making its opinions felt and a bike ride today might seem more like a swim. Max had given the odd triathlon a go, but never while quite so jaded. Getting on two wheels was forbidden, anyway, by his lovely wife, for whom he really should feel nothing but gratitude.

So, what could he do? Something to make it up to Jess, to reach across the divide and draw them back together. Buy her flowers? No. She'd consider that a needless extravagance when stocking the nursery and putting food on the table were the primary concerns.

That was it! Instead of the emptiness of a chivalrous gesture, he'd attempt something mundane yet meaningful. A domestic task to both ease her hectic agenda and display his own wide-ranging prowess as a mate. He would do something 'grown up' as penance for his piss-up. He would cook for her, lay on an intimate little feast. And not just a barbie, but something she wouldn't normally expect of him, something special they loved to indulge in together.

⫘⫘

Here she comes... Hello Bright Eyes! What, no smile for Eddie? But one for Calumn, eh? Alright then, on you go, Sweet Sister Jessica. See you round... and getting rounder by the day!

Oi, Cal, you want some of that, don't you, my friend? I could get it for you, you know. Easy. We could catch her in the chapel, alone. I could make sure she gives you what you want.

Because you do want it, don't you? Even all blown up and about to burst like that. Oi, Come on, Calumn, mate. Oi, come on, I was only joking, mate. OK. Bad joke, sorry. Not got the hang of this good disciple thing yet. Still too much of the old devil in me, I suppose, but I'm trying. Come on, Calumn, a bit of forgiveness, a bit of redemption and all that? I know... why don't we pray about it? Save this rotten old bastard from burning in hell? But then, come to think of it, maybe you'd really like to see me burn, eh? Or her? Roasting and crackling on Old Nick's spit, eh? Ever caught a whiff of human flesh on fire, Cal? It's something else, I tell you. Bacon sandwiches on steroids, mate... What was that? 'Get thee behind me?' You dirty old sod! Though I could oblige if that's what you're really after? Swipe a bit of butter from the kitchen... Oi, come on you humourless ol' git. Come back, Cal, it was only a bit of banter...

❂

Whatsapp: JessicaRabbit to MadMaximus

> Hey how you feeling, recovered from the hangover yet or still feeling sorry for yourself? On my way home but running late. Had a bit of an episode. Don't worry, none of my so-called "weirdness" just a bit of breathlessness. Stopped for tea and a pump or two after Mothercare. Intrigued by this surprise you've mentioned tho?

❂

What the hell was missing? Max tasted it again as each portion was served. The folding table was fully opened out and set with whatever mismatched pieces he could pull together. The candles were lit, a nice Burgundy had been opened to breathe, but the ambience was tainted with disappointment. And not just from Jess casually playing down another asthma attack.

Max had succeeded at everything he'd ever had any desire to do, and while under normal circumstances the culinary arts would not have been a chosen pursuit, he knew he couldn't abandon this particular mission. Duty was coming down on him and when it came to cooking, he'd just have to keep trying.

It seemed to him that as a physicist he ought to be meticulous at following a recipe, managing the measurements, the precise timings and the accurate delivery of energy, but he'd failed to factor in the alchemy of the unexpected. Something wasn't right, his process had been perfectly ordered but the tagine tasted nothing like when Jess made it in her mind-boggling world of mess. So he wasn't in the mood for her news.

'Oh no, babe, come on, you can't be serious! You promised you'd finish well before now.'

'I can't Max, not yet, not while I'm so needed. We're so understaffed. The cuts, the PTSD and post-Covid exodus, the constant staff sickness, the mental health crisis in the general population – and the better pay and hours offered by the private clinics. It's all part of the great run-down, of course, to increase privatisation, but I'm not letting them win. I'm not abandoning my patients. Conditions for them are crap enough as it is. Feels like everything there is crumbling. Anyway, it's only a couple more weeks.'

'No way. I'm sorry, Jess, but I really don't get why any of these nut jobs are more important than our baby, than *your* health! I mean, Christ, you had an asthma attack today! It's *you* that needs your head read, not them.'

'I'm fine, Max, the baby's fine. They need me.'

'I need you.'

'I know. But it'll be OK. I've still got six weeks until the due date. Plenty of time.'

TO: RevJohnEvesham@bettering.world.org
FROM: calumnberryman@patient-secure.hmhosp.org

Dear Rev John

I was hoping u might come and see me sooner. Their is something I need to talk about. I need to ask you about temptation. Their is something truly troubleing me.

Thank u. Calumn

Somewhere Else

This land is rich. The one who had led all those weak fools in this direction was maybe not so foolish after all. He had escaped, yes. He had run, yes. So impossibly fast. But he could not always run. And they have an idea now, from his terrified woman, where the runner is headed, even if she has long since become of other use. They can follow, taking their time. Meanwhile there are enough other sources of meat here, four-legged, easy to spear and no trouble to find along the way of water. This is easy going. Too easy? Some of them are getting fat. But also strong. Strong enough not only to live – but to live always? Yes, he feels it. He is beyond the reach of death now. He has become more than a man, better than any man. He has the strength of everything he has ever devoured. Maybe soon he can keep some women? Stop somewhere good. Breed. And not only for what the women can carry until both become bone. Maybe he can breed other men, like him, who can never be beaten. His own sons to guard him. Or daughters to serve him? Yes. Maybe daughters would be better than sons who might one day turn to fight him? Both or either would be better than the useful fools who follow him now. Those so easily lost along the way... or had they been taken? He must consider, are they now stalking the runner, or is the runner stalking them? If so, is he alone? Maybe another of his wandering, hopeless clan had somehow escaped unseen and they had found each other? So far, they have found only one strangled corpse from among their own number. Perhaps throttled by one of their own and perhaps he had deserved it. Maybe the others who are missing had simply been careless or stupid. Or ungrateful? Could they have slipped away to find their own path or form their own gang? But how could they find or make anything to match what he could give them, had already given them. Whatever, whoever may be pursuing them now, in body or spirit, whatever is reducing their numbers, *he* will not fall prey to it. He is too cunning, too powerful now. He will never again bow to the blow of another. Never again bear a scar like the one that serves to terrify, even if it can never bring him willing, living love. The wound that almost cleaved his head. No. He will never be hurt again, never lose anything else. He will love only those as invincible as he. Then the spirits of death will worship *him*, fear *him*. Protect him from the eyes of fire he feels upon him in his sleep, the snatched, scarce moments that never bring true rest. No matter. Soon he will need no sleep at all and will be completely free. Once he has found the runner. The man whose eyes now follow him, whether awake or in feverish dreams. The runner's mate did not wear those yellow eyes, but his children did. This man is now his last enemy, the one whose conquest will finally set him free. Yes, free even from those other distant and ancient eyes. Like the runner's but looking down from a different sky, hunting him through the blackness. Perhaps his enemy's shadow spirit? Those eyes now are the only thing he fears, the only thing he *needs* to possess. To consume. And when he is done with them he will need only what he *wants*. He will command their fire and their light. He will command the Sun. He will serve no one, fear no one. Cower before nothing living or dead. He will hunt forever, even more than his fill – and he will always tear out the first bite.

25

MANCHESTER

It had none of the attractions of that hidden gem of a church behind the shopping centre, but Jess was choosing to spend more and more time in the hospital chapel. If only to sit and be, away from the hum of the staff canteen. She was enjoying her mindfulness sessions and this seemed as good a place as any to practise.

It was clear this strange little room was an afterthought, however, not planned as part of the original building. Too big for a storeroom, too small and windowless for a workspace, though someone had made an effort. A calming baby blue on the ceiling, a soft fresco of clouds. Pleasing lighting. The small second-hand pews may well have been retrieved from an inner-city church, long since revamped into more valuable accommodation.

This particular place of worship – if one really could call it that – tried hard to cause no offence. A mock stained-glass artwork rendered on unshardable Perspex offered some pastoral scenes and a rainbow. While clumsy and naïve, it had a certain charm. The wall behind the picture needed repainting, however. It retained the dusty shadow of a cross, removed no doubt for reasons of non-denominational sensitivity.

Jess was settling into a comfortable stillness, and apart from the inward gymnastics of her growing cargo was learning to accept whatever conditions were present, and simply observe them with a kind curiosity. Until a 'condition' punched itself upwards from the primal source of her defence systems. Without turning, she knew that Eddie Briggs had entered the room. Not alone. There was another presence, powerfully eclipsed but reeking with fear – her own supply of which now surged through every neural pathway.

'Hello sweetheart. Fancy seeing you here. Fancy, indeed, eh Calumn? Ah, look at her. Lovely isn't she? Even if too bloody stuck up to turn around. We've come to pray, you see, Nurse Jessica. Me and the Apostle Pisspants here.'

'That's good,' she managed to say as she stood up, her back still turned. 'I'll leave you to it then.'

'Oh, no, don't go. Calumn's got something for you – haven't you, mate? Something very special he's been saving up.'

Sniggering was a sound more associated with schoolboys. To hear it rumble through the hard-baked tones of a grown man set up a dissonance that did nothing for Jessica's heart rate. But soon all her training was booting up and beginning to run. She pressed the silent alarm button on the pager tucked out of view in her waistband, beneath her white maternity smock. Then she twisted awkwardly, forcing an expression of placidity she hoped might fool them.

'No, really, I'm done here, it's all yours. Calumn... are you OK?'

'Yes. Thank you.'

She thought her legs might fail, but they held firm. The weight of her belly was a good excuse to hold onto the back of the pew. Could she walk? Yes. And her breathing was fine. But Briggs now filled the narrow aisle with his malevolent mass. There was no way past.

Jess felt a weakness in her bladder and the thought of such humiliation seemed worse than violence – and there would be violence because there was no way she would submit to any violation.

But then something extraordinary happened. Calumn found his voice. A new voice, not the cracked and thin delivery of his regular complaints or the hushed yet forced solemnity of quoted scripture.

'NO. NO. NO.'

Each beat burst from his throat like gunfire, shocking even Eddie Briggs it seemed, who turned slowly towards Calumn.

'You what?'

'You will not touch her!'

Calumn was trembling but steadfastly pointing at Eddie Briggs as if identifying the Devil for the Archangel Michael.

'You will submit to the glory of God and you will repent your wickedness here in His house!'

'You little weasel.'

It seemed to happen so slowly but so inevitably, the searchlight of mesmerising focus distorting her perception of time. Briggs needed no weapons beyond his own body. Each swing, each kick, each grimace of gleeful fury, each bewildered absorption of unthinkable force into Calumn's opening flesh and bone was minutely detailed. His nose burst, his lips disintegrated, his eyebrow opened, his ribs snapped. An arc of blood spurted across her smock and upwards over that lovely rainbow.

She had never seen such violence before, though she had tended to its results. How sheltered she had been. A thought that seemed out of place to her now, floating like a stray comma over the chapters of her life. But for Jess this horror was more than a repulsive spectacle. It reeked of rotting meat. It tasted metallically vile. Its sounds were a physical sensation, like a cheese grater over her skin.

She wanted to help but every instinct overrode this moral urge and she slid backwards, waiting in complete faith, despite the stubborn drag of dysregulated time, for help to arrive.

SMS message to Carl (Climbing)

> Hey Marce, great news that you'll be in town! Hope your meetings at the Salford Beeb go well. Do you have time to come out to Jodrell Bank? Be happy to give you a tour. Otherwise I could meet you near the train station for a quick bite / coffee / early beer?

> Have bike will travel!

> Let me know and I'll make it happen.

> No worries if not, but it would be great to see you. There's much to talk about and it's really cool that we're on the same page, about so many things! Anyway gotta go, incoming call from Jess's work phone, talk soon…
> Max

⚕

Jess walked beside the gurney to the emergency room, holding Calumn's hand, reassuring him. She stayed as they cut away his grey tracksuit to examine the full extent of the damage from the beating.

The sight of his thickened, rippling, devastated skin was unsettling. She knew that Calumn had burns, it was in his notes, but to see them stretch over his stomach, disappear under the hospital issue underpants and emerge again over his upper thighs, brought home the reality of a lifetime of suffering. A childhood scalding. It was unclear whether this had been deliberate or accidental, he had always refused to discuss the scars, or their history, with anyone.

Then she understood that Calumn did not want her to 'see him'. Certainly not the scars that would grant her a conduit to his soul. She decided to respect his privacy, to spare him her pity and the deeper gaze of her new gift, so she acquiesced to the demands to attend her own medical checks, and then talk to the police about the assault.

Before accompanying Calumn to the infirmary, Jess had asked the duty manager not to call Max, saying she would do so when ready – but in the confusion someone had called him anyway and he'd turned up in a wild panic. When she left the infirmary, she was told that her 'anxious' husband was waiting for her in the office. Knowing she could not avoid him, knowing he would drag her home as soon as he could, knowing that the board would now bring forward her maternity leave, Jess sent a message that she would see Max as soon as she could – knowing she would also return to Calumn as soon as she could.

After getting the physical all-clear, and after her interview with the police – where she'd found herself oddly moved that they were taking this as seriously as any other assault upon the 'innocent' – Jess found, and then left, a bewildered and agitated Max alone in a corridor under a flickering light, with a few firm assurances that she was fine. She instructed him to find her coat to cover up the blood on her smock, convincing him none of it was hers. She asked him to wait in the empty canteen, to get her a coffee she knew would go cold, telling him she needed one more quick check on her broken patient, her brave saviour, but after that she would be good as gold. She promised.

Now, at Calumn's bedside once more, holding his one undamaged hand, she felt a raw and welling rage. With Briggs, yes, but also with herself, with the board, and even Calumn, whom she could see was shutting down again, and not only from the pain medication he'd been administered after the emergency examinations.

The bible he must have asked for, which was now resting like a breastplate on his chest, neither offended her nor gave him the protection he imagined from her insights. It was his likely escape back into misplaced piety that frustrated her, the excuse this disaster might give him to retreat even further. The last thing Calumn needed was confirmation of his martyrdom.

None of this should have happened, of course. Another failure that would put the unit under the spotlight. But for all Jess's unease about the problems here – the underfunding and staffing crises, the effectiveness of some of the therapies – she had to believe it was better than many alternatives and almost everything that had come before in the history of secure psychiatric care. That long slow road of 'mad doctoring', from the sickening public displays of the insane to the enlightened reforms of the Quakers. At least they were trying, even if the media, public and politicians had little sympathy for, or faith in, their efforts. This time, though, they really had failed their charges. Both Briggs and Calumn.

Jess was also smarting from the subtle 'I told you so' and the festering fury wrapped up as love in the desperate, suffocating hug her husband had imposed when she'd found him pacing the corridor outside the duty office. Max had never wanted her to work here. He'd always believed there were real and present dangers. Why couldn't she have signed on – like so many of her former colleagues – at some cosy, private facility for the wealthy depressed or addicted?

Ah, but that would have been too easy for Saint Jessica Wallace, not what she had trained for, not the most challenging use of her skills. And her husband's anger could not help her, it could only soothe and manage his own feelings of somehow failing her. Weirdly, his vexation tasted to her more like guilt, but what could Max be feeling guilty about? Jess was all too aware of her own stubborn streak and she accepted every decision, and its consequences, as her own. Her husband's clench-fisted yet impotent fury – and whatever else was lurking beneath that – was not helping.

Jess realised that her own rage wasn't of much use either, so let it weaken to sadness. Calumn did not deserve any of this but shutting down from her and his future carers could not help him to heal. She whispered his name, testing his resolve. He was out, or pretending to be. Comfortably numb at the very least, she hoped. But the swelling over his eyes was vivid and his nose was nastily bulged and twisted. His jaw needed to be wired and a couple of teeth had gone, but that was no great loss in Calumn's case. Perhaps now he might agree to some repair work.

The nebula around him – sometimes so volatile, sometimes so dense – was fading and streaked with rusty silt. Jess saw the undulating thread running between them, more strongly than ever, and knew that despite his attempts to disconnect, Calumn needed to draw from it, however uncomfortable and draining that had always been for her.

Briggs should never have been allowed back into the general population, should never have been left alone with Calumn, should never have been allowed out of sight. She hated being proved right in this way, but at least now he wouldn't be let loose into the wider world. They would probably transfer him to Broadmoor.

Jess found herself forming a silent prayer for him. He was beyond their current ability to cure, but she detected buried deep inside him the tiniest spark, an untouchable light. He was surely not beyond the help of a greater power, of forgiveness. Even if he had exploited such hopes so horribly by lulling his new 'friend' into the belief that his efforts at conversion might bear genuine spiritual fruit.

Poor Calumn. Poor holy fool. But then a man such as he would always be marked out for mistreatment. He might as well have had 'victim' tattooed on his forehead. The omega of the pack, always the one upon whom those frustrated by their own bad fortune would find a way to relieve it.

He needed X-rays but it was suspected his left arm was fractured, along with several ribs. Jess had seen, when they'd cut his clothing away, the concave indentation of his chest, another condition of his particular expression of Marfan syndrome. Calumn had suffered enough in life – this was too much. They'd also have to monitor him for pneumonia and a risk of peritonitis, even possible kidney damage from some severe blows to the back, which would be devastating to a diabetic. She prayed this would not be the case, feeling an even greater connection to him now, with her own experience of the condition.

He showed signs of coming around now and Jess had to pull his searching hand away from the tubes.

'Calumn... Calumn, it's Jessica. It's OK, you're in the infirmary, please just relax.'

'Jessica.'

She knew that was what he was trying to say, even if he couldn't form the correct sounds through his re-arranged oral cavity.

'Yes, it's me. Calumn, I've come to say thank you. What you did was so brave. I will never forget it. But I've also come to say goodbye, for now at least. Everyone has insisted after what's happened that I take my maternity leave from tomorrow. I'm so sorry. But I will stay in touch. I promise. I'll come and visit whenever I can.'

⫘

TO: SisterJessicaWallace@staff-secure.hmhosp.org
FROM: RevJohnEvesham@bettering.world.org

Dear Jessica

I tried to call you, but obviously you are needed on other calls! Thanks for your note, I am horrified to hear of what has happened. I know you tell me you're ok but surely some trauma will need attending to? It is quite right that you have been told to take your maternity leave early. I regret that I won't see you at the hospital but I will indeed come to visit Calumn as soon as I can. I will be in touch again shortly but please keep me updated about the last weeks of your pregnancy, the baby, and your thoughts about the baptism, etc. And if you need some counselling or a willing set of ears, please know that I am entirely at your disposal.

Yours, John

26

HERE AND THERE

TO: revjohnevesham@bettering.world.org
FROM: dreloisekluft@children.of.sarah.org

Dear John,

I hope you're well?

I write this in the departure lounge, with an unreliable wifi connection and unsure of my exact take-off time as it's a private charter (I know!). You may be relieved to hear that I'm on my way home. My colleague, KC, has already hopped on a red-eye back across the ocean. This transition feels decidedly strange, much as it has been longed for.

I cannot give you any details, but recently I saw a man change before my eyes (at least in terms of who he might "normally" be, or who he might ever have imagined himself to be.) While he is now, happily, fully recovered, the experience was transformative, both for observer and observed.

One day, perhaps soon, I will be able to tell you in person about where I've been and what I've been doing. Though, I've also really enjoyed this process of writing to you, it's taken our friendship to a new level, I feel?

Which brings me to the main reason for this particular epistle. Recent events have inspired me to continue our on/off conversation about the notion of selfhood and the idea, in particular, that there's no such thing as a "fixed" self. Can there ever be a fully knowable or realisable sense of personhood? Surely, we are more of a "process" than anything?

Whatever we think of as our self is merely the transient and variable combination of numerous factors and fabrications? From our particular set of conditions to our perception of experience, to the processing of information, to our own thoughts, emotions or reactivity… even down to the enzymes and proteins within our cells and the particles passing through us every millisecond.

We exchange gases every time we breathe and chemical information every time we eat. We undergo constant renewal, growth and decay. Perhaps one aspect of who we are is more fixed than others, but even our DNA can naturally alter - at least in the way it expresses and functions. Our brains are fantastically plastic, and both our memories and values are unreliable, filtered as they are through perception and prejudice. Everything moves through some kind of porous membrane, whether liquid or gas, microbe or molecule, information or imagination.

When I think about what formed me and what made me choose what I *believe* I have chosen, when I consider why I am such a perfectionist - hardest of all on myself - it feels like such a tangled web of pathways and influences. Much of it spun from the urge to emulate my parents. But how could I ever have been the best of *both* of them? How could I ever match a relationship that looked so good from the outside, an apparent rock of security, but which *must* have been illusory to some extent? Something Darius often tried to tell me, even if I refused to believe him.

There's so much personal history to choose from in this quest to root out my perfectionism, but one pivotal childhood moment stands out, something I was reminded about by an old photograph not so long ago. Actually, it's a scene you might well understand.

A memory of boiling-hot old "Bombay" (forgive the colonialism but that's how memory has etched Mumbai for me) and of a tiny child balanced precariously in a chair that was fixed to a long pole by her father - if that's who he was. A kind of performative begging so profoundly shocking, even through the fog of jet lag, to my six-year-old self.

My mother tried to explain the act and the desperation behind it, but what she could not have intended - and what I carried away from that experience like some crusted, malformed kernel deep within the ground of my being - was *guilt*.

Why should *I* be so lucky, so blessed? Why should I have such protective love from two privileged parents? Why should I be free to go to school, to have a career, to choose my own path or the people I walked with along it? Surely it is imperative that I make the absolute most of such good fortune? I must not fail, must not err, must not be lazy or take anything for granted, must not waste a moment's time or a single useful thought or idea. I must always be of use, of *service*. I must have a purpose and strive relentlessly to fulfil it.

I think a part of me is still up there, strapped into a cut-off baby chair with that poor little girl. I sit holding her hand as she wails in terror and resentment. I wipe her snuffling nose with my clean cotton sleeve because her own mismatched clothes are filthy. I tell her I will do what I can. I will take on some suffering on her behalf. I will not let her or myself down - in life, in love, in work, in body. I will earn my place and freedom on the pavement below her instead of up on that pole, balanced upon the palms, the head, the back and shoulders of a haunted, hungry man.

How could I have known that I had no business even attempting such perfection - or demanding it of others as apparently blessed as I? Impossible in a member of my species and in a physical world so precious and yet so fragile, constantly rediscovering its own equilibrium and experimenting with itself! That being the "saviour" was not my role, not needed, at least not in the way many of us carrying the guilt of imperialism had assumed. That all I had to do was get out of my own - and others' - way.

I do so want to forgive myself, John. And everyone and everything! I want to live without resentment for all the inevitable let-downs and disappointments, and anger with my parents for teaching me respect for "proven facts" but keeping me ignorant of certain emotional truths.

What's that saying you once shared? "Holding onto anger is like holding a hot coal in your hands, waiting for the opportunity to throw it at the other person."

I also want to cast off the notion that I'm only worth loving if I'm loved by someone whom I also deem "worthy" - whatever my conditioned perception of that worth may be. God, how much wreckage that car-crash of a belief has caused!

But I'm not alone, of course, and I suppose we just have to keep starting again from wherever we are? As challenging as it is to not get wrapped up in complex and embellished narratives. And we do love to tell ourselves stories, don't we, John? Making ourselves either the heroes or the villains. All too often the villain, I imagine, or at least worthy of a lion's share of the blame.

Ooops connection dropped out. As did my train of thought amid the swearing! So many things drop out, don't they? I think that's part of the problem. After my parents died, and after the split with Darius and other reversals, I felt so utterly *abandoned*. Gosh. That's a big thing for me to say, or rather write, out loud.

There was something else I wanted to say, but it's gone for now. Bloody bandwidth. There's never enough of it, is there? What slaves to tech we have all become!

I do worry though. I mean, speaking of a sense of self, what would happen to the generations that we've sacrificed to the overlords of the internet if it all went down? These wonderful yet weary young people, many of whom seem to know themselves only through the wax and wane of groupthink, or only recognise themselves in a filtered selfie, or only value a memory or experience if it has been digitally embalmed. How would they then compose themselves or their lives? With remarkable human adaptability no doubt, but a painful process nonetheless.

It seems I too have been writing a new narrative for my own life recently, even if the muses keep throwing curve balls my way. Mount Olympians hurling down thunderbolts, laughing at our folly. But how much

I need to laugh again, John! I'm so looking forward
to seeing Tom. And hopefully we can all meet up again
someday soon, my very dear friend?

There's my call, got to dash, E xxx

He breathes, but is broken beyond her skills to mend. Her grandson had helped bear this hero home on a bed of crossed spears. The Warrior was determined to share in that honour, regardless of his own wounds. Many others are limping back now who need her attention, but she has trained the rest of her family well enough. The Tall Girl's mother takes charge, always keen to be of use, always needing to redeem herself in some way for that dreadful day in the long grass.

Salves and splints and fresh skins are applied, numbing infusions administered. Parched mouths and horrified hearts will be well nourished by the gratitude of the clan. *All of them.* They have lost not a single one who stayed behind to await an unknowable fate and – provided all other wounds heal well enough – only two members of the group she'd sent to spring the trap in the valley have been sacrificed. One of those now lies in her arms.

Do those fire-lit eyes recognise her? They stare, but not in despair. Not like the day she first encountered them. Can he feel the pain? The Old Woman knows that sometimes, when injury is too great, the body discovers a river of hidden mercy and surrenders quietly to the coming peace.

As she looks into his eyes, she is lifted to borrow the eyes of a bird circling far above them. The eyes of this hopeful, scavenger bird are now flying into yesterday, far above the canyon. She sees The Outsider below her now, running, falling, rising, running again. And now she feels that strain within her own body. Feels each wound as it is delivered.

No. It is too much. She hears a roaring and a screaming. No, she cannot carry this kind of becoming, not today. Not while also holding the last shreds of his life. She will revisit these sensations another time, to honour him. But this story is too sharp to bear right now, as sharp as the spear which had crippled him.

There will be many different stories of this day, from many points of view. Her grandson shares his own account with her now, as his cousin dabs at the livid claw marks across his back and something shivers in the girl from a childhood memory. Can the Tall Girl remember the furious, frustrated paws that killed her grandfather while he shielded a much easier prey?

But the young Warrior distracts them both from such thoughts with his witness to fresher events. As he talks, The Old Woman wonders if he soon might take her place as the tribe's teller of tales. He has learned well at her feet.

The Warrior explains how he, The Scout – and The Tracker, the brother she'd easily found again as he shadowed the gang along a forested riverbank – had each played their parts. How they had taken first blood in the battle that ultimately followed, quietly and unseen, by ambushing one of their enemies in the night, with a silent slice across the throat. This task had been simpler than anticipated. The gang they were tracking had left the riverbank to cut across more open ground. From a hidden vantage point above the wind-sheltered dip, where these marauders were taking their rest, the three had watched as one of their quarry chose some thick bushes behind which to take his relief.

When he was done, the silent spies crept around and then behind those very bushes to use them as their own cover – upwind of the gang and further aided by a covering stink and the rustle of dung beetles – trusting that another mindless brute would be lazy enough to follow where one of his herd had gone before.

They did not have to wait long. The deed was easily done but before they could drag the dying man away, they were almost discovered by the first who had chosen these bushes, when he realised his companion had not yet returned. As that member of the gang came back to search, The Tracker instructed his sister and The Warrior to move on swiftly with the warm, blood-drenched corpse shouldered between them, while he stayed behind to take care of the dead man's friend before he could raise the alarm.

The others argued with him, warning The Tracker that finishing this one would not be so straightforward. The first had been easy, with the combination of knees pressing on the victim's back, a hand across the mouth and a stealthy slice across his throat while he was in the midst of his squat. But that well-rehearsed action would be impossible this time. This fellow had already taken his relief, was on the alert and remained upright and forward-facing, with two arms free to fight. What's more, though The Scout's brother would have the advantage of surprise, he would be alone.

The Tracker insisted. He had picked off a few others from the gang on his own before his sister had found him. A fiercely tightened bow string around the neck should both stop the man's mouth and distract those arms and hands, silencing him into his final breath.

A tactic achieved, but at a devastating cost. When The Tracker caught up with them, they saw with horror the deep wound he'd taken to the stomach, an injury bound to slowly poison and drain him. The remaining able-bodied pair – one fast and agile but also slender and light – would be unable to carry between them both an injured man *and* the vital bait, which was the very purpose of their mission.

They limped on even so, and as morning came, they knew the trail of blood would lead the gang towards both a corpse in the bushes and the knowledge that another of their number was missing. The Tracker insisted on choosing a different path, insisted it was the only way. He would stay behind once more and wait alone, but this time out in the open on a misdirecting trail, to both distract and delay the oncoming threat.

He assured his sister and The Warrior that these dead-hearted men would get nothing from him, and not only through his determination. The Old Woman had shared among all the adults of the clan a parting gift. Tied carefully into bladders, strung tightly to their plaited belts, a particular dried fungus for each to chew should their capture by the enemy seem inevitable. Something that would still their mouths, their fears, and – in good time – their hearts.

At first his sister could not accept his choice. But soon she realised it was indeed the only way. To make certain this sacrifice would work as it should, The Scout had given her brother half of her own supply of the fungus and half from The Warrior, knowing that to argue further against his heroic decision was a waste of breath.

She then untangled her boning flint from its place in her own hair and used it to cut loose one of her brother's tight, short braids. The braid that had been wound through with shiny green beetle shells collected for him by his lover.

Brother and sister clasped hands for a moment and touched foreheads before she dragged herself away, almost falling as one knee buckled beneath her. But then she moved on without looking back. She dared not look back for both their sakes. She told The Warrior there would be time enough to mourn her brother, to praise him in song, but only if the remaining pair could make up the time and distance they needed now.

As she listens to this tale, The Old Woman understands that she must find a way to give back to this girl some of the time her terrible loss had saved. To give her as much quiet care as she might accept, for such unseen scars were often the most difficult to bear.

Her grandson continues his story. Onwards, over the cliffs above the canyon, they had laboured, no weight to carry like a dead weight. First, however, they had smothered their skin with the mixture The Old Woman had supplied to all except The Outsider, the living bait who must be easily found. This thick and tarry mud mix would not dry on the skins of those in hiding and should disguise both the visibility of their flesh and its signal upon the air.

This extra touch of cunning was a great relief to the pair, knowing they would have little energy to spare if the yellow beasts caught *their* scent too and decided those still walking would be fresher meat than the gift they'd brought to offer them. At last, the two had found a good place from which to pitch the cadaver, down to where the beasts might easily find and accept such an easy meal.

They took no rest, but moved back along the bluff once more, retracing their steps to hide in a cut within the rocks, a shelf The Scout had spotted earlier near the mouth of the canyon. Each took watches through the night, spears ready, lungs and legs ready in case the gang chose not to take this tempting yet terrible path – or found a way to escape it in time.

By daybreak the pair knew the plan was unfolding as it should. The body was gone, dragged to some chosen place to be enjoyed at leisure.

Then they saw The Outsider, running. He and his small group of guardians must have found the trail in time, ahead of the gang, and positioned The Outsider as planned, alone and in the open, within eventual sight of the enemy.

And he had done as he had promised. He let them see and recognise him, then led them on. How he ran! The Scout had been amazed by how The Outsider could match even her speed, despite his age. And yet, they could see that he was tiring, slowing.

The watchers heard the oncoming enemy before they saw them. Screeching like the horned owl, wailing like she-wolves in heat. As they came into view they leapt and danced, frenzied in their will to feed. Foolish in their invitation to other predators, with their foul noise and stinking sweat. Deeper into the narrowing valley they came.

Then a slingshot found its aim, dislocating the shoulder of The Outsider as he scrambled ahead of them. He stumbled but ran on. Then a spear grazed his thigh, taking a slice of muscle with it, but he limped forward. Then another, smaller spear pierced his side. He fell but did not yet seem finished. He forced himself up, moved on.

Not yet! It was not yet time for those waiting at the other end of the canyon to come to his aid. Neither must the pair hiding at its beginning alert the gang to danger by picking them off with well-aimed arrows from The Scout's lethal bow. The great yellow beasts must do their work first.

At last, a different kind of scream. One of terror, not gleeful appetite. And another. Great confusion now as the dust rose from too many places, rockfalls scattering as the four-legged creatures left their stalking places and darted low, sleek and rippling with power towards their targets. The sounds of killing by tooth and claw, of bone breaking as it was rolled between mighty jaws. Geysers of blood spouting from ripped-open necks.

But what of The Outsider? It seemed he had struggled on, but he was out of their sightline by now. They could not know if he, too, was part of the feast. They hoped that even if any of the enemy had escaped this first rush of the beasts and continued to chase after him, The Outsider would soon be of no interest to them, while they ran for whatever was left of their own worthless lives.

The Warrior told his audience how he and The Scout noticed a handful of the gang turning to race out of the carnage and back towards the wider entrance of the valley from where they had come. So the pair broke cover and clambered down to meet them, two against four, but with the advantage of ready weapons, steady limbs and surprise. The Scout felled two in quick succession with the bow skills first brought to their tribe by The Old Woman's mother.

Meanwhile The Stranger's great-grandson took out another with his spear and then fell into close combat with the last of the would-be escapees, a huge and fearsome fellow with a vicious old battle scar across his head which, somehow, had not taken his life when the wound was delivered.

Yes, thinks The Old Woman, but it had long since taken his soul. A body driven only by the shadow she has been hunting in her fractured sleep, all these endless and terrible nights. She shivers, knowing the peril her grandson had faced.

Nevertheless, as The Warrior tells her now, he had the best of this man. Especially when his adversary had looked into his flaming eyes with a shocked and horrified kind of recognition. Until one of the yellow beasts chasing the fleeing group of four caught up with them and reared to tentatively swipe and slash at The Warrior's shoulders, unsure which half of this writhing new two-backed creature to strike first. But soon an arrow found the beast's neck and it yelped back towards its own kind again.

Another arrow from The Scout found the back of the scarred man as he ran away in white-eyed terror. He fell, cried in disbelief, scrabbled in the dirt and tried to crawl away. Until The Warrior's recovered spear opened up his ribs and found the depths of his empty heart.

Bloody and exhausted, her grandson had clambered back to high ground and along the upper edge of the canyon, aided by The Scout. Only once they found the rest of their party did they learn the full outcome of the battle. The beasts, it seemed, had killed their fill. The Outsider had made it as far as an oncoming rush from his adopted clan when the remnants of the fleeing enemy were felled by those ready and waiting hands. Hands which now took up their mortally wounded companion and carried him, in hope of a miracle, back to the mother of the tribe.

But there would be no miracle. The Old Woman understood that whoever was to be saved must also be hungry for life and must have more to offer it in return. The man in her arms was done. He was hungry now only for rest, the true rest of atonement. And he would find it. She smiled for him, knowing it could not be returned. Those eyes of sunset dimmed silently into night as she kept her watch, knowing many other such eyes would sparkle and widen to hear stories of this man. And that they would keep their sparkle, for a while at least, because of him.

⁂

Tom had wanted to drive in from the farm to meet her at the private airfield, but as much as Eloise had fantasised about that scene, and its rapture of relief, she's had to deny him. Their reunion will have to wait.

She has a secure delivery to make first. A tiny, sealed chiller strapped to her wrist – a sample of the virus and a sample of the DNA sequence able to fight it. This ancient thing and this new way of defeating it. She's being met by a medical security team and whisked to the lab under flashing yellow lights.

It's the smoothest landing she's ever experienced. While she's always frowned upon the indulgence of private air travel (despite the occasional privilege of 'turning left' when she was with Darius) she is disturbed by how easily she could become accustomed to its luxury.

A hushed and rushed escort through immigration makes her feel even more rarefied, giving her a sense of how the rich and famous become so swaddled against reality, so attached to their imagined superiority. She soon snaps out of it. Recalling those oddly stretched and hidden skulls in the classical *momento mori* paintings that warn against vanity, Eloise is haunted by the ever-present death's head she is battling to keep at bay.

There is so much work still to do. To understand exactly which proteins, molecules or antibodies the 'Sarah sequence' is encoding and expressing in order to fight both the infection and its effects, to learn how these defend against the ravages of the virus. Once identified, could they be replicated and delivered successfully as targeted therapy, eliminating the need to splice in the DNA sequence itself? How long might such treatments take to roll out widely and affordably, if needed? And would this only ever be a temporary rebuff against a virus that might become endemic? Would more permanent genetic protection always be preferable?

Either way, they would have to work fast and freely – and for far longer – than standard medicine, public or privately funded, had done so far against Covid. They could not rely solely on vaccines, if ever successfully developed, to keep pace on a wing and a prayer... Or hope that profit-driven pharma would develop and share both acute *and* post-acute treatments for its untold damage, or that these would be made widely and affordably available. Though the big players would reap the rewards, either way. A population with multiple functional illnesses was good for *some* businesses, after all.

No, as ever for Eloise, *prevention* must prevail – and must be many-handed, much like a favourite goddess in her pantheon of unbelief.

27

MANCHESTER

'Oh Max, no! Not now... have you been filming me while I was sleeping? You bastard.'

The video function on his phone was now an essential tool of impending fatherhood, and one part he could play that gave him some focus. But Jess had never volunteered to be his leading lady. She did not enjoy having her image immortalised and it was all becoming a bit intrusive and irritating. Especially now she'd finished work and had so much time on her hands. Max followed her everywhere – the minutiae of her life as lived through a lens.

'What time is it anyway?' she asked.

'Eight. I'm off. Got an early tutorial, then that meeting I mentioned. Will you be OK? I'll keep my phone on.'

'Yes, of course. Go on, off you go.'

'What are you up to today?'

'I'm catching up with Lisa for a coffee, then she's coming to the prenatal class with me. The one you can't make because of this very important and mysterious meeting? It is quite handy though, I suppose, having a maternity nurse for a mate. Then I'm hoping for a swim after the class and maybe some shopping, if I can bear it. But I also need to get back and get ready for Manda's visit tomorrow.'

'Oh yeah. When's she getting here?' Max was perhaps a bit too upbeat about the reminder of Manda's arrival, apparently glad not to be interrogated, or worse, passively-aggressively punished for skipping the prenatal class.

'Not sure exactly, but I know she's on an early train.'

'OK. See you later. Kiss me.'

'Well, I would if you'd put the bloody phone down!'

'Maximus!'

The knot of guilt tightened. Marcy had just greeted him with Jessica's favourite online hail.

'Hey, how ya' going' Marce? You're looking well!'

'Why thank you, you bloody charmer. You too.'

'Ah, you know, I do my best. How's your day gone?'

'Good, yeah. Plenty brewing. Very exciting.'

'Can I get you anything from the bar?'

'No thanks. Look, it's not that long before our train...'

('our' train?)

'...but it's really good to catch up. First let me reassure you. Sorry I couldn't make it out to the array today, but the funding cut doesn't have to mean that *you* are cut. You know that I think you've got something, Max, and I'd really love to somehow still have your special touch in unravelling the more complex stuff. Yes, it would be a shame if we can't make a connection to the work being done at your faculty, or to film at the Lovell, but the thing is, you also bring a certain international appeal... and you're happy to travel, right?'

(Tell her about Jess, tell her about the baby.)

'Yeah, sure, love it. No worries. Anytime, anyplace, anywhere!'

'Good, good. Oh, Gina, hi love...'

(That was no colleague-style kiss. That was a full-on pash.)

'Max, this is my partner, Gina. Get what you need, love?'

'Oh hi, Max! I've heard so much about *you*! Yeah, thanks, babe. All sorted.'

(Gina, eh. Bloody gorgeous. Now there was some tough competition for Marcy's attention.)

If he wanted to compete – which, of course, he didn't. Despite his powerful inklings about Marcy's sexual fluidity.

(Tell Marcy about Jess, about the baby. Just tell her.)

'So, Marce, when do you think you'll start filming?'

Home again, and after watching what she could of the sunset from the patio and resisting the evening chill, Jess was tired. It had been a good day. Knowing it might be one of the last she enjoyed with the luxury of so much leisure time and no Max to entertain, she'd been determined to make the most of it. The prenatal class and a coffee with Lisa, then a swim – so wonderful to surrender her bulk to the water and feel like her old self again, if only for a few moments – and then a wander around an overly air-conditioned mall.

Normally, Jess hated shopping, but it was an increasing necessity with the baby due in less than a month. She felt that every trip was another compromise of conscience, another auction of small sections of her soul. There was always just *too much* choice, an obscenity of choice. And even the most basic of comforts came at a price. After watching a documentary on the oil industry, Jess worried that every time she turned on a light switch someone somewhere might have killed or died to power it. Or that her small act of illumination might be enough to trigger another climate tipping point. Shopping for herself left a sour aftertaste and she felt left behind by fashion, offended by the throw-away, season-by-season tat, all destined ultimately for the landfill.

But today was different. She'd stocked up on some protein snacks and deli treats, a few more baby essentials, and then by chance had found the perfect gift for Max's birthday. A pocket-size replica of a 16th century astrolabe. He could carry it with him on his climbing or documentary-making or other adventures, so he could measure the celestial movements of any days without her. She would always be with him as he marked that time.

When Jess got home she was delighted to find that Max had cooked again. Shepherd's pie this time. He was getting better, even if digesting it was a challenge. He'd even made concessions to her 'alternative' tendencies and had the oil diffuser running, with her favourite rosemary fragrance misting the air. But Max was wine-woozy all too soon and crashed out before her, while she waited for the food to go down.

The fever came on so suddenly. Hot then cold then hot. The restriction in her chest, the scratchy inability to swallow her raspberry tea. The light from her phone became painful to her eyes and an ache was moving up and down through every bone. Then a rough rash sprang up over her chest and arms. She didn't want to think about what it could be other than tiredness, or maybe something in the meal? Surely just tiredness. She'd been through a lot lately.

She went to bed with some paracetamol, hoping to sleep it off, hoping the air purifiers they'd been running since her asthma flare ups might somehow help. But she couldn't sleep. Everything shifted when she tried to stand up and go to the bathroom. Jess now understood this was serious. She woke Max, put on a well-fitting respirator mask, made him wear his, sanitised while he called an Uber.

SMS to John Evesham, from Jessica Wallace:

> Hey Mate, not Jess here actually, it's Max on her phone. Sorry to bother you, not sure whether you keep your phone on at night, but Jess asked me to text. We're at the hospital cos she's feeling a bit crook. Not sure what it is but I'm sure she'll be right. Raging fever, but. Not like her to whinge about anything, she's a real stoic, so I am concerned. She might be a bit delirious too because she asked me to ask you to pray! Made me promise. So, I've asked. Never break a promise to the woman you love! Not a preggo one anyway. Righto. Cheers mate. Gotta go. I'll keep you posted.

'What is it?'

Lisa looked at him with the kind of anxiety he was not prepared to recognise.

'We think it's a particularly virulent flu virus, or something like that. Possibly something new. She's tested negative for Covid. It looks in some ways like meningitis, but we don't think it is. We've had a couple of cases like it in the last few days, a range of symptoms, but nothing that's become quite so severe, quite so quickly, apart from one older man. She's so vulnerable, you see, being pregnant – and with the gestational diabetes. Not to mention the asthma flare ups. The vaccinations she's had, as good as the new nasal ones are, probably won't have protected her against this. And she seems to be developing pneumonia now...'

'But she's going to be alright?'

'I don't know, Max. We don't know.'

'*What?* But she's strong and you can treat her. Right?'

'We've got her on antibiotics in case of secondary infections, but there aren't many antivirals approved for pregnancy and we don't know if anything will be effective against this. Max, I'm sorry, I feel like it's my fault. I might have been the carrier, though I've had no symptoms. I should never have...'

Max had failed to register the other masked person who'd walked into the blue-rinsed waiting room. The claustrophobic cube in which he had been asked to remain alone and to keep his own mask on. He'd called Lisa for back up, even so, knew she was on a night shift and would already be at the hospital.

'Thank you, Nurse, that'll be all. You need to quarantine too now. Hello, Mr Michaelson, I'm Dr Chan. I'm sorry to tell you, but your wife's temperature is dangerously high. She's hypoxic and some of her internal organs are struggling, shutting down. She's also losing clear mental capacity. The foetal heart monitor is showing that the baby is now also in some distress. Mr Michaelson, do you have anyone else you can call to come and be with you right now? Someone who would also be able and prepared to quarantine if needed? We may need to make a very difficult decision.'

'*What...* what are you saying?

'Greg, mate.'

'Max, how is she? How are you?'

'Yeah, yeah, thanks, I'm holding up... Look big favour – can you get to the station to pick up Manda and bring her straight to the hospital?

'Of course. Yes, of course. On my way. Anything else?'

'No thanks, not yet, just take care of Manda, eh? Good ol' Rev John is on his way up from London and changing trains to meet Jess's mum. Kind of him. Oh Christ, Christ, Christ. Don't tell Manda yet, mate, but it's bad. I can't believe it, but it's bad.'

'Oh God. OK. Look, try not to worry too much. She's a fighter, Max. She's in good hands. It'll be OK. We'll get there as soon as we can. OK?'

'Yeah, yeah, thanks mate, thanks.'

He waits. He waits some more, holding his impotent phone. But suddenly there is no time to consult anyone else. They are on their way, but now the decision is his alone. *The baby. The baby. Jess. Jess. What would she do, what would she want?* He knows, of course. He doesn't want to know, but he knows. They tell him now that he could lose them both if they don't act soon. *Jess. The baby. Both. Neither. Fuck everything.*

How can this be his choice? He tells them to go ahead. Wide blue eyes pleading for absolution. For confirmation. For deliverance. The day is rising, piercing orange through the gaps in the buildings, through the gaps in the blinds.

It takes a little over eight minutes for the light of the sun to reach the earth.

Eight minutes.

The time it takes to perform the emergency caesarean that plucks their tiny daughter out into its glaring luminosity as, for all their frantic efforts, Jessica's life ebbs quietly away.

The 'family room' is more private, more beige, more 'comfortable' than the little blue cube on the ward, even if everyone must be masked and remain within in its confines. But there is no comfort here. Only devastation.

Manda, red-eyed and white-faced, straight off the train, held together on the maroon two-seater sofa by Greg, who is in no better shape himself. John Evesham, somehow here from London, so quickly, despite his pit stop to accompany Mrs Wallace. He sits still and silent, except for a tremor escaping to the milky surface of his tea.

Her mother there beside him. Max cannot look at her.

He is tumbling over the event horizon, falling to a singularity he cannot withstand. A collapsing of space, beyond understanding, beyond here, beyond now, without light, without meaning. His beloved Jess is gone from him, into a place he cannot accept. So dense, so small, so infinitely overwhelming.

No. Some say it is the act of seeing something, of observing something that makes it real. If I refuse to see this, then it cannot be. You were brought into being for me and in all this great universe, we found each other. You cannot leave me now.

You used to say nature is wiser than we are. But this is a bankrupt concept. Nature is a callous bitch who cares nothing for the suffering of the individual, only for her precious equilibrium. A communist tyrant wielding her appalling power over the collective. There is no truth in this.

There is only you. Only this moment.

Live. Wake. Be with me again.

Are you swimming now? Is that where you are? In the place you loved the most, head underwater, sliding weightless through the blue. Where are you now, my love, where can I find you?

⫘⫘⫘

'Max.'

It is her voice, but he cannot see her. The image is blurred, it's dark, she never really knew how to take a simple selfie, never mind a video.

'Max. Oh bollocks, oh wait. OK. Max, I wanted to make my own movie. One where I'm not annoyed with you. Not grumpy about lugging my bulk around. Just a quiet moment to tell you that I love you. More and more each day. And this, this darling bump, how I love our child and can't wait to meet the little person we've made. So this is a surprise on your phone, for you to find in your library or the cloud, or wherever. You drive me crazy sometimes but I've never been anything but crazy in love with you. Never could be. From the first time you smiled at me, helping me up out of the surf. It could never have been anyone but you. Anything but us. I have no idea how I got so lucky, you seem way out of my league sometimes... And yet I know that you love me, I feel it so deeply even when we disagree. Maybe you even love me too much? But neither of us will live forever, Max, machine-enhancements, gene-hacking or no. One of us, one day, will have to let the other go. Impermanence. I'm learning all about that in my meditation studies. I'm not afraid of death, my love. I never have been. I've seen plenty of it as a nurse and it can be truly terrible, but far worse is to give in to a kind of living death. Like my mother. Neither of us must ever do that. We must make the most of every moment, every part of ourselves, our lives, every moment with our child. Promise? Well, it's late and you're already in bed. I'm coming to join you soon. I'll see you in the morning. My darling. My darling, Max.'

She blows him a kiss. Then she is gone. Again.

They cannot put her to rest until an autopsy has been performed. Until they have all safely passed a fourteen-day quarantine. Jess waits now in the limbo of the coroner's care. They are told nothing, the infection that ripped her from them remains a mystery, but there is something frustratingly peculiar about it all.

She would have wanted organ donation, he tells them that, knowing whatever killed her now rules her out. They say nothing. The quarantine means he can watch his daughter, wriggling calmly in her incubator, only from a screen. He cannot touch her, cannot hold her. But perhaps this distance is what he needs, what they both need. She does not deserve to sense even a whisper of his overwhelming rage.

She has no name yet. He has no idea what to name her. He knows that he loves her. But he cannot reach her yet. Grief ensnares him like brambles, unfurling from the darkest soil. He has no doubt that he loves her and that he can love her enough for both of them. But not yet. Not yet. He's not ready to lay down under that avalanche.

They each remain well, in body at least, and she grows by the day, only three weeks too soon into the world. But neither has the strength to lend to the other yet. This time is for waiting. Their little family separated but eternally bound together, each member locked away in their own private cocoons. Waiting. Waiting. Waiting.

When Jess's body is finally released, he has no will to fight the funeral plans. Gives it all over to Manda and her mother. He cannot care about any of that. Asks only for a Bowie song somewhere, sometime.

At last he is allowed to meet his daughter.

He knows her already, but to hold her is a miracle that threatens to blow him into a million pieces. She smiles. At least that's what he thinks he sees. It is too soon of course, but he swears that she has a smile to mirror his own.

Her eyes, of course, are Jessica's. How could it be otherwise? So. Amber it is, then. *Amber.* A precious, luminous being who deserves so much more than he will ever be able to give.

When the day at last comes, Max stands in the church, silent and numb, a crying baby in a sling around his chest. He listens to hymns sung surprisingly well by a group of people so destroyed. He stands in the commitment chapel of the crematorium without any sense of what is being said or done. He drinks the whiskey well-meaning men hand to him at the wake. Whisky, the 'water of life'. *Jesus.*

Marcy is there. So kind of her to come, but he is unable to talk to her. Manda sticks close by, gaunt but determined to be useful. He will not give his daughter up to anyone else, however, as much or as often as they offer to relieve him.

He feels in his pocket for the astrolabe, grips it tightly, feels its rings and marks and symbols. He'd found it that morning as he'd emptied out her sports bag, now reeking with rot from the wet swimsuit that Jess, typically, had forgotten to hang out.

The plush private function room at her mother's favourite hotel is too small to contain his fury. He relents and lets Manda take Amber for a while, she is quiet now, sleeping at last. He walks outside for a cigarette and sits on a pavement littered with feathers from a pigeon fight. Grey and filthy, bar a small and curling one at his feet that is hypnotically white.

He knows that John will follow him. That he will sit down beside him.

'So where is she, John? Tell me.'

'I wish I could, Max. Not lost, though, not lost. You know the universe wastes nothing, why would it waste consciousness? All information is conserved. Energy can be transferred but it cannot be destroyed, right? She hasn't been discarded, Max. And physically she's still here, in a way, in your daughter.'

'And what do I tell her? Sorry sweetheart but you'll never know your mother. She was amazing, but she's gone. She's been recycled. She's a bit of information somewhere. Actually she's quite a few bits of information on my phone. Christ, John. For fuck's sake, how do I live with this?'

'I don't know, Max. Just... love and be loved. As you did, as she'd want you to. You won't be alone. Manda is moving up from Bristol to help you, isn't she? And I know I'm probably the last thing you want, but I'm here. I'll take whatever fury you need to let out, whatever despair. Anytime. Because, you know, we're actually connected in another way that I've only recently realised. Old fashioned of me, but I had assumed your last name was Wallace, too, like Jessica's. Then when I met Mrs Wallace, and saw your last name in the obituary, it dawned. You see, I'm actually a very dear friend of Dr Kluft. Eloise – the geneticist? You would have met her when you made that documentary about the bones. I knew your face was familiar. But I didn't put two and two together until recently. So perhaps we were also always meant to be friends, Max, one way or another? But only in whatever way you feel is possible.'

Max arches his brows, snorts and nods, but cannot smile and does not reply. He drains his glass. Lifts it to the light to see if it might function as a prism. The glass is not dense enough of course, but on a whimsy he also looks for some bending of the light, the gravitational lensing that occurs when mass warps the fabric of space-time. Everything is warped now, beyond recognition. He needs another whisky.

'Did you know there are clouds of alcohol in space, John? Perhaps your useless god likes a drink or two himself.'

'Yes. Perhaps.'

It is dark. He might almost have missed him, despite his height, as he crouches into an approximation of prayer. But the wrecked shaking is unmistakable. John slides along the pew next to him. He does not flinch, even when a hand grips his shoulder. Instead, he responds by curling against John's chest with a wave of weeping dammed back since God knows when.

'I loved her, John.'

'I know, Calumn. I know. Me too, in my way. And I have rarely been affected by any loss in this way. It's so very, very hard. But the more I think about it, the more I think that in some way, she *knew*. Then again, how could she possibly have known and been able to bear that knowledge? It is beyond bearing. All of this.'

'John. Reverend Evesham. I'm ready to talk now. Not about Jessica, not yet. Maybe some time. You will come back, won't you? You will keep coming?

'Yes, Calumn. Of course. So who are you ready to talk about? Sarah... Dr Kluft?'

'No. About her – the "Scarlet Lady" as you call her. About them. I'm ready to tell you everything.'

28

HERE AND THERE

If she has doubted for a moment where she belongs, this has evaporated with the unveiling of a fresh English morning. She has returned to the half-renovated farmhouse, bags barely unzipped. But true home for Eloise turns out to be a wiry pair of tattooed arms. The particular musk of a beloved man. The comforting knowledge that a little boy sleeps contentedly next door, a dog at the end of his bed. The reminder to treasure and fully inhabit every possible instance of joy.

There are many such instances, inspired by delightful discoveries. Machine-made mandalas and Mandelbrot-inspired graphics adorn the newly painted corridors, experiments printed out by Tom and carefully coloured in by Josh. These have become her favourite artworks.

The chill of the stone floor in the kitchen first thing in the morning. A room soon warmed by the second-hand range that Tom had found on eBay. The wood he had chopped to stoke it.

The smell of spring showers irrigating the vegetable garden he had begun. Tomatoes waiting to ripen in time, but farm-shop purchased for now. The taste of fresh basil from the kitchen window boxes livening up the tricolore salad that Tom had learned to make after enquiring about her travels through Italy.

These simple pleasures, Tom's commitment to their new life, his enviable ability to forgive and forget, all of this can still surprise and delight, but she asks no more difficult questions of her tiny taste of nirvana. She knows how lucky she is to hold these loved ones close. She also knows this idyll cannot persist, but cherishes this fine foundation, the potential for its rediscovery, moment by moment, whenever possible. She cherishes this extraordinary man too, capable of loving her, *all of her*, without fear or reserve. Their mutual acceptance of what they can and cannot be, or do, for each other.

Other questions nag at her nonetheless.

What has become of Madame Scarlet, having gone to ground again after her disturbing reappearance? No more scares at the school gate, at least, nor any further sightings of anyone sporting her colours who might be targeting Tom or Josh. Other bullies were still safely behind bars, but what if the gangster who had taken up with Tom's ex, and taken a dislike to Tom's concerns for the welfare of his son, should be considered for parole?

Beyond personal threats, there are her fears for the wider world. She wonders whether all their work in the Arctic has been in time. The hunting lodge cases turned out to be a nasty flu, one this year's vaccine had not anticipated, but no more than that. A worry, yes, like Ebola, Nipa, Polio, Mpox, not to mention deadly Avian flu going human-to-human – and the latest Covid variant-soup – but not of the most immediate concern for KC and her.

What of the ice core sample sent to Manchester? Perhaps only a false alarm, not yet definitive. She'd been personally updated on a video call with 'The Suit' shortly after delivery of all the DNA samples, with iron-clad promises there would never be any 'gain of function' work on the virus. Nevertheless, it bothers Eloise, will not sit easy with her that she seems to be in a secretive loop with someone about whom she knows so very little, whose role and responsibility remain obscure.

Meanwhile the preventative work, the precautionary principle, must remain her key focus. A rapid test is being deployed and shared with public health bodies internationally, potential border controls and quarantines quietly discussed – even if many in power would prefer their scientists to be disempowered – and even if the most powerful of nations are playing deadly ideological games. Eloise laments how much could have, should have been learned from certain Asian countries, with their polite acceptance of community, of the need to protect one another – as compelling an economic argument as anything the 'let it rip' libertarians could muster.

Despite the politicking, a vaccine for the Arctic virus is underway, maybe only weeks away from trials. Tailored treatments are being readied for further trials, if needed. Maybe... just maybe, they've been lucky this time? No illness among her own team. And among the Sami, still no sign of infection.

But what of those from the research station? All those oddly-acquired new companions cannot help but invade her homecoming peace, to sit invisibly around the generous kitchen table that Tom has constructed from reclaimed wood found about the grounds. She studies the daily medical charts that are shared with her, both for the women who had spontaneously developed the 'Sarah sequence' and the men who had consented to the procedure to splice it in. The survivors.

There is nothing clinically significant to report. There is, however, a self-reported and anecdotal sense of enhancement in empathy, experienced by almost all the group. A fascinating contrast to what appeared to happen in so many after their supposedly 'mild' Covid infections, but perhaps in some of those cases any previous *performance* of compassion for others had been precisely that?

Understandably, in some of the Arctic group there has also been the suggestion of post-viral fatigue – but fortunately nothing resembling the hideous constellation of sequelae and damage from other recent waves of infection, whether viral, fungal, bacterial or parasitic. Nor did they notice any tendency to disinhibition or greater risk taking, the often seen push in the relief following survival to unconsciously spread any lingering pathogens. Nothing would be surprising to Eloise, considering what the group has gone through, but overall physical health seemed no better or worse than before infection or treatment.

And yet she can't help but hope for evidence of some kind of *measurably beneficial change*. Greater abilities, perhaps? Stronger resistance of some kind, even if that were as far-fetched but future-proofed as increased tolerance to low gravity, or extremes of temperature, or enhanced oxygen metabolism?

Something to help humanity either journey 'out there' or survive better 'right here', come what may. Something to really make the whole experience worthwhile.

Another outcome of the Norwegian adventure for Eloise is a new and pressing motivation to establish a network of clinics for post-viral research, treatment and therapy. An initiative that would aim to listen to, respect and learn from its patients. Staffed by volunteers if need be – and she'd be the first – if sufficient funding was not forthcoming. Or perhaps the idea could be realised through a combination of crowdfunding and crowdsourcing?

Humanity could hardly take flight into the full potential that, even now, she hopes for, if further hobbled by the mass trauma of diminished health and bereavement...

In the meantime, the recovered and the convalescing from the Arctic remain quarantined. They have agreed to move to a military rehab centre for a few months, where family can join them if so desired. From a medical perspective, their patients being science researchers by profession could not have been a more fortuitous accident.

For now, Eloise accepts that all anyone can do is watch and wait. Trial, test, observe, adapt.

But then, is that not the way of life itself?

⬤

It is a hard thing to ask of him. His grandfather had bequeathed it, the man who had given his life for a little girl, the man whose surrender to the yellow beast had been answered by the actions of an unexpected other. This other man, therefore, deserves to travel onward in spirit with the crystal white spearhead so treasured by a certain young Warrior.

He unbinds it silently, without complaint, though as he presses it to her wizened hand she feels the pain of his letting go. This beautiful object is a fitting tribute to lay with all the other stones the tribe will place around her mother's tree, in honour of The Outsider and The Tracker. She will lay a piece of her own shiny black stone, so preciously sharp, gathered by The Stranger a lifetime ago near a terrifying river of fire.

There is another thing she must ask, this time of The Scout. Her brother's braid. But this is not to add to the tributes around the tall, round trunk of the sacred tree. It is intended for the young man who had loved him, to ease his grief. Ochre and thick rendered fat can help to heal a flesh wound, but only a sense of worth can tether a weeping heart to this world. The Old Woman knows this pairing cannot be replaced. And with no other to sing to, a bird might easily forget its song.

She fears the boy will do something foolish and knows she must watch him closely, find a way for him to be useful. The Scout understands and does not hesitate. She has memory enough of the man they both loved as they mourn him today.

But as for wounds, The Old Woman notices something else, carved upon the swaggering young man who had doubted The Outsider and also on that boy's father. Six fresh cuts, three on each shoulder, not acquired in battle. They echo the scars of initiation The Outsider had borne. Such markings were not a tradition within her clan, although the Stranger had arrived with some of her own.

This is something new. Something good. Even if she must make sure these men take hot sticks to these tributes and keep their proud new cuts clean and dry.

⌒⧓⌒

TO: dreloisekluft@children.of.sarah.org
FROM: DrKCHarmon@viro.paleo.ac

Hey, how are you? Good to be home, huh? Looks like we caught a break this time? Still waiting to be sure about Manchester, seems they've had a few cases of *something* unusual up there. But, hey, did you hear? They found something else at the drill site, where they took out that troublesome ice core. Don't have much info yet, but as they were about to seal up the hole the drill

bit went down an inch or two more and got chewed up on
something hard. Something really hard. NOT ROCK.

Will update when I know more. Maybe the Suit will summon
us to another video call? Hey, you never know, we might
even get sent back to the Arctic, hopefully before the
coming battle for resources there. Or off to the other
pole to hunt through all the glacier cores getting saved
from the melt and stored in those ice caves. Because I
know how much you *love* the deep freeze, Dr Kluft ;)

Brrr… KC.

The ceremony for The Outsider and The Tracker is as essential
to the clan as the celebration of a birth. All had wanted to take
part but some were shocked by The Old Woman's insistence they
must honour *all* of the lost souls from the canyon. That with
their songs they must help the shattered spirits of their enemy to
become whole again too. By doing so, they can release their own
fears and not entangle them into their own hearts. Otherwise,
hatred might take root and strangle any new life waiting to
emerge.

     None of them can know who these people might have
been before they became what they became. Who might have
loved them and lost them. What of themselves they had lost by
choosing that bitter path. By turning away from the brighter trail
– which might seem harder, even impossible when all but a full
stomach is out of reach – but which offers timeless gifts along its
glowing way.

     The songs fall away now and the clan return to the camp, to
their tasks, their worries, their joys. One joy in particular brings
The Old Woman a small but satisfied smile. It seems she was right
to set a rift between her grandson and that giggling, doe-eyed,
hip-swaying girl that all the other young men ached for. She
thinks now that their coupling would never have lasted, that

another pairing had always been waiting, a bud slowly unfurling from a patient branch.

She watches their easy way with each other. She sees The Scout weave a victory feather into one of The Warrior's braids, then gently stroke the crusted scars along his grateful back.

Through everything these two have experienced together – the struggle, the loss, the injury, the triumph – a deep and potent bond has formed. A vigorous and a very useful one. They will work well together, these two, watch out for each other, hold each other's hearts. And such children they might make! Such a blending of strengths and skills.

So. Perhaps she will wander this blessed ground a little longer, after all. To watch and wait and find out. To ensure that any such offspring are shaped as they should be.

More than a boon for her own interests, this kind of happiness is important to the tribe. Two who can prize their harmony above the need to win a squabble. Two who will gaze into each other's eyes, yes, but who have also looked deep into the eyes of death and said, *I see you, I know you... but not yet.* These two have saved each other. There is little more beautiful, little more unbreakable.

Would this pair have been drawn to each other without her intervention? Impossible to know. But she thinks so, yes. Some connections, even if unexpected at the time, seem intended all along, once brought into being.

⌇

'Lolo?'

'Darius, hello!'

'Hurrah. Getting the hang of this new video calling software. But I'll make it quick. Reception's not great – dust storms. The cave – Yemen. As you know we've found some animal bones deeper within, though nothing human yet. But that's the weird thing. When we picked apart a rockfall, underneath it, in what looks like a fire pit, there was something not... well, not anything that we recognise.'

'What do you mean?'

'Looks like it could be skeletal in form but it's not bone. Not flint, not stone, nothing it wouldn't take a lab to figure out. So we're sending it to yours.'

'Darius, have you touched it? Has anyone touched it? Ungloved, unmasked, unsanitised afterwards?'

'Good God, Lolo, you look like you've seen a ghost! And sound like my worried mother every time I'm anywhere near the Middle East. I'm not a bloody amateur, my girl. Of course not. Of course we haven't. It's all well-sealed. All procedures are tickety-boo, thank you, ma'am.'

'Good. OK. That's good. Let me call the lab. Thanks... thank you, Darius. Wait, Darius, wait... Was that a sneeze? Darius?'

⣿⣿⣿⢸⣿⣿⣿

And what of The Tall Girl? Who will be the one for her? What shall unfold for her? The Old Woman has a sense that this one will wander, not in her heart, but in her need to know. She may remain here with the tribe and yet keep herself somehow apart, as her great-grandmother had done – or she may choose, as that same Stranger had done in her youth, to carry her gifts onwards and outwards to those who might benefit from and learn to value them.

She will take the girl to the cave. Soon. She is ready to know its secrets. To see what marks have been made there, to envision those she might make herself. The child has witnessed the marks her kind can make upon each other, for good or bad, within and without. And even before her true initiation, for which much more preparation is needed, the girl must seek out her own spirit animal. Her own scout to awaken her senses and lift them above simple desires or easy satisfaction. The girl must become grounded with seriousness to the earth, to its living heartbeat within her own body, before she is ready to fly its bonds in any other form.

There is a restlessness in so many of The Stranger's line. The Old Woman imagines that a handful of these, The Tall Girl or others, will choose – or may even be forced – to look beyond the safe and the familiar one day. And it is clear to her now that the world outside this refuge has need of certain skills, certain knowledge, certain blessings. So much was lost during the great dying, wisdom in particular, it seems. And the power of kindness. The sense of something outside the skin, an awareness of the fine, web-like bonds that stretch between life – and between lives.

The seeds of such understanding must be blown far and wide once again and with unstoppable courage. The Old Woman, too, aches to float apart, like so many seeds upon the wind. Like the feather-light spores of an early spring flower scattered by a single breath.

The morning star beckons to her now above the thin line of the dawn, enjoying its brief moment of magnificence before its radiance is washed away by the light of the Sun, rising so close behind.

She closes her eyes and reaches her mind like a searching hand, one willing to receive whatever comes, into the waters of the infinite. Her kind lives at the place where here and now meet, where flesh and fire, earth and air coexist, but it is not where they belong. She is here only to guide them back, to lead them forward, to remember what is to come. To do what is necessary but never without love.

She breathes as all breathe, bleeds the same red blood, seeks life with the same hunger, but also walks in and out of a hidden void. Between everything and nothing. She cannot know when her thirst for this world and all its wondrous work will finally be quenched but she understands how the same stream that awaits her own surrender will carry others with it, one by one, to slip into her empty place.

Acknowledgements

As Eloise says in one of her rants (yes, I know, sorry) 'The bad actors have done such a good job with misinformation that science is now seriously on the backfoot' – and while it has taken me seven years to complete the promised follow up to *Bone Lines* (for, oh, so many reasons) – that emergency has only increased with world events. I'd apologise for that too, because I'm like that, but I don't think too much of it is my fault.

It is my fault, however, for choosing to be so endlessly fascinated by subjects that constantly update and evolve. So, my first thanks must go to anyone who's urged me to keep going when I've wondered why I write about the things I do, in the way that I do, through the characters I do – but I am hopelessly compelled. And having mentioned them, I must also thank those same characters for their unfailing inspiration and company, even in the darkest of times. Yes, even Eloise.

Heartfelt thanks must also go to the early draft readers: Virginia Moffatt, Mary Monro, Alice McVeigh and Simon Stanley for their invaluable input and encouragement. Also to Michael Langan and The Literary Consultancy for a developmental edit that made me look painfully hard at everything, but in all the right ways. Writing about what I do also requires a painful confrontation of one's own past, particularly one's own hypocrisies. To Patrick Kincaid for the copy edit and several proofreads, and for general moral support.

Incalculable gratitude to Jamie Chipperfield, not only for the corker of a cover design and some complex typesetting, but also for putting up with my nit-picking – and for being my BB wingman in so many ways. I must not forget the inestimable

Lindsay Clark for his gracious words about *Bone Lines*, which have spurred me on through any kind of writing since. Cheers also to Jude Cook, Jane Johnson, Dr Linn Järte and Miles Hudson for being last minute readers and for such kind words.

Very special thanks are also due to the amazing Breakthrough Book Collective for keeping me afloat as part of a crew that helps each other navigate the ups and downs of writing, publishing and marketing. In you, I have found my tribe. (And I think Sarah would be proud of that journey.)

On a similar note, a hearty hurrah to all the authors out there who just keep at it, no matter how soul-destroying, especially while fiction may feed the soul, but rarely feeds the body! We are often up against immovable behemoths – not to mention the new plagiaristic, market-flooding threats of AI – and an industry that often seems to put its source material, the creatives, last. But we keep finding our way around the obstacles!

And another hurrah to scientists such as Mariam Al Astrulabi (yes, the astrolabe!), Caroline Herschel, Lynn Margulis, Rosalind Franklin and many more, who some have tried to erase from history or deny rightful credit to or suppress their contributions, but whose names I choose to shout out loud.

A note on research... and sanity: Thanks to the *New Scientist* for keeping me informed and inspired – and to all the other science communicators, too numerous to mention. To Gaia House for keeping me going through some difficult years and providing me with the skills and the community to keep *trying* to be mindful, no matter how often I fail. To family and friends... and some very particular online support groups (you know who you are.)

Lastly, deep gratitude to any readers out there who have stuck with me in the long but unavoidable gap between *Bone Lines* and *The Fire In Their Eyes*! You are all The Children of Sarah. And thank you just for being readers.

www.ingramcontent.com/pod-product-compliance
Lightning Source LLC
Chambersburg PA
CBHW030939120726
47906CB00002B/639